'An ac~~·~~~ ~~...~~ and intense pace
that kept me completely rapt'
 KL Slater, international bestselling author of *The Mistake*

'A gripping psychological thriller ... I just couldn't put it
down ... I am looking forward to more from Elle Croft'
 Patricia Gibney, bestselling author of *The Missing Ones*

'I couldn't put this down. Pacy and gripping'
 Cass Green, author of *The Woman Next Door*

'Full of twists and turns, *The Guilty Wife* is a gripping tale of
betrayal, deceit, and duplicity. The ending will stay with you
long after you've finished the last page. Fabulous'
 Jenny Blackhurst, bestselling author of *Before I Let You In*

'A gripping portrayal of a woman under fire, which explores
the blurry boundaries of innocence and guilt ... A brilliant
debut'   Phoebe Morgan, author of *The Doll House*

'Twisty and fast-moving, *The Guilty Wife* kept me guessing
until the very end! A great read'
 Isabel Ashdown, author of *Beautiful Liars*

'What a clever idea! This kept me reading through the night
to see how "the guilty wife" would get out of this one ...'
 Jane Corry, author of *Blood Sisters*

'A real edge-of-your-seat read, this is a book that ripples
with suspense right through to the gripping finale'   *Sun*

in South Africa, grew up in Australia and moved to the UK in 2010 after travelling around the world with her husband. She works as a freelance social media specialist and also blogs about travel, food and life in London.

Follow Elle on Twitter @elle_croft to find out more.

Also by Elle Croft

The Guilty Wife

The Other Sister

ELLE CROFT

ORION

An Orion paperback
First published in Great Britain in 2018 by Orion Books,
an imprint of The Orion Publishing Group Ltd
Carmelite House, 50 Victoria Embankment,
London EC4Y 0DZ

An Hachette UK company

1 3 5 7 9 10 8 6 4 2

A CIP catalogue record for this book is
available from the British Library.

ISBN (Mass Market Paperback) 978 1 4091 7546 9
ISBN (Trade Paperback) 978 1 4091 7545 2

Typeset at The Spartan Press Ltd,
Lymington, Hants

Printed and bound in Great Britain by Clays Ltd,
Elcograf S.p.A.

www.orionbooks.co.uk

The
Other Sister

Prologue

2018

GINA

My eyes fly open.

I've kept them squeezed shut for what's felt like minutes – but which must have only been for a couple of seconds – in a futile attempt to clear my head. To calm myself.

There's a thumping sound, and my head snaps up to face my bedroom door. I hold my breath as I imagine it flying inwards, revealing an intruder.

My eyes flit back and forth blindly in the dark, until I realise.

That relentless beating. It isn't coming from outside. It's my own thrumming heart.

Adrenalin seeps from my pores as my temple and my pulse pound aggressively.

I count backwards from ten. I close my eyes again and focus on sounds in a bid to combat the darkness that's threatening to control my senses. My breath, sharp and shallow; my heart, its beat settling to a low, steady march, like an army advancing into battle. A siren in the distance. A fox wailing, its harrowing cry echoing under my prickling skin.

Taking a deep lungful of air, my breath catches at the taste in my mouth. Metallic. Sharp. I've felt this before, this tingling on my tongue.

Carefully, deliberately, as though keeping my movements steady will somehow slow the passing of time, I turn my head to look. To see. My eyes have adjusted now, and I slowly take in the details of the tableau that's spread out before me.

My gaze drifts from the shoes strewn carelessly in opposite corners of my room, to the trail of clothing that lies in motionless heaps. Clues, all pointing my way.

And me. Hands in my lap, tense, my body barely perched on the edge of my bed. My fingers, dark and glistening.

I am naked. And covered in blood.

I make out thick, dark smears streaked across my walls, my pillow, my stomach. My hands are shaking, dark red droplets dripping from my fingers into a puddle on the carpet by my feet. I try to remove myself from the pool, its surface glistening in the glow of the street lamp beyond my window.

I push myself further onto the bed, and as I scrabble into the corner, clutching the bed covers, my fingers close on something warm and sticky. For a split second, I let my hand linger. But I don't turn around to look. I already know what I'll see.

How did things go so wrong?

I try to clear my mind, to follow the thread of events that led to this. But it's not a linear path. It's convoluted. A tangled mess that, if it was picked apart and laid out thread by thread, would probably all end up here, anyway.

Somewhere deep in my gut, an instinct nags at me, reminding me of what I'd rather not acknowledge. Reality is slippery, out of reach, an ever-changing shadow. But there are certain facts as solid as the body in my bed. They're circling me like predators, screaming the truths I can't ignore, no matter how much I'd like to.

2

This isn't over, they snarl.
You started this.
And only you can finish it.

Chapter 1

2017

RYAN

The smell is a physical force, stopping me mid-step.

I'm frozen in the hallway, nostrils flared, breathing deeply to absorb the scent of my childhood. I wonder if she knows just how much like Mum she's turned out to be, right down to her incredible cooking skills. I won't tell her, of course. She'd hate that. But some days, walking into this house, inhaling rich aromas wafting from the kitchen, I'm taken back to the years when this hallway was filled with laughter and love. Before it all fell apart, before sadness seeped into the walls and the thick silence of grief muffled any flickering of happiness.

I shake my head. That was then. This is now. I walk towards the clattering of pots and pans, the giggling that's erupting from my sister every few seconds, and sigh, relieved that joy has returned, swelling and filling each room, breathing life into a dusty skeleton of a home so nearly destroyed all those years ago.

I announce my entry by clearing my throat loudly, and the couple springs apart, feigning embarrassment.

'I didn't hear you coming in,' says Gina.

'Probably because you're making such a racket in here,' I joke. 'Smells amazing though, is that mushroom risotto?'

4

'Yep,' Julian says, greeting me with a firm squeeze of my shoulder. 'You hungry?'

'Starved. Is there enough there for me?'

'Of course there is.'

'Legends. Thank you. Anyone fancy some wine?'

Both Gina and Julian nod heartily, so I retrieve a bottle from the fridge and pour three glasses, watching them move around each other in perfect harmony, like dancers performing a well-rehearsed routine. A familiar pang of envy twists my stomach, followed quickly by guilt. I should be happy for my sister. I *am* happy for my sister. But watching her and Julian together only highlights what's missing from my life.

I've never had a relationship like the one they've got. It's easy. Effortless. They don't manipulate each other, and if they disagree about something, they talk about it rationally, listening to each other's point of view. The few girlfriends I've had were all needy and possessive, trying to control who I spent my time with, and allocating a specific number of my evenings to spend with them. With Gina and Julian, it's different. They never need to insist on spending time together. It's what they both want to do.

Julian leans across the counter to kiss Gina, quickly, as though it's an impulse rather than a conscious action, and then continues grating cheese onto the steaming bowls of risotto. Her fingertips gently brush his back as she walks past, taking an empty pan to the sink. I take a sip of the cold wine and imagine what it feels like to be as comfortable with another person as they are together. To not have to hide yourself, or constantly worry that they'll discover who you really are.

Gina doesn't know how good she's got it – no, that's not true. She knows that what she and Julian have is something special, she's never denied that. But it's not enough for her. She wants the career, the house, the respect of her peers.

But they aren't enough either. I know, because I have those things.

'OK, dinner's up,' she says, handing me a bowl.

'This looks incredible. Thanks so much.'

'You're welcome,' she smiles. 'Beats eating your cooking.'

I roll my eyes and follow her into the living room.

'So,' I say to Julian as we eat, 'are you all ready for your shows?'

I still don't quite understand how he makes a living from illusions and magic tricks, but judging by the planning and stress that's gone into creating his upcoming two week tour, performances must be a major source of his income.

'I think so,' he says, taking Gina's hand and rubbing his thumb across her knuckles. 'The set is as ready as it'll ever be. I've sold some tickets, but not enough, which means I'll need to do most of my promotion on the road. It'll be hectic once I'm out there.'

'Still no offers of representation?'

For as long as I've known Julian, he's been trying to find an agency to represent him. All the famous illusionists have managers and promoters and agents – it's the only way to break into TV shows and book deals and sold-out stadium tours.

He shakes his head.

'You'll get there,' Gina assures him. 'Soon you'll be a household name.'

'Have you got any new tricks?' I ask, changing the topic. I didn't mean to bring up a sore point.

'They're not "tricks",' Gina says defensively, using her fingers to make air quotes.

'Sorry.' I hold my hands up. 'I didn't mean any offence, I don't know the correct terms for magic.'

'It's not called magic,' Julian explains patiently. 'It's illusion.'

'OK. So do you have any new *illusions*?'

Julian pauses and briefly narrows his steely grey eyes at me, then decides to let my sarcasm slide. It wasn't directed at him, anyway.

'Actually, I do have a few new elements to my act,' he says. 'Do you want to see one?'

'Sure,' I say, not wanting to be a spoilsport. I'm not a huge fan of magic – sorry, illusions – but there's no need for him to know that.

'Great,' he says brightly, putting his bowl down and producing a deck of cards from his back pocket with a flourish. Gina sits up straighter, her eyes glued to Julian. I take a sip of my wine, hoping it'll relax me enough that I'll enjoy being the subject of his act.

Julian hands me the deck.

'Take a look through that deck, will you please, Ryan?' he says, his demeanour completely transforming. Until now he's been relaxed, slouching, his speech unhurried. Now his shoulders are back and his chin is lifted. His voice has assumed an air of authority, and his eyes are alert. I resist the urge to laugh at the theatrics of it all.

'It's just a regular deck, as you can see.'

He watches as I flip through it. He's right, it's just a pack of cards, nothing special, no trick cards, no duplicates.

I reach over to hand it back, but he holds a palm up towards me.

'Not just yet, Ryan. I'd like you to shuffle the cards really thoroughly. Take your time, shuffle them multiple times if you need to. Yes, just like that. Mix them up really well, make sure they're nothing like the way they were when I gave you that deck.'

I do as I'm told, shuffling clumsily until I'm certain they're in a totally random order. This time, when I hand them over, he accepts them, immediately spreading the deck across the coffee table in a fluid motion to create a wide, perfectly even arc.

'Now what I want you to do is select a card, whichever card you like,' he tells me, his eyes flashing as his voice rises and falls, almost lyrically.

I don't pretend to deliberate. I just pluck the first card my eyes fall on, and steal a look. It's the six of hearts.

'Have you taken a moment to memorise your card?' he asks. Before I can answer, he goes on. 'It's very important that you don't forget this card; it's imperative for what's about to happen next that you keep that card locked in your mind. Do you have it there?'

He taps his forehead and I nod, not trusting myself to speak in case I snort with laughter. I glance at Gina. She catches my eye and a smirk plays at the edges of her lips. She knows how unpleasant I'm finding this, but she also knows I'd never tell Julian how I feel about his profession. I scowl playfully back at her as Julian asks me to replace the card and reshuffle the deck. I do as I'm told.

'Now what I'm going to do, Ryan, is I'll select your card from the middle of this deck without any kind of indication from you as to which card that is. Do you think I can do it?'

If this is the best he can do, it's no wonder he's not filling the theatres on his upcoming tour. I've seen a teenager on a street corner in Covent Garden doing this one for a couple of quid in a hat at his feet. It's hardly impressive.

'Sure,' I say. 'I believe you can do it.'

'Well, great,' Julian says. He waves one hand over the

small deck in his hand and then pulls the first card from the top.

'Now, Ryan, was your card...'

There's a dramatic pause.

'... the king of diamonds?'

I'm disappointed, I realise. As much as I hate being duped, this somehow feels worse. I have no idea how to break it to him that he's wrong, so I just shake my head.

'No?' he looks dismayed. 'Hmmm, OK. Let me just have a think.'

He looks around, at the floor next to him, at the cards in his hand. I shift uncomfortably. There's something deeply pathetic about a man on the slippery slope towards middle age, who's failing to be a magician. If he didn't make my sister so happy, I'd be having serious words with her about her taste in men.

'Sorry, there seems to have been some kind of mistake. Except... Ryan, sorry, I've just noticed that there's something in your pocket there.'

I follow his gaze to my hip. Poking out the front pocket of my jeans is a card. Smiling out of sheer relief, I pull it out. Sure enough, it's the six of hearts. I hold it up, impressed.

'Is that your card?'

I nod. He's triumphant.

'What about this one?'

He slides another card from the top of the deck that's still resting in the palm of his hand. It's the six of hearts. I look down. The card hasn't moved from my hand, but now there's another, exactly the same, in Julian's. I look from my card to his, trying to process what I'm seeing. He flips another card over. Six of hearts. And then another, and another, and then he throws the whole deck on the table, and every single card is a six of hearts, apart from the single king of diamonds that he fooled me with at first.

I want to be mad. I've been played – spectacularly so. But to my own amazement, I kind of enjoyed it. I burst into laughter, and both Gina and Julian join in.

'OK,' I concede, breathless. 'I'll admit it, just this once. That was brilliant. And you definitely got me. This time, anyway.'

Chapter 2

GINA

'I'll take the gnocchi, please.' I smile at the waiter, snapping the menu closed.

'Certainly.' He nods, taking the leather-bound folder from me.

I glance around, taking in the soft jazz music and the occasional clink of a wine glass, the men in suits and the women whose jewels glisten in the glow of the candles flickering at each table.

I'm underdressed. Even in my classiest outfit, the one and only designer dress I own – triumphantly snapped up from a charity shop rack and worn to every upmarket occasion I've attended since – I'm decidedly shabby compared to the rest of the diners. I'm glad I thought to accessorise with some sparkly earrings that, to an untrained eye, could just about pass for diamonds.

Smoothing invisible wrinkles in my lap, I look across the table and relax as soon as my eyes catch Julian's.

'You're the most beautiful woman in this restaurant,' he says.

'No, I—'

'Gina,' he interrupts, taking my hand. 'That wasn't a question. It's a fact. Trust me.'

My cheeks grow warm under the intensity of his gaze.

'Thank you,' I manage. 'You don't look so bad yourself.'

I cringe internally. Julian always manages to say what he means, sounding genuine and romantic without being cheesy. And in return, I deflect. I make jokes that aren't funny. I'm like a teenager with a crush, only I'm in my thirties, and in a serious relationship.

He winks. 'It's a few days early, I know, but happy anniversary.'

I clink my glass against his.

'Happy anniversary,' I echo.

'Can you believe it's been two years?'

'Best two years of my life,' I say.

And it's true. Because before I walked into that small, dark theatre, armed with a notepad, pen and cynicism to spare, I'd been wading through life. Getting by. My job was mediocre at best, my flat was little more than a shoebox with a microwave, I'd given up on the notion of romance in my future, and I had just an acquaintance or two at work. I wouldn't have called them friends.

There was no drastic moment in my adult life that I can blame this complacency on. I'd just slid into hopelessness without realising. For years I'd dreamed of more, I'd longed for a bigger life, a more meaningful existence – a legacy – and then I'd just stopped. Those things weren't for me, I'd figured. I'd tried, but they hadn't happened, which meant – in my perpetually sceptical mind – they simply weren't meant to happen. And so I'd been showing up every day, existing, doing what I needed to, going home to a ready meal and the evening news, followed by hours of mindless Netflix bingeing. It was my daily routine, and I barely gave it a second thought.

And then I sat in the front row of Julian's show, ready to cover just another local event that would appear on page sixteen of the paper I knew hardly anyone actually read. When he walked onto that stage, the floorboards creaky and sagging, I recognised in him something that I hadn't seen in myself for years. He was vibrant. Alive. And I was captivated. He was like a gust of wind, blowing open the doors I'd closed so firmly, scattering the debris that littered my life, filling me with hope again.

He insists that it was love at first sight when I approached him after the show for an interview, but I know that I fell first. That day in the theatre, and every day since.

'I'm sorry I won't be with you for our real anniversary,' Julian says, interlocking his fingers with mine in the middle of the table. 'I'm going to miss you. I hate that I have to be away from you like this.'

'Me too,' I admit. 'But it's only for a couple of weeks. And it won't be like this for ever.'

'I know. But two weeks is still far too long to be apart. Which is why . . .'

He lets go of my hand and reaches into his jacket pocket, one eyebrow raised theatrically. I laugh, too loudly, only realising how conspicuous I am when heads turn our way. I take an embarrassed sip of my Prosecco, but Julian waves his hand dismissively.

'Forget about them,' he says. 'We're having a good time.'

He's right. I need to calm down. I'm wound so tightly with anticipation that I haven't let myself relax into our last evening together. Even after being with Julian for two years, even when he tells me every single day that he adores me, I still struggle to believe that it's really happening, that he's really chosen to be with me.

I place my glass back on the table, and notice a small velvet box sitting in the middle of my plate.

'What?' I gasp.

'Just a little something to remind you that I'm always thinking of you,' Julian says.

'Good sleight of hand,' I say, impressed, as I pick up the green cube. I open the lid quickly, and draw in a quick, delighted breath. Hanging off a delicate chain is a gold pendant, about the size and shape of a bullet, engraved with an intricate pattern of tessellated triangles and small, perfectly parallel lines.

'What is it?' I breathe.

'It's a capsule necklace,' Julian says, holding his hand out. I place it in the centre of his palm and he unscrews the top section to reveal a small chamber inside.

'Back in Victorian times it was fashionable to wear a piece of a loved one's hair in a locket. I wanted to get something we could both wear, but a locket didn't seem quite right. This is used for keepsakes. Sometimes a scroll with a note written on it... but I put a lock of my hair in yours. That's not creepy, is it? I thought it sounded romantic, but now that I'm saying it out loud...'

I hesitate. Julian will have spent weeks researching this gift, making sure it's laden with meaning, and utterly unique. I love that about him – his insistence on not just buying a present, but an item that's been carefully considered and that will still be relevant in years to come. This, coupled with his natural flair for theatrics, makes for some unusual gifts. Our first Christmas together, he presented me with a framed print showing how the stars looked at the exact date and time, and from the precise location, where we met. It was the most romantic thing anyone had ever done for me. This necklace is just as thoughtful, and I know he will have put far more effort into choosing it than any gift I've ever bought for him.

'I mean,' I say slowly, 'it *is* a little bit creepy.'

Then I see his expression falling and I add quickly, 'but I absolutely love it.'

His shoulders drop in relief. I stand up, no longer caring what any other diners think of us, and move around the table to kiss him. Then I crouch down and lift my hair up, indicating for him to secure the chain around my neck. It's cold against my skin, and heavy. I like the weight of it, the gentle press on my sternum. It's comforting.

'Thank you,' I say as I move back to my seat. 'I'm never taking this off.'

And I mean it. I *do* love his gift. I love the meaning behind it. I love the way the pendant looks. I don't ever have to open it, don't have to acknowledge what's inside.

'You're welcome,' Julian says. 'It's so we can be close to one another. Even when we're far apart.'

He looks into my eyes again, his gaze sending fire through my veins. I want to spend for ever in this moment. I want to capture it; find a way to hold onto how happy I am, the way I'm bursting with hope for our future. I try to push down the terror that's always lurking, not too far behind my joy, telling me that this won't work out the way I imagine.

'When we get back to yours,' he says with a smile, 'you owe me a piece of your hair.'

He reaches into his shirt and pulls out a matching capsule, his silver rather than gold, but identical in every other way. I can't keep the smile off my face.

A waiter arrives with our meals, the smell of pumpkin and sage greeting me from my plate. I inhale deeply, closing my eyes to savour it.

'So,' Julian says as we both tuck into our food, 'what are you going to do without me?'

'I'll have you know I have a full schedule of social activities planned,' I say, mock insulted.

15

'Really?'

'No, not really,' I admit. 'But I *am* going to speak to Jacqueline later this week, about my social media idea.'

'You've worked really hard on that,' Julian says, attacking his steak as though it's his last meal on earth. 'She'll have to say yes.'

I sigh. Julian and I have differing opinions when it comes to my boss at Channel Eight, the successful and celebrated Jacqueline Davies. To me, she's a tyrant. She frequently makes staff members cry, has absolutely no tolerance for mistakes of any kind, and in the decade she's been there, she's never given out opportunities that she feels are undeserved.

But to Julian, she's a friend. No. Perhaps friend is overstating things a bit, but an acquaintance at the very least. Close enough that he could ask her for a favour: hiring his girlfriend as her personal assistant. But he's never seen her at work, doesn't know what she's like to deal with day-to-day. She's the older sister of his closest university friend – a friend whose family he spent every Christmas with until he was well into his twenties – so he's only seen her when she's relaxed, not when she's on the warpath, as she seems to be most days of the week.

I'm not at all confident that she's going to say yes, no matter how much effort I've put into creating a pitch that I think could actually help the channel. But I have to ask.

Jacqueline might not give me the chance I've been craving. But what's that saying that Tash once spouted at me during a particularly infuriating day at work?

Oh, yes. *If opportunity doesn't knock, build a door.*

It's about time I built myself a damn door.

Chapter 3

1996

SHARON

'Gina! Cassie! Come and get your lunch!'

I throw the tea towel down onto the kitchen counter and roll my neck around to relieve the tension that's been building since the start of the school holidays. I know I'm an awful parent for even thinking it, but I can't wait for them to go back to school.

'Ryan,' I say, trying to stop the patience from escaping my tone. 'Please could you go fetch your sisters and tell them that lunch is ready?'

He barely looks up at me from the Game Boy I now thoroughly regret buying him for Christmas.

'I dunno where they are,' he mumbles.

'I can hear them from here. They shouldn't be hard to find,' I explain. 'Besides, I didn't ask where they are, I asked you to please go and fetch them. And I don't mean in ten minutes when you've reached the next level of Donkey King.'

'It's Donkey *Kong*, Mum.'

There's no disguising his disdain for me and my complete lack of cool, but I don't care. As he slouches off to find the girls, I start folding the washing that's been waiting for me in the hamper on the floor since this morning.

Once that's done, I get a head start on washing the dishes.

I'm on autopilot, thinking about my to-do list as I mechanically dip bowls and wooden spoons in the soapy water. I need to buy cat food, and prepare a menu for Saturday's dinner party, and get invitations out for Cassie's eighth birthday. It's only once I've dried everything that it dawns on me how long it's been since Ryan walked off.

Wiping my hands on a towel, I listen as hard as I can. There's no sound of feet running down the hallway, none of the girlish giggles that have driven me crazy for the past week. I groan. All they want is food until I've actually made some for them, and then they're nowhere to be found.

'RYAN!' I scream at the top of my lungs. 'GINA! CASSIE! LUNCH!'

The neighbours will be judging me. But I can't muster the strength it'll take to walk up the stairs and search for them. I hold my breath, counting for ten seconds, mentally bargaining with them to just come downstairs without making a scene. If they do, I promise myself, I'll give them ice cream as an afternoon treat.

But they don't appear and I'm forced to go looking for them, feeling about as enthusiastic as my son was when he left the kitchen table.

I trudge up the stairs, still calling their names as I go, hoping they'll realise that I'm at the end of my tether. I get to Gina's room first. Empty. Ryan's is the same, and so is Cassie's. I frown, checking my bedroom in case they've decided to get up to mischief somewhere they know they shouldn't be. That would explain the eerie quiet. But that's empty, too. Cursing under my breath, I make my way back down the stairs, expecting my offspring to jump out at me in a fit of high-pitched squeals. Gotcha, Mum. Fooled you. I half-smile, just thinking about the descent into proud giggles that will no doubt follow, and I brace myself for the attack.

But there's no incursion, and they're still nowhere to be found. Not in the kitchen, not in the bathroom, not in the living room. I'm starting to feel uneasy now, that sense of discomfort that comes from not knowing where my children are for every second of the day. Like the first morning I dropped Ryan off at nursery all those years ago. I'd spent the next four hours convinced that he was hurt, or neglected, or crying because he missed me so much. Of course he was fine, and so were the other two when they started. But that fear, I can't ever eliminate it. All I can do is manage it.

Which is what I'm trying to do now, but my thoughts are running ahead of me. How long has it been since I saw Gina and Cassie? Why didn't I bother to find them sooner? They must have heard me calling, so why didn't they come, or at least call back to me?

I fling open the door to the utility room and relief floods me as I see their three little bodies huddled together con-spiratorially, just outside the wide-open back door. They're peering down at something, and my stomach churns in anticipation. Over the past year or so, Pickles, Gina's lovable tabby cat, has taken to leaving 'gifts' just outside the back door. He's always so proud of himself, and I really can't be mad at him, but the sight of the poor little broken mouse or bird always fills me with grief.

I don't have the energy today to dispose of another tiny fragile body. I'll just keep the kids inside so they don't have to look at it, and make Bill take care of the mess when he gets home. And I really must get Pickles a louder bell.

The relief I felt when I first saw my children safe and out of harm's way is swiftly replaced by indignant anger.

'What do you think you're doing in here?' I begin. 'I've

been calling you for ages. Now come and have some lunch before—'

I don't get to finish, because Cassie turns to face me and her eyes, so full of distress and pain, tear my heart wide open. Her cheeks are red and wet with tears, and she's crying as though her future has been destroyed before her very eyes.

'Darling.' I rush forward to hold her. 'What is it? What's wrong?'

It's only then that I notice the other two. Gina looks shocked. She's frozen in place, staring at me with her eyes wide and her body trembling. And Ryan, with snot running into his open mouth, is sobbing with such force that he looks like he might be sick.

Dread washes over me as I peer over Cassie's shoulder, and then I see it.

It's not a mouse. Or a bird.

It's Pickles. He's dead.

Not just dead.

Butchered.

And lying in a pool of his own blood.

Chapter 4

2017

RYAN

In a city that's home to millions of people, in a place like London where you're exposed to countless new faces every day, spotting the doppelgänger of someone you know every once in a while is inevitable.

I've been sure I've spotted old school friends before, the recognition clicking just a second too late to call their names, their faces swept up in the crowd with no time to check. I've been convinced I've rubbed shoulders with a celebrity or two in my time. There was a woman on the Tube once who looked so much like Madonna that to this day I still tell people I saw her. It might have been a random woman with a gap between her front teeth and an expensive-looking jacket, but no one can prove me wrong.

I used to think I'd seen Gina, too, after she left all those years ago, before she came back. On street corners, out the window of my bus, a glimpse, fleeting and impossible to catch, like smoke in the wind.

But I've never seen Cassie.

Until today.

It was the mundanity of it all that caught me off guard. I'd left the house at 8:04 precisely and walked to the Starbucks closest to the station. I'd ordered my usual grande caramel macchiato, but today I'd asked for an extra shot.

It had been another night of broken sleep, thanks to the nightmares that have been keeping me up in recent months, as well as Gina and Julian giggling when they'd arrived home, tipsy. I'd need all the help I could get to make it through the day.

As I'd waited for my coffee and cheese and Marmite toastie, I'd tapped away at my phone, familiarising myself with the day ahead, checking emails and deleting anything that wasn't relevant. I like to be ready to go when I reach my desk at ten to nine. It takes a certain personality type – someone who craves precision – to manage digital advertising for a massive agency like the one I work at, and I wouldn't be able to do it without keeping a strict routine. It's the same every working day: coffee and a toasted sandwich, emails on the train, ready to hit the ground running by nine, gym for forty minutes at lunch, the same salad from Pret every day, then back to it until six. It's not exciting, but I love my job and the routine soothes me.

And it stops my mind from going to places I've spent years trying to avoid.

I'd been huddled on the platform this morning with hundreds of strangers, jostling for the prime position to get on the 8:29 train via the back doors of the third carriage from the front.

The train had slowed as it approached the station, the driver looking nervously at the clusters of workers creeping closer to the edge of the platform, all determined to get to work, no matter the cost. I'd only looked up from my phone for a heartbeat, just long enough to see the faces whipping past me in the first two carriages of the train.

It had been little more than a flash of blonde curls, green eyes like my own, a smattering of freckles across her nose.

My eyes had caught hers. I don't know if she truly saw

me or if she was looking through me, absently getting on with her day, but as she'd flashed past, time had seemed to slow and bend, to collapse on itself so that the past and the present collided, unfelt by anyone else but me.

I must have only locked eyes with her for a second, probably less. I barely saw her, hardly had a chance to absorb her features. But I'd known, with a recognition I can't explain, that it was her.

It was Cassie.

The very idea of it had knocked the breath out of my lungs.

'Are you OK?' someone had asked me as I'd doubled over from the force of emotion that had just slammed into me. I'd nodded, not trusting myself to speak, and was swept onto the train by jostling commuters. I'd let myself be crammed into the centre of the carriage, propped up by bodies pressing against me from all sides. I don't remember the journey. I was paralysed by one fact, the impossible truth I'd just been faced with.

Cassie was on my train.

Even as the words had run through my head, I'd known they couldn't be true.

Cassie is gone.

Cassie has been gone for a long, long time.

But knowing the truth did nothing to stop what I'd seen from feeling incredibly real, setting my heart thrumming and my stomach churning.

As the train had pulled into my station, I'd elbowed my way through the tightly packed mass of commuters to get to the door.

'Excuse me,' I'd muttered, as a woman had rolled her eyes at me and shifted a millimetre to the left.

'You've got to wait for the doors to open, mate,' a voice

23

had called from behind me, causing a ripple of sniggers throughout the carriage. I'd barely even heard them as I'd shoved through gaps that didn't exist to make sure I got off the train first. As soon as the doors chimed, I'd punched the button and forced my way off the train. She'd probably got off at one of the previous stops, the ones where I'd been too stunned to move or think or look. But I'd had to see; had to know.

I'd shoved past people, ignoring their protests, searching for those blonde curls in the throng of bodies around me. Glancing into the train carriage, there was no sign of her.

And then a gap had opened up in the crowd ahead of me and I'd caught a glimpse of straw-coloured ringlets, an echo from my nightmares, bouncing in time with the steps of the other commuters. I'd surged forward, determined to reach her, to find out what the hell was happening. I'd locked my eyes onto the back of her head as she'd swept through the ticket barriers, moving closer and closer as people had walked in separate directions, clearing the way for me.

I'd only looked down for a second, just to check that my card had registered on the barriers. But when I'd looked up again, she'd disappeared.

Hurrying out of the station, I'd looked left and right, frantically trying to work out which way she'd gone.

I'd yelled her name, knowing as I did so how completely insane it was.

'Cassie!' I'd screamed, breathless, confused.

But, of course, there was no response. How could there be? I'd run one way, and then turned back on myself and tried searching in the other direction, but there was no sign of the woman with the blonde curly hair.

I'd had to give up then. I'd walked on trembling legs to work, reeling from the encounter with Cassie.

Not Cassie. Cassie is gone, I'd repeated to myself, over and over and over again, as though somehow saying the cold, hard truth would erase what I'd seen – what I'd felt – when I'd locked eyes with that woman.

By the time I arrive at the office I'm shaking so badly I have to sit down in the reception area. I take greedy gulps of air, keeping my eyes fixed to a point on the floor, desperate to retain my grip on reality. Only when I'm sure I won't pass out, when my brain has stopped whirring, do I walk slowly, methodically, to my desk.

'Are you all right?' asks Maddie, peering over the side of my cubicle, where I've hidden myself, hoping that the trembling stops before I have to go to my first meeting. Maddie doesn't care whether I'm OK or not. She just wants a bit of gossip. 'You look like you've seen a ghost.'

I almost laugh at the irony of the statement but instead I tell her I'm fine, and when she's walked away I bury my face in my hands. Sweat has soaked through my shirt. It's dampening my jacket, the heat of it seeping up to my collar, choking me. I loosen my tie and take a few deep, juddering breaths.

I saw a woman with curly blonde hair. I probably see hundreds of women with curly blonde hair each week, but not once have I mistaken anyone for the sister I've spent years trying to forget.

It's not possible for it to have been her.

So why, in that instant when I locked eyes with her, did every cell in my body scream an impossible truth? It wasn't a hunch, or a feeling.

It was fact. As solid as the chair I'm now sitting on. My baby sister was on that train.

But the woman I saw this morning could not have been Cassie.

Because Cassie is dead.

Isn't she?

Chapter 5

GINA

There are times when I can will myself into forgetting just how pathetic my career really is. Days when I can throw myself into the tasks I've been given with the kind of vigour that drowns out the voices telling me I was made for so much more than this.

Today is not one of those days.

So far, I've spent an hour typing notes from yesterday's meeting that was so dull the first time around that someone in the corner – strategically placed to be close to the pastries – actually started snoring.

Reliving it again today, without any snacks or comic relief, made me consider stapling my hand to the desk for some excitement, as well as for the chance to get the hell out of here for a day. Too bad I hate hospitals, or I might have actually been tempted.

My reward for finishing that task was to format a Power Point presentation that Jacqueline had hastily created. I did a good job. I always do. If there's one thing I can be proud of day to day it's that I always put my best into my work. Even if it's not what I want to be doing.

I'd thought, before I started this job, that working in television would be glamorous. A world apart from the budget-stretched local newspaper offices I've known for the past decade or so. Watching Channel Eight almost every day of my adult life – always the news at six, learning how the presenters composed themselves, the way they spoke, their posture – had made me believe that the world of TV was a worthy dream to aim for.

Every evening, when I'd sit in my faded, tattered armchair, eating whatever could be microwaved in order to avoid being in my tiny, grimy excuse for a kitchen, I'd dream of being the face that appeared on television screens all across the country, the name that first came to people's lips when they discussed breaking news stories. I'd dream that one day it would be me smiling at the camera, perfectly groomed, with an enviable wardrobe and an apartment that didn't resemble a student bedsit.

I'd tried to make that dream a reality. More than once. But apparently I'm not the only one with ambitions to be a news presenter. Competition is stiff. And young. If I'd made the right choices when I was twenty, I might have been a household name by now. Instead, I wasted my early career reporting local events and petty crimes, deluding myself into believing that my big break was just around the corner.

When I met Julian, I realised that I'd been waiting for opportunities to come my way rather than fighting for what I wanted. He helped me to rekindle my ambition, to unearth a long-forgotten determination to become who I've always known I was meant to be. But when I found myself up against women over a decade my junior, whose degrees were selected for the very purpose of becoming a news presenter, I gradually came to accept that my only way in was to know the right people.

Isn't that what they say? It's not what you know, it's who you know.

And so I found myself taking a side-step that I hoped

would one day lead to a step up. I finally admitted to Julian that I could use his help, and I let him use his connections to secure me this role as a personal assistant to the most notoriously unlikeable channel director in the industry. The plan was to worm my way into her favour, become a kind of protégée to her.

It wasn't just news she was working on – Channel Eight has an entire catalogue of shows, from comedy to drama to reality TV, and masses in between – but Jacqueline was known for her expertise in breaking the hottest news stories. She was brought in to revive the flagging news segment of the channel, to bring it up to date. To beat our competitors. I knew that if I could get on her good side, I could find a way into presenting.

As it turns out, though, she hates me, just like she hates everyone else in this godforsaken place. Her favour to Julian, it seems, extended only to hiring me. Personal connections counted for nothing once I started, and it didn't take long for me to see there was no glamour in TV, not unless you were the one in front of the camera.

At least in those hack publications I used to work at I had the freedom to come and go as I pleased, to choose the stories I covered. To at least fool myself into believing that I was following my dream, albeit on a much smaller scale than I'd ever hoped.

Here, I spend my days in mind-numbing strategy meetings about viewer figures and programme acquisition, silenced by my lowly position. I'm not entitled to an opinion. I take notes, and then I type them up, and all the while I amuse myself by mentally composing my resignation letter, just for fun.

I know I won't write it, though.

I never have, not even in the most soul-crushing moments

when I've felt like my dreams were shrivelling up and disappearing altogether. Because while there's even a whisper of a chance that this role could somehow lead to something more... well, I can't let that go, no matter how misguided my hope is.

Besides, I need the money. Meagre as it is, I can't afford to give up my income. This is London, and even living rent-free doesn't make the cost of living here much easier.

So I don't write that letter. I won't. Instead, I grit my teeth, reapply my lipstick and moan to Tash.

She's busy today. Her curt *mmhmms* are meant to indicate that I should walk away, get on with my work and leave her alone. But I need to talk to someone, and in this office she's my only option. The sooner she lets me get this off my chest, the sooner she'll get back to whatever task it is that she's taking so seriously.

Eventually, she stops typing, breathes in deeply as though resisting the urge to sigh, and offers me her full attention.

'She just doesn't see my potential,' I complain. 'Case in point, I took care of all of the social media while you were away—'

'And I'm truly grateful for that, I really am, and I'm sorry it added to your work—'

'Oh no,' I interrupt her interruption. 'I'm not saying this to make you feel bad, Tash. I was more than happy to take that on for you, it gave me a chance to prove that I'm capable of a bigger workload. But she doesn't see that. She just sees a personal assistant who constantly blends into the background. I could walk in here naked and no one would notice.'

'I'd notice. And I'd definitely tweet that.'

My shoulders relax as a laugh escapes my lips. Tash joins in, covering her mouth with her hand as she giggles.

'You just need to be patient,' she advises, sticking to her usual script. 'We both do. You *will* be a presenter one day, and I'll be a marketing manager, and we'll look back on these days and laugh at how impatient we were. Just keep your head down and do the work. Don't make waves. I know it'll pay off in the end.'

It's easy for her to say. She's still in her twenties, still has her whole career ahead of her. A career that doesn't rely on looks.

'I wish I could believe that,' I say. 'I have no doubt that you'll get what you want one day, but I just can't sit on my hands and wait for something that might never eventuate on its own. I have to make it happen.'

'What are you planning, Gina?' she asks, narrowing her eyes in suspicion.

I hesitate as she tucks a stray strand of hair back into the intricately braided bun she somehow has the time to create each morning. If I tell her what I'm going to ask of Jacqueline, she'll tell me not to bother. But I need an outlet for this anxious energy that's coursing through me. I feel like I could burst.

'I'm going to speak to Jacqueline today. About my career progression.'

She groans. She thinks she knows how this is going to end. But just because it hasn't gone to plan before, doesn't mean it'll be like that now.

'No, Tash, it's going to work this time. I can feel it.'

She narrows her eyes.

'You're an assistant. That means you do what's asked of you, you don't get to ask for things. I know you're ambitious, and I admire that, but whatever you've got planned, it's not going to end well, and you're going to end up back here in tears, feeling worse than you do now. Please, just don't go in

31

there asking Jacqueline for something she's already said no to. I'm begging you. Not just for your sake, although I am obviously concerned about you, but for the rest of us, too. I can't deal with her at the best of times, but when she's in a bad mood you know it ruins everyone's day. Do you really want to be the cause of that?'

'It'll be different this time. Trust me,' I insist, hoping I sound more confident than I feel. My stomach is churning, and I'm light-headed, probably because I haven't managed to eat a thing all day.

She nods in resignation. She doesn't believe me, and I can't say I blame her. But I have to do this.

'Well, you deserve success, so I hope it goes really well,' she sighs.

Returning to my desk, a hard ball of anxiety fills my otherwise empty stomach, growing larger and larger by the second. I have to do this now, before I lose my nerve.

I stand up resolutely, not giving myself the chance to back down before I've even tried. Jacqueline is at her desk, her face a silhouette against the sunlight streaming in behind her. I can't see her expression to gauge her mood but it doesn't matter. I need an answer, and waiting for the right temperament to strike could mean standing here for ever.

My heart hammers as I rap my knuckles on her open door, and I walk in before she has the chance to invite me.

'Do you have a minute, please?' I ask.

'What is it, Gina?'

Her tone is sharp. This isn't how I was hoping to find her, but it'll have to do.

I close the door behind me. Jacqueline stiffens in her seat and juts her jaw out. Not a great start. I ignore the sudden flash of doubt that hits me, annoyed at myself for even feeling it, for being intimidated by my boss. But she's the only person with the power to grant me the career I first dreamed of when I was a young woman. She has the power to change my future.

'I'd like to speak to you about an opportunity that I think could benefit both of us,' I begin as I sit down, crossing and uncrossing my legs.

She narrows her eyes and raises an eyebrow, but she doesn't stop me.

'My responsibility, as your personal assistant, is to make your job and your life easier, and to anticipate your needs,' I say. 'And I understand that one of your main priorities right now is to increase viewer numbers and ratings for Channel Eight.'

Her face is steely, devoid of all expression. I can't be certain that she's even listening to me, or if I'm just an annoying buzz, like a fly slamming against her window, barely punctuating her thoughts.

'I believe that the best opportunity to achieve this goal lies in digital media, which is an area I've proven my proficiency in, having recently managed all of the channel's social accounts in Tash's absence.'

Jacqueline opens her mouth, probably to end my well-rehearsed monologue, so I keep talking before she has a chance.

'With that in mind, I'd like to propose a project, for which I would take full responsibility, to host a daily news snippet live on Facebook, featuring the topics that will resonate best with the millennial audience we're trying to reach.'

'Gina—'

'Before you say anything,' I cut her off. 'This wouldn't take away from any of my existing responsibilities, and I know that it's within the digital marketing budget to pay for promotion, which is the only additional cost. The production is simple, and I would present, which means we wouldn't need to take away from any of our existing presenters—'

'Gina! Stop.'

I freeze. My mouth dries out, like it's been filled with sawdust. Jacqueline slowly smooths the ruffle that runs down the front of her pristine white shirt, letting the silence close in on us. The anticipation is torturous.

'We've already talked about this, Gina.'

She's speaking slowly, as though that's the only way I'll comprehend such a complex topic.

'What I need isn't another presenter. I can find one of those anywhere, one with experience and qualifications, even. I need an assistant who actually wants to do her job, who wants to go above and beyond to meet my requirements. I need you to schedule my appointments and sort through my emails and take notes in my meetings and field my phone calls, and whatever else I tell you to do. I don't need you to dream up completely unnecessary projects just to launch your own unreasonably ambitious career.'

The deflation is almost physical, like all the confidence I've ever felt has withered inside me in this one mortifying moment. Heat begins to rise in my face. I know I'm flushing, but I can't let her see how much her words have stung. A professional newsreader would stay composed, so I make myself stare straight into Jacqueline's hazel eyes, hoping my silence will make her uncomfortable.

'I know you think I'm being unfair, but if you really care about this channel, you'll know that *this* – this *project* of yours – is exactly what I don't need right now.'

She spits her words out, as though my proposal is nothing but a childish dream.

'Actually,' I begin, but she holds her hand up to silence

me. Her shiny black nails glint in the light, winking like they're in on some conspiracy against me.

'Actually, nothing, Gina. Are you going to do the job you were hired to do? Or am I going to have to find someone who will?'

I can't stop my mouth from falling open.

'You'd fire me for being ambitious?'

'Of course not. I'd fire you for not doing your job. You're not a presenter, Gina. You're a washed up journalist with a few too many years under your belt. Once you realise that you're a PA, and start acting like one, then I can actually get on with my job of making this channel successful. And then, *maybe*, if you've proven that you can be loyal, and that you can do your job with excellence, we can talk about your career progression. Until then, forget it. And don't think for a second that I'm going to extend you any privileges just because I know your boyfriend. I took a risk as it is when I hired you, and I'm starting to think that was a mistake. Now, I need those minutes from yesterday's meeting by two o'clock. Do you think you can do that, Gina?'

Her patronising tone isn't lost on me. I'm helpless to stop the burning of my cheeks, and the tears of shame and anger that sear my eyes. Nodding once, I get up without speaking. I don't trust myself to open my mouth.

Yanking the door open, I rush out of Jacqueline's office and ignore a concerned-looking Tash as I sweep past. At least I manage to keep the tears in until I reach the ladies' toilets. Safely locked inside a cubicle, I press the flush button until the sound of rushing water drowns the sound of my hate-filled sobs.

Chapter 6

RYAN

The blade slices cleanly through my flesh.

Dropping the knife with a yelp, I wrap the fingers of my right hand around my left index finger, gritting my teeth through the pain.

I should have known better than to try to cook a meal from scratch. That's Gina's skill, not mine. As I run my bleeding finger under a cold stream of water, I wonder if there's still time to get a takeaway instead. But Gina will be home any minute now, and with Julian away, it's a rare opportunity to spend some time together.

It's been six months since Gina's been back in my life, but it's still a surprise when she walks in the door each evening. I never thought I'd have a sister again, and I certainly never imagined I'd have the chance to make things right.

The day I got that phone call will forever be burned in my memory. My work phone had cut through my concentration. The call had been directed through the switchboard, so I couldn't see the number.

'Ryan Mills.'

'Hi, Ryan, it's me. Gina.'

My brain had clutched for a business associate called Gina. I mentally ran through my client list, but came up short. I was about to ask for her company name when the voice, clear and confident, came down the line again.

'Your sister.'

I'd sat in mute shock while my only sibling, the one who had been gone for fifteen years, kept talking, told me how she wanted to reconnect, how she missed me, how she needed to speak to me about something.

I'd agreed to meet, mostly because my brain refused to process the information it had just received, and I couldn't think of a response more sophisticated than 'OK'. But I'd had enough presence of mind to pick somewhere public, just in case her friendly tone concealed a rage I knew she had every right to feel.

I'm wary of things that seem too good to be true, family reunions included.

I'd arrived at the pub early the next evening, dressed in chinos and a cashmere jumper, an outfit that I'd spent hours deliberating over. I couldn't control the sweat that was making my palms slick. It was hard to hold my pint. What would we say? What *could* we say? I'd never allowed myself to imagine how this would go, because when Gina had left, she'd made it clear that it was for good. For months afterwards, I'd convinced myself that I'd spotted her out and about, but I knew that it was just wishful thinking. She was true to her word, too. Not once had she been in touch. Not a postcard, not an email. Not even a friend request.

And yet here she was, walking through the door of my local pub, looking almost the same as when she'd left. A few lines around her eyes gave away the time that had passed between us, but she was still unmistakably Gina. Bright red curls. Emerald eyes. Freckles. Beautiful . . . just like Mum.

'Hi.' She'd stopped opposite me, smiling broadly.

'Hi.'

'I'm just getting a glass of wine,' she'd said, so casually, as though we'd only just seen each other. 'Another beer?'

I'd nodded mutely, and she'd disappeared to the bar, leaving me reeling. For the first time since I'd picked up the phone, I allowed myself to believe that this really was Gina, and that she really was back. Not just back, but smiling. Which meant maybe she didn't hate me after all. Was that even possible, after everything?

She returned with two drinks, which we clinked together. I took a deep gulp from the new beer, needing the fortification, hoping that she'd start talking first.

'You're probably wondering what I'm doing here,' she'd begun.

'The question had crossed my mind,' I said. She'd laughed, and the familiar sound made my stomach clench. Not with tension. With hope.

'I heard about Mum and Dad,' she'd said.

'How?' I'd asked, confused. I didn't know that my sister still cared what the rest of us got up to, never mind keeping up to date with our news. Not that we often had much to share, but about two months before Gina's call, our parents had upped and moved to Florida.

Retirement, they called it. Their life's dream, they tried to convince me. But I knew the truth. They were running away. From that house. From their past. From their grief. An invisible captor they'd never found a way to evade after all these years. I'd tried to be supportive but I was devastated. Not even their parting gift of our family home could alleviate my sadness. I was losing what little family I had left. I wanted them to be happy, but didn't I deserve happiness, too?

I already knew the answer to that.

'I get curious sometimes,' she'd admitted, looking uncomfortable. 'Dad's Facebook profile is public.'

'You're on Facebook?' I'd yelped. I'd looked for her so many times I'd lost count. She was never there.

'I'm not searchable.' She'd shrugged, offering nothing more.

I'd nodded, not wanting to push too hard, in case I scared her off. But I'd felt an unmistakeable flicker of envy. I'd never had any way of getting in touch with her, of knowing what she was up to, or even if she was OK, but she'd been keeping tabs on us, finding out what was happening in our lives, as long as we'd posted it online.

'I could never have come back, with them in the picture,' Gina had said to me across the sticky table. 'Not after everything. I'd always wanted to get in touch with you, but I didn't want you to be put in that awkward position.'

'But you just left. You could have sent me an email, or a letter, or ... *something*. It's been so long, Gina.'

'I know, and I'm sorry. I am. I should have been better. I told myself I was protecting you, that you were happier without me. You had their love, at least.'

My stomach contracted with guilt. It was true, I did have their love. All of it.

'Well, I missed you,' I said. 'And Mum and Dad were ... well, you know how they were.'

Grief-stricken, hollow. Empty versions of their old selves.

Gina had closed her eyes briefly and taken another sip of her wine.

'So tell me what you're up to these days. Where are you living?'

I'd swallowed hard, using my thumbnail to scratch a line into the grime that formed a cover on the tabletop. She wasn't going to like this. There was no way to say it delicately, so I just blurted it out.

'I'm living in their place. They gave it to me when they left.'

She'd raised her eyebrows, her eyes flaring with indignation. She didn't say anything. She didn't need to.

'How about you?' I'd asked, a lame attempt at moving on.

'Actually,' she'd said, 'I just moved back to London, so I'm looking for somewhere to stay.'

I'd laughed, then. It wasn't out of bitterness, although I had felt an undeniable flicker of that, too. Of course she hadn't just come back into my life because she missed me. She wanted something – and not just anything. She must have already known about the house, and she was looking for somewhere to live. It was a big ask, we both knew that.

I enjoyed living alone, having my own space, answering to no one. There was no way to know if Gina and I would get along, if we'd drive each other crazy, if I'd regret this after a few days. But despite the inconvenience, and the risk, I wouldn't say no. I couldn't.

Because I owed her. Whatever she asked, I'd say yes. Moving in, and anything after that, and even then we wouldn't be even. We'd never be even.

Besides, I *had* missed her. And after so many years apart, I wasn't going to be the one to drive a bigger gap between us, whether she was using me or not.

'You can live with me,' I'd said.

'No, that's not what I—'

'It is,' I'd argued. 'I may not have seen you for a long time, but I still know you, Gina. Besides, I'd love for you to come live with me. The decor is terrible, and so is my cooking. But the rent is free and you can have your old room back.'

She'd jumped off her chair then, walked around the table and flung her arms around me. The warmth had started from somewhere deep inside, somewhere long forgotten, and spread throughout my body, all the way to my fingertips, which had tingled with possibility. I'd hugged her tightly. Gina was back. I finally had the chance to make it right. An opportunity for redemption.

As I wrap a plaster around my sliced finger, the unmistakable jangle and click of keys reaches me from the front door. Throwing away the garlic, now ruby red like tiny chunks of flesh, I call out to Gina to let her know I'm in the kitchen.

All I see when she walks in is a cascade of red hair, but as she looks up, her eyes are red and her face is blotchy, with smudges of mascara like small bruises under her eyes.

'What's wrong?' I ask, dread hitting me in the solar plexus. No matter how old we get, I still feel protective of my younger sister. Maybe now, as an adult, I'll do a better job of it than I did all those years ago.

She sighs and flops onto a stool at the breakfast bar.

'It's nothing. Well, it's not nothing. It's just that I tried to get Jacqueline to give me a chance. And she said no. Again.'

Relieved that it's nothing more serious, I step into the space between us and reach out to hug her.

'Sorry,' I mumble awkwardly.

'It's OK,' she says as she pulls back and her green eyes look into mine. 'I kind of expected it, but it still sucks. I'm just really done with being a failure.'

'You're not a failure,' I say forcefully.

'Thanks,' she says, clearly unconvinced. 'Anyway. I'm not going to let myself mope. I had a cry – at work, embarrassingly – and now I just have to move on. This doesn't change anything. My plans haven't changed. I'm not going to be stuck as an assistant for ever.'

'That's the spirit,' I say, handing her a bottle of red wine. 'Sounds like you could use some of this though.'

'Definitely,' she says, pouring herself a glass. 'Anyway, enough about me. How are you?'

'Fine,' I lie. The truth is, since the incident on the train yesterday morning, I've felt uneasy, on edge, like the world is slightly out of kilter. I've spent years carefully constructing walls around my past, protecting myself from those memories, building a routine that pacifies me into numbness, and in one moment it all came tumbling down.

All I can think about is Cassie.

What would she be like now? Would we get along? Would she still make me laugh and infuriate me in equal measure, like she used to?

I want to talk about it with Gina, but I can't risk it. There's no casual way to mention that I thought I saw our sister on a train yesterday. Or that I spent last night in the attic, desperately searching for Cassie's death certificate, telling myself even while I was doing so that it was crazy. And unnecessary.

I saw my sister's body, I saw the blood, and I know she was gone. She *is* gone.

I didn't find that certificate, in the end. Mum and Dad must have taken it with them, must have thought it precious enough to take to Florida. It's the only explanation.

But I can't tell Gina any of these things. I can't dredge all of that up again.

It would ruin us.

It would ruin me.

Chapter 7

GINA

'Come on, Gina,' Tash complains, sliding a bottle across the table towards me. 'We left work an hour ago. Put that thing away.'

'Sorry.' I give her my best apologetic look as I slide the pen into the elastic on the side of my notepad and slip it into my handbag. 'I just overheard those guys over there talking about their boss investing in some shady—'

'Gina,' Tash warns sternly.

'Sorry,' I repeat with a laugh. 'I guess I can't just turn it off.'

'You're the most journalisty journalist I've ever met,' she says, clinking her bottle against mine. 'Always a story going on in that head of yours.'

'Yeah, well, pity that's not all it takes to get a proper bloody job,' I grumble. Then I mentally pull myself together. I've done enough complaining. I need to move on.

'Anyway,' I say brightly. 'Cheers! Thanks for the drink.'

'Thanks for doing my job while I was away.'

'You're welcome. I actually kind of enjoyed it,' I admit, taking a swig. 'And if it means I get free drinks, I'm up for it anytime.'

'Well, the drinks are partly to say thanks, partly to help you commiserate after yesterday.'

I groan. 'You can say it now.'

'Say what?' she asks, all mock innocence. 'Oh, you mean "I told you so"?'

I laugh, hoping it sounds light-hearted. 'That would be the one. Seriously though, you were right. It wasn't good timing. I'm just sick of waiting. But please let's not talk about work, it's boring enough from nine till six every day. Tell me about Mexico!'

'Well,' she begins with a smile, 'you will never believe what Belinda did at the hotel bar...'

I try to relax as Tash launches into story after story of her sister's over-the-top hen party in Cancun, but I can't enjoy myself. There's too much swirling through my mind.

'Did you and Julian have a nice dinner the other night?' she asks when I get back to our table with another round.

'It was lovely, thanks,' I say, my fingers finding their way subconsciously to the weighty charm that's hanging from my neck.

'Did he give that to you?'

'Yeah, he has a matching one. It's got—'

I stop myself before I blurt out the part where we carry a lock of one another's hair around our necks.

'It's got what?'

'Oh, nothing.' I tuck it back beneath my shirt and take a sip of my beer.

'So he didn't pop the question, then?'

Tash wriggles her eyebrows and I squirm in my seat.

'No,' I admit. 'I've told him not to.'

'What? Why? You guys are perfect for each other.'

'I know,' I say. I don't even try to deny it. There's no one on earth who could complement me better than Julian does. I know without a doubt that I want to be with him for ever. I hope he feels the same way.

44

'But I don't want to *just* be someone's wife. Even if it is Julian's. I want my own achievements, something to my name besides a wedding.'

'You can still achieve things once you're married.'

'I know that,' I say defensively. 'But when I *do* get married, or even if I just move in with him, I want us to be equal partners. As it is, I'm sponging off my brother, which is bad enough at my age. I won't do that to Julian, too.'

'OK.' Tash raises her hands, as though in surrender. 'All I'm saying is, if I ever find someone who I'm as madly in love with as you are with Julian, I'll marry him in a registry office the next day just to lock him down.'

We both laugh this time.

'Man, is that the time?' Tash cries abruptly, looking at her phone. 'I've gotta go.'

'Good point. Me too,' I say, typing out a quick text to let Julian know I'm leaving. 'Julian's got his first show of the tour tomorrow, and I want to catch him before he goes to bed.'

'Wish him luck from me,' she says as she orders herself an Uber. 'How are you getting home?'

'I'll walk.' I shrug. 'It's stopped raining, and it'll only take me half an hour.'

We move towards the exit, pulling on our coats and scarves, and Tash gives me a tight hug as her driver arrives outside the pub.

'You sure you're OK to walk?' she calls back to me as she opens the door.

'I'm good, I promise,' I assure her, waving goodnight.

As soon as the car disappears around the corner, I dial Julian's number.

'Hey baby,' I say, grinning into the phone as he picks up.

'Gina! I miss you.'

I focus on the sound of him shuffling a deck of cards in the background. I picture him, propped up with pillows on a hotel bed, his hair ever-so-slightly out of place from where he's run his fingers through it, a barely touched room service tray beside him and the cards being riffled absent-mindedly.

'How was your night with Tash? Have you left?'

'I'm walking home now,' I say. 'It was good, thanks. I didn't really fancy it but I'm glad I went, it took my mind off things for a bit, you know?'

'Yeah, I bet. I know yesterday didn't go well for you, but it's all going to work out in the end. You know that, don't you?'

'I hope you're right. I wish I had your confidence.'

I want to believe him but I can't ignore the doubts that are following just a few steps behind me – silent, but unmistakably present, like shadows.

'Well, I can't give you confidence,' Julian says, his tone brightening. 'But I have something else that might help. I made you a playlist today. It's just a little something to remind you that I believe in you, and to help you to keep going, even when it gets hard. Here, I'm sending it now.'

My phone buzzes against my cheek as the playlist arrives in a message, and my smile returns.

'You're the best. I love you.'

'I love you too. I should go now though. I'll call you tomorrow.'

'OK. Break a leg.'

I hang up, wondering if that's the correct term to use for an illusionist, or if it's reserved just for actors. Have I just jinxed my boyfriend? Mentally waving the question aside, I open Julian's message and tap the link to 'Gina's Just Do It Tunes'.

I press play and as the first song begins a giggle escapes

my lips, startling the couple walking ahead. They jump and turn around, glaring at me.

'Sorry,' I mutter, not meaning it. I shake my head at Julian's brand of motivation. He knows how much I hate Kanye West. At least, he's heard me proclaiming that I can't bear the man's music. But when he walked in on me belting out a karaoke version of 'Stronger' one day, he teased me about my hypocrisy for weeks. This song is the single exception to my Kanye ban.

As I walk, the determination that waned yesterday begins to return, a tide coming in, growing with every stride. Julian's right. Yesterday's failure is irrelevant in the grand scheme of things. What's ahead is more important.

I concentrate on my favourite line of the song, the one that tells me that whatever doesn't kill me will make me stronger, as I cut through an alleyway that shaves a good ten minutes off the walk home.

Most of the time, I'm far too scared to walk this way at night. Not that anything bad's ever happened here. It's just creepy, and I know better than to venture down a dark, dimly lit, abandoned alleyway at night.

Because if something did happen, I'd feel like a fool for willingly stepping into danger. Tonight though, I'm bold. Invincible. I pick up my pace, keeping time with the rhythm. My heart rate responds in time.

I barely notice the adrenalin blooming in my veins as I move deeper into the darkness. I'm so consumed by the idea of what my future might hold, so absorbed with the lyrics about doing anything when the time's right, that I almost don't see it.

I stop mid-step, hairs needling at the back of my neck. It takes a few seconds for my brain to register the details of what my eyes have already detected, but when it does, my blood surges, hot and fast, starting in my chest and bursting through my veins.

I tug the headphones from my ears and step tentatively towards the silver satin heels. Such an innocuous sight: a pair of pretty shoes. But not here. Not like this. These heels, worn no doubt for a fun night out, are peeking out from behind a pile of black, bulging rubbish bags. My heart pounds in my mouth.

There's a sharp snap, something breaking under my heel. I jump backwards, startled by the crack, the noise out of place in the eerie silence. It's a compact mirror, silver, like the shoes, lying in a small red pool. Blood.

The sight brings with it a wave of memories, a flood of emotion, and for a second it threatens to overwhelm me, to pull me under. But I fight the sensation, mentally battling to reach the surface, to return to the present. This isn't a moment for remembering a time I tried so hard to forget. I need to move.

The shards of mirror – and the dark droplets clinging to them – create a distorted reflection, flashes of light and dark that are glinting at me, winking, like I'm being mocked.

I follow the trail of blood from the compact to the silver satin shoes.

From where I'm standing, she could just be drunk. Passed out. I force myself to imagine this scenario for a second, clinging to the details to test them for truth. Her friends, two other women in impossibly high heels, are on the street flagging down a taxi. They'll come back, and together they'll heave their friend onto their shoulders, sharing the weight of her, tucking stray curls behind her ears. They'll rummage in their bags for a plaster, and they'll mend her sliced finger, promising they'll buy her a new compact tomorrow. I'll hold the door open for them as they stumble to the main road, then close it after they're safely inside the car. I'll apologise for jumping to dramatic conclusions, and I'll wish them a safe journey home.

Except there are no friends. I know – I'm unshakeably certain – that she's not just intoxicated. It's the angle of her legs that gives it away. The way they're bent. It's unnatural. One foot points up, towards the heavy clouds overhead, and the other is twisted, toes facing down, pressed into the cold cobblestones. The heel from her left shoe has snapped. I spot the satin-wrapped spike lying a few feet away, in the widest part of the alleyway.

Expecting what I'm about to see does nothing to minimise the reality that hits me when I peer past the garbage bags. I hear myself gasping out loud, and my stomach dances wildly. The first thing I notice is how pale her face is, like a porcelain doll, eternally frozen. But then my eyes are quickly drawn to her neck, to the dark, sinister bruise that circles her skin. There are grazes along her arms and chest, and strips of her navy blue dress have been torn away as though she's been dragged along the ground. A cluster of jewels glints at me, winking in the green glow that bathes us from the grim light above the back door of a pub. My breaths are shallow. I gulp a lungful of oxygen to stop the spinning in my head.

My eyes flit back and forth in the dark, exploring every corner of the alleyway to be sure that the person who did this is gone. There's no sign of another human, not a living one, anyway. It's just me. And her.

Time hangs in the air as I absorb each detail in turn, and then it rushes forward all at once, and I'm kneeling next to the woman, feeling for a pulse that I'm certain no longer exists.

It takes three attempts for my fingers to stop trembling

enough to dial 999. My body is cumbersome, as though I've never had to complete such a delicate task before. I'm hardly aware of what I say, but I think I tell them to hurry.

And then there's nothing.

My own rapid breathing is the only sound echoing in my ears. My skin prickles and my heart beats so violently that my vision begins to blur, a dark mist closing in around me. Sirens wail mournfully in the distance. I think they might be for us. Me and this woman. We're in this together, somehow.

Blinking away the blackness, I force myself to pick something – anything – to focus on. I choose a mural painted onto the wall straight ahead of me. I direct every molecule of my being towards it, forcing myself to concentrate, to get a handle on my senses.

It's new, I think – the mural. Street artists love this alleyway. For years they've used it as their canvas, recycling the space whenever new inspiration hits. I trail my eyes slowly from the top, which is a dark green, to the point where the wall meets the ground. It's bright blue, the same shade that tints the lips of the woman I'm crouching beside. My body tingles violently.

I breathe deeply, riding the wave of emotion that washes over me. Fumes of fresh paint hit my nostrils, and my head spins again. I narrow my eyes, fixing them on the huge, cartoon-like pocket watch sprayed onto the grimy wall, a flock of birds flying off the face, leaving empty spaces where the numbers should be. There are words underneath it in angular, sharp letters.

My skin tingles as they jump off the wall towards me, screaming their message until it's all I can see, all I can hear, the words playing on a loop in my mind.

Your Time Is Now, it says.

I blink. I need to stay alert but my limbs are frozen, the adrenalin paralysing me. I close my eyes for just a second, to compose my thoughts, but the words follow me into the darkness.

Your Time Is Now.

Chapter 8

DETECTIVE ADAM ADEBAYO

This case couldn't have come at a better time.

There's no way to even think such a thing without sounding callous, I tell myself as I switch on the car's sirens to move past a slow-moving van ahead, but it's the truth nonetheless.

Guilt tugs at me as I remember the victim. And worse, her loved ones. There's a family to be told, people who are, right now, unaware that their lives are about to change for the worse. For ever.

Still. Circumstances aside, receiving that call from my detective inspector telling me I've been assigned to a new case is the distraction I've been hoping for, something to focus on that's not my latest failed relationship.

I don't offer much in the way of conversation on the drive over to the scene. I'm too busy watching the footage on my phone, starting it over and over again, my disbelief growing with every fresh replay.

'Who *does* that?' asks my partner Christine, trying to sneak a look at my screen as she pulls to a stop at an intersection.

I shake my head. People react in countless different ways when they're confronted by death. Tears, shock, laughter, even. But I've never come across a reaction quite like this.

'That's social media for you,' I say, as though I come from

a generation that's removed from the dangers of constant connection. The truth is, I'm guilty of it too, of spending late nights scrolling through Instagram instead of going to sleep, of promising myself I'll look at just one more post.

'I love a good selfie as much as the next person,' Christine says. 'But I wouldn't live stream a bloody crime scene.'

'Well yeah, we're the police, so obviously *we* wouldn't. But haven't you seen those people with selfie sticks when there have been terror attacks? It's more common than you might think. People just want to feel like they're part of the action.'

'How does taking a picture make you part of it? And why would you *want* to be part of something like that?'

'I'm not a psychologist,' I say. 'But maybe it's the shock that makes people do something they'll later regret. Or, I don't know, their lives might be so utterly dull that a crime that has nothing to do with them really is the most interesting thing they'll ever be associated with. Or maybe sharing every bit of our lives has just become such an instinct that this is our natural reaction now.'

She tuts, and checks the rear-view mirror.

'Well, I'm pretty sure filming or live streaming a crime scene wouldn't be my natural reaction.'

I tip my head in agreement as I hit replay again.

'Is there anything useful we can glean from the footage, at least?'

My screen is filled with a woman's face. She's young, my age at a guess, with cascading red hair that falls in layers around her face, framing her pale skin and bright green eyes. If it weren't for the flush in her cheeks and her dilated pupils, there'd be no sign of stress. She's composed, and her mouth is held in a kind of restrained smile. It's like watching the news, which makes sense, as it's published on the Channel Eight Facebook page. I have a suspicion this is unauthorised, however. If it's been posted with permission, our lawyers will have something to say about it.

The camera is fixed on the woman, who's standing with her back towards a large, colourful mural. She's in a dimly lit space – an alleyway, I've learned, after multiple times watching it.

'This is Gina Mills,' the woman's voice announces from the tiny speakers in my phone, 'reporting live for Channel Eight from west London.'

She takes a deep breath, whether to calm herself or to build suspense, I can't be certain.

'While walking home this evening, I stumbled upon what appears to be a murder scene. I contacted emergency services as soon as I made the gruesome discovery, and I'm now waiting for the first responders to arrive.'

She shifts slightly, and I spot something silver glinting in the corner behind her. It could be a mirror, or perhaps just a piece of broken glass. I'm itching to get there so I can see for myself, the adrenalin that comes with the announcement of a new case making me twitchy and impatient.

'The victim – a female who I'd estimate to be in her late twenties – appears to have suffered a blow to the head, and is showing signs of bruising around her neck. I found her here in an alleyway in west London, behind a busy neighbourhood pub, concealed from view of the main street. If you know anything about this crime, please contact the police immediately to assist them with their investigation.'

I groan.

'There's literally nothing of use in this,' I say. 'And yet, hundreds of thousands of people have watched it already.'

'Slow news day,' Christine snorts.

And a beautiful woman breaking the story, I think. It can't hurt.

We turn onto a high street that's crammed with emergency services vehicles and pedestrians trying to get a sneak peek at the drama. Christine hits the kerb, swears, reverses, and parks perfectly parallel to the footpath. My door makes a crunching sound as I fling it open. I wince, pulling it towards me, away from the post box on the kerb.

'Sorry,' I mutter, not waiting for a reply as I step out of the car, observing as much as I can as I walk towards the scene. The first responders have already secured the area. Police tape keeps the small crowd of rubberneckers from spilling into the crime scene; the alleyway behind a row of pubs and bars that already looks so familiar from the footage on my phone.

I don't recognise the officer standing just inside the tape, but I nod at him like we go way back as I flash my badge in his direction. He gestures towards the crime scene log which I sign before stepping into a protective suit and slipping a pair of covers over my shoes.

The clouds are low and heavy above a white tent that dominates the area. It makes the alleyway feel claustrophobic. As I move closer, a flash blinds me temporarily and when I blink, shadowy silhouettes lurk in my vision. When I open my eyes again, Detective Inspector Mia Bristow steps out of the tent in front of me. She beckons me over.

'Hey, Adam,' she says as I approach. 'Did you see the video our witness made?'

I roll my eyes. 'Yeah. She said it looked like an injury to the head, or maybe strangulation?'.

'Bingo,' Mia says as Christine appears by my side. 'We won't know which one actually killed her before the autopsy, but either way, someone tried really hard to make sure she was dead.'

My partner and I peer into the tent at the same time.

There's not a lot of room in the small covering – it's mostly here for privacy – so I can hear her breath, a quick hiss, as the victim comes into view. I get it. No matter how many bodies I see, it doesn't get any easier for me, either.

There's something grotesque about the way the woman is lying, the way the temporary floodlights are casting a cold glow over her. She's blonde, and was probably beautiful when she was alive, although it's hard to tell now. Her face is swollen, her lips tinged blue. Her hair is matted to the side of her head with blood. It's thick and dark, contrasting with her skin. Around her neck is a ring of bruising, dark and sinister, a necklace of pain. She's propped up awkwardly next to a pile of rubbish bags, and her limbs are at strange angles.

I follow the blood that marks a trail from her feet across the tent, disappearing under the canvas. She must have been dragged, or perhaps she dragged herself, from the other side of the alleyway to where she now lies.

'Do we still have the witness here?' I ask.

'Yeah,' Mia sighs. 'I'll let you two get acquainted while we take care of the forensics, then you can take her back to the station.'

'Is she a suspect?'

'Could be. Too soon to tell, but we're not ruling her out. See what you can get from her, and check her phone for any more evidence she may have recorded.'

She points towards a small cluster of camping chairs that have been set up as far away from the body as possible. I spot a redhead covered in a silver blanket who's being handed a cup of something steaming by a member of the medical team.

I stroll over, trying to imagine what kind of personality it takes to start a live stream after seeing something as distressing as what I've just been looking at. Being hooked on social media is one thing, but there's sharing the high-lights of your life with your family and friends, and then there's desperation, a need to be part of something bigger than yourself so deep that you can't see right from wrong. If that's the kind of witness we're dealing with, we're in for an infuriating night.

'Shall we?' I ask Christine, and she indicates for me to go ahead.

'Miss Mills?' I ask gently, taking a seat next to the woman I recognise from the video on Facebook. 'I'm Detective Constable Adam Adebayo, and this is my partner, Detective Constable Christine Taylor.'

She looks up at us, her face ghostly pale under the harsh lights. In the video she was oozing confidence, her tone assertive and her voice unwavering. The woman in front of me seems fragile, as though the slightest touch will shatter her until there's nothing but microscopic fragments tinkling on the ground beneath our feet. I should know better than to believe appearances, but still. She doesn't *look* hungry for fame.

'Can I ask you a few questions about what you saw this evening?'

She nods, barely, and holds my gaze.

'Could you describe to me how you found the victim?'

'I was walking home,' she says, her voice low and calm. 'I was out with a colleague for some drinks after work, and then I was walking home.'

There's no emotion in her words. She's telling us the facts, but she seems completely detached from what happened.

'I don't usually take this alleyway, but I knew it would save me time, and I just wanted to get home to bed. I was listening to music, so I was distracted, and I suppose I wasn't really paying attention to what was going on around me. Then I saw her feet. Her shoes. And I stepped on a compact mirror. That's when I saw the blood.'

I can barely see the green of her eyes, her pupils are so large. It's one of the most common symptoms of shock, I remember.

'It's OK,' I assure her as gently as I can. 'I know that what you saw is really upsetting but can you tell me what happened next?'

'I got closer, and that's when I saw her. I knew she was dead.'

Christine looks over at me, and I give her the smallest of shrugs. Gina's demeanour is certainly unusual but when it comes to witness reactions I've seen a full spectrum in my time as a detective. There are those who become fact-focused, and seem to be numb, like Gina, and then there are people who become utterly hysterical, complete with fainting or crying. There's no right way to react, but calm witnesses certainly make our job easier.

'There was the blood,' she continues, her voice devoid of any inflection. She sounds almost robotic. 'And there were bruises around her neck. I could just tell she was dead. I called the police. Or the ambulance. I don't remember who I spoke to. They asked me to check her pulse, but there was nothing. She was gone. I think the call got cut off then, although I can't really remember.'

She looks off into the distance, frowning slightly, as though not quite sure what's happening.

'OK,' Christine says, leaning across me to get closer to Gina. 'And then what?'

'Then I started the recording.'

She shows no hint of embarrassment. Or remorse. But at least she's not trying to deny it. I follow Gina's vacant gaze

58

over my shoulder, in the direction of the tent. She's probably got an identical mental image to the one that's hovering at the periphery of my imagination. I blink it away.

'Why?'

'Pardon me?'

'Why did you decide to share what you'd found on social media?'

She looks at me blankly.

'I'm a journalist.'

'Do you work for Channel Eight?' Christine asks.

'Yes.'

'As a reporter?'

'No. As a personal assistant.'

Christine and I exchange another glance. This woman is nothing like the vivid reporter we just watched in the car on the way over. It's hard to imagine the Gina we're speaking to mustering up enough energy to lift a phone, never mind record a crime scene live. She looks like she might fall asleep, or topple off her chair.

'So how are you a journalist, then?'

'I was a reporter at a local newspaper in Sussex for ten years,' she says. 'I moved back to London recently and found a role as a personal assistant at Channel Eight.'

I raise my eyebrows.

'There were no newspapers in London hiring someone with that kind of experience?'

'I'm looking to get into television journalism,' she says simply.

'And breaking the story of a murder was your way of getting the job you want,' Christine fills in the gaps.

Gina looks impassively from Christine's face to mine, and then back again.

'You might not believe me,' she says. 'But that's not why

I did it. I can't ignore a story. And I wanted to make sure her story was told. That's all.'

I look at my shoes to rearrange my instinctive reaction. Showing my true feelings about journalists would be unprofessional. I've had to work with them from time to time, and every one has been the same. Always acting as though they're doing the world a favour, while simultaneously screwing over anyone who comes between them and whatever information they want. I hope my dealings with this one are short-lived.

'We'd like you to come with us to the station for processing, Miss Mills,' Christine says.

'Why? I've done nothing wrong.'

Even when she's defensive, it's as though she's feeling nothing. I wonder if I should get the medical team to check her again. Although there's no such thing as a normal reaction to discovering a dead body, there's something off about the way Gina's acting.

'You're not under arrest. We'd like you to come in so we can get you checked again by the medical team, and then take your DNA and fingerprints. That way, when forensics come back with DNA from the body we can rule yours out right away. It just means we won't be chasing our tails. Plus, we need an official witness statement. Is that OK?'

'Yes, that's fine.'

I shake my head as Christine leads a passive Gina towards the car we arrived in. I signal to our boss that we're heading back to the station, and she nods her acknowledgement.

I take one last look at the alleyway before I turn to follow my partner. A shiver hits me in the small of my back, and I tug my jacket tightly across my chest. As I turn around, I notice the mural I saw in Gina's video.

It's bursting with bright colours, at odds with the moody

darkness of its surroundings. There's a giant clock face, and a flock of birds.

Your Time Is Now, it says to me.

As I walk away, I can't help but wonder.

Is that encouragement . . . or a threat?

Chapter 9

RYAN

It takes longer than usual for my consciousness to drag me from the depths of sleep.

When I finally wake up, groggy and slow, I slap at my phone until I manage to find the button that turns off my alarm.

The blood behind my eyes is pounding a steady, painful beat. My muscles ache and my mouth is dry. I frown. I'm not hungover – I can't be. I only had one small measure of whisky, my usual nightcap. I steal a glance at my bedside table. There's an empty glass, evidence that it was an average night. But there's nothing average about this headache.

Heaving myself out of bed, I pocket my phone and trudge to the kitchen, desperately hoping that coffee will make whatever this is better. I can't afford to be sick, there's too much going on at work. Absently, I press a pod into its place in the coffee machine and push the button for the largest size, placing a mug underneath the dark brown flow. As it whirrs away, a sense of unease settles over me, spreading and intensifying.

It's the same feeling I get every time I go on holiday, the utter certainty that I've left something essential at home. Only I haven't booked any holidays for the rest of this year. I mentally check off the things that could be causing this feeling. Mum's birthday isn't for months. My bills have all been paid. Maybe I missed a client call yesterday, although I'm sure I would have remembered that by now. I check my phone, hoping my notifications will offer the answers.

I spot a message first. It's from David, at work. *That's your sister on TV, right?*

I frown, more unsettled than before. Why would Gina have been on TV? David must be confused. He probably just saw someone with red hair and jumped to conclusions. I take the first sip of my coffee and relax as the hot, bitter liquid hits the back of my throat. I know that it's only in my mind, but I'm immediately more alert. The pounding behind my eyes has receded slightly, although it's still there, nagging at me, begging for my attention.

Trying to ignore it, I open Facebook. I hate myself for even having it installed on my phone, but there's something compelling about watching other people's lives unfolding. I know that's not why I still look at it every day though, no matter how many times I promise myself I'll stop. It validates me. I know my life is better than theirs, those people I used to go to school with, or who I partied with at university. I'm not proud of this insecurity in me, but when I see someone whose life hasn't turned into anything even close to extraordinary, it makes me feel better. Like maybe I'm doing OK after all.

Today though, as I open my feed, feeling superior doesn't even cross my mind.

Because all I see is Gina. Her face, smiling at me from a video thumbnail in a post published by the official Channel Eight page. According to Facebook, it's been shared by eight of my friends. And eleven thousand strangers.

I tap the play button and watch with mounting incredulity as I learn what Gina was doing last night while I was asleep.

I run down the hallway and hurl my fist at her bedroom door, my headache drowned out by greater concerns.

'Gina! Gina, are you home?'

There's a disgruntled moan, which I take to mean that she is, and that I can enter. She's nothing more than a lump under the duvet, her hair fanned out across her pillow.

'Gina,' I say, more gently now. 'I just saw. I'm so sorry. Are you OK? You should have called me.'

She mumbles something incoherent as I sit down next to the lump of covers.

'I have coffee,' I say, waving my mug close to where her face should be. She slowly peels the duvet down to reveal smudged, dark eyes. I hold my half-drunk coffee out.

'Are you all right?'

She sits up and grabs the mug, taking a deep gulp. She looks at me for a few seconds, her eyes red and swollen, still smeared with last night's make-up. Then she sighs and nods.

'I'm fine. I think. Just exhausted, really.'

'Why didn't you call? I could have . . .'

I trail off. I'm actually not sure what I could have done. My sister raises her eyebrows at me, her face echoing my thoughts.

'OK, I couldn't have helped, exactly. But what the hell happened?'

'You've seen the footage?' she asks, her voice barely louder than a croak. I nod. 'So you know most of it already. It's all a bit of a blur, to be honest. They told me I was in shock, so I don't think I was really comprehending anything that was happening. I do know I had to go to the police station. They wanted an official witness statement, and I had to provide my DNA and fingerprints and stuff so they can eliminate me from any forensic evidence they found at the scene.'

'But what made you *film* it, Gina, especially from Channel Eight's account? And what were you doing walking down that alleyway on your own at night? I thought you avoided it, you said it gives you the creeps.'

Gina stares into the coffee mug, like she hopes she'll find clarity in the pitch-black liquid.

'I know this doesn't really make sense,' she says wearily, 'but I'm a reporter, Ryan. You don't understand it, and that's OK, but I saw that woman...'

She trails off, swallowing hard. She closes her eyes for a second and takes in a shaky lungful of air.

'I saw her, and I just followed my natural instinct. My gut told me to report it. Maybe it was my brain's way of processing what I was seeing. That's the best explanation I can give. And I was logged into the Channel Eight accounts because I'd been looking after them while Tash was away.'

I weigh up what she's saying. She is a reporter at heart, I've seen that. She carries that tatty notebook everywhere, and she's always scribbling things down, always finding an angle.

'And that alleyway does give me the creeps,' she adds. 'But I just wanted to get home. I was hoping to get a good night's sleep.'

'I know that feeling,' I laugh drily. Her expression doesn't change. She's motionless, her eyes fixed on the mug in front of her.

'Have you spoken to Julian?' I ask gently.

She looks up at me, her eyes red-rimmed.

'Yeah, I called him last night, on my way back from the police station. He wanted to come home, but I told him he should stay. His show...'

She trails off, and I feel helpless to comfort her.

'Here, I'll go make you another coffee,' I say, holding out

my hand for her mug. I've never been good at emotions. Practical help is the best I can do. 'I need one myself.'

I'm almost out of her bedroom when she calls my name. I turn around. She looks so small and fragile, wrapped up in her duvet and surrounded by pillows.

'Thank you,' she whispers.

'It's just coffee.' I shrug. 'After the night you've had, it's the least I can do.'

As I wait for our drinks to pour, I watch Gina's video again.

'Before I begin my report,' she says sombrely after introducing herself, 'I must warn you that this video may contain content that disturbs some viewers, so discretion is advised.'

She spins around, the camera still focused on her face, her expression the perfect combination of respectfully distressed and warmly open. I have to hand it to her: she's a professional. She's captivating to watch – even I can see that – which must only be adding to the number of views this video is getting.

She's trending on Twitter. She's all anyone is talking about on Facebook. And I haven't even looked at the news yet.

Gina's sitting upright when I walk back in, her face glowing by the light of her phone. She takes the second coffee with a thin smile and cradles it against her chest with one hand, putting her phone beside her.

'It's everywhere,' she whispers in disbelief.

'I know,' I say. 'You're trending.'

Her eyes widen and she covers her face with her free hand.

'I just keep seeing her. Her lips ... they were so blue ...'

I pull her hand away from her face and squeeze it.

'I'm so sorry you saw that,' I say, knowing that there's

nothing I can say that'll reverse what she's seen. I desperately wish there was something I could do that would make things better for her.

'Thanks,' she croaks. There's a pause as both of us consider the horror of what happened last night. I can't imagine how it would feel to make a discovery like that, the fear that must have gripped her, the knowledge that what had taken place there could never be taken back. I don't want to ask too many questions, to make her relive it. She'll talk if she feels ready. And so we sit in silence, until finally she speaks again.

'What did you do last night?'

'Oh, you know, it was pretty wild,' I say. 'I napped in front of the TV.'

'Sounds perfect to me.'

There's another pause.

'I know it's awful of me to be worrying about this right now,' she says hesitantly, 'but I have to admit I'm kind of nervous about what's going to happen at work today. I don't think they'll be too pleased with me. I haven't checked my emails yet, I'm not ready to face it.'

'Take the day off,' I say. 'They'll understand. After what you went through last night, you need to rest, to let yourself process it all.'

She shakes her head firmly. 'I can't. That would make it worse. Trust me, you don't know Jacqueline.'

I frown. From what Gina's told me about this woman, she's not particularly tolerant of mistakes, although Julian insists she's not as bad as she sounds. Still. I don't expect she'll take kindly to her assistant hijacking the company's social channels.

'But Gina, what you saw—'

'What I saw was unthinkable,' she interrupts. 'But if I

stay home I won't be able to take my mind off it. Going to work is at least a distraction, even if it means getting in trouble.'

'I can understand that,' I say. 'But look on the bright side: you went viral. Their stats must be up, surely?'

She laughs, but there's no humour in it. 'Yeah, along with their lawsuits, probably.'

I tap the duvet where I estimate her knee to be.

'How about I go make us some breakfast while you shower and get ready? It sounds like there's not much you can do but face the music on this one. So you might as well be prepared.'

She nods and stares at me, unblinking, as though she's trying to work me out.

'Thank you, Ryan,' she says. 'I don't know what I'd do without you.'

'It's fine.' I dismiss her with a wave. Now that my initial shock has worn off, the headache I woke up with has returned, and my muscles are tight and knotted. I didn't think I went particularly hard at the gym yesterday, but my body is telling me otherwise. I need painkillers. And more coffee.

'You just worry about getting ready,' I say. 'And let me worry about the eggs.'

Chapter 10

DETECTIVE ADAM ADEBAYO

'OK, settle down, what have we got?'

The chatter in the room simmers to a murmur and the few people milling around the coffee pot drift back to their seats.

DI Bristow is standing at the front of the room, beside a giant whiteboard that's been plastered with photos, notes and forensic memos. Front and centre is a picture of the victim.

Michelle, I silently correct myself. She's no longer just *the victim*.

She was identified in the early hours of the morning as Michelle Everard, a complete person with hobbies and friends and quirks and bad habits and hopes and now ... nothing. It wasn't much of a challenge to work out who she was; her wallet was still in the clutch bag she'd had with her, complete with cash and credit cards. Her phone was right there next to it, so we knew it wasn't a robbery we were dealing with.

Because we were able to identify Michelle so quickly, we could also piece together the key details of her life almost as fast. She was twenty-nine, an insurance broker with a passion for hiking, according to her Facebook profile.

Right beside the photo on the board, the one of her

smiling, there's another one that was taken at the scene, a gruesome juxtaposition of life and death. A reminder of what we're all here for.

'That wasn't rhetorical,' Mia calls from the front. 'What do we have so far? Go.'

I clear my throat. 'The witness,' I say, 'Gina Mills. She's been cleared, her alibi checks out for the time of death.'

No one really suspected Gina, but we had to check nonetheless. It wouldn't be the first time a killer had 'discovered' a body, when really they just wanted a front row seat to watch the destruction they'd caused. But we contacted the bar she told us she'd been at with her colleague, and they sent their footage over almost straight away. Her alibi is rock solid.

'Right, so she's not a suspect,' Mia says, crossing her name off the whiteboard. 'Do we have any leads on who did it?'

'We've just pulled the victim's phone records.'

I look to my right to see who's speaking. It's Ali Khan from Forensics, and he's waving a wad of paper towards the front of the room.

'Looks like she was meeting someone she had been talking to on Tinder. A guy named Martin Lloyd. We're tracking his email address now.'

'Good,' says Mia as she writes the new name on the whiteboard. 'Prash, Dave, work with Ali on finding this date of hers, and keep me posted. Anything else?'

'Preliminary cause of death is bleeding from the brain, not asphyxiation. Looks like she was knocked over first, but the blow didn't kill her initially. She bled out while she was being strangled.'

Just imagining her final moments sours the coffee that's just settled in my stomach.

'Do we have the footage from the alleyway yet?' someone across the room chips in.

'The camera's a fake,' Christine groans beside me. 'The guy who owns the bar said he used to have a real one but it got vandalised so often he doesn't bother any more.'

'He might now,' says someone behind me, and sniggers ripple across the room. It's not funny, but we all need to get rid of some of the tension that's built up over the past few hours. Laughter seems as good an outlet as any.

There's always outside pressure on us to solve a murder quickly. But thanks to Gina's stunt last night, that demand for a solution is even worse than usual. The public was aware of the murder almost at the same time as we were, which means interest in the case is already far more intense than it would normally be. And that means we'll be working around the clock to close it as quickly and efficiently as possible.

'Did we pull anything useful from the Facebook footage?'

'Nothing,' Ali groans. 'All that drama and there was absolutely nothing we could use. There was no one else in the footage, and nothing we don't already know. So that's a dead end.'

'Press?' Mia asks.

Emma from the public relations team stands a little straighter as she talks.

'We're issuing a press release this morning to assure the public that we're doing everything we can. There's no sub-stance to it whatsoever but we need to get these journalists off our backs, they're worse than usual.'

'OK. Adam?'

'Yes?' I reply.

'I want that witness statement filed this morning, please. With all this public scrutiny, we need our paperwork in order. And keep an eye on the comments around Miss Mills's video for any new information. Ali, I'll need those forensic notes too, please. Great work everyone, let's get back to it and we'll meet again this afternoon for another update.'

There are murmurs of assent, and the room thins out quickly as everyone heads back to their desks. I stop to refill my coffee cup before returning to my own cubicle.

Overnight, the office has become a hive of activity. It's always busy, always bustling, but a new sense of purpose has descended on us all. I know it well, that determination to get to the bottom of a case, to find justice. Phones are ringing, people are yelling across the room and despite the lack of sleep, the energy in here is palpable.

It's hard to focus on paperwork when there's so much going on. I'd much rather be out interviewing, or finding that Tinder date, but Mia's right. There will be scrutiny on this case, so my documents had better be in order. There's no point procrastinating.

Sighing, I open the manila file on my desk and start typing up my almost illegible notes from late last night. Interviewing Gina had been equal parts frustrating and fascinating. I'd tried to sympathise with her. After all, she'd made a gruesome discovery, and there's no doubt that the image of Michelle's body will haunt her for a long time to come, but her complete lack of emotion made it difficult to gauge anything from the answers she was giving us. She'd offered all of the facts, describing in detail what she'd seen. She was trembling, but she carried on. The medical team determined that she was suffering from shock, and plied her with sugary tea and chocolate, which she ate compliantly. She was brave, and resilient.

But still. She filmed a crime scene, and streamed it live on social media. She wasn't too shocked for that, apparently. There's no law against what she did, and as Christine pointed out to me after Gina had gone home, if she hadn't covered it, someone else would have. She was simply the journalist who got there first. But the interview left me with an uneasy feeling, like I was missing something important. I just couldn't work out what that was.

I take a break from typing and skim the comments under the Channel Eight video instead. There are thousands on Facebook now, along with endless tweets and comments on news sites. I scroll through them, hoping something will stand out, but they mostly follow the same few themes. There's a heated debate going on about violence in London, and whether or not it's caused by immigrants. I don't allow myself to spend too much time on these ones. They just make my blood boil.

Then there are the generic comments from people wanting to be involved, no matter how loosely: strangers offering thoughts and prayers, those who claim to know Gina, or Michelle, or those who live anywhere within a mile of the scene wondering if it could have been them.

And finally, there are those who have taken offence to Gina's actions and who have no qualms about telling the world what they think. They claim to be upset on behalf of the victim's family but it's hard to see any kind of benevolence in amongst the unfiltered venom of their words.

The mildest are simply questioning what she did.

What kind of person finds a murder victim and then films it for the world to see? Something wrong with this 'journalist'. I hope she's fired for this.

It's not altogether surprising. I can't pretend I haven't had similar thoughts myself over the past few hours. But it's the more aggressive comments that are so unexpected.

Fame whore! Get off our screens and let the family of the victim mourn in peace. No one wants to see your ugly mug on our screens.

Who is this bitch and why is she disrespecting the dead like this? It should have been you, you filth.

I find myself hoping that she isn't reading these. She has enough to deal with today, including explaining herself to her boss. I can't even imagine how that conversation's going to go.

This footage has made our job a whole lot harder, there's no denying that.

But as much as I wish she hadn't done it, I have a sneaking suspicion Gina's regretting it far more.

Chapter 11

GINA

Despite my initial insistence to Ryan that I had to go to work, I'd briefly weighed up calling in sick this morning.

Over breakfast, I'd made the inadvisable decision to read the comments that people were leaving under my video. To my surprise, it was still there, gathering views. I'd expected the Channel Eight legal team to demand its immediate removal, but it seems that ratings have trumped reason in this case.

And those views, inevitably, were followed by opinions. As I'd scrolled through the increasingly irate messages people had left, safe behind the shield of their screens, my stomach had flipped over. I regretted the beans and egg I'd already eaten, and left the rest of my plate untouched.

'I don't think I can go in,' I'd announced to Ryan, shoving the remains of my breakfast towards him.

'You have to,' he'd said. 'You said so yourself: if you put this off, it's only going to get worse. Besides, everyone knows you shouldn't read the comments.'

He was right. I'd have to face Jacqueline eventually, and staying home wouldn't stop the tide of opinions. Besides, I know what my boss is like. She'll respect me more – not that she respects me much to begin with – for not running away from conflict.

And so I'd got myself ready and put on the outfit that never fails to make me feel confident – a black pencil skirt I'd snapped up in a sale, an emerald green silk shirt I'd bought at a charity shop, and the black pointed court shoes I'd spent part of my very first Channel Eight paycheque on. Then I'd marched out the door, ready to face whatever was coming my way today.

When I'd spotted my face on the front page of the *Metro*, and noticed people's furtive glances above their papers on the Tube, I'd had to close my eyes and focus on my breathing to stay calm. My heart was in my mouth the whole journey, my stomach a fluttering mess.

As the train had stopped at a station, I'd held onto the pole beside me to avoid being swept off with the crowds. Someone behind me had breathed against my neck, the warmth of it making me cringe. They'd breathed again. Weren't they getting off, along with the surge of passengers? There was plenty of space now. Half the carriage had disappeared. I'd turned to glare at the stranger who was invading my personal space when I'd heard his low, raspy voice in my ear. It was little more than a whisper, a hot, clammy breath just centimetres from my skin.

'If you know what's good for you, you'll stop.'

I'd frozen, too startled to turn and face him. The voice came again, urgent and angry.

'Attention-seeking bitch.'

And then the doors had beeped and the man behind me ran for the opening, disappearing behind the closing doors in a flash of blond hair and a black jacket. I was left clinging to the pole, trying to stay upright.

My legs are shaking now, as I walk out of the elevator and into the office. I try to remain inconspicuous as I make my way towards my desk. I need a few minutes to process what just happened before the inevitable barrage of questions from my colleagues about last night. But I've barely sat down when I sense a presence. My head snaps up.

'Tash,' I say, relieved. 'Oh, it's you. I'm so glad you're here.'

Her eyes are narrowed, her jaw set, and her arms are crossed over her chest.

'Are you OK?' I ask.

'What the hell is wrong with you?'

'Sorry?' I blink. I was expecting sympathy, someone I could talk to over a cup of tea in the kitchen, away from nosy colleagues. I wasn't prepared for combat.

'I said, what the hell is wrong with you?'

'I don't... what are you talking about?'

'You know she was a *person*, right?'

'Tash, I really don't—'

'She deserved dignity. Not for you to use her body as some kind of entertainment.'

She's shouting now, bright red spots appearing on her cheeks and little flecks of spit flying at me as she unleashes her venom. Heads have turned. I look around, my eyes flitting from person to person, hoping for an ally. One by one, they all look away, embarrassed to be caught eavesdropping.

'Look, Tash, can we talk about this somewhere else?'

'No, I don't want to talk anywhere else. I don't want to talk to you at all,' she says haughtily. 'I prefer friends with morals.'

And with that she stalks off, all eyes following her as she makes her exit.

My stomach sinks. I'm suddenly drained, ready to go home, although I still have the whole day ahead of me. As the sounds of the office recommence, I let my eyelids drop, and the same vision that stopped me from sleeping

77

all night swims in my imagination. Michelle's vacant eyes, her bruise-coloured lips, the way her legs were twisted and her hair was matted with blood. Every time I close my eyes her face hovers in my vision, larger than life, making my heart pound.

'Gina!' Jacqueline's icy voice snaps me out of my thoughts.

I stand up, smoothing my skirt.

'Yes?'

'I'd like to speak to you. Now.'

She spins around and I follow her into her glass office, wondering if I'll be allowed to rest at all today, or if I'm going to be shouted at by everyone I encounter. I close the door behind me and wait for my punishment.

'Would you like to explain to me what happened last night?'

Her tone is cold and measured, as always. As I sit down in her visitor's chair, I study her face for signs of anger, or even disappointment, but there's no emotion showing. Emotion wouldn't suit a woman like Jacqueline, it would soften her too much. The only word that comes to mind whenever I look at her is 'sharp'. Sharp edges, sharp words, sharp nails, sharp shoes. Even her hairline is a pointed black widow's peak. She's all about precision. Perfection.

'What would you like to know?' I ask. I shouldn't be anything other than deeply apologetic, I know, but I can't bring myself to play the meek assistant today. I'm too tired, and too full of emotion. I feel like I'm going to snap, like the last twelve hours have stretched me to breaking point. If I'm going to get fired, I'd rather she just got it over with instead of toying with me.

'What I'd like to know,' she replies coolly, 'is why you decided to use the channel's Facebook account – without permission – as your own personal news reading platform.'

I weigh up my words before I speak. I know that Jacqueline responds best to bare facts. There's no point trying to sugar-coat the truth.

'I'm sorry I didn't ask for permission,' I say. 'It didn't really cross my mind to call you while I was standing over a dead body.'

'But it did cross your mind to broadcast it live?'

'It was an instinct, honestly. I know what people are saying, that I did it for attention, but that's not what happened. There was a story that needed to be told, and I spotted an opportunity.'

I hold her gaze as she stares back at me, unflinching, daring me to say another word. I stay silent, hoping my answer was the right one.

'I'm not sure if you understand just how serious this situation is, Gina,' she says eventually. 'You've put the reputation of this whole channel on the line for five minutes of fame, and you expect me to, what, thank you? Do you have any idea what's been going on behind the scenes to try to fix this mess of yours?'

I open my mouth to answer, but she doesn't wait.

'Of course you don't. You have no idea what damage control even means. I told you, Gina. I told you just a few days ago to get on with your job and not make waves. And instead of listening to me, and recognising that I'm trying to help you, you did the exact opposite, and now you have the absolute cheek to sit there and expect me to let you get away with this because you *saw an opportunity*?'

'I'm not expecting thanks,' I say wearily. 'I'm just telling you what happened. You asked why I filmed it, and that's my answer. I'm a journalist, Jacqueline, although I know you try your best to forget that.'

She flares her nostrils, and I know I've gone too far.

'I've just been on the phone with Frank Coulter,' she says unexpectedly. I was convinced the next words out of her mouth were going to be used to fire me. I definitely didn't anticipate her telling me about her phone call with the head of the station. 'And it seems he'd like us to build on the momentum of your footage. He actually used the words "capitalise on the buzz".'

I can't help it. A bark of surprised laughter fills the room. I clamp my hand over my mouth.

'I'm glad you're enjoying yourself,' Jacqueline says sarcastically.

'Sorry, I just—'

'In any case,' she continues, 'the public are absolutely eating up your coverage. I have no idea why, it's completely unprofessional, but I think people love a villain, and they see you as a bit of an anti-hero. Whatever it is, though, the numbers are up. There's no chance I'm going to let this kind of opportunity go to waste.'

I frown. Is she complimenting me for the video, or insulting me? Perhaps she's doing a bit of both.

'I've checked with our legal team, of course, and they assure me that you didn't actually cross any legal boundaries with your little stunt. Ethically, it's another story, but that won't get us in trouble with the law, so we don't need to worry for now. You didn't show the body, and you didn't include any descriptions that could identify the victim.'

She's talking as though this was entirely by accident, rather than a conscious decision I made based on my years as a reporter. I let it slide. Silence falls over us, and I wonder for a second if she's waiting for me to say something. Then she sighs, as though what she's about to say pains her.

'You're being interviewed on *Afternoons with Lucy* today.'

I blink. 'Pardon me?'

'You'll need to go down to the studio now so they can get your hair and make-up done, and you'll be briefed by the team there.'

'So you're not firing me?' I ask.

'Not yet,' she says simply.

I nod, a mixture of elation and nerves pulsing through me. The man on the Tube this morning pops into my mind, his threatening voice warning me to stop. What did he mean by that? There was nothing specific in his threat. It wasn't even a threat, as such. I know I shouldn't let him get to me. He was a stranger on the Tube, an opportunist with a bee in his bonnet. He probably just didn't like the idea of a woman being on his screen, I decide. He doesn't deserve another thought.

I let myself out of her office, my heart in my mouth. I'm dazed by Jacqueline's revelation. *Afternoons with Lucy* is one of the highest-rated talk shows in the country. It airs right about the time when mums are getting home from school and fixing their kids a snack. The host, Lucy Klein, feels like a friend, like someone you'd like to share a bottle of wine with while you debrief your day.

I'm ecstatic, but then I remember how this all came to pass, and my smile drops from my face. I'm thrilled, of course I am. But I also can't forget that this is happening because a young woman was murdered. There's a time and a place for celebrating success at work. This is neither.

I wish I could talk to Tash about what just happened – she of all people would understand how I can be pleased amidst such distressing circumstances – but she's clearly livid about my decision to live stream from the alleyway. I'll need to give her a few days to cool off, and find a time to explain myself, to help her understand.

Right now though, I have bigger things to worry about.

Like being interviewed for a national television show. My stomach writhes, but I tell myself that what's about to happen is what I've always wanted. National television. My face in people's homes, my voice telling them the facts.

I've never believed in fate but I do believe in grabbing whatever chances life throws my way. And, although the way I got here was a little unconventional, no one could deny that this is an opportunity.

And I'm definitely going to take it.

Chapter 12

1996

SHARON

The last cigarette in Bill's emergency packet is almost down to a tiny, smouldering stub, and now my lungs are screaming silently, my head spinning.

I haven't smoked since I found out I was pregnant with Ryan. Fourteen years ago. God, has it been that long? I close my eyes and breathe slowly, deeply, trying to extend the exquisite pain of the last few puffs. Over the years, whenever I've cleaned out that top drawer in our wardrobe, I've always announced to Bill that I'm throwing out the small, crumpled box. And every time he laughs and tells me he needs it in case of emergencies. I'd say that this constitutes an emergency.

I've been pacing for an hour, since I settled the kids into the living room with a duvet and a cup of hot chocolate each. It's much too warm for such cosiness, but they didn't seem to mind. The shock has knocked them out cold, all three of them asleep with mugs still in their hands, tears drying on their cheeks.

Bill walks through the front door as I'm stubbing out the tiny nub of the cigarette that remains between my fingers.

'Have you been smoking?' he asks, frowning. 'It stinks in here.'

I run to him and fling my arms around his neck, sobbing.

'Hey, shhhh,' he says, squeezing me with one arm and stroking my hair with his free hand. 'What's wrong? You said on the phone it was about Pickles?'

I nod, unable to speak for fear of breaking into a fresh wave of sobs, and start walking towards the utility room. I stop at the door. There's no way I can bring myself to look at that again. I flap my hand to gesture him inside.

'Outside. Out the back door.'

My husband looks at me quizzically, hesitates for a split second, then opens the door. There's silence as he crosses the room, and then a pause as he takes in the scene on our back doorstep. I hear him groan. I close my eyes and try to ignore the image that's stuck in my mind, the same scene Bill's seeing now. When I'd looked through my children's shoulders and spotted Pickles, Gina's sixth birthday present and the sixth member of our family, I'd wanted to scream, to claw my way out of the room, away from his poor, stretched-out body. But the instinct to protect my children won over, and I bustled them out to try to offer them comfort.

Since then, though, I've been going silently crazy, asking myself again and again who would do something like this. It can't be a fox. The cut along Pickles's belly was far too precise for it to have been made by a wild animal. The thought makes my stomach churn again, and the anger flares up once more in the pit of my stomach.

When Bill's face reappears from behind the door, the colour in his cheeks has drained away.

'What happened?' he breathes.

'I don't know,' I admit. 'The kids found him like that, but they were too traumatised to answer any questions.'

He nods, frowning.

'But that's not just a dead cat, Sharon. It's not like he was hit by a car and brought home, that's . . . well, I don't know what it is, but it's twisted.'

I already know this. It's why I called him home early from work. He's right, it's not just a dead cat. It's something dark and sinister and sickening. I look at him for answers. I need him to have the answers.

'I'm calling the police.'

'Bill, do you really think . . .' I leave the question hanging in the air, but he knows what I mean. Do you really think the police care about our dead cat? Do you really think this is serious enough to bring the police into it? Do you really think it's necessary?

'Yes, Sharon, I do. Think about it. If someone is out there harming an innocent cat, what else could they be capable of?'

I feel a shudder running from the top of my spine to the small of my back. Bill curls an arm around me and kisses the top of my head.

'Leave it to me,' he says, always capable, always in charge. 'I'll call the police. They might want to come and take a look, but why don't you go have a bath in the meantime? Where are the kids? I'll keep an eye on them.'

'Thank you,' I whisper, wanting nothing more than to go to sleep and wake up with this all just a bad dream.

As I lie in the hot water later, listening to Bill's voice drifting up the stairs, explaining what's happened over the phone to the police, I remember his words and I feel my body go cold, in spite of the heat that's enveloping me.

If someone is out there harming an innocent cat, what else could they be capable of?

I squeeze my eyes closed.

What kind of monster is lurking outside my back door?

Chapter 13

2017

GINA

I glance at my watch for just a second before pulling the heavy door open. It swings easily and I step inside, my stomach grumbling as the smell of something frying hits me.

'Hi.'

A bearded man behind the bar is smiling in my direction. 'Here for lunch?'

I look around. There's an old guy in the corner, nursing a Guinness, and a woman in round-rimmed glasses tapping away at a laptop with a salad in front of her, untouched. The pub is otherwise empty.

'Uh... actually, I was wondering if I could speak to the manager?'

'You're looking at him,' he says, squinting slightly as he looks me up and down. Then, as the penny drops, 'You're that reporter, aren't you? The one from Channel Eight?'

'That's me,' I say, holding out my hand. 'I'm Gina.'

I brace myself for this guy's reaction. So far, people seem to have had strong feelings about my live stream, and they're not shy about sharing them with me. Everyone I've met over the past few days has had something to say about the ethics of my actions, and most of them haven't been favourable.

'Todd,' he says, taking my hand and shaking it firmly. 'What can I do for you?'

I try to conceal my surprise at his lack of reaction. My muscles relax as they stop bracing for an attack.

'I just have a few questions about the other night,' I say, perching on one of the stools at the bar.

'What kind of questions?'

I flip my notepad open and click the top of my pen unconsciously.

'Well,' I say. 'Had you seen Michelle Everard here before?'

Todd frowns and begins wiping the bar down.

'I've already answered this,' he says. 'When the police came in here.'

'I know. I appreciate that. I'm just trying to get some answers for myself.'

'The police are getting answers,' he says bluntly. 'Don't you think you should leave them to get on with what they do best?'

'Of course,' I say quickly. 'Absolutely. And I'm not trying to get in the way of their investigation, it's just that...'

I pause, switching my tactic. He's suspicious of me. Fine. But I can appeal to his emotions, if I can't get through to him with logic. I look down, and force my eyes to well up. Not everyone can cry on cue, but my secondary school drama teacher insisted that our class had to learn how. I'm not about to win any Oscars, but I can usually procure a tear or two, enough to convince someone of my distress.

'I was the one to find her, you know? And I know the police are investigating, and I know they're the professionals, but I just need some kind of closure. Something to help me to understand what happened.'

I look up to gauge the impact of my emotional appeal. His face has softened, and he's stopped cleaning.

'To help me understand *why*,' I whisper.

His shoulders drop and he sighs heavily.

'OK, fine. But can you make it quick, please? It's almost lunchtime and it'll be getting busy soon.'

'Of course. So . . . had you seen Michelle in here before?'

'Like I told the police, I didn't recognise her. That doesn't mean she'd never been here before, of course, but she definitely wasn't a regular.'

I take notes as he's talking, enjoying the thrill of doing the work of a real journalist, uncovering the truth of a case most reporters would only dream about working on. I push aside the nagging thought that I'm not really working on this case. Not officially, anyway. But what I do in my lunch break is my own business.

'And did you notice her on the night she was killed? Or did you notice anyone with her, or paying attention to her?'

'Yeah, I noticed her,' he says. 'And I'm sure a lot of other people did, too. She was beautiful, dressed up like she was going somewhere fancy. So she stood out, yeah. But she left after just a few minutes. She walked in, ordered a gin and ginger, and had barely sat down when she was out of here, didn't even touch her drink.'

He shrugs.

'I just figured she changed her mind, left to find somewhere a bit more suited to her outfit. I never could have guessed . . .'

He trails off and clenches his jaw, a muscle in his cheek pulsing as he stares at a point over my shoulder.

'Did anyone use the back entrance that night, the door that leads out to the alleyway?'

'Probably,' he says, focusing on me again. 'In fact, definitely. Even I used that door. It's where we take the rubbish out, as I'm sure you noticed when you were back there. Most of my staff would use it during a shift.'

'What time did you use the door?'

Todd rubs his beard.

'I have no idea,' he says. 'It was before Michelle was killed, I can tell you that much, because there wasn't a dead body outside.'

'OK. Who else was working here that night?'

He looks at me, his eyes narrowed, for a couple of seconds.

'No,' he says. 'I'm not doing this. I've given their information to the police, but I'm not risking my staff members' names being dragged through the mud for some story.'

'That's not what I—'

'I think we're done here,' he says sternly.

I clench my jaw. Todd's muscular arms are crossed over his chest and his stony expression leaves no doubt that he's not going to be swayed. I breathe in slowly.

'Fine. OK. I'm sorry I pushed it. I'll get out of your hair. Could I use your bathroom before I go though, please?'

He nods and points towards the back of the pub. I smile and dart off in the direction he indicated, looking over my shoulder to check that he's not watching me. There's a dark corridor that leads to the toilets, the gents' and ladies' marked clearly, the other two doors left blank. One of them has to be the kitchen, judging by the clinking of cutlery and glassware coming from beyond the wooden door. The other must be the office.

I look around quickly but there's no one else in sight. I try the handle. It twists easily, and I open the door a crack to be certain the office is empty. Satisfied that I'm alone, I let myself in and close the door quietly behind me, concentrating on keeping my breathing steady. Todd might not be willing to give me his staff records, but that doesn't mean I can't get them myself.

The office is a mess. There's a small desk with an old computer and printer, a filing cabinet, and piles of paperwork cluttering every available surface. On the wall is a staff rota, which I quickly photograph with my phone. Then I pull open the filing cabinet, rifling through the hanging folders, moving as quickly as I can without missing anything. I stop when I reach one called 'Staff', and pull it out of the cabinet. There doesn't seem to be any order to the paperwork inside, but I photograph every page, shove it all back inside, and let myself out. I hope I have what I need, but there's no time to look any further. I have to be back at my desk before Jacqueline returns from her meeting, so this will have to do for now. I can always come back, I suppose.

I wave at Todd as I leave, desperate to get out before he suspects anything. Tonight, I'll sit down and cross-reference the people on the rota for the night of Michelle's murder with the contact details that were in the file. And then I'll start making phone calls, finding out who saw what. Because someone must have seen something.

But for now, I need to get back to the office.

Jacqueline can't know I'm doing my own investigation. Not until I have everything I need.

And then I'll take my story to the world.

Closing the front door behind me, I slide my shoes off and pad down the hallway in bare feet.

As I pass the living room, I'm distracted by a flicker of movement in the corner. My heart jumps, but it's just Ryan, rummaging in the chest of drawers in the corner, the one that stores decades of junk that no one has bothered to touch for years.

'Hey,' I say.

It's as though my words are electric. Ryan leaps up, yelping. As soon as he catches sight of me, his whole body seems to exhale in relief.

'Oh my God, it's only you,' he says, breathless.

'Who the hell did you think it was?'

'No one,' he says.

I study him closely. He's back on the ground now, hastily shoving items back into the drawers where they came from. Strewn on the carpet around him are old magazines, notebooks, home video tapes that we can't watch because we no longer own a VHS player, pens, files and board games we haven't played for years.

'What are you doing?'

'What?'

He looks up. His face is pale.

'Oh. Nothing. Nothing, just looking for, um . . . a hammer. A picture in my room came loose.'

'The hammer is in the shed out the back,' I say, crossing my arms over my chest. 'You know that.'

He doesn't reply. He just stares at me, like it's one of those games we played as a kid, to see who would crack first. Whatever it is he's doing, he clearly doesn't want me to know about it. I shrug and break eye contact.

'Do you want a beer?'

Trying to force an answer out of my brother won't work. It never has. Better to let him tell me in his own time, on his own terms.

'Yeah, I'll be there in a sec,' he says, putting the last of the knick-knacks back where they'll probably stay untouched for another decade.

When he joins me in the kitchen, he's a little more composed, but he still seems rattled.

'Are you OK?' I ask, passing him a beer.

'Yeah, fine. Why?'

I look into his eyes, the same green as mine, and search for clues in their depths. He stares back, his jaw out slightly, defiant. I consider pressing him for information. He's acting strangely, and he knows I know it, but clearly he doesn't want me to ask. And really, right now, I don't have room for any more drama in my life. I decide to let it go. For now.

'Nothing. Just asking.'

'OK. How are you?' he asks.

I shrug. That's a complicated question to answer. On the one hand, I'm fine. I'm alive. I have no right to complain about anything, not when I'm still living and breathing and working and sitting with my brother in our kitchen. Not when Michelle doesn't get to do any of these things any more.

And yet these truths don't change the fact that I'm so busy at work that I have no idea how to get all of my work done, I feel constantly sick about the abuse I've been receiving online, and I'm missing Julian.

'I'm all right,' I say after a second. 'I just wish I knew what happened to Mich—'

I never get to finish the rest of my sentence. My words are swallowed up by a deafening crack, followed by a crunching, metallic tinkling. A window breaking.

I shriek and jump off my stool, my arms flapping wildly as though somehow that will protect me from this unseen, unknown attack. Ryan yells at me to stay where I am, and runs out of the kitchen towards the sound. A sob bursts from my chest, loud and sharp, and my heart rate spikes. It hammers at my throat while I wait in the terrifying wake of whatever's just happened.

There's a shout from somewhere outside, the aggressive roar of a car engine, and then silence.

After a few seconds Ryan swears loudly, and then there's the crunch of footsteps across glass.

I hear the front door opening.

'Ryan?'

'It's OK,' he yells back from the hallway. 'Just stay there.'

I couldn't move if I wanted to. I'm paralysed, rooted to this spot on the kitchen floor. But then, after a few seconds, my brain begins to work again, and I realise that I never heard the sound of the door closing. Ryan has left me here, alone, with the front door open. Panic forces me to leap to my feet, and down the hallway, blackness creeping into my vision. I blink it back just in time to see Ryan stepping back inside. He locks the door and refastens the chain. I'm trembling all over.

'What happened?'

'Someone threw something through the window. I tried to get a photo of the car, but it drove off too fast.'

'Did you see anyone?'

He shakes his head. 'By the time I got outside, they were already driving away. I'm going to check out the damage.'

He gestures into the living room, but I make him go first. I tiptoe in behind him, dread balled in my stomach like a stone, smooth and solid. Cold air whistles in through a jagged hole in the window, and the curtains stream in response, a taunting dance that makes me feel edgy, exposed. In the living room, surrounded by shards that were once the window, is a brick wrapped in a piece of paper.

I stare at it, as though it might jump up and assault me. Ryan steps towards it, the crunch of the glass under his shoes making me grind my teeth. He lifts the brick to inspect it. Unwraps the paper. Recoils.

'What is it?'

He turns his body away, as though shielding me from something.

'It's nothing,' he says. He's lying. I step towards him, but he moves away.

'Come on,' I say. 'Just tell me.'

'No, Gina, it's—'

Before he can protest again, I step into the space between us and snatch the paper from his grip. He looks at me, his eyes wide and laden with apology.

I smooth it out with shaking hands, and feel the dread inside me growing larger and larger, pressing against my organs as I read the words, written in thick black lines.

Fame loving whore! I know where you live, and I'm telling you to stop. Stop investigating or I'm going to live stream your demise. And don't worry, I'll make it worth watching. You'll get the ratings you've always wanted.

'I'll call the cops now,' Ryan says.

I look up at him. His face is a kind of grey, a colour I've never seen on skin before. He looks like he's going to be sick. I feel like I might be, too.

I read the message again, my horror mounting with every word.

I close my eyes tightly. Now, as well as the image of Michelle's lips, there's another picture that's been plastered onto the walls of my imagination. It's that gaping, yawning hole in the middle of the glass, shards glistening sharp and threatening from the light outside. Nothing but blackness beyond, nothing between me and whoever it is that wants to hurt me.

Ryan's voice drifts towards me from the kitchen. I hadn't even noticed him leaving, but now that I realise I'm alone, I scurry back into the safety of company.

The only person who knows I'm investigating Michelle's murder is Todd, the guy from the bar. He was the first witness I interviewed, the first person I admitted my mission to. He wasn't happy about me asking questions, but surely he wasn't angry enough to do something so violent, so extreme?

So who would care this much? Who would be this desperate to shut me up, to stop me from investigating?

'Tell the police to hurry,' I say to Ryan, my voice catching in my throat as I try to form the words I know I need to say. 'Tell them this note is from the killer. It has to be.'

I pause, watching Ryan's eyes widening with fear.

'Tell them I think he might be watching me.'

Chapter 14

RYAN

Michelle.

I repeat the name over and over in my head, until it's all I can hear.

The woman who was killed. Her name is Michelle. Not Cassie.

So why, every time I see a photo of her – and her face is everywhere – do I see my sister?

It's not just that I notice the resemblance between Michelle and Cassie. Anyone could see that. Curly blonde hair, green eyes, about the age my sister would be now. I don't see someone who *looks* like Cassie. I see Cassie. My brain screams at me that it's not her, that it's someone called Michelle Everard, a woman who worked in insurance, who had her own family and friends and siblings. But my body's reaction tells another story.

I can't avoid her, as much as I've tried. She's everywhere – on my news feed, on the front page of the newspapers, trending on Twitter – haunting me, forcing me to remember, to confront my past. And every time I spot that face, it comes as a total shock to me.

I got through the whole morning without even thinking about Cassie, which felt like an achievement, even though it wasn't through anything I had done.

I've been too distracted by the brick that sailed through our window, by the idea that there might be a murderer watching my sister, to worry about my strange delusions.

When the police arrived, not long after my phone call, they'd listened attentively to my explanation of what had just happened, and my description of the white car I'd seen disappearing around the corner. Then they'd turned to Gina.

'What does the sender of this note mean by asking you to stop investigating?'

My sister had blushed. 'I went to speak to the owner of the bar today.'

'Gina!'

I'd been appalled. I'm meant to protect her – I owe her that, at least – but there was no way of helping her if she insisted on being so reckless. She'd looked at me, stubbornly.

'I just want some answers.'

'How could you do something so stupid? This isn't some petty crime, it's a murder! You're putting yourself in danger.'

'Your brother's right,' the officer had said. 'And not only is it dangerous for you to be running your own investigation, it could also hinder what we're doing.'

Gina had looked at the officer meekly.

'I'm sorry,' she'd said. 'I'm not trying to hurt your investigation. It's just not easy for me to sit around and do nothing . . . not after what I saw.'

'It may be hard, but please trust me, we're doing everything we can, and we will find whoever did this.'

He'd looked at me, then. 'Here's my number. If either of you feel threatened again, call me. My mobile's on that card. And, Gina?'

'Yes?'

'For your own safety . . . leave us to do the investigations. Please.'

Remembering her expression, the utter resignation that had flashed across her face, a fresh wave of sympathy washes over me. The consequences of her decision – of the moment she decided to step into the alleyway instead of taking the long way around – keep multiplying and expanding, like ripples on a pond.

I'm wondering whether we should get security bars installed on our ground-floor windows as I step out of the office to go to my usual Pret, to get the same salad I eat every day for lunch.

And that's when I see her.

Someone's discarded newspaper, swept along by the wind, is skipping across the pavement in a sudden gust, heading in my direction. I watch it making a beeline for me. It looks purposeful, I think. And fast. Before I can react, it's attached to my leg, wrapping around me, clinging on for dear life.

I peel it off, glance at it without any real interest, without thinking. And there she is. On the front page. Smiling, alive.

Cassie.

My heart starts beating too quickly. It's speeding up, faster and faster, until it's buffeting my ribs so violently that I'm scared it will simply run out of steam and give up. My chest aches and my head is spinning. My whole world is whirling, out of control, and suddenly I'm panting and sweating and completely incapable of functioning.

I sit heavily on a stone bollard and try to take deep, gulping breaths.

An inexplicable sense of danger has descended on me. I can't describe it, I can't explain it, but I'm completely consumed by fear. Because it's not Cassie I see staring back at me.

Michelle.

Her name is Michelle, I tell myself.

I keep repeating it, over and over again, until the physical symptoms pass. I drag myself, on shaking legs, back up to the office, and Google sweating, chest pain and dizziness.

A heart attack, the results tell me. Only I know it's not a heart attack.

I rest my head on the top of my chair, looking up at the ceiling. Why is my body reacting so powerfully to pictures of Michelle? Her looking vaguely like Cassie doesn't explain it. The two women have nothing to do with one another.

I think back to the woman on the train, to the absolute certainty I felt, a knowledge so strong it permeated down to the marrow of my bones, that it was Cassie. But I can't make sense of it.

All I know is that my past is coming back.

It's hurtling towards me, threatening to derail my life, to take away everything and everyone I love.

I have to stop it.

Before it ruins everything.

Chapter 15

DETECTIVE ADAM ADEBAYO

'Shit.'

I know it's bad when Christine starts swearing. She reserves her curses for special occasions, insisting that when she does use them, she wants them to count, to have an impact.

'What?'

She sticks her head around the side of my cubicle.

'Have you seen the email from Emma in the press team?'

I scan my inbox, and click on the latest unread email.

Dear All,
We've just been informed that the *Daily Mail* will be publishing an article imminently, to disclose that victim Michelle Everard was meeting a Tinder date on the night of her death.

I don't bother reading the rest.

'*Daily* bloody *Mail*,' I say.

'I guess we can't really blame them,' Christine argues. 'It's news. People will go crazy for it. It's going to spark debates on whether online dating is safe, and happily married

100

millennials will mourn the good old days when people used to meet in real life. It's going to be fun.'

I roll my eyes. 'Sounds like a blast. Do we have any news on the account?'

The forensics team got hold of the email address associated with Martin Lloyd's Tinder account yesterday, and since then they've been trying to find the guy's location.

'Nothing.' Christine grimaces. 'I just got off the phone with Ali, and he says it was created using an IP blocker. It doesn't appear to be used for anything else, so that's a bit of a dead end.'

'OK, how about the photos on his account?'

'He didn't come up when we ran the images through the database, so he doesn't have a record, but now the press are onto it, maybe we should release them, see if anyone can identify him?'

'Good idea,' I say, and I offer my clenched fist for her to bump with her own.

'I'll go run it past Mia,' she says, walking in the direction of the incident room.

I'm on edge, desperate for a break in this case, frustrated at what has been a run of dead ends. The initial twenty-four hour period is always the most crucial in solving a case, and that slid away last night. It's hard not to treat it like a failure, and react accordingly.

The evidence we've gathered so far is threadbare at best. The victim's body was clean. No DNA, no fingerprints. Easy enough to do when the victim is strangled with an object – not rope, that would have left fibres, but something like a cotton cloth or towel – the way Michelle was. The hard part about pulling something like this off is doing it without being seen, which somehow her assailant managed to do.

No matter how many times it happens, I'm always amazed when someone gets away with a horrific crime like this in London. It's a city that offers the ultimate form of anonymity, of being swallowed up inside the tide of the crowd, and yet somehow you can never go completely unnoticed.

Whenever I fancy a bit of peace and quiet – some space away from the chaos of home – it's impossible to find. I'll go for a walk to clear my head, but wherever I go there are people there, too. I've tried tiptoeing out at sunrise to go for a run and breathe my own air for just a minute, but I've never managed to make it to the end of my street without seeing someone else out and about, cluttering my serenity. So how anyone can commit a murder without another soul catching wise is completely beyond me.

But that seems to be what's happened here. The forensic evidence gathered at the scene isn't getting us anywhere. All we've got is this guy on Tinder, Michelle's mystery date. According to the messages on her phone, they'd been chatting for weeks. He sounded like a nice enough guy: polite, asking questions, complimenting her. He claimed to work as an estate agent, but we haven't found a Martin Lloyd who matches that description yet.

His whole profile seems to be fake, and our current working theory is that he created it for the sole purpose of getting women to trust him enough to meet him alone. He – well, so far all of the evidence is pointing to a male, although that could be false, too – chose the location for his first date with Michelle: the pub that backs onto the alleyway. It's public and casual, and probably wouldn't have given her any cause for concern. A pub seems like a safe place to meet. But after Michelle arrived, Martin didn't show. Ten minutes after their arranged meeting time, he sent her one final message.

> So embarrassed, I'm out the back, in that alleyway,
> I nipped back here for a cigarette (nervous, lol) and
> tripped on something. Think I may have broken my
> ankle? So sorry, could you come give me a hand?
> Some first date, hey...!

I wonder if any alarm bells went off for her as she sat in that pub, reading his message. Or whether she was just so relieved not to have been stood up that she went along with it unquestioningly. If she hesitated, it was only for a few seconds because the CCTV camera at the front of the pub registered her leaving just a minute later.

Frustrated, I close the file containing Michelle and Martin's Tinder conversation, and open Facebook to check the comments again. They've slowed down a little after the initial flurry, but they're still trickling in. Someone's posted a link to an interview Gina gave yesterday on *Afternoons with Lucy*. I recognise the name, it's one of those after-school shows my mum used to have on when we got home, while she was making dinner. I click the link.

Gina's looking polished and professional in a grey dress adorned with ruffles down one side. She's alert. Present. Nothing like the dazed woman we interviewed less than forty-eight hours ago. Her hands are folded neatly in her lap and she's perched at an angle, facing towards her inter-viewer. Between them is a glass coffee table topped with an explosion of white roses. She smiles as she's introduced, and crosses her legs delicately at her ankles.

'Gina, tell me,' urges Lucy in a tone that is probably

supposed to convey empathy. 'How did you feel when you made your discovery last night?'

'I was terrified,' Gina replies. 'At first I didn't know what I was looking at, but once I realised . . . I didn't know if I was in danger, if the person who did that to her was still around. I was scared, Lucy.'

'That's understandable. So what did you do?'

'Once I understood what I'd stumbled onto, and after I got over the initial panic, I called nine nine nine right away. They wanted me to check her pulse. I knew she was dead – I could just tell – but I needed to be sure. I was nervous to touch her, in case I hurt her, or damaged any evidence, but I felt for a pulse, and there was nothing. Her lips were so blue—'

She stops mid-sentence and reaches for a tissue. She dabs the corners of her eyes, her hand shaking. It seems her shock has well and truly worn off now. She's full of emotion, nothing like the woman I spoke to in the alleyway, or back here at the station.

The presenter leans over to press her hand onto Gina's shoulder, to comfort her.

'I know this is hard,' she says, well rehearsed to sound warm and caring. 'Take your time. Can you tell us what happened next?'

'I don't remember exactly what I said, or what they said. It was all a bit of a blur, but I know I asked them to hurry. I just wanted them to arrive, so I wasn't left alone with her.'

'How long after the call did someone come to help?'

'They arrived within minutes,' Gina says, looking down at the tissue she's shredding nervously in her lap.

'Gina, I think what our viewers are really interested in knowing, is why?'

She looks back towards Lucy, sniffing a little.

'Why what?'

'Why you chose to broadcast the scene live while you were waiting for the first responders.'

'Well, although I'm not currently working as a journalist, I was a reporter for a newspaper in Sussex for almost a decade. I covered local events as well as crime. So I suppose it's second nature for me to want to tell the world what's happening if there's a story to be told. It might sound strange to you, but it was an instinct, really, that made me decide to do it.'

Lucy raises her eyebrows slightly, but doesn't show any emotion.

'You must know that there are people who are saying your actions were unethical, that you should be charged for making a crime scene public like that?'

'I understand people's concerns,' she says. 'And I am sorry for any pain I caused anyone. But I was careful not to show anything that could have given away the identity of the victim, and I simply reported the facts. That's a journalist's job, and I stand by that. And I hope that Channel Eight will stand by that, too.'

I almost jump out of my seat when a hand swipes across my vision.

'Dammit, Christine,' I say, clutching my chest. I close my browser window as she returns to her cubicle, laughing at my reaction.

'Mia liked my idea,' she says. 'She called Emma while I was with her and the media team agreed to issue a press release with the photos from the Tinder profile.'

A current of hope runs through me, but even as it does, I know that I should know better. The killer would have to be incredibly stupid to use photos of himself in his profile. But right now it's the only lead we've got.

No suspect, no magic CCTV footage showing us a murderer, no DNA, no fibres, no witnesses.

Just a handsome young man on Tinder, with brown hair, brown eyes and a killer smile.

Chapter 16

GINA

Even as I'm doing it, I know I shouldn't be.

But it's so hard to resist. Knowing that people are talking about me online is like an itch I'm trying not to scratch. The more I refrain, the more it torments me until I'm ready to burst with discomfort.

And so, inevitably, inadvisably, I find myself furtively scrolling through the comments. Most of them are harmless enough, people airing their opinions, nothing new. There are a lot of people simply discussing the crime itself, or expressing fear for their safety, or for the safety of their loved ones. But the majority of the comments are about me. I've become a subject to debate hotly, my morals have been laid out for anyone to pick through. Since my interview on *Afternoons with Lucy*, the intensity of the comments has increased, as has the ferocity. There's a minority who seem to understand my reason for reporting Michelle's murder the way I did, but they're getting harder and harder to spot among the vitriol.

I've never paid much attention to these people before, the kind who leave nasty comments behind a cloak of anonymity. It's never mattered much because it's never been personal. Now, however, it's all aimed at me, all about me, and it has my blood pulsing furiously. I should just close this tab, walk away from my desk, and get a cup of tea. But instead, I keep reading.

Haha never trust a redhead am I right?

Does someone have some Daddy issues, love? You're looking for attention in all the wrong places. Get some therapy.

She clearly couldn't find a boss who would sleep with her, so she had to find another way to get ahead in her career. Lol, good luck to her.

I probably should have expected this, but I didn't. Maybe I'm naive, but I could never have foreseen the level of public interest, the sheer volume of opinions hurtling towards me. If it's not in the comments, it's on Twitter, or via email, or published directly to the Channel Eight Facebook page. We're reporting them as soon as we see them, but they're coming in thick and fast.

I open my inbox, a place that's safe from the trolls, safe from abuse, thanks to the obscure use of middle initials in all Channel Eight employees' email accounts. Here, there's something soothing about opening a message, completing the task, and moving on. There's a new message at the top of my inbox, from a name I don't recognise.

I feel a flicker of excitement as I click it. Maybe it's one of the staff members from the bar, with information about the night of Michelle's murder. Despite the police's – and Ryan's – insistence that I leave my investigation alone, I can't. The brick, and the awful note designed to scare me off, isn't going to work. I can't let myself be put off. A real reporter would push through, would keep digging. And that's exactly what I'm doing.

Thankfully, my snooping in the pub office wasn't for nothing. In amongst the photos I'd taken of jumbled paperwork, I found the email addresses of the employees whose names were on the rota for the night of the murder. I got in touch with each of them, appealing for any information they might have about that night, about the back door, about Michelle. I didn't know if it would yield any results, but it was worth a try.

I don't recognise this name though. M Smith. I rack my brain as the message opens, trying to remember who I emailed. The text appears all at once.

So you call yourself a real journalist, you stupid bitch? Think you're so great at investigating? If you don't shut up and disappear this is what's going to happen to you. Oh yeah, and maybe I'll live stream it too, if you're lucky.

My heart pounds as a series of photos begin loading beneath the message.

The pixels in the first one clarify to show my face. My jaw clenches. It's me, this morning, leaving my home and stepping into the Uber I'd called, too fearful to walk to the station alone.

I breathe deeply. It's no surprise, although it still makes my stomach churn. The brick through my window showed that my home wasn't off limits. Someone must be staked out, taking photos of my comings and goings. Anger burns in my throat at the idea. I'm about to pick up my phone to call the police when a second photo loads, all at once, the image forcing a gasp from my lungs.

It's me again. But I'm not at home. I'm at work. At my desk. Where I'm sitting right now. In the photo, I'm frowning at my screen, one hand at my keyboard and the other wrapped around my pendant. I'm wearing a black dress and winged eyeliner, which means this photo was taken yesterday.

I look around me without moving my head, without wanting to appear obvious. There are about twenty-five people in my direct eye line. Any one of them could have snapped this photo of me. But why would they? Perhaps it was someone external, someone who came in for a meeting, or in the guise of a facilities staff member. Or maybe it was someone who works on another floor. Which means, really, it could be anyone.

The third and final photo loads, and this time my eyes fill with tears, and my vision is so blurred that I have to squint to see it properly, to check that I'm really seeing what I think I'm seeing. A sob beats at my chest, and my insides twist.

It's another photo of me.

But this time, I'm not at home, or at work. I'm dead.

My head is bleeding, and there's a ring of dark bruises around my neck. My eyes are glassy, unseeing. My hair is matted with blood, and my skin is a sickening grey, like the water that gurgles out of the bottom of the sink after washing a load of dishes.

I know it's photoshopped. But the threat is real. And the sight of me like that makes something deep inside me tear open, like I'm trying to claw my way out of my own skin, starting from the most hidden, innermost part of myself.

Snatching my phone from my desk, I rush to the bathroom and make it into the cubicle just in time to empty the contents of my stomach. I throw up again and again, until my ribs ache and there's nothing left but bitter bile, and then I sit on the cold tiles and cry. I can't stop shaking, and as I recall the message, its threat burned into my memory, icy fear grips me.

Is it safe for me to step outside? Can I even go home? Should I be here, at work? And then there's the question that's floated to the top of my mind, the one I'm not sure I want to know the answer to. Is this what being a news presenter really means?

I dial Julian's number, unsure if I'll even be able to speak when he picks up but needing to hear his voice anyway. He answers after the third ring and his simple 'Hey, babe,' opens the floodgates, and I'm weeping and trying to speak and it's making me choke.

'Gina? What's happening? Are you OK?'

His concern soothes me enough to get a couple of breathless words out.

'I'm OK. I just . . . someone threatened me.'

At this, I dissolve once again. The threat is on replay in my head, the image of my mangled body like a chorus, a tune so catchy I'm terrified it'll never leave me.

'Babe, who threatened you? Are you safe?'

I nod, snot sliding down my face and into my mouth, before realising that he can't hear me. I need to pull myself together. I'm safe.

'I'm safe right now,' I say out loud, and the panic that had crippled me begins to fade. 'It was an email. They know where I live. They've been to my work. They photoshopped . . . I'm sorry to call—'

'Don't be sorry,' he says firmly. 'I'm glad you called. Have you reported this to the police?'

'No, I only just got it. I'm at work, I called you first.'

'OK, well promise me you'll report it. Being threatened is not OK, and it needs to be taken seriously. You don't deserve this, Gina.'

I was prepared for Jacqueline's anger after what I did. And I knew there would be some people who disagreed with my decision to live stream from the alleyway. But I was completely unprepared for this. It's rattled me far more than anything else that's happened over the past few days.

'I'm going to book myself a flight home,' Julian says firmly.

'No, don't do that,' I say. 'I promise, I'm fine. I just really needed to hear the sound of your voice.'

'I'm worried about you,' he says. 'You're dealing with so much down there and I should be with you. It's not right for me to be away when you're going through this.'

'Your shows,' I say. 'You can't miss them.'

He's spent such a long time perfecting this show, I can't let him give that up. There's nothing I want more than for Julian to be here with his arms around me, but I have the presence of mind at least to know that him being here won't change a thing. He can't stop the threats from coming.

He starts to protest, but I don't let him.

'Honestly. Julian, listen. I'm not going to let you change your plans just because of an email. That means they win, and I'm not letting that happen. I promise I'm OK. You've made me feel so much better, really.'

'Are you sure?' He doesn't sound convinced.

The bathroom door squeaks. Someone's coming. I reach up to flush the toilet, and whisper into my phone, 'I have to go. Call you later.' I hang up, and stay still as footsteps approach.

Whoever it is stops outside my cubicle. My stomach sinks. I recognise those pointed, patent leather pumps. If she knows I'm in here rather than working, I'm going to be in trouble, and this time she might not be so forgiving. I try desperately to keep my shuddering breaths quiet.

112

'Gina?' Jacqueline's tone isn't caustic, like it usually is. It's almost gentle. 'I saw what was on your screen. Are you OK?'

Her concern is so unexpected, and I'm so overwhelmed with gratitude that she's not angry, that I break into a fresh wave of sobs.

'Open the door, Gina. Come on.'

Sniffing, I pull myself up and unlatch the door. My boss is standing in front of me, all sharp angles and harsh lines, but there's something else in her eyes, too. It's not sympathy. I think it's understanding.

'Here,' she says, handing me a bottle of water. 'Splash your face, and let's go and talk in the meeting room next door.'

I nod, and follow her instructions like a child. I'm strangely glad she saw that message, relieved that someone else knows and isn't trying to dismiss it, or telling me to toughen up.

Jacqueline leads me into the small meeting room and closes the door behind us. She motions for me to sit down.

'First of all,' she says, 'I'm sorry you received that message. It was completely unacceptable. Abuse is never OK, and I'll be personally reporting this to the authorities.'

I almost break down again but I manage to keep my emotions in check for long enough to thank her.

'How are you doing?' she asks. 'Aside from this email, I mean.'

I let out a sound that's half laugh, half cry.

'Well, aside from that, I guess I'm OK,' I say weakly. 'I still keep seeing visions of Michelle every time I close my eyes, and I'm finding it hard to sleep...'

I stop, realising that my boss doesn't want a play-by-play of my emotions. Stick to the facts.

113

'But I'm coping,' I say. 'Thanks for asking.'

Jacqueline sighs. 'Look. I know I've been working you really hard since the other night, and I know it hasn't been easy for you, especially given what you saw, and all of this backlash. I can't imagine everything you're having to process right now, but you've been doing a really great job.'

I look at her suspiciously. There has to be a *but* coming soon.

'I mean it,' she says. 'And you know it pains me to say so.'

I laugh again. I've stopped crying now.

'I'm still not thrilled about what you did,' she continues, 'but I can recognise a job well done, and you've been brilliant in all the interviews you've given.'

'Thanks,' I say, still bracing myself for the bad news I know must be coming.

'I know you're having an awful day,' she says, 'but you've been invited to give another interview this afternoon in light of the news about Tinder. Think you can do it?'

I pause. The abuse and threats aren't going to go away if I keep putting myself out there. But they might not go away even if I turn into a hermit. Besides, if Jacqueline says I'm doing well, then I must be doing *really* well.

And isn't this what I've always wanted? Every job has its downfalls. Perhaps the dark side of presenting is online hatred. But that doesn't have to stop me. I can report anything abusive that comes in to the police, and I can make sure the security team is extra vigilant about who they let into the building. This doesn't have to end my career before it's even truly started.

Jacqueline seems to take my hesitation as a no.

'Gina,' she says, leaning in close, 'I know you have enough to worry about now, and I didn't want to have to bring this up, but this channel . . .'

She stops, twists her wedding ring nervously, as though deciding whether or not to speak. I've never seen her like this. It makes me anxious, and I find myself unsure where to look, what to do.

'Not many people know this, Gina. But Channel Eight is on the brink of collapse.'

'I... I'm sorry...' I say, at a loss for words. Why is she telling me this?

'I've been given the unenviable task of saving it, of getting our numbers up to where they need to be. I thought it was impossible. I thought my career was over...'

She trails off again, and for a second I'm genuinely worried she might cry. But she pulls herself together, sits up straighter, clears her throat.

'I'm telling you this because your news story, distasteful as it may be, could just be the miracle we need. The numbers are improving. They're not where we need them to be, yet, but they're a step in the right direction. Which is why I'm asking you to do this. I know the interviews are hard for you, but I need you. The channel needs you.'

I nod. 'OK,' I say. 'I'll do the interview.'

Jacqueline smiles. I think it's the first time I've ever seen a smile from her directed at me, and I don't know whether to be pleased or disturbed.

'Thank you,' she says as I stand up. 'Really.'

'It's fine,' I say, smoothing my skirt. 'I'm happy to help.'

As I turn to leave, she calls out again.

'Oh, and Gina?'

I turn back, my hand hovering over the handle of the meeting room door.

'Yes?'

'I can trust you, can't I? To keep this conversation between us. No one else needs to know.'

I'm suddenly itching to get out of this room. I was pleased to have Jacqueline on my side but I don't like the hint of desperation in her tone. I don't know what to say to this version of my boss.

'I won't say a word,' I say, pulling the door open wide so our conversation is no longer private. She stands as well.

'Thank you, Gina. I really hope I can count on you.'

She says it with a smile.

So why does it feel like a warning?

Chapter 17

RYAN

It's a dream.

I know it's a dream, because Cassie's in it. Not the woman I saw on the train the other day, or the murder victim who looks a bit like her. This is the real Cassie, the little girl I knew, who delighted in teasing me, in tickling me until I cried, in stealing my favourite toys until I'd go red in the face with fury.

In my dream, she's running at me in our back garden, her blonde curls bouncing on her shoulders, her pink dress flying behind her like a cape. She's screaming something, but I'm trapped in silence. I can see her eyes, wide and angry, and her mouth moving to form words, but I can't decipher them. I want to run but I'm paralysed. All I can do is stand and watch her coming for me, fear rooting me to the spot.

I wake up panting and soaked through with sweat. I glance at the clock. It's two o'clock. I sit up in bed and the cold night air hits my damp chest, making me tremble. I'm too wide awake to go back to sleep now, so I get up and put on my warmest jumper, usually reserved for the coldest winter nights, then go to the kitchen to put the kettle on.

When my tea is ready, I cradle the steaming mug and settle onto the sofa, enjoying the warmth that spreads across my palms. Mum used to say that there was nothing in the world a cup of tea couldn't fix. She was wrong, of course. Tea is the perfect remedy for a bad day, or a bit of sad news, or a broken heart. But she never found the cure for a shattered soul. I hope that whatever it is, she finds it over there in Florida.

I miss her, I realise. Of course I miss her. Maybe that's why Cassie's been haunting me lately. These dreams I've been having, convincing myself I'd seen her on the train, mistaking the murdered girl for my sister ... there's got to be a reason why she's on my mind so much. She's been interrupting my sleep almost every night for months, and every time it's the same thing – Cassie, furious, screaming something I can't hear. And me, stuck in the same spot, powerless to act, terror flooding me until I wake. Every time, I'm left breathless and empty, like the nightmares are opening up a chasm I tried to patch up a long, long time ago.

I check the time in my parents' new city. It's still evening there – they're probably getting ready for bed, but they should still be awake. I dial my dad's number, my stomach fluttering as it rings. I haven't spoken to them for months.

Things have been strained between us since Gina moved in. She was right. Her being back in my life did drive a wedge between our parents and me, but they'd left me anyway, so it was a price I was willing to pay. Besides, the debt I owe Gina is so much bigger, and the scales still tip entirely in her favour. I have no right to wish that things were different.

I almost change my mind about the phone call. My thumb is hovering over the end call button when it starts connecting. A second later, my dad's chin comes into the frame.

'Ryan? Hello?'

I smile automatically.

'Hi, Dad, you have to hold the phone up a bit higher.'

It's the same routine every time, his awkwardness with technology never failing to amuse me. He adjusts the camera, eventually working out how to get his entire face onto the screen. He looks good.

'Nice tan!' I say. 'Florida looks good on you.'

'Thanks, I'd almost forgotten what a tan actually looks like.'

'I'm still dreaming of the day I'll get one,' I joke.

'Keep dreaming,' he hits back. 'With that red hair, you have no hope.'

It's true. Mum, Gina and I are cursed to permanent paleness. Whenever we went on holidays as kids, Gina and I would have to stay in the hotel with Mum for an extra ten minutes to make sure no square inch of skin was left bare, while Dad and Cassie would run off to the beach, armed with factor fifteen that would be immediately abandoned. At the end of the day, inevitably, those of us with sunscreen on would still be burned and sore, and the others would be a lovely deep brown, no trace of pink in sight.

'How are you?' he asks. Then, frowning, 'What time is it over there?'

'Oh, it's late,' I say, waving my hand dismissively. 'I just couldn't sleep.'

'Everything OK?'

'Yeah, fine. Just one of those nights. How's everything going over there?'

'Good, good. Can't complain. There's been a lot of golfing from me. And your mum's made some new friends at the club, they've started playing tennis.'

'Sounds good,' I lie. It sounds utterly boring, but if they're happy then I'm pleased for them. 'Is Mum OK?'

'She's very well,' he says. Then he looks away and shouts 'Sharon! It's Ryan.'

I can hear her voice, but I can't make out what she's saying. Dad frowns.

'She'd come and chat to you, bud. It's just that...'

He trails off, but he doesn't need to finish.

'You guys know about Gina, don't you?'

He sighs. 'It seems that even the other side of the world isn't far enough. News travels.'

'Dad—'

'Ryan, look, I know she's your sister, and that you're enjoying having her back in your life, but you need to be careful—'

'No, Dad,' I say firmly. 'You're wrong about her. You always have been. And what's happened here has absolutely nothing to do with before, you must know that.'

'We thought we knew things twenty-one years ago, too, but—'

'Stop,' I interrupt him. 'Just stop it, OK? I'm sorry I called you. I thought I missed you guys, but now I remember exactly what things were like, and I want no part in it.'

A memory bubbles to the surface, one that's threatened to appear many times over the years. I've always shoved it back down, unwilling to face the repercussions of what it means. But now, well, now I'm angry. I'm ready to face my past – this part of it, at least. It plays in my mind like one of those old VHS home videos Dad used to play of us kids – of Cassie – when Mum wasn't there to stop him. It's a little wobbly, and terrible quality, but it's clear enough. I was fifteen, which means Gina was only thirteen, the same age I'd been when Cassie died. It was Christmas. What had once been a season of excitement and treats and raw anticipation had turned into just another occasion that Mum would spoil

120

for everyone else by crying. We were all sad. We all missed Cassie. Only Mum made it her personal mission to ensure no one in the house had any fun, lest it somehow degraded our grief.

We always took a family photo at Christmas. It was Dad's thing. He'd spend hours setting up his camera on the tripod that only came out for this one annual occasion, making sure the tree was in view, and lining us all up squarely for the shot. He'd use us kids as props to measure where we'd all stand in the frame. Of course, at the time, we hated it. Looking back, it's one of my fondest family memories. Before 1996, anyway. Since then, they'd been getting gradually more traumatic for everyone, no one more so than Mum.

She'd fight with Dad for the whole morning, muttering words like 'farce' and 'disrespectful'. He'd carry on, acting cheerful for us kids, as though we couldn't taste the tension that now filled our house like a cheap perfume, cloying and stifling. Inevitably, as Dad pressed the shutter and came running to take his carefully planned place, Mum would burst into tears and the whole shot would be ruined.

'It's just not the same,' she'd wail, and we'd have to try again. He'd use a whole roll of film, but in the end we all looked miserable in every single one, Dad included. Looking back, I think he kept the tradition going in the hope that, one day, Mum would move past whatever stage of grief it was that she was stuck in, and we'd all enjoy the family photo shoot once again.

But he couldn't have been more wrong. The day that's just emerged in my memory was the last attempt. We'd gathered, as we always did, in our festive finest. Gina was shaking presents under the tree and I was pestering her by untying the bow she'd so carefully arranged in her hair.

We were laughing and squealing when Mum had appeared in the living room. She'd been calm. Poised. This got our attention more than any of her screaming or crying.

Maybe this was the turning point we'd all been waiting for.

'I'm ready for the photo,' she'd declared, and Dad's face had lit up like the tree behind him.

'You look beautiful, Sharon. Truly.'

She'd smiled, then. Touched a nervous hand to the sparkling squares adorning her ears and leaned over to kiss Dad. Right on the lips. I remember being taken aback by that, by her affection.

'I don't want her in it.'

She'd said it so matter-of-factly that we'd almost missed it. Gina and I were busying ourselves, taking our allotted places on the sofa, the ones we'd agreed on with Dad. It took a few seconds to process what I'd heard. Dad got there first.

'What's that, love?'

'I don't want her in it.'

She'd pointed at Gina then, and time had stood still. The pounding in my ears had started, the guilt had risen up, the confusion had practically blinded me.

'What do you mean, Sharon? That's Gina.'

'I know who she is,' Mum had said coldly. 'But I won't be in the photo with her.'

'She's your daughter.'

'She's a monster.'

I'd risked turning to look at Gina. Her face had been bright red, her hands clenched by her sides. I'd wanted to reach across, take her hand, tell her it would be OK. But of course it wasn't OK. And besides, I was too scared to move, like if I showed any sign of life, Mum might realise the

122

truth. And if she did, she'd turn on me instead. So, like a coward, I'd stayed motionless, not even daring to breathe.

'Sharon, please,' Dad had begged.

'Bill, I've made my decision. If you want this family to continue to be a family, then it needs to be on my terms.'

'Darling, let's go upstairs and talk—'

But Gina had heard enough. She'd pushed past my dad, and without acknowledging any of us, had walked quietly up the stairs, her head hung low.

'Gina!' Dad had called out. But he hadn't followed her. He hadn't fought for her. And neither had I.

Dad pleads with me now. 'Ryan, don't be like that. We miss you.'

'You know who missed *you*, Dad? Gina. For years. But guess what? You weren't there for her, and now you don't get to have either of us. Call me if you change your mind, but otherwise I'm done.'

Dad opens his mouth to argue but I press my thumb down on the red button instead. I'm trembling again, this time with rage. I'm annoyed at myself for being weak enough to forget. To forget why I was OK with cutting them off. To forget how completely willing they were – and still are, apparently – to think the absolute worst of their children.

And to forget just how guilty I feel about everything.

Because even though Mum acted awfully, even though what she did, and how she treated Gina, was completely unforgivable, the burden was still mine to bear.

This was all my fault.

Chapter 18

GINA

'Don't get up,' Julian groans, his arm curling around my stomach, locking me into place next to him.

I reach over to turn the alarm off and mentally calculate what I can sacrifice in order to spend more time in bed. I'll skip breakfast, I decide. And dry shampoo my hair instead of washing it. I won't wear make-up – I have more interviews today, and they always take off my make-up to put more on anyway. It's a waste of time.

I turn over and nuzzle into Julian.

'I missed you so much,' I say.

He wasn't due home for another week, so when the doorbell rang just before midnight last night, dragging me from dreams of blue lips and blood-matted hair, I'd been terrified. What if the person who sent that email was here to make good on their threat? What if the person who threw the brick was back, willing to do more than just break a window?

'Ryan!' I'd screamed.

He'd come running, his hair wild, his eyes still half closed with sleep.

'What?'

'Who's at the door? Should we call the police?'

'Hang on,' he'd said, wide awake all of a sudden, and

had jogged towards the front door, which I'd double-bolted as soon as I'd got home from work. I'd hovered at the end of the hallway, 999 already keyed into my phone, my finger over the call button and my heart in my mouth. I'd watched as Ryan had peered through the peephole. He'd laughed, and his shoulders had relaxed.

'It's for you,' he'd said, turning around.

'Who is it?'

My head had started buzzing as my body screamed for air. I let out the breath I'd been holding in and filled my lungs again shakily.

'Just trust me,' he'd said wearily. 'You're going to want to open the door.'

He'd walked right past me, muttering something about needing a good night's sleep for once, and I'd tiptoed to the door, my heart pounding. As soon as I'd looked through the peephole I'd screamed.

'Julian!' I cried, unfastening the chain as quickly as I could, fumbling with shaking hands. 'What are you doing here?'

'I knew you were struggling, babe. I have to get a flight back up tomorrow in time for the show, but I just couldn't be away from you for a whole extra week. I couldn't leave you on your own. I missed you too much, and I needed to know that you're OK.'

I'd sobbed into his chest with relief, and then his mouth had been on mine and we'd stumbled into my bedroom. Needless to say, we hadn't done much talking last night.

We have a lot to catch up on this morning.

'How are you?' he asks me. 'And don't give me the usual "I'm fine."'

I sigh, letting my eyes drift from his steely eyes to the dark stubble on his dimpled chin. It's hard enough trying to get my emotions in order mentally, never mind articulate them.

'I think I'm all right,' I say eventually. 'I mean, I'm all over the place, but I know I'll get through this. I was rattled by those photos yesterday though. It's scary to think people genuinely want to hurt me, just for doing my job.'

'I know,' he says, squeezing my shoulder. 'That must have been horrible. But you have to remember, a woman was murdered. People are going to be angry about that. I'm not saying it's right that they target you – obviously that's never OK – but the emotion, however misdirected, is natural.'

'True. I guess I've been so caught up in how scared I was that I hadn't really stopped to consider that.'

'That's also perfectly normal, Gina.'

'Anyway. How's the show going so far?' I ask, ready for a subject change.

'Really good, thanks,' he says, shifting his weight so he's on his side, elbow on my pillow, head resting on his hand. 'There was this YouTuber who came to my Manchester show. He does hypnosis and illusion tutorials mostly, but he's got a really big audience. He posted about my language hypnosis segment, and it's had loads of views already.'

'That's great,' I say enthusiastically. For as long as I've known Julian, he's been trying to make a name for himself. He spends months creating his shows, and then pitching them to agencies in the hope of finding management who will take control of marketing, ticket sales, and most importantly of all, paying the venues. But their answer is always the same: he's not unique enough. Which is total bollocks, of course, but he keeps improving, keeps learning, keeps tweaking, keeps promising the agents that his next tour will be the one that proves he's got something different to offer. And I know he's right.

'Do you want to see it?' he asks, reaching for his phone.

'Of course I do,' I say, resting my head in the crook of his arm as he lies back and holds the phone above our faces.

He must have watched the video recently, because as soon as he opens YouTube, it's there, ready to go. He fast forwards through the introduction.

'He just goes on a bit,' he explains, and then the image transforms to one of Julian on a stage in a fairly unimpressive theatre. He presses play.

'Now, I need a volunteer from the audience,' he's saying from the stage. 'But before anyone puts their hand up, I want to prove that I'm not using paid actors, mostly because I can't afford them.'

A laugh rises up from around the camera.

'When you came in tonight, I asked you to pull a token from a box. You couldn't see inside that box, so there was no way of choosing which one you selected, but someone out there has a red token. Who chose red?'

He peers out towards the camera, and focuses on someone to his left.

'You down there, yes, you in the blue shirt. What's your name?'

'Gary,' the man says loudly.

'Gary, you have the red token? Great! Are you on a date? Who's the beautiful lady next to you?'

'Amanda,' she calls out.

'Amanda!' exclaims Julian. 'I knew a girl called Amanda once. She was a nightmare, but I'm sure you're lovely.' I smile at his stage presence. It's the first impression I ever had of him, and it was one of the reasons I fell in love with him. He's animated, confident, and totally in control. It's mesmerising, and I'll never tire of watching it.

'Now, Amanda, how long have you known Gary?'

127

'Eight years,' she replies.

'OK, great, so you know him pretty well then, you'd say?'

She shrugs. 'I think so.'

'It's not a trick question, Amanda,' Julian says, and there are smatterings of laughter. Amanda giggles.

'So you know Gary quite well. Can you tell me, does he speak another language?'

Amanda shakes her head.

'No? Not even *un peu français*?'

'I have no idea what that means, and neither will he,' she calls back.

'Perfect. Gary, can I get you to join me on stage, please? Give it up for Gary, everyone!'

There's light applause as a slight, blond man walks up the small set of stairs on the right-hand side of the stage. He shakes Julian's hand.

'Nice to meet you, Gary, thanks for joining me. Now, what I'd like to do next involves a bit of casual hypnosis.'

Gary laughs and looks back at Amanda nervously.

'Have you ever been hypnotised before?'

'No, never.'

'OK, well there's nothing to be worried about. I'm not going to make you do anything you don't want to do, that's not how this works, all right? I'll walk you through it all, but by the end of it you're going to be speaking entire sentences in Russian. How does that sound to you?'

'Sounds impossible,' Gary says, laughing.

'Well, as Audrey Hepburn once said, "Nothing is impossible, the word itself says 'I'm possible,'" so I'm keen to give it a go if you are. What do you say, Gary?'

Gary shrugs his shoulders and lets out a little puff of air from the side of his mouth. 'Yeah, why not?'

'OK, Gary, what I'd like you to do here is to press down

on the palm of my hand, press it as hard as you can, keep pressing, that's right.'

Julian's arm is outstretched, his palm facing upwards, applying equal pressure to the downward force Gary's exerting, so their hands remain in place. Their eyes are locked, as though facing each other in preparation for battle. Suddenly, Julian drops his arm so Gary lunges forward, and as he does so, he taps Gary on the shoulder and says, 'Sleep.'

Gary's arms and head go limp, and aside from the gentle swaying of his limbs, he's motionless.

'That's it, Gary, as you fall deeper and deeper into this sleep, you'll feel more and more at ease, and all of your muscles in your neck, your arms, your fingers, will keep feeling looser and more relaxed. That's it.'

He turns to face the audience.

'Now, in just a moment, I'm going to ask Gary to speak some phrases in Russian. As you'll remember, confirmed by the charming Amanda, he doesn't actually speak any other languages, but that will all change in a moment. Now, to make sure I'm not just getting him to speak in gobbledegook and calling it Russian, can someone help me out by pulling up Google translate, please?'

He casts his eye over the audience again, and points to someone off camera, to his right.

'The woman in the green dress, yes, do you have it up on your phone? Great, come and join me on stage.'

She's introduced as Rabia, and instructed to look up the Russian translation for each of the phrases Julian is about to say. She'll then play each one back to the audience after Gary's attempt. She looks sceptical.

'Right, Gary,' Julian says, turning his attention back to the man in the trance. 'I'm about to say a phrase, and then I'll tap you on your right shoulder. When I tap you, you're going to repeat what I've just said in Russian. If you understand, lift your head.'

Gary's head rises so he's face to face with Julian, but his eyes are still firmly closed, and his mouth is hanging slightly open. He looks incredibly relaxed.

'OK, Gary, the first phrase is "Hello, my name is Gary."'

He reaches out and gently taps the shoulder of the man in front of him.

'*Privet, menya zovut* Gary,' Gary says, without a second's hesitation.

Several people in the audience gasp audibly. Gary doesn't move or react. Rabia's mouth has dropped open. Julian turns to her.

'Rabia, for the sake of the audience, would you type "Hello, my name is Gary" into Google translate, and play the audio version into my microphone, please?'

She types for a couple of seconds and then holds her phone up towards the microphone, tapping her screen as she does so. The robotic voice is crystal clear.

'*Privet, menya zovut* Gary,' she recites.

The applause is thunderous this time.

'I don't want anyone to think that was a lucky guess by Gary, so shall we try again, for argument's sake?'

More applause, accompanied by whistles and cheers.

'OK, Gary,' he says, turning back to the man in the trance. 'Your next phrase is, "This is the best magic show I've ever seen".'

He taps Gary on his shoulder again.

'*Eto luchsheye volshebnoye shou, kotoroye ya kogda-libo videl,*' Gary says, without pausing to think.

There are more squeals and gasps, and people stand up to give Julian a standing ovation. I turn over and kiss him.

'I'm so proud of you,' I say. 'I knew people would sit up and pay attention sooner or later.'

He kisses me back. 'Thanks, I can't believe it. It's had ten thousand views already, and that was just a few days ago.'

'You're brilliant.'

'Well, not everyone thinks so,' he says, exiting the app and putting his phone down. 'Some of the commenters are saying that I used an actor, that it's all fake.'

'You shouldn't read the comments,' I say, recognising the irony in my statement even as it leaves my lips. I can hardly dish out advice that I'm so blatantly ignoring myself.

'I know,' he sighs. 'I'm just frustrated that people don't take me seriously.'

'They will,' I say, kissing his nose. Then I glance at the clock and sit bolt upright. 'I have to go!'

'No,' he moans. 'Stay. Can't you just take the morning? Be with me until I have to fly back?'

'I so wish I could,' I say. 'Honestly. But I have more interviews today.'

Jacqueline had called me – again – late last night, once the day's figures had come in, to talk me through the topics that had elicited the biggest reaction from the viewers. The strategy, she told me, was to replicate those moments to gain more viewers, to build more buzz. Today's selected topics included online dating safety, again, and how social media interacts with modern journalism. As pleased as I am to be let in on some of the inside workings of the channel, these nightly calls from my boss are starting to grate on me. After all, she's still only paying me a PA salary.

Julian groans and tries to pull me closer again.

'Shall I call Jacqueline, tell her you need the day off?'

'No!' I cry immediately. I'm mortified by the idea of him using his personal connection to secure any kind of privileges for me. Besides, Jacqueline has already made it abundantly clear that a play like that won't work. 'No, please don't do that.'

'I'm only joking,' he says, although I'm not certain he means it. 'What are they interviewing you about this time?'

'I'm on a panel. It's all about social media and journalism.'

'Sounds like they're really milking you for all the ratings they can get.'

'Yeah, but it won't last. Once this story dies down, I'll be back to my personal assistant duties like nothing ever happened.'

'I'm sure that's not true,' Julian says.

'Well, I hope not,' I say, my lips brushing his. 'But all I know is that I have to ride this out till the end, whenever that is.'

I don't know why I omit the detail about the dying channel, about Jacqueline's strange plea for me to keep our conversation secret. It's probably not important, anyway. This isn't about her.

'I get it,' he says. 'I'm just being selfish. I just want to be with you.'

'Trust me, babe,' I say. 'I'd rather be here. But I have to run.'

'OK,' he whispers, kissing me quickly. 'Go get 'em.'

Chapter 19

RYAN

I almost don't see it, hidden among the pile of junk mail and bills.

Tossing the handful of envelopes I'd gathered from the hallway onto the kitchen bench as I sweep past, I grab a beer from the fridge and enjoy the silence of an empty house. I lean against the breakfast bar and let the stress of the day wash away as I sip the cold beer.

Absently, I rifle through the mail. A phone bill for Gina, a council tax bill, a Florida brochure addressed to Mum and Dad.

And that's when I spot it.

It looks harmless at first; intriguing, even. A small, pink envelope with my name and address scrawled in spidery black ink. There's a small heart above the i in Mills. I smirk, and put my finger under the flap of the envelope to open it.

What flutters out, whirling to the floor and landing on my foot, makes my throat close over and my heart stop mid-beat.

It's a newspaper clipping, old and tattered along the edges where it was cut, years ago, judging by the condition it's in. But it's not just any newspaper clipping. In the millions of newspapers that have been published in my lifetime, the billions of words and pictures and stories, this one I'd recognise anywhere. This is the only one that matters. It's a photo of a little girl, smiling broadly at the camera, a tooth missing and a stray blonde curl hanging across her left eye.

She's so full of joy, her vitality so palpable, that a solid ball of emotion catches in my throat. It hurts, every time I see a photo of Cassie, to know how full of life she was. How truly, how completely, she lived. I know she was only eight when she died, and I know all kids are full of life. And maybe I do see her through rose-tinted glasses because her life was cut short so unexpectedly, so horrifically. But I also genuinely believe that she saw things differently, that she lived life better than I do. That she deserved to live instead of me.

I reach down and pick up the photo, black and white and grainy, but still unmistakably her. My sister. My finger brushes her smiling face gently, and another tiny piece of my heart tears away. Then I remember the envelope, and I snatch it up and pull out the small card that's nestled inside.

The front of it is simple. It's white, embossed with two words in black: *My brother*.

The hairs on my arms stand upright. This is either some kind of uncharacteristically cruel prank by Gina. Or... but I don't want my mind to stretch to the alternative. Because the alternative is ... what? That my dead little sister is alive and sending me a card? I'm tired, and I'm stressed, but I'm not delusional.

Holding my breath, I open the card. There are just a few lines of the thin, spidery writing inside.

I know you're a killer, Ryan. Don't you think it's time the truth came out?
Love,
Your Other Sister. x

I slam the card closed on the kitchen bench, my heart creating its own erratic rhythm. I squeeze my eyes closed to try to halt the dizziness but it's not helping. I have to sit. Supporting myself on the edge of the kitchen island, I find my way to the bar stool and collapse on it heavily. I reach for my beer and finish the bottle in one long gulp.

What the hell is going on? Who would send this to me, and what does it mean?

You're a killer, the words taunt me. But I know those words aren't true. They can't be. Cassie's death was a horrible, tragic accident. It wasn't a murder. The news article that this clipping belongs to even says so. I remember it, word for word, although I haven't read it for years.

Cassandra Joy Mills, a local girl who recently celebrated her eighth birthday, died yesterday afternoon following a tragic fall while she was playing in her back garden with her siblings. Her death was deemed to be an accident, but child safety advocates are calling for tighter laws around child supervision.

That's all she got. A tiny snippet on the second page of our local newspaper, to push an agenda by mum-shaming groups who believed they were better parents than those whose lives had been hit by tragedies like this one.

An accident, that's all it was.

So who sent me this letter, and what do they mean by it?

I turn the envelope over. There's no return address. The stamp is British, but that doesn't tell me much. I don't recognise the handwriting, and there's nothing else that gives me any clue as to who sent this, or from where.

I think back to my unquestionable certainty that the woman I saw on the train was Cassie, that the woman in the papers was Cassie, and not for the first time I wonder if I'm going crazy. But whatever hallucinations I was having those other times, this card in my hands is real. This newspaper clipping, it's not a figment of my imagination. Which means I'm not insane.

But that leaves me sitting in my kitchen, trembling from head to toe, not wanting to ask myself the most troubling questions of all.

Who elsc knows about Cassie? How did they find out? And what do they want from me?

Chapter 20

DETECTIVE ADAM ADEBAYO

I slam the paper tray closed and furiously hit buttons until something whirrs inside the printer. There's a crunching noise that makes me wince, and then a single piece of paper is spat out.

'Finally,' I snap, snatching it up and stalking back to my desk.

'What's up your arse?' Christine asks as I slap the paper down on top of the case file in frustration.

'Just another bloody dead end,' I complain. 'The guy whose photos were used for the Tinder profile, his work just sent through his time cards. He was definitely on a shift all night. It wasn't him.'

I'd known it was too good to be true when a woman called our tip hotline saying the photos we released to the press were of her ex-boyfriend, Riley. She'd given us his details, and we'd turned up at his house to question him.

'Yeah, that's me,' he'd said matter-of-factly, when we showed him the photos.

'We can see that,' I'd replied drily. 'Can you tell me anything about a Tinder profile under the name Martin Lloyd?'

'Nope,' he'd said. 'I've never used Tinder. No need. I have no trouble getting laid.'

I'd ignored that.

'Any idea how someone might have got hold of these photos?'

'Sure,' he'd shrugged. 'They were from a photo shoot I did a few years ago. For one of those stock image websites. I think I got, like, three hundred quid for a few hours' work. But anyone can get hold of them, if they pay for the download. Whoever it is must be dedicated though, it takes a bit of effort to find multiple stock photos with the same person in them.'

We'd asked what he was doing on the night of Michelle's murder, and he'd claimed to be at work. He gave us the name and phone number of the restaurant he worked at as well as the photographer who took his photos, and then we'd thanked him for his time and come back to the station to verify his information.

'What about the photos?' Christine asks.

The photographer had sent us the images she took at the photo shoot with Riley, and sure enough, all of the Tinder images were included in the album.

'We've contacted the stock photo companies where the pictures are listed, to get user information from anyone who's downloaded them in the past. I'm not holding my breath for a breakthrough there though.'

'Aren't we Mr Positive today?' she asks, and I shoot her a warning look. I'm too tired for banter, and far too frustrated to mess around. I pull my glasses off and pinch the bridge of my nose, an attempt to ward off the headache I can feel building behind my eyes.

'What are you working on?' I ask.

'I was going through the blood spatter report again,' she says. 'But it wasn't telling me anything I don't know. I haven't quite finished, I'll get through it soon, I just got distracted.'

'By what?'

She looks embarrassed. 'Another Gina interview.'

I roll my eyes. 'Are you kidding me? How long is she going to milk this for? And why are you even watching that?'

She shrugs. 'Honestly, no idea. But there's just something really watchable about her. Look.'

Reluctantly, I roll my chair around the side of our adjoining cubicles until I'm sitting behind Christine. She pulls her headphones out of the computer and turns the volume up.

'No, I don't think Tinder is inherently dangerous,' Gina is saying to a man in a bright red tie. 'But I think more should be done to ensure accounts are properly verified.'

Her eyes are alive, and her face is animated. Not in a distracting way, but in a way that captivates me, and makes me want to be right there with her, learning more. I study her black fitted blazer and crisp white shirt, and realise with embarrassment that I'm utterly absorbed with the way she moves, her voice, those emerald eyes. Christine's right. She is incredibly watchable.

'Well, let's move on to that night, and the discovery you made,' the interviewer says, clearly keen to avoid offending online dating companies. 'When did you first know that Michelle was dead?'

'I wasn't paying attention at first,' she says, her tone becoming more serious. 'I had just gotten off the phone with my boyfriend, and I was listening to music. I was distracted. And then I stepped on something, it crunched under my foot. I looked down to see what it was, and it was this little compact mirror, it was all shattered, and there was blood on it. I followed the trail of blood and at first what I saw was something glinting. I stepped closer and I saw what it was, it was Michelle's necklace, this chunky thing with loads of sparkles...'

I don't hear the rest of her sentence. It's like someone's injected caffeine straight into my bloodstream.

'What necklace?' Christine and I yelp in unison.

We stare at each other for a second, and then we both stand up and rush through the office to the incident room, where Mia is sitting at her makeshift desk. She looks up at us but before I say anything I glance at the photo held with a magnet to the top of the whiteboard. I must have seen it a hundred times already, but I need to check. To be sure.

Michelle's slumped onto the bulging bin bags, her legs at unnatural angles and one arm thrown across her torso. But there's no jewellery.

'Gina just said Michelle was wearing a necklace when she found her,' I say, panting.

'When? What?'

'On a TV interview just now,' Christine says, as out of breath as I am.

'Bring her in,' Mia replies without hesitating. I nod, and run back to my desk.

Less than two hours later, we're sitting across from one another in an interview room. Christine shifts in the uncomfortable plastic chair beside mine as I try to get a read on Gina.

To her credit, she came in as soon as we asked her to. She's still dressed in a slim-fitting black suit, a white shirt, and make-up that looks far too heavy away from the heavy lighting and camera lenses. Here, under the glow of fluorescent strips, her skin looks almost orange. But her eyes are the same striking colour. She keeps them locked on mine, and for a split second I forget what brought us here.

Instead of digging for the truth about her statement, I want to know everything else about her: her hobbies, her ambitions, her taste in music, her sense of humour. Where she grew up. Her favourite food.

'Thanks for coming in today,' Christine begins, and Gina drops her gaze. The spell is broken and I'm suddenly embarrassed by my own thoughts. 'I should note that this session is being recorded.'

Gina nods.

'I understand that we've been through this already, but could you take a moment to walk us through how you found Michelle and exactly what you saw that night?'

A frown flickers across her face. 'OK,' she says slowly, uncertainly. 'Well, I was walking home from drinks with a colleague. I was listening to music, and I took the alleyway as a shortcut. I stepped on that shattered compact mirror, and then I saw droplets of blood, which led me to behind the bin bags.'

She hesitates, taking a deep, shaking breath.

'Am I . . . is this what you want me to tell you again?'

'Yes, please continue,' Christine says.

'All right. So I stepped around the bins, and that's when I saw Michelle. I called emergency services, they asked me to check her pulse, and I confirmed that I couldn't feel one. And then while I was waiting for help to arrive, I did the broadcast.'

'Can you tell me what Michelle was wearing?' I ask.

'It was a dress, short, and fitted. Navy blue, I think. And silver satin heels, one of them had broken off and was further into the alleyway. A clutch bag, I think, that might have been navy blue as well.'

'Any jewellery?'

She doesn't react. Doesn't pause.

'She had on a really sparkly necklace, but I don't remember seeing anything else.'

I pull a sheet of paper out of my file. It's on the top, already prepared for this.

'In your original statement,' I say. 'You didn't mention any jewellery.'

She tilts her head as though trying to remember.

'What I saw that night was really traumatic,' she says after a couple of seconds. 'You saw me. I was in complete shock. I don't know why I wouldn't have mentioned seeing it, but I guess I must have forgotten.'

'That could explain it,' says Christine, sliding a photo across the table. Gina's eyes widen when she sees it. 'But can you explain this?'

Silence falls over the room for a few seconds as Gina studies the photo of Michelle's body, taken at the crime scene. Then she looks up, her eyes wide.

'Explain what?'

'The necklace. Where is it?'

'I don't know, someone must have taken it off, for forensics or whatever.'

'There was no necklace found at the crime scene, Gina.'

'I don't understand,' she says.

'Neither do we,' I say, leaning over and resting my elbows on the cold metal table. 'You see, these photos were taken when we first arrived at the scene. You were the only person there, and you told us no one else had been with you.'

I wait for her to react, but she remains calm.

'What we're asking you, Gina,' says Christine, 'is whether you took that necklace from Michelle's body?'

'What?' She looks aghast. 'Why would I do that?'

'Some kind of trophy, maybe?' Christine offers. 'Or maybe something to hold onto until you could sell it off. There are people who buy murder mementos, you know.'

The corners of Gina's mouth turn down in disgust.

'I don't have the necklace,' she says. 'I didn't sell it, and I didn't keep it as a souvenir.' She spits the word out in distaste. 'You guys clearly don't think much of me, do you?'

'What we think is irrelevant,' Christine says lightly. 'But were you lying about someone else being there at the crime scene?'

'No, it was just me.'

'Then where the hell did the necklace go, Gina?' I say, my voice rising. 'Jewellery doesn't just walk off.'

'I don't know,' she repeats. 'Anyway, you're the detective. Isn't it your job to figure that out?'

I clench my jaw together, infuriated.

'Am I under arrest?' she asks. 'Or can I go now, please?'

Christine sees her out, but I remain in my chair, fists clenched, seething. In part because Gina offered us absolutely no useful information, but in part because I expect more from myself. I became a detective to solve cases, to get justice for victims, to stop more crimes from happening. But working on this case feels like running up a hill that's made of soft sand. Every step I take towards the top sends me sliding a few feet backwards.

This necklace feels important, perhaps because it's a new lead, something to chase that isn't my own tail. Of course, it could turn out to just be a missing necklace, a red herring that sends us into a frenzy of activity for nothing. Or it could be the key that unlocks the case.

I can't even begin to guess which one it is. But after this interview, I do know one thing for certain. Call it a cop's intuition, because it's not based on fact.

Gina's hiding something.

Chapter 21

GINA

For one hopeful moment, I'm certain that Tash is going to forgive me.

It's been a week since we last spoke – properly spoke, not just her yelling at me – at the bar. Before. That's how I measure my life now. Before I walked down that alleyway. Before I saw the woman, and the blood, and the blue lips. Before I made the irreversible decision to press that 'Live' button on Facebook.

And then there's after. Since that moment, my world has been turned upside down, shaken around like a snow globe and tipped back upright. Everything's the same, only it's completely different, too.

Before, Tash and I would talk about everything from our careers to our families and our weekend antics. But in this new world, she's mad. She's taken it all so personally, as though I've somehow slighted her, or done her a huge injustice. She started a petition – it was anonymous, but I spotted it on her screen, so I know it was her – to have me fired for professional misconduct. There's no grounds for it but it's gained a hundred thousand signatures already. Thankfully, the ratings are still high enough that the channel isn't taking it seriously. Yet.

I've tried talking to her but she just walks away, as though

I don't exist. So I went with a different approach, emailing her to apologise, despite not being quite certain of exactly what I'm sorry for. Is she mad because I used the social media account that she's responsible for? Or because she has a moral objection to what I did? I just wish she'd talk to me so I'd know, so I could explain. I even considered buying her flowers, although that seemed like a bit too much. Besides, I can't afford extravagant displays of repentance, my bank balance is dangerously low as it is.

To add insult to injury, all of this chaos has created piles of additional work for her. After any of my online question and answer sessions or TV interviews, there are hundreds of comments to moderate. And thanks to the onslaught of threats the channel is receiving, there are daily reports to fill in, accounts to flag to Facebook, and users to block.

It's keeping her so busy that most evenings we're the last two people in the building. Although Jacqueline showed me a glimpse of her softer side last week, she's been back to her usual self since, and she isn't showing any lenience when it comes to doing my actual job; the work I now don't have time to do during regular office hours, thanks to the endless stream of interviews.

This evening is no different to the last few. Ordinarily, this would be the perfect chance for Tash and me to talk, to work through our issues, for me to help her understand why I chose to film the scene. But she won't even look at me.

She bundles up her coat, throwing her phone into her bag as she holds down the power button on her computer. She really should shut it down properly but I know that she has a dinner she's running late for. She didn't tell me that. I heard her explaining her evening plans to one of the other girls as they returned from their tea break. A break I wasn't invited to join them for.

The ghostly glow of her monitor cuts out, and for a second she hesitates. This is the part where we say goodbye, or when we used to, anyway. I stop typing and pause, anticipating a break in her frosty silence. I want my friend back, and I allow myself to believe, just for a moment, that she wants me back, too.

She seems to be deciding whether to smile or walk away, but then the moment's over and she's turning away from me, her shoulders slumped.

I breathe out slowly, expelling my disappointment. It feels like everyone hates me these days. Even as I think it, I know I'm being melodramatic. I still have Julian.

And, of course, Jacqueline's pleased with my work, as are the rest of the channel bosses. I'm not sure what will happen when the momentum runs out though, as it inevitably will. The Tinder angle breathed fresh life into this news story, but that'll die down soon, too, and the world will move on to another story, another scandal. Of course I'm hoping the killer will be caught, that justice will be served. But selfishly – and I'd never admit this to anyone – I know that when that day comes, I'll be forgotten. Discarded.

At least once I've faded from the public eye, the trolls might leave me alone. Thankfully, there haven't been any more emails, but the messages on Twitter have been as plentiful as they have been horrific. The police assured Channel Eight's legal representative that they've taken each of the threats seriously, and will be finding the users and charging them. But I can't help replaying them over and over whenever I'm alone with my thoughts.

You'll get what's coming to you, bitch

I hope you get raped and murdered in your sleep, you fame whore

It should have been you who was strangled, the world doesn't need inbreds like you walking around, I hope you're next

No matter how much everyone tells me not to worry, or assures me that they're just anonymous cowards who want to feel powerful by scaring me – no matter how badly I want to believe them – I feel like I might suffocate in the terror of their threats.

Because it's not just anonymous trolling online, and it's no longer removed from me. My safety is at stake, all because of a video. People know where I live. I was followed. I was being watched. Who was watching me?

I've been too scared to go outside, too nervous to be home alone, or to go out at lunch, or even to catch the train home, in case there's someone following me, trying to catch me alone. Instead, I've been catching Ubers to and from work.

But it's almost the end of the month now, and I have no money for another taxi. I'm only just scraping by until payday comes around next week, which is just another painful reminder of how badly I'm failing as an adult. I'm in my thirties, for goodness sake. I should be able to afford as many taxis as I want.

And yet here I am, skint again, and forced to walk home in near-crippling fear, due to a dying bank account. Yesterday, for the first time since the night of Michelle's murder, I walked home after I'd finished all of my work. My heart was beating so hard I thought it would tear through my flesh, and I'd been convinced every shadow was an imminent threat, but I'd arrived intact.

As soon as I'd bolted the front door behind me, I'd gone straight for Ryan's whisky, gulping back a generous glass of the stuff and wincing as it went down. But I'd made it. Nothing bad had happened.

Today I've been telling myself it was a sign that life will get better soon. Better, not normal. Because life will never go back to how it was before all of this. I have to settle for better, and I almost believe it when I tell myself that's possible.

I shut down my computer and pull my heels off, throwing them under my desk and changing into my trainers, moving quickly because I have no idea if I'm being watched again. Being alone doesn't help my fears. I need to get out, in public, where I'll be protected by the very presence of other people. I heave my bag onto my shoulder, take the elevator to the ground floor and swipe out of the turnstiles, trainers squeaking on the shiny tiles as I wave goodbye to the security guard at reception.

I call Julian as soon as I step outside. His voice instantly comforts me.

'Hey, it's late, are you just leaving work?'

'Yep,' I sigh. 'I couldn't stay another minute. I'm done.'

'Busy day?'

'Same as every other day for the past week,' I say wearily. 'How about you? How's Edinburgh?'

The part of me that still feels unsafe is mad at him for leaving again so soon, right when I need him. But I know that holding him back won't help either of us. He needs to chase his dreams. And he definitely needs to make the most of the publicity he's getting from that YouTube video. His

Edinburgh show tomorrow night is already sold out, which is a first for him.

'Edinburgh's . . . cold,' he laughs. 'But fine so far. We did a lighting and sound rehearsal this morning, so now I'm just resting up ahead of tomorrow, taking it easy.'

'You're going to do so great,' I tell him.

'Thanks,' he says. 'But I just feel so guilty being away from you right now. I'm still tempted to cancel the show.'

'Don't you dare,' I say firmly. 'This is a huge opportunity. Think long term, OK? I got to see you the other day, and that was an unexpected bonus. But now you have to focus on your career. We'll be together again before you know it.'

I'm trying to convince myself as much as him, but as the words come out I know they're true. I want him with me, but I want him to succeed even more than that.

'Are you walking home again?' he asks.

'Yep.' I try to sound brave. 'Time to get back on the horse, or whatever the phrase is.'

'OK. Be careful,' he says. 'And remember to stay calm.'

I'd called him the previous evening, breath shallow, on the verge of tears, unsure that I could carry on. He'd calmed me down, convinced me I could keep going, but I'd been a mess.

'I'm OK,' I assure him, not wanting him to worry. Besides, he's hundreds of miles away. I have to do this on my own. 'I can do this. I promise.'

'I know you can,' he says. 'You're the strongest person I know. I love you, Gina.'

'I love you too,' I say, hanging up.

I'm walking too quickly, as though I can escape my nerves by outrunning them. I'm soon out of breath, a stitch stabbing my torso. I drag my headphones out of my bag, then decide that it's better to be alert and aware of my

149

surroundings, and settle for counting each step as my foot hits the pavement instead. My lungs loosen as my breathing slowly grows deeper and more controlled. It's not enough, though. I'm still wound tightly, ready to fight, ready to run, ready to scream at the slightest hint of the unexpected.

I can do this, I know I can. I just need to be determined. I clench my jaw and increase my pace as I stride through the dark.

I've taken a longer route – to avoid going anywhere near the alleyway – which takes me through a park with a small playground. Anticipation tingles in my toes. I'm almost home.

I step onto the spongy play surface, the kind that makes sure that kids bounce when they fall off the equipment, and I keep counting. Two hundred and seventeen. Two hundred and eighteen. Two hundred and nine—

I freeze. Movement streaks along the edge of my vision, triggering a commotion behind my ribs. Should I run? But my feet are planted to the ground, and I'm paralysed by anxious indecision. A flicker of a shadow darts in front of me, and I open my mouth to shriek, but the scream catches in my throat and withers away.

A scrawny fox slinks past, its eyes trained on me as though I'm the predator. I almost laugh, but the noise dies in the cold air, coming out as a frightened wheeze and a puff of breath.

I let out a deep lungful of relief as I watch the brush of its tail disappearing behind a shrub. With trembling legs, I keep walking. The shock of the fox's appearance has left my lungs burning, and my body tight, like strings on a guitar, stretched until there's no more flex. I feel taut, on edge, ready to snap.

I step past the swing set, around the merry-go-round and turn right to reach the path that will take me to my street.

But my brain screams at me to stop. To pay attention. I don't need to look twice. I already know what it is. I know by the whisper of electricity that tingles softly across my neck; the sharp slap of recognition that reverberates deep in my bones.

For a split second I consider leaving, pretending I never saw this. Running home and locking the door behind me. But I can't. I've seen it now. There's no turning back.

I squeeze my eyes tightly closed but I can still picture her clearly, the image burned into my brain. She's in a dress, red and floral, but it's been ripped and torn, marked with patches that are so dark they're almost black. It's blood. I know it, just like I know that the dark circle around her neck isn't just a shadow. She's propped up against the playground equipment, but she looks broken, her arms and legs forced into unnatural positions. Like a doll, dropped and forgotten.

My chest squeezes tightly until I'm sure my ribs could crush my frenetic heart.

It's happened again.

It's the only thought my brain will allow to cut through the roar of my blood rushing and the hammering of my pulse. They're so loud it's all I can focus on. That, and the one fact that matters: it's happened again.

I'm not the target, I tell myself. If I was, I'd be dead by now, instead of the woman in front of me. But I was meant to find her. My stomach flips at this truth, at the idea that this woman was murdered right in my path, on my way home, just in time for me to discover her. My whole body is trembling.

There's a sudden, shrill sound, and for a split second my brain thinks it is the dead woman, screaming. But then my

151

logic kicks in and I can see the bright light in my hand, and feel the vibrations through the bones in my arm, and then I understand that it's just my phone ringing. Still, knowing what's happening doesn't help me make sense of it. Why would my phone be ringing now? Who would call me in the midst of this? I glance at the name.

Jacqueline.

She doesn't know what I'm in the midst of, of course. How could she? She's just calling to update me on numbers, to talk through tomorrow's interviews.

My thumb hovers over the reject call button. I take a deep breath, willing myself to calm down, trying to find clarity. I need to reject Jacqueline's call, use my phone to contact the police. But part of me wants to speak to someone, to tell someone what I've just walked into without them taking it down as an official statement, without my reactions being on the record. I don't want the full weight of responsibility to fall on me. Without thinking, I press the green button, pulling the device towards my face instinctively, my muscle memory taking over.

'Jacqueline,' I breathe. My voice is raspy, like I've been smoking for the past twenty years.

'Gina,' she replies, all crisp efficiency, no acknowledgement of the distress in my tone. 'So we have today's numbers and I'm afraid—'

'There's another one,' I wheeze, interrupting her. 'Another body.'

The silence that follows is somehow deeper than the emptiness that surrounded me before my phone rang.

'How do you know?' Jacqueline's words are slow and precise.

'I've just found it,' I gasp. 'I was walking home. She

was . . . she was just . . . here. I think it's the same person who did it. It looks the same.'

'Have you called the police?' Her tone has changed now, from steely and businesslike to something that sounds a little bit like panic.

'No, I was just about to when you called. I'm . . . how is this happening?'

'Gina, listen to me,' Jacqueline says urgently. 'I need you to listen. You need to call the police. And once you've done that, I need you to broadcast it, just like you did last time.'

'What? No! Why would I . . . what?'

'Our ratings are down again, Gina. The story is losing momentum. Remember what I told you about Channel Eight?'

My mind is clawing for answers, regretting the moment I answered the phone. I should have rejected it, like my instinct had screamed at me to do.

'I don't . . . Jacqueline, I can't do that.'

'Why not?' Her voice is calm again, commanding. 'It's not illegal, we already know that. Filming it isn't going to hurt that woman. Think about it: by getting the news out, we might be able to find the killer more quickly.'

'But . . . the threats . . .'

I'm struggling to process information, my thoughts moving slowly, as though they're being pressed in on all sides.

'The threats aren't going to stop, either way,' she says patiently, like she's explaining the concept of sharing with a toddler. 'But what can change is your future at the channel. Your career. You told me that you broadcast the murder last week because of your instinct as a journalist, Gina. This is a story, it's a huge story, and it needs to be told, you know that. And you're the one to tell it.'

'I don't know . . .'

'What are the chances of you finding two bodies, Gina? There's a reason why you're the one who's getting to these scenes first.'

A shiver trickles down my spine. I know it's true, but hearing her say the words somehow makes this all feel so much more real.

'Don't waste this,' she says. 'I'm counting on you. The channel is counting on you. Call the police.'

The line goes dead. I hold the phone at arm's length to look at the screen, as though the answers might be found there, but my hands are shaking so much that it slips right through my fingers. I swear, not recognising my own throaty voice. It takes me three attempts to pick it up from the ground, and when I do, I only know one thing. I need to report this.

There's a crack slicing through the surface of my screen. With clumsy hands, I dial 999.

'Hello, emergency service operator, which service do you require: fire, police, or ambulance?'

'Ambulance, please.'

'I'll connect you now.'

I hear a click, and a pause that feels like it takes minutes to end.

'Hello, ambulance service, what's the address of the emergency?'

'Oh God, um, I don't know the address, it's the park just off Caseley Road in W12.'

'OK, that's fine, we're locating you now. What's the nature of your emergency?'

'There's a woman. I think she's dead. It looks the same as the other time.'

'Are you with her? Is it safe for you to check her pulse?'

I glance around me, to be certain I'm alone.

'I . . . yes, I think it's safe.'

I edge closer to the woman and reach for her wrist. I flinch as my skin touches something cool and smooth. I glance down. It's a silver bracelet, crowded with delicate charms that rattle when I touch them. I find the space on her slim wrist where her pulse should be, and press my forefinger and middle finger down, holding my breath.

Nothing. Her blood is stagnant, useless inside her veins. Mine, by contrast, is coursing furiously from my thumping heart.

I vaguely remember that I'm still on the line to the emergency operator. I can hear him talking to me, but I don't hear what he's saying.

'She's dead,' I say, keeping the emotion from my voice as much as I can. 'There's no pulse.'

I don't hear another word because I hang up and stare at the woman beside me. She's dressed as though for a night out, her neck circled in thick, black bruises. Her lips are blue, her body covered in scrapes and grazes. Her hair is matted with dark, glistening blood.

My head buzzes, the noise building to a roar. I think about what Jacqueline said to me just moments ago: *By getting the news out, we might be able to find the killer more quickly*. I don't know if she's right, or if she was just trying to manipulate me. There's no way to tell, and there's no time to think it through.

The rational part of my brain tells me that I shouldn't do what she asked, that it's too risky, that the consequences could be too great. But another part of me – the part that agrees with Jacqueline that it was no accident I found this body – screams at me that I have to do it. That it's the only option.

Through shaking breaths, I unlock my phone and turn the camera to face me. A crack slices through my face.

I look broken, but I smile anyway. And I begin.

Chapter 22

DETECTIVE ADAM ADEBAYO

I'm tidying my desk, drained and miserable from another day of getting exactly nowhere on this case, when Detective Inspector Mia Bristow walks into the office.

'Incident room. All staff. Now!'

Christine and I exchange confused glances. She shrugs as we stand up and follow our boss. About half of the team has gone home already, so there are only a few of us milling about, looking unenthusiastic and weary.

Mia doesn't bother with preamble, or tension-building.

'There's been another murder,' she announces.

The transformation in the room is electric, the anticipation tangible. Spines straighten and eyes widen. It's like we've all simultaneously downed double espressos.

'Looks like it's the same killer, from what we know so far.'

Gasps ring out across the room. I'm equal parts desperate to know more and willing Mia to tell us she's joking. I can't imagine a worse scenario than us not solving this case in time to prevent another innocent person from being killed. But Mia doesn't joke.

It hits me like a kick to the ribs, knocks the wind out of me. One glance at Christine tells me she's feeling it just as keenly as I am.

But there's no time to dwell on our guilt. That'll come

later. For now, we have to harness the energy we're all feeling, the drive that you only ever get from a case like this one, the kind of case that will slip through your fingers if you don't put everything you have into it. We all get it. We're all coiled tightly, ready to spring into action, to nail the bastard who's doing this.

Once the room has settled down, Mia hits us with another bombshell.

'The person who found the body is none other than our friendly neighbourhood journalist, Gina Mills.'

This time the room explodes, the air crackling with indignant energy.

'Settle down!' Mia yells, and we fall into a restless silence.

'First responders are at the scene, and I'm sending forensics down there. Carl, Ben, go with them. Jimi and Elizabeth, I need you on CCTV in the area. Grab as much footage as you can and scour it with a fine-tooth comb. Adam and Christine? I want you two to interview the witness. Officers at the scene arrested Gina, and they'll be on their way here shortly, but for now, check the footage she posted—'

'Wait, she filmed it again?' Ben asks incredulously.

'Seems like it. So I need you guys to watch it carefully, and come back to me with your initial observations. Check the database for similar cases, make sure we don't have a serial killer on our hands. Make a note of any leads or angles we can follow up on, and get ready for the interview. I think we should hold her for the full twenty-four hours, make her sweat. She knows something.'

There are smatterings of 'yes, boss', and then we all spring into action, buoyed by a second chance to get whoever this is. They might have slipped through our fingers the first time round, but there's no way we'll let that happen again.

We leave the incident room completely changed from

when we first walked in, transformed by a shared sense of purpose. Christine goes to the canteen to get us coffees while I pull up the video on my computer. It's easy enough to find: it's trending on Twitter, and is at the top of my Facebook feed.

'Here you go,' says Christine, handing me a steaming mug of black, potent coffee. 'I put a couple of extra sugars in it.'

'Thanks.' I take it gratefully. 'Ready to watch tonight's show?'

'Should I have brought the popcorn?'

I laugh and press play.

Gina's face smiles back at us, looking well put together, as always. Her hair is perfectly straight and slick, a curtain of bright colour against the dark night. Aside from the glossy lips framing her smile, she's not wearing a lot of make-up, not like when we brought her in for questioning.

As the video plays, I try to take in as much detail as I can. There are flashes of fuchsia pink as her top peeks out from underneath her jacket whenever she moves, clashing with the bright red post box just over her left shoulder. Watching her move, and speak, and smile, I can only think of one way to describe her appearance: camera-ready.

'Good evening,' she greets me from my computer screen. 'This is Gina Mills, reporting live from Channel Eight. As you may already know, I was walking home last week when I discovered the body of Michelle Everard in an alleyway in west London. I'm reporting live once again, to share the distressing news that I've just discovered what looks like another murder victim, killed in much the same way, in west London, another female, this time left in a child's playground in a residential park.'

I clench my teeth as I watch her reporting this unexpected turn of events. The chances of a person discovering a dead body in their lifetime must be astronomically low, but then to find a second, appearing to be killed by the same person, and then just happening to film them both . . . impossible. My hunch the other day was right. She's hiding something, and I'm not going to let her leave the station without finding out what it is, without knowing exactly how she's involved.

'The woman appears to have been strangled,' Gina continues, 'as was Michelle Everard, who was murdered not far from here. The similarity of the crimes leads me to question whether we have a serial killer at large in London.'

'Bloody hell,' mutters Christine in my ear, echoing my thoughts.

Those two little words – serial killer – they're easy enough for Gina to say, even if they're technically untrue. The definition of a serial killer is someone who's committed at least three murders, but it's a natural conclusion to jump to, given the circumstances. What she also doesn't know is that those two little words are going to create an absolute nightmare for us. The press will be working themselves into an absolute frenzy after hearing this.

We watch the full video, two minutes of it, and then press play again. We're not the only ones watching; it's racked up 500,000 views and it's less than an hour old. We make a few notes but there's nothing that jumps out at us immediately, so we start preparing for the interview.

I flip through Michelle's case file, thumbing through the pages that are now soft and slightly creased from overuse. I already know every word of every report, but I'm hoping something new will leap out at me.

Someone calls my name from across the room, and I look up expectantly.

'She's here.'

I stand, my stomach squirming with nervous energy.

We let her sit in the interview room alone for a while, partly because we want to go through our key questions before we barge in there, but partly because we want to make her nervous.

When we do finally enter, we don't say a word. We take our seats, shuffle paperwork, play with the recording equipment, smooth down invisible creases on our uniforms. Only then does Christine speak.

'Gina. I have to say, we didn't expect to see you again. Especially not so soon. And certainly not under these circumstances.'

Gina says nothing. She's completely still, apart from her fingers, which are shaking. I notice a sheen of sweat glistening on her top lip.

'Before we begin,' Christine continues, 'I need to inform you that you do not have to say anything. However, it may harm your defence if you do not mention when questioned something which you later rely on in court. Anything you do say may be given in evidence. And once again, this session is being recorded.'

'I understand,' she says. She doesn't seem worried about being here again. Not yet, anyway. A night in a cell usually fixes that for stubborn witnesses.

'Can you please describe to us what happened tonight?' I ask.

'I was walking home from work—'

'I'll just stop you right there,' interrupts Christine. 'Why didn't you just get public transport? It'd be quicker, and much warmer in this weather.'

'There are a few reasons,' she replies. 'I've been getting Ubers home, but I can't afford to do that for ever. I've been too scared to take the Tube or the bus after the threats. And

I wanted to chat to Julian along the way. I can't do that underground.'

The emotion I saw when she was here last has completely drained away. She's back to the shell-shocked, fact-driven Gina we first met.

'Julian's your boyfriend?'

'Yes.'

I scribble notes as my partner is talking. We'll switch soon, to keep Gina on her toes, to try to catch her off guard.

'Where is Julian?' Christine asks, her questions coming more rapidly now.

'In Edinburgh. For work.'

'So were you on the phone to him when you discovered the body?'

'No, we'd hung up by then.'

'OK,' Christine says, flipping through her notes. 'Let's backtrack for a second. You said you were walking home from work. What time did you leave the office?'

'Around eight thirty,' she says. I flick my eyes up towards the camera in the corner of the room. I'm confident that the guys behind me, the team that's watching through the two-way mirror, will have already noted the time Gina claims to have left. I'm hoping they'll waste no time in checking her alibi. We have none to spare.

'Is it normal for you to work that late?' I ask.

'No, I've been busy this last week,' she says, still not moving. She's rigid in her seat, and only her eyes and lips show any sign of life. 'I still have my regular job to do on top of the interviews.'

'So why were you walking home the way you were?' Christine asks. 'That's not your usual route, is it? I'm just looking at a map here, and it looks like it's out of your way.'

Gina blinks. 'Yes . . . I mean, no it's not my normal route. I

162

didn't want to walk anywhere near the alleyway. I went the long way round, which meant walking through the park.'

'OK,' I say. 'Can you describe how you found the body?'

'There was a fox. It startled me as I was walking through. I was on my guard. I was almost at the gate when I spotted her. Jacqueline called me just as I was about to call the police, and I told her what happened and she told me to call you. That's what I did, as soon as she hung up. They asked me to check her pulse, so I grabbed her wrist. It was icy cold, but then I realised that it was actually her bracelet I'd touched. When I did feel for her pulse, there was nothing. I told the guy on the phone that she was dead, I hung up, and then I recorded the broadcast before the first responders arrived.'

Her sentences are clipped, each one relaying a fact. There's no feeling in her words. It's like she's in some kind of trance.

Christine leans back in her chair and folds her arms across her chest.

'Did you know what you were going to find when you left work tonight, Gina?' I ask.

'What do you mean?'

'Did someone tell you that there was going to be a dead body in that park?'

'Who would tell me that?'

'I don't know. The person who killed her, maybe?'

'Why would the killer contact me?'

She seems completely oblivious to the fact that her actions are suspicious. She's confused, as though my questions are unreasonable.

'How are you involved in these murders, Gina?'

'I'm not,' she says. 'Can I please go home?'

I almost laugh, but Christine cuts in smoothly.

'Actually, we're going to keep you here. We're not done with questioning you yet.'

'You'll keep me here . . . in this room?' she asks.

'No. You'll be processed, and then you'll be in a holding cell unless we're interviewing you.'

There's a sudden bang from behind the steel door that leads to the corridor. It's another interview door slamming, but in here the sound has nothing to be absorbed by. It echoes, like a gunshot. Gina jumps. It's the first sign of life she's offered since she arrived.

She looks between Christine and me, blinking.

'Do I get a phone call?' she whispers.

'Yes, you're legally entitled to one.'

'I'd like to make my phone call, please,' she says, and her eyes fill with tears. It seems that, finally, the reality of what's happening has caught up with her. Hopefully this means she'll be more cooperative when we interview her next.

Christine and I glance at each other. We don't need to say anything. Both of us know precisely what the other person is thinking. We've got her exactly where we want her. She's scared.

And if there's one thing I've learned from years on the job, it's that scared people talk.

Chapter 23

GINA

'Julian,' I say urgently. 'Thank God you picked up. Did I wake you?'

'Gina?' he asks, no trace of sleep in his voice. 'Where are you calling from?'

'The police station,' I say. 'I was arrested, and I'm being held in custody overnight.'

'Because of your video? I saw it. Are you OK?'

I imagine him sitting up in bed, running his hands through his hair as he frets.

'I'm scared,' I admit. 'It's just hit me, that this is really happening. Julian, I don't want to sleep in a cell.'

I haven't seen it yet; the cell where they've said they're going to keep me. But I have no doubt they'll show me to it soon. For now, I have two minutes to speak to Julian, and then it's back into that interview room for more interrogation.

'I'm so sorry,' he says. 'I wish there was something I could do. Just stay calm, and take the legal advice they offer, OK?'

'Won't that look like I have something to hide?' I ask. 'I haven't been charged with anything, and I don't want to look guilty.'

'Guilty of what, Gina? You haven't killed anyone,' he says

firmly. 'And what they think doesn't matter. Facts are what matter, and the fact is that they've got no reason to charge you, do you hear me?'

I nod, even though I know he can't see me. I'm overwhelmed by everything, wishing there were magic words I could tell the police to make them let me go and move on. Wishing I'd thought this through better. But I know it's not that easy.

'Can you come and pick me up tomorrow when they let me out?' I say. 'Please?'

'Of course. I'll fly home first thing.'

'I'm sorry,' I whisper. Now he's going to miss his sold out show, all because I've messed up. I hate myself for even asking, and I hate myself more for letting him. But I can't do this alone. Not any more.

'Don't be sorry, Gina,' he says gently. 'We're a team, which means we're in this together. Crazy times and all. I know you'd do the same for me.'

He's right. Of course I would. But that doesn't make me feel any better. Constable Taylor, who's been standing over me this whole time, taps her wrist. Time's up. My stomach sinks.

'I have to go,' I say. 'I love you.'

'Be strong, Gina,' he replies. 'You'll get through this. I love you.'

I'm led by the detective back the way we just came from. She opens the door on our right and gestures for me to step inside. I hesitate at the entrance, knowing what's inside. It's a cold, brightly lit room, stark, with cameras mounted in two corners of the ceiling. It's sinister, and being in there makes me far more vulnerable than I'm comfortable with. I want to run, but instead I roll my shoulders back, as much

166

to convince myself of my confidence as to show the detective that I'm not intimidated, and walk inside.

Constable Adebayo is already sitting on one of the rigid plastic chairs, reading his notes. I feel sick as I take my seat opposite him.

'I'd like to remind you,' he says, 'that you have the right to legal advice, and we can offer this to you if you don't have access to a lawyer.'

I chew the inside of my lip. Julian said I should take the legal advice. But I didn't kill those girls, and I don't want to have to explain myself to someone else. I'm supposed to be considered innocent unless proven guilty, and they can't prove me guilty. Besides, only criminals need lawyers.

'I don't need a lawyer,' I say.

He raises his eyebrows, but he says nothing. Instead, he shuffles through some more papers. Constable Taylor is completely still beside him. The silence is excruciating, which I'm sure is the point. I focus on the dark brown roots protruding from the top of the detective's bright blonde ponytail, and try not to picture the blonde hair cascading down the shoulders of the woman whose broken body I can't stop remembering. I shudder involuntarily.

Eventually, she breaks the silence.

'We've been in touch with the security team at Channel Eight. And they confirm that you swiped out of the building at eight twenty-three. There's also a security guard who says he saw you leaving at around that time.'

'OK,' I say slowly. I know all of this already. I told them this. So I don't know why they're relaying it back to me as news.

'And our forensics team have offered us a preliminary time of death, although this could change once the full

167

autopsy is done, but they're estimating that the victim was killed between eight and eight fifteen tonight.'

The penny drops. They know that I'm not the killer.

'So we're not suggesting that you are a murderer, Gina, do you understand? But we don't think it's a coincidence that you were the person who found both victims.'

Of course it's not a coincidence. I'm not stupid enough to suggest that it could be. I can see how this all looks from their point of view, but they're wasting their time.

'Why did you film the scene again, Gina?'

I close my eyes to try to get my thoughts in some semblance of order. They're scattered, strewn across my mind. Should I tell them about Jacqueline, about what she said in that phone call? She implied that my career was at stake if I didn't film the scene . . . Does that mean my career would also be at stake if I told the police about our conversation? As Jacqueline said herself, what I did wasn't illegal. I haven't done anything wrong. Telling them the details of that phone call will only bring up more questions, which won't help anything, or anyone. What *will* help is for them to accept what I did and move on, so they can focus on what's important: arresting a murderer.

'I almost decided not to,' I admit. 'I knew it wasn't a coincidence that I found both of these women, but I couldn't explain it, either. But I knew that there must be a reason it was me. And I figured the sooner I could break the news of this killer striking again, the less likely it would be that whoever did it would get away with it.'

'So you were trying to help us?' Constable Taylor asks sarcastically.

'Look,' I plead, 'I'm not trying to convince you that I'm virtuous or anything, and I know you disagree with what

I did, but reporting is all I had to offer, it's the one thing I knew I could do to make a difference here.'

The detective looks sceptical, but she doesn't argue the point further.

'Were you scared?' Constable Adebayo asks.

'Of course I was!' I cry. 'I still am. I can't believe this has happened. But just because I reported an event doesn't mean I can't also be affected by it. Look at war correspondents: they're scared, all the time, but they see reporting what's happening – unpleasant and terrifying as it may be – as more important than their feelings.'

The detectives glance at one another, shuffle some paper-work.

'I'm not trying to claim that I'm some kind of hero here,' I add. 'I just want you to understand.'

If they do understand, they don't offer me any indication.

'Is there anything else you'd like to tell us?' Constable Adebayo asks.

I don't reply. I concentrate instead on trying to pinpoint his ever-so-slight accent. Nigerian? Ghanaian? I'm not sure why I'm even trying to guess, it doesn't matter right now. I pick at my cuticles, hoping he can't see how much my hands are shaking.

'No?' he asks, leaning forward and opening a file. 'OK. Well, I have something that may be of interest to you. We've just received the first photos from the crime scene, and I notice that there's no sign of a bracelet on the victim. Can you tell me what happened to the jewellery you claim to have felt on the victim's wrist?'

'I don't *claim* to have felt it. I *did* feel it,' I say, looking from his face to Taylor's. They're not letting any hint of what they're thinking break through their stony expressions.

'I saw it,' I insist. 'It was a silver bracelet, full of charms. Loads of them.'

They don't believe me.

'Well, where is it now?'

'How would I know?'

'You'd know,' Constable Adebayo says quietly, leaning forward once again, 'because you were the only person to have seen it, and because you were – according to your own statement – the only person on the scene between when you called for help and when our team arrived.'

'Well I don't know what to tell you, but I don't have it. My bag was taken away from me at the scene, so the guys who took my stuff can tell you that I never had a charm bracelet on me. Or a necklace.'

There's a pause as the detective assesses me.

'Would you give us permission to search your home?'

I study his face to see if he's just testing me, but his jaw is set and his eyes show no hint of mirth. He's serious.

Julian said I should seek legal guidance, and I know exactly what he'd tell me to do now. He'd insist on me getting a lawyer, refusing the search, fighting this invasion of privacy until they have a warrant and there's no other choice. But I'm not Julian. I want them to see that I have nothing to hide. I want them to know, with absolute certainty, that there's nothing incriminating in my home. But most of all, I want this to be over. I want my life to move on.

'OK,' I say. 'Yes, I give you my permission.'

'Well in that case,' says Constable Taylor, whose thick south London accent sets my teeth on edge. She pronounces 'that' as 'vat'. I suppress the urge to correct her. This isn't the time. 'We have no more questions for you at this stage, so you'll be processed and taken to your holding cell until we need to speak to you again.'

She pauses, and then adds, 'And I'm sure we'll need to speak to you again.'

I'm led out of the room, and into another room with a sign on the door that says 'Processing'. Here, another officer who I haven't met before takes photographs of me, makes me press my fingertips against a glowing scanner, and swabs the inside of my mouth. The officer searches me, checking my pockets and looking for a belt. Then she gets to my pendant.

'I'll need you to remove the jewellery, please,' she says, her palm outstretched.

'Please don't take this,' I plead, wrapping my fingers around it protectively. 'It's really important.'

Her face remains expressionless. 'The necklace, please.'

I cry as I unclasp it behind my head. I'm so alone, and taking away the one link I have to Julian is torturous. But they can only hold me for twenty-four hours without charging me, so I just have to get through this, I have to be strong. I'll be out of here tomorrow, and then I'll get my pendant back. I take a deep breath to compose myself, and wipe my eyes with the back of my hand.

I'm led along yet another corridor, through a thick, metal door and into a bleak-looking wing of the station with six identical doors, all a sickly green with a small slit about halfway up. Like narrowed eyes, watching me. One of the doors opens to my left.

'In there,' says the officer, gesturing for me to enter. I take a hesitant step towards the door. It's tiny, and dim, with just a single fluorescent light overhead, enclosed in a metal cage. There's a metal bed with a plastic mattress, and a stark metal toilet without a lid.

'Now!' she barks, and I stumble forwards, into my cell.

The door slams behind me, footsteps echo, and then another door slams. Then nothing. I stand completely still in the middle of the room, waiting. For what, I don't know.

I'm frightened – of course I am – but it's a different kind of fear. The fear I feel when I'm outside, when I'm looking over my shoulder, expecting someone to jump out at me, that's a fear for my life. For my safety.

In here, it's a fear of the unknown that's burning a hole in my stomach, acidic and sharp. I have no idea what's coming next, so I can't prepare. They aren't going to charge me with murder, I know that, but what if they come up with another way to keep me here, to hold me for longer than the twenty-four hours? I dismiss the thought. I'm not a murderer. I don't belong here. The person who killed those women is still out there, still free to kill again. Sweat tickles my top lip. I wipe it hastily, determined not to break down in here.

I focus on Julian, on the fact that he's coming for me. Some of the tension in my shoulders loosens. Once he arrives, everything will be OK again. He's all I need. And then I realise, with a clarity that surprises me, he is really, truly, *all* I need.

It shouldn't have taken two murders, death and rape threats, and an arrest for me to come to this conclusion, but nonetheless, the revelation hits me here, in a cell at the back of a police station.

I don't care about the fame.

I don't care about progressing in my career. I don't need to be a newsreader, and I don't need to earn a certain amount to have 'made it'. I have everything I need already.

I've had it all along, I just never appreciated it. I was too desperate for more to just accept my happiness. I was waiting to tick certain boxes, achieve specific things, before I allowed myself to believe that I really do have it all. I was an idiot. A desperate, reckless idiot.

And look where it's got me.

Chapter 24

RYAN

Cleaning was supposed to be a distraction; a way for me to clear my head. Instead, all it's doing is giving me room to think, and that's the last thing I need.

I've created a mess.

I'd been looking forward to an early night, desperate for this to be the night that I finally slept through, free from nightmares. But then the news broke, and all hope of rest evaporated.

When I'd arrived home from work last night I'd flopped onto the sofa, telling myself I'd get up soon to make dinner, that I was just resting my eyes. Next thing I knew, my phone was ringing under my head, the vibrations jolting me awake. I must have drifted off.

'Julian,' I'd said groggily into the phone, wincing at the pounding in my head. I've always hated taking naps. I always feel worse when I wake up than I did before, and this was no exception.

'Hey, Ryan, look, I just had a call from Gina. She's at the police station, being held there overnight.'

'What? Why? Is she OK?'

'She's fine, apart from being totally shaken up,' he'd said. 'It happened again. She found another body.'

I'd turned the TV on while Julian was still on the line, and watched the footage with a growing sense of panic.

'What the hell?' I'd asked. 'How is that even possible?'

'I have no idea,' Julian had said, sounding weary. 'But I can't chat right now, I have to go. I'm coming back in the morning so I can pick her up when she's released, but that means I have to cancel my show, so I have a bunch of calls to make now. I just wanted to let you know.'

I'd thanked him and hung up, and then gone into the kitchen to pour myself a drink, any thoughts of dinner forgotten.

My mind has been racing ever since. Gina, on her way home from work, somehow, *somehow* discovered the second victim of what's now being called a serial killer. A monster, they said on the news. But how could she have been the person to find both of these women? Is she a target? Or worse – is she somehow involved?

I'd felt like a traitor for even thinking it, and so I'd turned to cleaning as a way to keep myself busy, to keep my thoughts in check, until Julian brought Gina home from the police station. I'd started with the kitchen, pulling pots and pans from cupboards, scrubbing the inside of sticky drawers and throwing out long-forgotten jars of sauces and half-used jars of spices that went out of date years ago.

Then I'd moved on to the lounge, dusting and hoovering and tidying bookshelves, and now I'm on my hands and knees in the bathroom, inexplicably obsessed with getting the grout between the tiles to turn white again.

The inky light that's beginning to soak up the final traces of night-time tells me that it must be early in the morning. I ignore the fatigue that's settled over me and work away at the grout, hoping, if nothing else, that Gina will be pleased to come home to a clean house later. She'll have had a hell of a night, and I'm completely helpless to make it any better for her.

The doorbell rings, startling me, and as I get up, too quickly, I almost knock the bucket of sudsy water over. Holding the edge of the bathtub for balance, I manage to slide my way across the slippery tiles.

Is Gina home already? Julian said she was being held for twenty-four hours, but maybe they released her early. She should have called me – I'd have got in a taxi and picked her up. I dry my feet on a hand towel near the sink and dash to the front door.

'Gina,' I say, breathless, as I pull the door roughly towards me.

I stop dead, all the blood in my body flooding towards my toes. It's not Gina at the door.

'Mr Mills?' asks the police officer mildly. I glance over his shoulder and notice another officer behind him. I'm too stunned to react, or to think clearly.

The policeman tries again. 'Are you Mr Mills?'

I nod dumbly, my brain still frantically trying to piece everything together.

'We are here to search your property, Mr Mills. May we come in, please?'

I continue to stare, not comprehending his words.

'Mr Mills, we have permission from Gina Mills to conduct a search of this property in relation to a murder investigation. Please can you step aside so we can commence our search?'

I do as I'm told, my movements sluggish and distant, as though they're not my own. I watch in silence as they walk past me, down the hallway, and into the living room. After a few seconds I force myself to focus, and rush after them, heart pounding.

'What are you searching for? What is this about?'

'As I said, it's in relation to a murder investigation,' the second officer says unhelpfully.

I try to make sense of what's happening. They're searching our home, which means they think they'll find evidence. Does that mean they believe Gina really does have something to do with the women whose bodies she found? But they said Gina gave them permission. So maybe this isn't serious after all.

They're moving around the living room in a kind of choreographed dance, working from the two far corners, searching quickly but methodically, leaving nothing unchecked. It's lucky I just spent so long clearing the space, as there's not much clutter for them to wade through. As they finish the room we're in, the officer who rang my doorbell peers into the bathroom.

'Cleaning up, are we?' he asks, one eyebrow raised.

'Do you have a problem with me cleaning?'

'Bit unusual, isn't it? To be cleaning at this time of the morning.'

'Bit unusual to be searching someone's house at this time of the morning, too, but you're doing it anyway.'

He says nothing but treads heavily into the room, the soles of his boots squeaking on the still-wet tiles, leaving dirty footprints all over my hard work. I tut loudly as I hover behind, watching them work, the knot in my stomach growing larger and larger. They move on to the kitchen, checking the washing machine, opening cupboards, banging doors, but their search proves fruitless.

When they reach Gina's room, I'm frantic with worry. Not that they'll find anything, I remind myself, but that they'll ruin her perfectly ordered space. With every surface they touch, every notebook they rifle through, every pair of

177

underwear they lift from her drawer, anxiety draws closer and closer, ready to pounce.

As the minutes tick by, my apprehension builds. The note that calls me a killer, the one from whoever is calling themselves my other sister, is behind my closed bedroom door, tucked under my pillow, along with the newspaper clipping of Cassie. The knowledge of its presence is so huge, so frightening, that I'm sure the officers must sense it there, too.

I open my mouth to ask if they're going to search my room as well, but then I snap it closed again. Asking the officers would look suspicious; like I have something to hide. Instead, I take out my phone and look for answers online.

My shoulders collapse in relief when I discover that my room can't be searched. They're here for evidence relating to Gina, which means they can look in her room, and any common areas of the house. But not my room. Not under my pillow. They won't see that note. I won't need to explain the impossible.

After what feels like hours, the searching stops. They take a DNA sample from me, to make it easier for them to identify unknown DNA, they explain, and then they hand me a sheet of paper with an itemised list of what they've taken. It's mostly jewellery of Gina's and, oddly, a towel that was hanging on the airer in the living room.

When we're finally done, I show the officers to the front door, grunt a goodbye and close it firmly behind them.

The silence they've left behind feels charged with meaning. What did they expect to find here? And when will this be over?

I walk to the bathroom and stand in the doorway, surveying the damage. The dirt from the police officer's boot has mixed with the overly soapy water I'd been far too liberal with, creating a brown, silty sludge. My head hurts from lack of sleep and my muscles ache from all my scrubbing. I want to stop, to make a giant cup of coffee and try to make sense of whatever just happened.

But Gina can't see this mess – it will only make things worse. So instead, I grab the scrubbing brush, still lying in the middle of the bathroom floor, and erase all evidence of the officers' visit.

Chapter 25

DETECTIVE ADAM ADEBAYO

'Is that everyone?' Mia asks as Christine walks in, closing the door behind her.

'I think so, boss,' someone says from behind me.

'OK, we're twelve hours in on the second murder. What have we got?'

Behind her on the whiteboard is a photo of the second victim, a woman we've now identified as Angela Delaney, thirty, a recruitment consultant who had just moved to London from Dublin.

'MO is the same,' says Ben, to my left. 'White female, blonde, curly hair, late twenties or early thirties. This was another Tinder date, although the profile she was talking to was for a...' He consults a piece of paper in his hand. 'Lee Maclean. Her phone and wallet were still on her, so again, this wasn't a robbery.'

Mia writes *Lee Maclean* and *White, Blonde*, on the board where there's still space.

'So our killer has a type,' she says. 'Did we find any similar killings in the database?'

'Nothing that matches the MO,' Christine says. 'A few west London murders, but they were mostly stabbings, or domestic violence. We'll keep running searches though.'

'OK, thanks. Anything useful found on the scene?'

'No fibres or footprints. We're still working on DNA.'

'Keep me posted on that. How about cause of death?'

'Same as before,' says Jimi. 'Head wound, caused by a fall after she was forcefully shoved to the ground, hitting the edge of the metal slide on the way. But there's evidence of strangulation again, too.'

Mia writes *Head wound + strangulation* in bold, scrawling letters across the whiteboard. Then she turns back to face the room.

'What about our witness?'

'Gina's still in custody,' I say, 'but we haven't found anything to charge her with yet. Her alibi checks out, but there's a missing bracelet that she can't – or won't – explain. We got permission to search her home early this morning. The guys picked up a few necklaces and bracelets, but nothing that matches the ones we're looking for. There was also a towel with a stain that looked like it could have been blood, so that's with forensics now.'

'OK, good,' Bristow says. 'You still have twelve hours, so make her sweat, see what you can get out of her. Ali, where are we at with Gina's phone?'

'We've cloned the contents,' he says, 'so now we're just going through it to see if there are any links to the Tinder accounts, or anything else that could explain how she knew where the victim would be. Nothing so far, but I'll let you know if anything comes up.'

'Emma,' barks Mia. 'What's happening with the press?'

'They're all over us,' Emma sighs. 'Gina said it could be a serial killer, so the morning papers are running with it, calling him the Tinder Ripper.'

The whole room groans in unison. We all hate the nicknames the press comes up with. Not only are they cheesy as hell, but they give the killer notoriety, a sense of status.

'Well there's no point trying to fight it,' Mia sighs. 'Let's issue a statement asking the public to be extra vigilant and to report anything suspicious to the tip line.'

'Done,' says Emma.

'Great work, everyone.' Mia claps her hands together once, a sign that we're finished. 'Let's keep pushing. We're all tired, but we'll sleep when we catch this guy.'

A few people leave but most, like me, just head straight for the coffee machine and pastries on the table at the side.

'Shall we bring her up for a fresh round of questioning?' Christine asks as she joins me at the coffee machine, the dark circles under her eyes visible through the extra make-up she applied just before the meeting.

'Yeah,' I say, looking at my watch. 'We don't want her to get too comfortable in there.'

We request for her to be transferred to the interview room, and then we leave her alone for twenty minutes or so while we scoff a couple of pastries each, and I change my shirt.

'Good morning,' I say as I walk in. I try to sound as fresh as possible, despite the fatigue that's threatening to knock me over. I want Gina to feel like she's the only one who hasn't slept, like she's at the disadvantage. And she clearly hasn't rested. Every time I've seen her before now she's looked impeccable, without so much as a hair out of place.

This morning though, she's dishevelled, her skin dull and mascara streaked across her eyes. Her shirt is creased, and her hair has been pulled into a simple ponytail. She looks much younger, and much less assured.

I take a long sip of my coffee. She looks across the table at it longingly. I pretend I don't notice but I pull the lid off and leave it within smelling distance of her.

'We recovered some interesting evidence from your house,' Christine says to get the ball rolling.

182

Gina looks confused.

'Is there anything you want to tell us about before we draw our own conclusions?'

'There's nothing in my house that has anything to do with those women,' she says, her voice scratchy.

'Well, we'll be the judge of that, if you don't mind.'

'What did you find?'

Christine pauses and pretends to shuffle through her paperwork, but I know she's just trying to rattle our witness.

'Blood,' she says eventually.

'Where?'

'Should we have looked in more than one place?'

'I'm not trying to hide anything,' Gina explodes. 'I'm only asking where because I'm curious. I probably cut myself or something.'

'So when we test it, it'll be your DNA on that towel?'

'Mine, Ryan's. Julian's maybe. I don't know. I don't remember getting blood on a towel. But if I did, it's not relevant to any murder. Why aren't you out there looking for the killer instead of going over the same things with me?'

Exasperation radiates from her, and her eyes fill with tears.

I want to believe her, to just let her go and find another angle to delve into, I really do. Part of my brain is telling me to trust the woman across the table from me, to accept her story and let her go home, give her the space she needs to recover from the trauma of what she's seen. After all, we know she's not the killer. Her alibis are indisputable. She didn't murder those women.

But then I remind myself that she discovered two crime scenes – two scenes that do, in fact, appear to be the work of a serial killer – and filmed them live for the whole world to see. I'd have to be an utter idiot to believe that she's not tied up in this somehow, even if she doesn't realise it. So no matter how much I'd like to write her off and move on to another, more cooperative lead, I can't help feeling that if we ask enough questions, eventually we'll shake an answer out of her that will unravel the truth of all of this.

Christine is now peppering Gina with the same questions we've asked over and over again, hoping persistence and a night in our holding cells will yield a different result to our previous interviews. I'm trying to focus on her answers, but they're all the same as before. Despite a night in a cell, she's giving us nothing new. And the clock is ticking. Time is draining away, slipping through our fingers, and when it runs out we'll have to let her go, without charges, with no new information, and with a killer still on the loose. My stomach turns at the thought, and I push my coffee aside.

I need to concentrate. I lean across the table and listen carefully. This might be our best chance to get the truth from Gina.

Our twenty-four hours is officially up, which means that Gina is being released. And we still don't have the answers we need.

It's late, and I need to go home, get at least a little bit of sleep. Today has kicked my arse. I'm emotionally battered from the events of the past twenty-four hours. We tried to get something useful from Gina but we failed. We sent other officers in, in the hope that a new approach could yield better results, but they, too, were unsuccessful. I'm frustrated that I can't see a clear answer, I'm angry that whoever is doing this is getting away with it, and I'm desperate for a long run and an ice-cold beer.

I haul my backpack over my shoulder and wait for the lift to arrive, hoping that the officers I sent to question Gina's boss will come back with something useful. I'm in a world of my own as I ride down to the lobby, questions on a loop in my head, taunting me, the answers nowhere in sight.

As I walk through the reception area, a woman squeals and runs towards a man who's just walked through the sliding glass entrance doors. She launches herself at him, and throws her arms around his neck, her legs around his waist.

I look around to see if anyone else has noticed this bizarre display of affection. Everyone's heads are turned towards the couple, who are acting as though they've been reunited after years apart.

Then, with a start, I realise that the woman who's making out with someone in the foyer of the police station is Gina. If only Christine were here to see this, I think with a grimace. She hates any kind of public display of affection, and she's not so fond of Gina, either. I move towards the door, chuckling to myself at the reaction I know I'll get from my partner when I tell her tomorrow, when I catch a glimpse of Gina's boyfriend.

Julian.

The facts click into place in my brain. She's mentioned him in her interviews, but I didn't catch the connection. I've seen him before. The video my sister sent me. It's him. Before I can stop myself, I'm stepping towards them.

'Miss Mills,' I say, and the pair spring away from one another.

'Oh,' she says. 'It's you.'

'This must be Julian,' I say, ignoring her hostility and offering the tall, dark-haired man my hand. He takes it, and shakes it firmly.

'I'm Detective Constable Adam Adebayo,' I say, and he smiles thinly without a word. 'You're that magician guy, aren't you?'

'Oh, we actually prefer the term illusionist,' he corrects me. I raise an eyebrow. I thought they were the same thing.

'Right. But you're the one who made that guy speak Russian, aren't you?'

'That's me,' he says, his smile turning genuine now. 'You've seen the video?'

'Yeah, I watched it a couple of days ago. That's crazy. You're quite the famous couple now, aren't you?'

They exchange a glance, but I can't read their expression. They don't respond.

'Did that really happen?' I ask.

'Of course it did,' Gina says defensively.

'It's true,' Julian says with a laugh. 'It did happen. I've performed that a few times, actually. Sometimes I try Russian, sometimes Swedish, sometimes Swahili. It gets the crowd going, that's for sure.'

'Yeah, but how do you do it?' I ask.

'Constable,' he says scoldingly. 'You should know that someone in my profession would never give away his secrets.'

I laugh, but his answer frustrates me.

'I get that,' I say. 'But can you at least tell me if it was a set-up? Was that guy an actor?'

He narrows his eyes at me.

'Just because you don't like the idea of something,' he says calmly, 'doesn't make it impossible.'

'That's not what I—'

Gina interrupts me.

'Look,' she says bluntly. 'Julian's not a fraud. He's the most talented man I know. But he's also not here to be questioned. And I'm kind of ready to get out of here, as I'm sure you can understand.'

I nod, uncomfortable now that I got so excited over a

magic trick. I've been put in my place, and fair enough. I shouldn't have questioned his authenticity; that wasn't fair.

'Thanks,' Julian says. And without another word, he turns around, grabs Gina's hand and walks out the building.

Chapter 26

GINA

I stand behind the crowd, shaking with anger and fear and disbelief, completely unprepared for this.

Honestly, I don't know how anyone *could* be prepared for this. It's not something you ever expect to happen to you.

As I'd walked up to the office, coffee in one hand, phone in the other, ready to dial the police if I needed to, I'd heard the yelling. Was there an event I wasn't aware of this morning? I was too distracted to give it much thought, so I kept on striding towards the Channel Eight building, an imposing seventies monstrosity created by a famous architect back in the day. It's nothing short of hideous.

When I'd rounded the corner, the cement block towering in front of me, I'd seen them. Some kind of demonstration, judging by the placards and chants. Occasionally, groups trying to get publicity for a cause would show up like this, hoping it would garner enough attention that they'd end up on the news. It didn't work. Disrupting our lives wasn't going to make headlines. The smart ones knew this, and they'd take their marches to the most public of places, inconveniencing as many people as possible. That definitely got our attention.

I'd been tapping away at my phone, texting Julian to let him know I'd arrived at work safely, when I'd heard it.

I'd stopped dead in my tracks, and listened again.

'Give Gina Mills the sack, we don't want no journo hack!'

My spine tingled. Did I really hear that correctly?

Their voices had rung out again, loud and clear, just metres away from where I was standing. There was no mistaking it this time. They were here to demonstrate but their cause wasn't some obscure conflict halfway across the world. Their cause was *me*.

Fighting nausea, I try to make out the signs some of the demonstrators are holding.

'Mills has no morals,' says one in angry red letters. 'Long live ethics,' screams another.

I don't have a clue what I'm supposed to do. The blood drains from my face, leaving me weak, like a slight breeze could knock me over. Can I walk past them, or could they actually get violent? I've seen reports of so-called peaceful protests and demonstrations taking a terrifying turn before. People can get worked up when they're passionate about a cause, as these people clearly are. And when you add crowd mentality to the mix, things can get messy.

'Gina?' A voice next to me pulls me out of my thoughts. It's Jacqueline. 'You look terrible,' she says, never one to skirt around the truth. 'What's wrong?'

I can't find the words but I make a vague flapping gesture towards the crowd. She looks confused for a second. She, like I did, probably assumes it's just another random demonstration, not worth even mentioning. But then the chants drift our way, and understanding floods her face.

'Oh,' she says, a frown momentarily breaking through her usual poise. It takes her a couple of seconds, but then she takes charge.

'Don't worry, Gina, they're just small, angry people with

nothing better to do. Let's get you safely inside, and then we'll get them taken care of, OK?'

'But how will we get in?' I whisper.

'You know the best way to deal with people like this?' she asks, and I shake my head. 'Pretend they're not there. We're going to walk in, you're going to keep your eyes straight ahead, your shoulders back, and we're going to the office.'

'I can't,' I say. I can barely squeeze the words out. They all seem so angry, so vehement.

'You can,' Jacqueline says simply. 'They're just here to protest, not to hurt anyone, all right?'

I nod slowly. I don't want to walk past them, but I want to stay with Jacqueline. She's so calm, so assured. I don't demur as she rests a palm briefly between my shoulder blades, and I let myself be led, like a child, towards the seething cluster of demonstrators.

'Don't listen to them,' she says, her words clipped, as we get closer. 'And don't respond. Just walk. Just keep going. They can't follow us inside.'

They almost don't see us. They're so absorbed in their hatred that they almost miss the two of us walking right past them. I start to think we might get inside unnoticed when someone yells out.

'It's her!' a man screams. 'It's the bitch herself.'

My cheeks grow hot.

'Keep walking,' Jacqueline says.

'Don't you have any decency?' a woman's voice cuts through the yells.

We're almost at the door, almost safe, when it hits me. My vision jolts, and it takes a second to realise it's because I've been hit, right on the back of my head. I scream, and run inside the doorway, holding the back of my head, tears streaming down my face.

I collapse onto the cold, tiled floor of the lobby, bringing my hand in front of my face to check for blood. It's clean, although the spot where I was hit is throbbing.

Jacqueline bends down so she can look me in the eye.

'Are you OK?' she asks. I don't know if I am. I don't know how to answer her. I stare up at her, pitiful.

'It was an umbrella,' she says with a grimace. 'Luckily it looks like just the fabric bit got you. Could have been worse. I've asked security to call the police, they're on their way.'

The woman in front of me steps back for a second to assess her work, then leans in to dab lipstick onto my bottom lip with a tiny brush.

'There,' she says, looking pleased with her handiwork.

I swivel the chair so I can see myself properly in the mirror. As has been the case before every interview, I look far too made-up, with foundation so thick I could scrape it off with my fingernail, and my eyes so dramatic I hardly look like me.

These days, though, I'm struggling to recognise myself even without the help of these extra layers. I used to look at my reflection and see something like hope staring back from my green eyes. There was more for me, I knew it. I believed that my future held bigger and better things, and I was itching to tackle them all. The optimism shone from me. I radiated excitement. Now, I don't see the promise of what's ahead. It's been replaced with something smaller, something cruel, an emotion I don't like to look directly at, in case it takes hold, burrows deep, stays with me for ever. At first I thought it was fear. But it's not that, even though that's a feeling I'm all too familiar with. No. This is worse than fear. It looks a little bit like regret.

'What do you think?'

'You've done a great job,' I say half-heartedly, reaching for my cup of tea. 'Thanks, Georgia.'

'Anytime. What are you talking about today?'

'The same, really,' I say. 'Tinder. Women's safety. I don't know how much they care what I'm saying, it's more just to wheel me out for ratings.'

She laughs, and Tamara, who's teasing and spraying my hair, joins in. I've spent so much time in hair and make-up over the past week or so that these two women have become the closest thing I have to friends. Tash is still giving me the cold shoulder – any hope of our friendship being rekindled was lost when I filmed the second murder scene – and after this morning's demonstration, which I'm convinced was orchestrated by her, I'm not sure I want her in my life again, anyway. But Georgia and Tamara aren't mad at me. They treat me like they would any other guest who walks into the studio, not like someone to be prodded and questioned and handled with suspicion. I can relax with them, and for that I'm grateful.

Until all of this happened, I never took the time to realise how small my circle of friends really is. Or maybe I did, but I didn't think it mattered. When I moved back to London, I'd left behind a life that I wasn't happy with, an existence that never really fitted me properly, anyway. I was happy to make a clean break, get a fresh start. Besides, it's not like I had a lot of friends back there, either.

There was Sophie, my next-door neighbour, who I used to speak to almost every day. Some days we'd catch each other on the way out in the morning, or as one of us was coming home. Other times, probably twice a week, we'd share a bottle of wine after work and chat about life and men and work and anything else we could think of. We mostly hung out in her flat, because it had real furniture and nice decor, unlike my shabby, dark basement space. Then I met Julian, and she met Craig, and they got pregnant, and twice a week turned into twice a month, turned into 'we really should catch up soon', and then I moved away and the convenience was removed from our friendship, showing its true colours. These days, we text each other every few weeks but our lives look so different now that there's increasingly less to talk about. She messaged me when the news first broke, to check that I was OK, but texts aren't the same as a good old face-to-face chat.

I had other friends, too. Mostly colleagues. They'd heard me talking about my dreams for years, and although they were encouraging at first, even they got sick of pretending to believe in me, failure after failure. They were a reminder of everything I didn't want to be, and so I'd not really kept in touch with them when I left. The occasional Facebook like wasn't really grounds for friendship, and I was all too happy to let those relationships fizzle.

Since moving back to London, I've been living in a bubble that consists entirely of Julian, Ryan and Tash. I have acquaintances at work, and the odd friend of Ryan's who comes around. Julian's illusionist buddies. But they're not my friends, as such. They're not the people who will stick by me through something like this, who will check in to see if I'm coping.

Besides, I didn't feel like I needed anyone else, not really. Everything was so new – this job, the city, my renewed relationship with my brother – that I've been distracted. I've never once felt lonely. Until now.

'I hate to tell you,' Tamara says, 'but you have a tough act to follow.'

She points her comb towards the small screen above our heads, which shows what's being recorded right now, just a few metres away from us. The host, Lucy, is speaking to a woman, a bit older than me, who's sobbing into a tissue. She's blonde and slim, and although her hair has been straightened, I can see the resemblance from the photos that have been splashed across every news article for the past few days. She must be a relative of Angela's, the second woman who I discovered. My body stiffens. Georgia reaches above her to turn the volume up.

'And did Angela tell you,' asks the host, Lucy, her tone warm and sympathetic, 'anything about the man she was meeting that night?'

The woman sniffs and looks up from the tissue. Her eyes are red, and her mascara is running down her cheeks. I feel sick all of a sudden, the tea curdling in my stomach. I don't think I can cope with her grief, it makes everything so much more tangible. If I concentrate hard enough, I can just about manage to separate the women I found, those crumpled, broken bodies, from the real people they were. The bodies I stood over weren't alive. They were vessels, nothing more. Empty of their essence. But seeing the loss written all over the faces of the families, hearing their stories, it brings those bodies to life. The thought is dizzying.

'She mentioned that she'd been chatting to a guy on Tinder,' the woman says. 'But I didn't know she was meeting him. She's usually so careful about things like that.'

'Were there safety precautions your sister would have taken before meeting someone she'd only spoken to online?'

The woman nods. 'She'd only have met him in public, and she would have told someone – in this case one of her friends – where she was going, and at what time. Only that did nothing to protect her.'

She breaks into a fresh wave of sobs, and Georgia turns the volume back down.

'I deleted Tinder,' she announces. 'It's not worth the risk. I'm blonde, I'm thirty. It could have been me.'

'I was supposed to meet a guy last night,' says Tamara as she pins my hair in place. I wince as she pushes a pin into the spot where the umbrella hit me this morning. 'But I chickened out. After all of this, it's too risky. And I don't even have blonde hair.'

Georgia and I murmur our agreement, although I'm only half listening to their chatter now. My eyes are still glued to the grieving woman.

'I always thought I was being safe,' Tamara continues. 'I'd do the same things – meet in a public place, tell someone where I was going, let them know the name and details of the guy. But these women did all that and look how it turned out.'

'I just don't get it,' Georgia says. 'They arranged to meet at a bar around the corner. How did she end up in an abandoned park?'

'He must have lured her there somehow,' Tamara replies as she replaces lids on pots of creams and palettes of eyeshadow. 'Like with the alleyway the first time.'

'Well, until they catch this arsehole, I'll stay happily single, thanks very much. You're lucky you're in a relationship, Gina, you don't have to put up with the dangers – the literal, life-threatening dangers – of dating.'

'I know,' I admit, snapping back into the conversation. 'I couldn't be more grateful for not having to deal with online dating, especially right now. But I'd be terrible at it, anyway.'

'No one's *good* at it,' Georgia scoffs. 'We all just muddle through in the hope that we'll find someone else who's muddled through well enough to catch our eye.'

'So true,' Tamara laughs. 'I went on a date last month

where the guy actually got up and left halfway through, that's how bad at this I am.'

'He didn't!' Georgia cries.

'No joke,' she laughs as Georgia's jaw drops open in disbelief. 'Halfway through, he did the whole "my housemate's locked himself out, I have to go," routine and bolted.'

'No! I've used that excuse,' Georgia squeals, and dissolves into a fit of laughter.

'Enjoying yourself, are we?' A cold, angry voice cuts through her giggles.

I look to my left, to the source of the intrusion, and flinch. The woman who was just being interviewed is now standing beside me. Angela's sister. I glance up at the screen and, sure enough, Lucy has moved on to another interview. I don't know what to say, so I stay quiet and look at the floor.

Tamara and Georgia quickly busy themselves, fiddling with make-up brushes and hairdryer cords to avoid the awkwardness that's radiating between us.

'I hope you're happy,' she says, her eyes narrowed. 'I hope you're enjoying your little moment in the spotlight, using my sister as a way to launch your career.'

'That's not—'

'I don't care what you have to say for yourself,' she says icily. 'You have something to do with what happened to my sister. I know you did. And I'm not going to stop looking until I find out what it is. When I do, I'm going to tear down this little platform you've built for yourself so everyone knows who you really are.'

'Excuse me,' says Georgia, stepping between the woman and me. 'You have no right to talk to her like that. I'm sorry for your loss, but I think you should leave.'

The woman snarls, her face twisted with grief and anger, mascara rivers tracing down her face, her eyes red from sobbing. She hesitates, looking between Georgia and me, deciding what to do, whether to push it or leave. I'm frozen in place, my heart pounding in my ears, unsure whether she's a real threat, someone who could do me genuine harm, or simply a sister crazed by grief. I stare at her, taking in the tiny veins in the whites of her eyes and her black pupils, which almost overtake her pale irises. My muscles are clenched, my body poised in fight or flight mode.

Finally, after what feels like minutes locked in this stand-off, she breaks eye contact and hangs her head, as though defeated. She breathes deeply, like she's steeling herself for something, then looks up sharply, her eyes meeting mine.

I don't see it coming. By the time the wet, slimy spit lands on my face, hard and fast like a bullet, Georgia and Tamara are screaming, throwing themselves at her, restraining her. She falls to the floor with a thud, and there's a scuffle at my feet, limbs tangling with the straps of my handbag. I'm too stunned to move. The ball of saliva slides slowly down my cheek as I stay frozen in place. I can see security guards running towards us in my peripheral vision.

They descend on the knot of women at my feet, pulling them apart, trying to quiet their screams. The two guards manage to separate the women and the squealing dies down. The sister is led away, to be escorted off the property, muttering profanities as she goes.

'Oh my God,' says Georgia, brushing herself down indignantly. 'She's crazy.'

I reach up to touch my cheek. It's wet and warm, like it's bleeding. Only I know it's not. I let out the breath I didn't realise I'd been holding in. Georgia turns her attention to me.

'Are you OK?'

'I'm fine,' I say, my voice shaking as violently as my hand.

Georgia gently dabs at my cheek with a tissue. 'You didn't deserve that.'

I manage to pull my lips into a thin smile. Georgia's just trying to make me feel better, but I'm rattled. The studio felt like a safe place. When I was here, I was protected from the people who wished me harm online. And the security to get into this part of the building is tight. You can't get in unless you're really meant to be here. But I'm just as vulnerable here as I am when I step outside, and the thought terrifies me.

'Gina Mills?' A voice to my left makes me jump. I clutch my chest as a man wearing a headset pops his head around the corner.

'You're on in five.'

Chapter 27

1996

SHARON

I close the front door behind me and breathe a little sigh of relief.

It's not that I'm happy about being separated from my kids for hours on end, it's just that ... well, dealing with their emotions on top of my own has been overwhelming. So it was as though a physical burden had been lifted from me when I finished the school run this morning, kissed them goodbye, told them I loved them. After all, with everything that happened last week, it's been an emotional time for all of us. Poor Cassie has been virtually inconsolable, crying for days on end. And Ryan and Gina have been processing their grief through anger, bickering constantly, picking at each other and turning on me when it's too much for them to deal with.

I thought our little funeral service would help bring them some closure – or maybe, if I'm being honest, I begged my husband to do it because I was the one who really needed it – but watching Bill shovel wet clods of dirt over our family pet just made us all feel sad and scared and depressed all over again. Poor Pickles. And those poor kids, for finding him like that. As I sip my third coffee of the morning, I think back to what the police said when they came to see the scene I couldn't bear to clean up.

'Probably just some kids, bored in the school holidays, you know?'

I'd wanted to scream at the officer for his idiocy. Bored kids steal sweets from the corner shop, or spray-paint fences, or destroy garden gnomes. They don't kill cats. Psychopaths kill cats. Hurting innocent creatures isn't a recreational activity, and I'm appalled that they're trying to convince me to treat this like it's no big deal.

Once the initial shock of the kids' discovery had subsided, I'd become more and more convinced that someone had done it to send us a sinister message. What that message was, or why anyone would need to send us one, I had no clue.

Bill agrees that it was more than bored kids but that's where the similarities in our opinions end. He tells me I'm being paranoid; jumping to conclusions. But every time I close my eyes, I still see that black and white fur soaked in red, those golden eyes open wide with fear, his mouth stretched in a screech that did nothing to help him, his belly gaping from bottom to top. My stomach writhes, and my vision mists again as tears threaten to spill into my coffee.

I shake my head and stand up. I have too much to do today to sit around feeling sorry for myself. And besides, I need to stay busy, stay distracted, keep my mind away from that relentless loop of horror. I flip on the radio to hear Celine Dion singing about something all coming back to her. I roll my eyes, thinking that I know exactly how that feels, but soon, despite my best efforts, I find myself singing along as I gather washing from the kids' rooms, make the beds, collect stray toys from the floor. Ryan's room is, predictably, the worst of the lot. I can barely find carpet for the random assortment of junk that covers his floor.

I begin picking up toys and socks and bits of sporting

equipment, trying to find the correct home for each new item. I think it's time we had another garage sale, or at least a proper clean-out. Maybe this weekend I can get Ryan to fill a bag to take to the charity shop.

I spot something poking out from under his bed and get down on my hands and knees to grab it. His Game Boy. I tut out loud, wondering how long it'll take him to step on the damn thing and come crying to me for a new one. I pull it towards me, shifting the weight on my hands and knees to get up again, and that's when I spot it.

The sight makes my skin crawl, like it's alive and trying to remove itself from my body.

Bill's hunting knife.

I've argued with him so many times about keeping that thing. The sharp, serrated edge and pointed tip are far more deadly than any of our kitchen knives. And Bill doesn't even hunt. He insists on keeping it, though, as a memento from the days when he and his dad used to go deer hunting, some kind of macho bonding time that I'll never understand.

He knows how much I hate the idea of it being in our house but he promised me it'd stay locked in the safe at the top of our wardrobe, out of reach even for me. Despite this precaution, my mind would occasionally flash to how things could go wrong. I'd pictured one of my babies, covered in blood, crying, needing stitches. While I'd argued with Bill, that was the worst-case scenario. One of our kids getting hurt was the most terrible thing that my imagination could conjure.

Not this. I could never have foreseen this.

My muscles scream with dread as I flatten myself onto the carpet to get a closer look.

It's not fear for myself that's caused my blood to pump violently against my temples, my heart to thrash. My eyes absorb the dimly lit scene under Ryan's bed, and I'm frozen to the spot, held in place by indecision.

I could just pretend I haven't seen anything, I tell myself.

Walk out of here, clean and hide the knife back in the safe, shove this to the back of my mind. Life will go on as normal, and my family will be safe.

But I know, without understanding how, that nothing will be the same any more.

It can't be the same, because the blade of Bill's hunting knife is covered in blood. Even in the shadows beneath my son's bed, there's no mistaking what I've stumbled upon.

The deep red liquid has seeped into the carpet, creating a dark, dangerous-looking stain that's surrounded by crumbs and toys and small balls of dust. And stuck to the blood, to the blade, the handle, the carpet, is something soft and wispy.

It wasn't the blood that caused my hair to stand on end. It's this.

As I stare, horrified, a sob rises from somewhere deep inside me, escaping as a scream, primal and wounded.

Those wisps that are stuck in dried-up blood . . . they're black and white. Fluffy.

It's Pickles's fur.

Chapter 28

2017

DETECTIVE ADAM ADEBAYO

I glance behind me. I know the team is there but I need to check just one more time, to be certain of their presence. Christine is by my side, as always. Solid. Dependable. And behind her stand Prash and Dave, dressed, as I am, in protective vests. We don't expect to need them, but we don't take any risks on days like today.

I knock on the wooden door. For a few moments there's only silence, laden with anticipation. And then footsteps. Someone reaches the front door and there's a pause, and a shadow passes over the peephole. It's the moment before we know if there's going to be trouble.

There's a metallic scrape and rattle as a chain is released, and the door swings open slowly.

Before I can stop myself, I smile. Then I realise where I am and what I'm here for, and I rearrange my face into a sombre expression.

'Gina. Good morning. Is Ryan home?'

Her gaze slides from my face to my protective vest, and then behind me to my team. Her face, open and pleasant when she first opened the door, shifts and hardens.

'What is this about?'

'Is your brother home?' I repeat, not answering her question. It'll be far more complicated if she insists on answers.

We need to establish if he's home first. The questions can come later.

'Why aren't you answering me? You can't just show up here like this demanding to see Ryan.'

Her voice is raised. I need to make sure she stays calm. Hysterics aren't going to help anyone in this situation.

'Please, Gina,' Christine chimes in next to me. 'We will answer all of your questions as soon as we can, but for now it's really important that we find Ryan.'

'No,' Gina hisses. 'I've told you, you can't just barge in here like this. Haven't you harassed me enough?'

'Miss Mills,' I say. My tone is stern, but calm. 'We have a warrant, so we have the authority to come in, with or without your permission. If you try to stop us, I'm afraid we'll have to arrest you, so I strongly suggest that you allow us inside.'

There's a sudden flurry of movement from the end of the corridor. Ryan appears around the corner, looking as though he's just woken up, his red hair sticking up at odd angles, his feet bare, wearing jogging bottoms and a threadbare jumper. My whole body tenses for what's coming.

'What's this all about?' Gina demands. Then she seems to sense her brother's presence, and she swivels her body to face him.

'Oh, thank God,' she says, her shoulders dropping in relief. 'Ryan, they're saying they have a warrant.'

She says it so innocently, her voice so filled with trust, that something tugs at my chest. I shove the thought aside. This is not the time for sentiment.

'What's this about?' Ryan asks, stepping beside Gina, looking me square in the eye and crossing his arms across his chest. Anger flares inside me. How can he be so arrogant?

'Mr Ryan Mills,' I say roughly. 'You're under arrest for the murder of Angela Delaney.'

'What?' Gina cries, her voice brittle. 'What are you talking about? This doesn't make any sense! Murder?'

The look in her eyes is wild. Primitive, almost. She turns to her brother again.

'What are they talking about, Ryan?'

'There's been a mistake,' he cries, his voice coming out as a high-pitched squeak. Not so cocky now that he knows we're on to him, it seems.

I ignore his protestations, stepping into the space between us and reaching behind me for the cuffs that are attached to my belt.

'Your hands, Mr Mills.'

He staggers, then reaches out to steady himself against the wall. I take the opportunity to secure one ring of the cuffs around his wrist.

He tries to pull his arm away but I'm stronger than he is. He's not going anywhere.

'I'm not a murderer,' he gasps. He's panting, and his legs are buckling at the knees. It always amazes me when criminals are surprised by their own capture. As though it's somehow a common misconception that getting away with murder is easy.

Gina tries to shove me, a brave but ineffective move. Prash steps between us and moves her aside easily, keeping her separated from her brother.

'We have an arrest warrant, miss,' he says to her. 'You can follow us to the police station, if you like, and one of the team will explain what's happening there.'

'But he's done nothing,' she argues.

No one says anything. I reach around and grab Ryan's other wrist. He doesn't struggle this time, and I restrain him quickly. I let out the breath I've been holding in. As far as arrests go, this one has been pretty painless.

'Ryan Mills,' I say, steering him towards the open front door. 'I must inform you that you do not have to say anything. But, it may harm your defence...'

I recite his rights to him, although I'm not certain he's really paying attention. As I lead him away, down his front path and towards the car we arrived in, he turns back, just for a second. I follow his gaze. Gina is standing in her front doorway, her eyes wide, looking vulnerable, like all she wants is for someone to fold her in their arms and tell her it's going to be OK. But it won't be OK. Not once she learns the truth about her brother.

When we arrive back at the station, Christine leads Ryan to an interview room, while I grab us a cup of coffee each. She returns a minute later, grimacing.

'What's up?' I ask.

'He wants a cup of tea,' she says.

I frown.

'And?'

'And a lawyer,' she adds. 'I've called the duty solicitor.'

I sigh in frustration. I'm itching for answers and a lawyer will slow this entire process significantly. Especially a duty solicitor, who could take hours to arrive, depending on their current caseload.

Thankfully Thompson, the tall, slim solicitor with the pointed face and nasal voice, hurries in half an hour later.

He's left alone with Ryan for a few minutes. We watch their interaction through the two-way mirror that overlooks the interview room, with the sound off. Ryan looks flustered. He's sweating – there are dark patches where his stress has soaked through his jumper under each arm – and his face is flushed.

He's shaking his head as Thompson is talking to him. I wish I could hear them. A few seconds later, the solicitor nods in our direction.

'Ready?' Christine looks at me.

'Been ready for hours,' I reply, and I follow her through the door into the small, cold room. We introduce ourselves to Ryan and nod at Thompson. We tell them that the session is being recorded, and I point towards the cameras in the corners of the room.

'Mr Mills, let's start with some basics, shall we?' Christine asks.

He stares at us, his face wiped of any emotion other than fear.

'Where were you last Wednesday, the eighteenth, at around eight o'clock at night?'

He doesn't hesitate.

'I was at home,' he says.

'Was anyone else with you?'

'Well, no, I live with Gina, and she was ... well, you know where she was.'

'So no one else can vouch for your whereabouts?'

He frowns, as though coming up with an alibi has only just occurred to him.

'No, but that doesn't make me a murder—'

'What my client is trying to say,' Thompson cuts in, 'is that he'd like to know the grounds on which you've arrested him. You must have some evidence if you've brought him in. He'd like to hear it.'

'Fine,' Christine says lightly. I think she's enjoying this. If I'm honest, so am I. 'We found Mr Mills's DNA on the body of Angela Delaney. He's being charged with murder.'

When we'd searched Gina's room we'd been there to find the missing jewellery. The officers had spotted a towel

207

hanging out to dry, with a blood-like stain marking a corner of the fabric. They knew there was a high chance that it was just Ryan or Gina's blood. A shaving cut, a kitchen accident. Nothing sinister.

We'd taken a sample of Ryan's DNA to test the stain against. In the end, it had been Gina's blood, an old mark, our forensics team had explained. At the time, we'd been disappointed that the search had been a waste of time. That was until we found the DNA on Angela's body and the system had alerted us to a match.

'But how can my DNA be on her if I never even saw her?' Ryan cries. 'I don't know her.'

Thompson begins to protest, but Ryan ignores him.

'I wasn't there! I didn't do it. I'm not a murderer – there's been a mistake.'

'This interview is over,' Thompson says forcefully, silencing his client.

'That's fine,' I say, although it's not fine. I want more time with him. I want to get Ryan alone, without his lawyer, and pressure him until he caves. I won't tell them that, of course. 'He'll be taken through to processing now. You can speak to him after that if you need to.'

Ryan looks like he's just been punched in the face, as though the shock of his situation is physical. His reaction needles at me. He looks genuinely distraught, like he honestly has no idea what's happening, or how he's ended up here. But then I think about the evidence, and I know that this is just an act. It has to be.

'Wait!' he yells, and the three of us give him our full attention. My heart pounds. Are we going to get a confession so soon?

'Gina was there, right?' he cries. 'At the crime scene, I mean. What if some of my DNA was on her, you know, from living in the same house, or from coming into contact with each other, and then it was transferred from her onto that girl?'

Christine looks at him and her voice is icy cold when she says, 'We've not arrested you on a whim, Mr Mills. Our evidence is strong.'

And with that we stand up and walk out of the room, Ryan's cries following us all the way down the hall.

Chapter 29

1996

SHARON

'Are you calling our children liars?'

Bill's nostrils are flared, his voice dangerously low. I'm trying to keep myself calm and rational, but beneath my stony expression is a panic like I've never known before. What is happening to my family?

'Bill, I don't want this to be true any more than you do, but there aren't very many possible explanations.'

'They all said they had nothing to do with it.'

'I know that,' I say as patiently as I can manage. 'I was there. But what's the alternative? That some stranger stole your knife from our wardrobe, brutally killed our cat, then snuck into our home and planted the knife under the bed of a thirteen-year-old boy?'

Silence stretches between us, taut as a steel wire. I feel like I could reach out and pluck it, listen to the note ringing out through our bedroom.

I have no idea what to say, which combination of words could make this all right. Either I believe my children, and therefore believe that a murderous psychopath has been in our home, or I believe that one of my kids is that murderous psychopath.

Pickles wasn't killed by accident. It wasn't some kind of tragic misunderstanding. He was murdered, deliberately and methodically. That's a fact. And the only other fact we knew for certain is that it was Bill's hunting knife that did the job. And that knife was in Ryan's room, hidden under his bed.

'I just...' I begin, not wanting to voice the thought I can't get out of my head, because I know exactly how my husband will react. 'It has to be Ryan, doesn't it? The knife was under his bed.'

'That doesn't actually prove anything,' he points out.

'OK, but how do you explain getting hold of the knife in the first place, then?'

When I'd first found it, I'd been furious with Bill. How could he be so careless, taking such a dangerous item out of the safe and leaving it within reach of the kids? I'd called him, hurling my accusations down the line. He'd denied them all, claiming he'd not so much as thought of the knife in months. As far as he knew, it was still safely tucked away behind an inch of steel. Lucky for me, Bill is a terrible liar, so I'd have been able to tell from his tone, from the pauses between his sentences, if he wasn't being truthful. But that still leaves us with the question of how the knife was accessed. The kids don't know the code for the safe... do they?

'Why couldn't it be one of the girls?' Bill asks me now.

'Really?' I ask, my voice now simmering with barely contained rage.

It's a rhetorical question but my husband stands on the other side of our bed, arms crossed over his chest, legs slightly apart, battle-ready.

'Fine,' I seethe. 'First of all, Pickles was Gina's cat. She loved that stupid fur ball. And besides, she's scared of knives. You've seen the way she acts in the kitchen when there are sharp blades around. And Cassie... well, really?

I mean, she's just a little girl! I just don't see how you can even consider it for a moment.'

'Well if you're so willing to point the finger at Ryan, shouldn't you at least consider the possibility that it could be one of the girls?'

'Cassie's seven, Bill. She runs away from *butterflies*.' My voice catches and I close my eyes to compose myself.

Bill sighs. 'I know,' he says, his shoulders deflating and his arms dropping to his side. 'I know you're right, but I just . . . Ryan?'

'I'm not saying it's definitely him,' I say lamely, all the fight drained out of me, too. 'But I just don't see how it could be either of the girls. And the alternative is that a stranger has been in here, and that seems even more unlikely.'

I think back to the looks on my children's faces earlier that evening when we confronted them. After calling Bill I'd sat on the sofa, shaking, until I could think clearly. But even after the trembling had subsided, I had no idea what to do. No parenting course or book could prepare me for a situation like this one, where I suspected that one of my children could be capable of something so dark and hideous that I could hardly bear to think it.

I'd carried on as normal, waiting for the moment when Bill walked through the door and took charge, but it was excruciating. I could barely look my kids in the eye when I picked them up from school. I watched them with the kind of intensity I'd employed when each of them had still been a newborn, my eyes flicking towards them every few seconds, checking that they were breathing, alert to any sign of danger, fretting that they were too hot, or too cold, or too hungry.

Only now I was looking for different signs. Was one of my

children capable of violence? Of killing something innocent in cold blood? And what would give that away?

They'd spent the afternoon as they usually did: eating their after-school snack as though it was the only food any of them had been given all day, complaining about homework so much that it doubled the time they took to complete it, then collapsing onto the sofa, the girls watching a Disney film, Ryan playing his Game Boy.

Was his favourite game inciting him to violence? I read a study recently in a parenting magazine I'd flicked through in the dentist's office that suggested video games could be linked to aggressive outbursts in teenagers. Could Donkey Kong cause violent behaviour in an otherwise gentle kid?

'Ryan, that's enough of your Game Boy for today,' I'd called from across the room, where I'd been watching and waiting for Bill's return.

'But, Mum,' he whined, 'I've finished all my homework.'

'I know,' I said, 'but I'm asking you to please put it down. Now.'

'But why?'

'Because I say so,' I'd snapped, and he'd looked like he was about to cry.

Guilt had weighed heavily on my chest until Bill walked in.

After he'd inspected the knife, after we'd had a family dinner, during which I couldn't eat for the lump that was lodged in my throat, we sat the kids down at the kitchen table and showed them what I'd found – the blade – cleaned of all evidence of Pickles's murder, of course. I looked around the table to measure the reactions of each of my children. Cassie shrank away, tears threatening to spill onto her cheeks. Gina's eyes grew enormous in her tiny, innocent face. And Ryan yelped in recognition.

'Cool, that's Dad's knife!'

He'd reached over to try to snatch it, but I'd placed a hand over his wrist, stopping him.

'Yes, it is.'

He'd noticed the tone in Bill's voice, realised this wasn't a game. I let go, and he slowly pulled his arm back to his lap.

'Why do you have it here?' he'd asked.

'Can any of you explain to us,' Bill had asked patiently, 'how this came to be under Ryan's bed?'

Three heads shook in unison. The fear in Ryan's eyes was real. I knew it, instinctively, in the pit of my guts. I knew he wasn't lying when he insisted to us that he didn't know how it got there, or why it had been removed from the safe. He was worried that he was in trouble, but he didn't understand what for.

Bill and I looked at one another. He nodded. We couldn't tell them the rest, couldn't bring ourselves to share exactly what the knife meant, how it had been this blade that had ended Pickles's life. We let the kids drift off to bed, telling them that if they had anything they wanted to tell us, we'd always listen, and we wouldn't be mad. They'd nodded solemnly, and within minutes the whole encounter had been forgotten, an argument over toothbrushes taking precedence in their minds.

Which means either there's a dangerous person getting into our home, and into our son's room without us knowing.

Or one of my children is a liar. And a killer.

Chapter 30

2017

GINA

'Where's Julian?'

I'm pacing around my living room while strangers finish their search of my brother's bedroom.

I've tried to tell them to be careful with his things, to handle his laptop and games console gently. They're his most prized possessions. But they hardly notice my existence. I'm an annoying noise that they're trying to tune out, like a mosquito buzzing in their ears.

My calls to Julian haven't been getting through – I kept getting his voicemail – and I'd been frantically hitting redial until the device was gently removed from my iron-like grip by Tash.

I hadn't known who else to call when Ryan was arrested. I'd been trying Julian over and over again, without any luck, until eventually I stood in the hallway with utter loneliness swelling inside me. Ryan was gone. Arrested for murder. Julian was unreachable. Police officers were searching my home.

Fighting off an onslaught of despair, I'd called Tash, expecting her to reject my call.

'Hi,' she'd answered, sounding suspicious.

'Tash, it's Gina,' I'd said, believing that she'd picked up

without looking, and now would be the moment she'd hang up.

'I know, I have caller ID,' she'd replied sarcastically. 'What do you want?'

There was so much to say, so much to fix between us. But in that moment, I'd just needed a friend.

'Ryan's just been arrested,' I'd said, still in disbelief about what had just happened. 'I can't find Julian, and my house is being searched.'

'Oh,' she'd said, her voice full of emotion again, the past few weeks of frostiness completely erased in two sentences. 'Oh. OK, don't worry, Gina. I'm on my way over, hold on.'

She'd turned up fifteen minutes later and found me still standing in the hallway, phone in my hand, trying to get hold of Julian.

She'd pulled me into a massive hug while I'd stayed motionless, too surprised to return the affection.

'I thought you hated me,' I managed to wheeze eventually. She'd let go and stepped back, assessing me from arm's length.

'I never hated you,' she sighed. 'I was angry, yes, although I can see now that I probably overreacted. I just ... Oh, Gina, I don't want to burden you with something else, but when I was younger, an aunty of mine was killed. Hit and run. And the press made it all so much worse for us. So I took it all a bit personally when you made these murders so public.'

'I'm really sorry,' I'd whispered. 'I didn't know. I wasn't trying to upset anyone.'

'No, *I'm* sorry,' she'd replied fiercely. 'You've been going through hell. You needed me, and I wasn't there for you. I made it worse. But I'm here now, and I'm not going any-where.'

She'd hugged me again, and this time I'd returned her embrace, grateful to have my friend back.

Now she's standing in the living room hitting redial, apparently having just as much luck as I did.

'I'm sorry, Gina. I'll keep trying. I'm sure he'll be here really soon, he's probably just run out of battery.'

I almost laugh. The excuses we make for people when they're uncontactable. I played this game with my girlfriends in high school when a boy we liked wasn't texting back.

'Probably dropped his phone in the bathtub,' we'd joke.

'He could have broken all of his fingers.'

In the end though, they just weren't that into us. Back then, people weren't attached to their phones like additional appendages. These days, there's really no excuse to be offline, broken fingers or not. Unless you're on a flight, or in some kind of maximum security situation, the one thing we all have in common is our phones, and our constant attachment to them.

So for Julian to be completely unavailable isn't easy to explain.

I sigh and throw myself onto the sofa, incapable of doing anything else. Tash rushes over and takes my hand.

'It's going to be all right,' she says. 'I'm here. I'm not going to leave you alone, don't worry.'

'Thanks, Tash,' I say, grateful to at least have someone here to comfort me, even if it's not the person I really want. 'I'm glad you're here. Having these guys going through all of Ryan's stuff just feels . . . I feel violated.'

'I know,' she says, rubbing my arm. She can't possibly know, but I let it slide.

'Have you eaten?'

I shake my head.

She hovers at the door to Ryan's room and asks one of

the officers if she can use the kitchen. I hear a murmur, she nods, and then disappears down the hallway to rustle up something to sustain me.

The officers walk in and out of Ryan's room, taking notes, nodding to one another, inspecting ordinary items as though they hold the secrets to Ryan's past. I glare at them while they work, willing them to just leave so I can process the events of today in peace. Right now, I'm completely numb, unable to feel much of anything. There's too much information to process, too much happening for my brain to settle on any one thing.

'Excuse me, miss,' a lanky officer who looks like he's just left high school interrupts my thoughts.

I stare at him in silence.

'Um . . . Sorry to bother you, even more I mean, but I was just wondering if Mr Mills has a car?'

I shake my head.

'OK, thanks,' he says, walking away.

I sigh as Tash walks over and hands me a plate.

'I made you a sandwich. It's just chicken salad, I hope that's OK.'

I take the plate from her and look without interest at the sandwich. I want to throw the plate, food and all, against a wall. I want to hear it smash, to revel in the destruction, to let the shards collapse to the ground. But I don't. Instead, I lift the sandwich to my mouth.

'Thanks, Tash,' I say, nibbling the crust. My stomach roils, and I put the plate down on the coffee table.

'Of course.' She smiles, and I desperately want her to leave. Except then I'll be left here with no one but the police to keep me company. I turn to her, my eyes filling with tears.

'Can you try to call Julian again, please?' I ask, my voice wobbly. I hold my breath while she taps at my phone. He'll answer this time, I tell myself. He'll be here soon. I can send Tash home, and then everything will be OK.

Tash's mouth tightens into a grimace, and my stomach plummets.

'Voicemail,' she announces.

'Leave a message,' I instruct. I can hear the beep from where I sit.

'Hi, Julian. It's Tash here, I'm a friend of Gina's from work. Please do call back as quickly as you can. It's really important.'

She hangs up and plasters a smile on her face.

'I'm sure he'll call back soon,' she assures me brightly.

I smile weakly in return.

'Thanks, Tash,' I say for the hundredth time today, wishing I could be as positive as she's being. 'You're probably right. He'll be here any minute.'

Chapter 31

DETECTIVE ADAM ADEBAYO

'Of course he's lying,' Christine insists. 'There's no way they would have found his DNA if he hadn't been on the scene.'

I grunt. It's true that the DNA is compelling, although when I saw the stunned look on Ryan's face when we told him his DNA was at the scene, I could have sworn his reaction was real. His skin became the colour of bone, his eyes grew wide, and he looked like he was going to be sick.

'It could have been touch DNA,' I offer, playing devil's advocate, wanting to explore every possible option. What Ryan mentioned, the transfer of DNA between people, is possible. We need more than just some DNA fragments to be able to say definitively that Ryan did it. Which means, until we know for sure, we have to explore the option that he really is innocent.

'That would be a little bit convenient though, wouldn't it?' Christine asks.

'It would,' I admit. 'But a jury might not agree. It does offer reasonable doubt. If we're going to bring this guy down, we need more.'

As if somehow I willed it into happening, there's a sudden flurry of activity from the far corner of the room.

'New evidence,' someone yells, and I stand up too quickly, smacking my head on my desk lamp in the process. I rub the spot that's stinging as I follow Christine and the rest of the team towards the incident room.

'What do you think it is?' I ask, as I catch up to her.

'No idea,' she says. 'But I'd say we're about to find out.'

Everyone arrives within seconds. There's a buzz of excitement rippling through the team. After weeks of what's felt like slamming our skulls against solid walls, we're now so close to solving this. One brick has been pulled away from the wall this sonofabitch has built around himself, and the rest is about to come tumbling down.

'OK, settle down,' Mia yells from the front of the room. Our chatter dics instantly.

'The team at the Mills household have just called in to let us know they've found something.'

No one speaks. No one moves. And yet there's a shift in the room, an electricity. The sudden surge of hope this news offers also brings with it a tide of conflicting emotions. Obviously I'll be glad when the killer's caught. Of course I will. But this feeling of living on a knife edge, of not being able to relax, of knowing that I need to find justice for those women . . . it's become my new normal. Going back to a life without the Tinder Ripper will feel strange. Empty, almost.

Even as the thought runs through my head, I kick myself mentally for even thinking something so insensitive. It's just the stress talking.

'There was a note found in Mr Mills's bedroom.'

I throw Christine a look. She returns it with a shrug. Mia is looking at the screen at the front of the room and clicking her remote control.

'Here's what the team just sent us.'

It's a clear plastic evidence bag, filled with a small piece of white card covered in thin, sloping handwriting. The photo

221

we're looking at was just taken on a phone, so it's not great quality, but we can all read the message clearly:

I know you're a killer, Ryan. Don't you think it's time the truth came out?
  Love,
  Your Other Sister. x

'Who the hell is his other sister?' Christine yells.

'We're not sure yet, but I expect you and Adam to find out. When the team gets back from the search, get forensics on this for prints. Elizabeth and Jimi, I want you to find any CCTV cameras near the Mills residence, map out the route Ryan would have taken to each of the crime scenes and see if you can find him on camera for either of the murder dates. We need to prove his alibi is false, and we need to do it soon. We don't want his lawyer thinking he can get away with this, OK?'

We all agree and start moving, single-minded, and collectively buoyed by the thought of closing this case, of getting to go home tonight.

'Keep me posted, and if anything else comes up from the house search I'll call you back in,' Mia shouts as we start filing back towards the office.

As soon as I get back to my desk, I rummage through my paperwork for Gina's first witness statement. It's handwritten, but the careful print on the sheet in my hand looks nothing like the thin, spidery writing on the card found at Ryan's house.

'It's not Gina's writing,' I announce to Christine.

'OK,' she says, clicking away at her own computer. 'I'm just checking Ryan's social media, but there's no mention of another sister here.'

'What are their parents' names?' I ask.

'Uh... give me a sec... Bill and... Sharon, if his Facebook is to be believed. Looks like they live in Florida, maybe they have another kid out there with them?'

I type their names into our search database, expecting no results, same as Gina and Ryan. But there's a hit. A report, from 1996, about a child's death. I click the link.

'There's something in the system,' I say, and Christine jumps up from her chair to read over my shoulder. I scroll through the report, whistling through my teeth when I get to the end.

'So there *was* another sister,' Christine says. 'Who died twenty-one years ago.'

I turn to face her.

'But it says it was an accident, that the kids were playing and she fell and hit her head. I don't see the connection.'

'Adam,' Christine says as she reaches over to click my mouse. Her voice is low and urgent, and I spin my chair back around to see my screen. She's opened a photo that was attached to the file. A picture of Cassie, the dead child. Ryan's other sister.

'Look familiar?' she whispers.

The child is eight, according to the report, and smiling at the camera, with a missing tooth. But I don't see any of that at first. All I see is her mop of unruly hair.

It's blonde, and cascading across her shoulders in tight, wild curls.

Just like Michelle's.

And Angela's.

'We've got him.' Christine grins. 'He's our guy.'

Chapter 32

1996

SHARON

'Do you think they're OK?' I ask, for what's probably the eighth time tonight. I lost count after three.

'Sharon. They're fine,' Bill says patiently, reaching for my hand from across the table. He massages it gently with his thumb.

'I know you're worried,' he says, 'but we haven't had a date night for so long, and I was hoping we could just enjoy each other's company tonight.'

'I'm sorry,' I begin, 'I'm trying, I really am. It's just that—'

'The timing's terrible, I know,' he finishes my sentence. 'But it is our anniversary, and I don't want to let that slide, no matter what's going on. We should celebrate. And besides, the kids are safe at home with Teresa. I got the alarm installed so that you'd be able to relax and feel comfortable about things like this.'

I exhale slowly. He's right. Our babysitter is responsible, she's been looking after the kids for years. And the new alarm system, blinking at me from beside our front door, has set my mind at ease a little. Still. I can't shake the sense of dread that's been building since I kissed the kids goodnight. Guilt washes over me, out here dressed in my best black dress, with heels and lipstick on, sipping wine and eating steak, when there could be danger lurking around my children.

I try to shake the feeling off, and force myself to smile at Bill. After all, he's made such an effort for our anniversary this year. There were the roses that he produced with a flourish from behind his back when he walked in the front door this evening, and the earrings he presented to me when we sat down at our candlelit table. Crystal, for fifteen years. All I've offered in return is worry and nerves. And a card that I hastily bought along with the groceries today.

'You're right,' I admit, taking another deep breath and letting it out again slowly. 'I'm so grateful for everything you've done for me tonight, and I adore my earrings. Thank you. I'm sure the kids are fine.'

He smiles and keeps stroking my hand.

'You're welcome,' he says. 'Now can I interest you in another glass of wine?'

We get home late, around midnight, tipsy and giggling. It was the wine that finally allowed me to relax, sinking deeper into its velvety softness with every sip. We shared a dessert and then moved over to the bar, where we sipped cocktails and flirted like we had all those years ago. As the night wore on and nothing terrible happened, I realised how silly I'd been for worrying. Of course the kids were fine. Of course I was allowed a night off with my husband. Things were getting back to normal.

We find Teresa asleep on the couch, with a late-night drama on in the background. Bill flicks the TV off and I shake our neighbour awake gently.

'Teresa,' I whisper. 'It's Sharon. We're home.'

Bill giggles beside me, and I shush him, suppressing a giggle myself.

'Go and make some tea,' I say, as Teresa stirs and opens her eyes.

'Hey,' I whisper.

'Oh, hi, Sharon.'

'How was it?'

'It was all right,' she says, rubbing her eyes.

'Come into the kitchen. Bill's put the kettle on.'

She nods and follows me, sitting heavily at the kitchen table. As she wakes up, I pour a small pot of milk and put it in front of her, along with the sugar bowl.

'So they were well behaved for you?' I ask as we stir the steaming cups Bill's just put in front of us.

'They were a little . . . agitated,' she says. 'Cassie and Ryan got into a massive fight.'

'Really?' I ask, taken aback. Cassie believes that the world begins and ends with her big brother. And Ryan adores his baby sister. If a fight breaks out at home, it usually involves Gina. Classic middle child, I suppose, overshadowed by her older sibling and not as babied as much as her younger one. As a middle child myself, I understand the struggle.

'Yeah, Cassie was really wound up. She told Ryan that she hated him, which really upset him. I had to put her to bed early.'

I glance at Bill, who raises his eyebrows at me.

'Did she say why she was so upset with him?'

'Well, she did. But it didn't make much sense.'

Teresa takes a long sip of tea, looking like she'd rather do anything than tell us what had happened between the kids.

'It's OK,' I encourage her. 'You can tell us what she said.'

'She said . . . she said she knows who killed your cat.'

My heart leaps into my throat, threatening to choke me.

'Who?'

There's a pause, heavy with tension and fear, and mingled

with a sense of understanding. I know what she's going to say before it leaves her lips, but I'm hoping against all hope that I'm wrong.

'She said . . . she said it was Ryan.'

Chapter 33

2017

RYAN

I thought I'd experienced fear before. If you'd asked me even yesterday, I'd have told you that I understood what terror meant, how it felt, what it could do to your mind and your body.

And then I spent a night in a holding cell, with a murder charge pressing down on me, the weight of it buckling my legs at the knees and threatening to crush my lungs. Now I truly know fear, and I understand that it's not an emotion, like joy or sadness. It's a physical presence, an all-encompassing knowledge that pervades my thoughts, my movements, my future. All I know is fear. And confusion.

My stomach growls, and I'm angered by my body's inability to pause. My future is about to go up in flames, and yet I'm hungry. How is that even possible?

There's a banging sound, followed by a mechanical crunch, and then the door to my cell swings open. An officer appears in the frame of the doorway, backlit by fluorescent strips.

'Mills. Out,' he grunts. I stand, my muscles screaming in protest. Since being brought to the cell last night, I haven't moved. Pins and needles surge through my arms and legs as I follow the officer out into the hallway.

My lawyer, Carl Thompson, is waiting for me.

'Are you OK?' he asks as I sit in the rigid plastic chair next to him.

'I don't know,' I say. 'What's happening?'

'The same detectives from yesterday, they're going to come in here shortly and ask you some more questions. As I advised yesterday, don't answer anything that could be incriminating, do you understand?'

I nod, not comprehending his words. My mind is thick and slow, a mire of terror and questions. Then, as I process what he's said, I shake my head.

'No, nothing I'll say *will* be incriminating, because I didn't do it.'

'Look, I understand this is confusing and stressful, but I'm here to help you, and to make sure your legal rights are adhered to. So if in doubt, we can stop the interview at any time and you can consult with me. And if I tell you to stop talking, you stop talking, do you understand?'

I nod again. My heart is hammering but I pull my shoulders back and grit my teeth. They can't just decide I'm guilty.

'Morning,' says the female detective as the two of them walk in. 'Just to refresh your memory, I'm Detective Constable Taylor, and this is Detective Constable Adebayo.'

Taylor. Adebayo. I won't forget them this time. They sit down opposite my lawyer and me and run through the procedure that's starting to feel frighteningly familiar: stating our names, the date and time, my rights, reminding me that we're being recorded.

'Tell us about Cassie,' Constable Adebayo says, taking me completely by surprise. Without any warning, I'm plunged into fresh panic, unable to move or think or breathe. How do they know about Cassie?

'Here,' Taylor says kindly, pushing a styrofoam cup across

the table, along with sugar sachets and little plastic milk capsules. 'It's coffee. Thought you might need it.'

My arm reaches for the cup, but my movements are imprecise, like I'm intoxicated. I take the coffee gratefully and gulp it down. It's bitter and burnt, but I barely notice.

'We found this in your bedroom,' Adebayo says, flicking a photo across the table towards me. I peer at it, and my heart contracts. It's the note I got, the one calling me a killer. And the photo of Cassie.

'I don't know who that's from,' I manage to say, my throat closing over my words.

'Why would someone call you a killer?' Constable Taylor asks.

'I ... I don't know,' I reply weakly. It's a lie.

'Tell us about Cassie,' Detective Adebayo asks again. This time, I'm expecting it. I'm still not prepared, but at least now it doesn't feel like a punch in the guts.

'She was my sister,' I say.

'What did she look like?'

'She was ... she was a little girl, you know? Blonde, curly hair—'

'Just like the women you murdered?'

'Don't answer that, Ryan,' Thompson cuts in sternly. 'It's leading.'

'Where were you on the night of the eighteenth?' Taylor asks calmly, without hesitating.

'I've already told you,' I say, reeling from the change in direction. 'I was at home. I had a nap.'

'And you didn't leave the house at all?'

'No, not after I got home from work.'

'And what time was that?'

I'm more confident now. These are questions I know the answer to. They're not ambiguous.

'Around seven,' I say.

'So you weren't walking around your neighbourhood at around eight?'

'No,' I say firmly.

'How do you explain this, then?' Constable Adebayo opens the manila file in front of him and pulls out a handful of photos. He spreads them out in front of me so I can see them all, a story unfolding frame by frame.

They're all pictures of me, walking on streets I recognise, places I'm intimately familiar with. It's the area I live in, the roads I walk along every day. It's definitely me. In a couple of the images, my face is clear. In the others, my features are obscured from view, but the clothing is the same, and I know it's me. I frown, trying to understand the significance of what I'm seeing.

Then I spot the date and time stamp in the bottom right corner.

All of these photos were taken on the eighteenth of the month.

And they were all taken between eight and eight fifteen in the evening. When I was asleep on the sofa at home. I look up, aghast.

'How could this . . . ? I don't . . .'

I let my words die. I have no idea how they've found these images, or what's going on, but I know I'm beyond talking my way out of this. Whatever's happening to me, I'm in it far too deep to claw my way back to solid ground. I need help.

I look over at Thompson, and he must see the distress in my eyes.

'I'd like to speak with my client alone,' he says, and Constable Adebayo simply nods.

'Thought you might,' he said. 'But before you do, we

thought you might be interested in seeing a few more photos.'

He pulls another handful of glossy images from the top of his pile, and dumps them in front of me. This time, he doesn't bother fanning them out in order. He doesn't need to. The picture at the top is another still from a video camera, this one just metres from the pub that backs onto the alleyway. It shows me walking past, towards the crime scene, on the evening of the first murder. Right before that woman was killed. When I was at home, watching TV. I'm certain of it.

But now, looking at these images, I don't know what to think. The police wouldn't fabricate evidence . . . would they? Maybe they're just doing this to try to get a confession. Maybe they really have nothing, and this is their way of pushing me to the edge. I've seen the cop shows. Sometimes they play dirty.

'I don't know where you got these,' I say forcefully, 'but I was at home on both of these evenings. I didn't kill those women. I wasn't walking around my neighbourhood. Whatever you think you know, it's wrong. You've got the wrong guy. I didn't do it.'

'That's enough,' my lawyer says, standing up. 'We're done.'

Constable Adebayo sits back in his chair, crossing his arms across his chest, assessing me.

'So that's how you're playing this?' he asks, a smile twitching at the corner of his mouth. 'Well, just so you know, we're officially charging you with murder, which means you'll be appearing before the magistrate's court tomorrow. With this evidence, we don't expect you to get bail. Your DNA is on the crime scene, there are notes in your home calling you a killer, and we have footage of you from multiple cameras proving that your alibi for both evenings was a lie. We can prove that you were out, alone, in the vicinity of both of the murders, within minutes of the crimes. It's pretty compelling, don't you think?'

I don't answer. All I can do is stare, aghast, as he leans his forearms onto the table, sneering at me.

'Well, *I* think it's compelling,' he says, narrowing his eyes at me. 'And the judge will too, I'd say. So you go ahead and chat, the two of you, but it's not going to do you any good. We've got you now. You're not going anywhere.'

Then he gathers up the photos in front of me, places them back on top of his pile of paperwork, slams the folder closed and walks out without another word. Constable Taylor follows right behind him. It's just me and my lawyer now.

'I'm sorry to tell you this, Ryan,' he says, leaning on the table and speaking slowly. 'The detective was right about the evidence being compelling. They've asked me to negotiate a plea deal with you.'

'A plea deal?' I ask.

'Yes, it means that you confess, plead guilty, in exchange for a reduced sentence. I can help you through it.'

I frown. 'Why would I confess to something I didn't do?'

'The evidence,' he says, 'tells a different story. With what they've just shown us, I'm afraid I don't see you getting through a trial without a guilty verdict. If you don't take the plea, I'll fight for you, Ryan. I will. But I want you to have all the facts before you make a decision. Their case is compelling.'

'But I didn't do it!' I yell. My stomach is heavy, and there's a pounding behind my eyes. How is this possible?

Thompson isn't fazed by my loss of control. I'm shaking, the blood pulsing around my body so violently I wonder if it's possible to explode.

'I'll give you some time to think about it,' he says, gathering his things and nodding towards the two-way mirror. 'This is a very big decision but you don't have long. You'll stand before the magistrate tomorrow and they'll expect you to plead either way.'

'I don't need to think about it,' I say. 'I'm innocent. I'm not pleading any other way.'

Chapter 34

1996

SHARON

'Coming,' I yell, popping the cake back in the oven.

I glance at the clock. It's two in the afternoon, which means I have just over an hour to get this cake out of the oven and iced. It's Cassie's eighth birthday, and I want it to be perfect. After all of the turmoil of the past months, after everything we went through with Pickles, and the fear that stayed with us since that awful day, now is the time to move on. I can feel it. I need it.

The day after our anniversary date, I'd sat Cassie down and told her what Teresa had said about her fight with Ryan.

'I hate him,' she'd said simply, no shades of grey about it.

'That's a very serious thing to say, Cassie. This isn't a family that hates. We're a family that loves.'

'I don't care. I hate him.'

'OK,' I'd said solemnly, trying to reason with my stubborn seven-year-old. 'Why do you hate him?'

'Because he killed Pickles.'

'Why do you think that?'

'Because I heard you and Daddy. You said it.'

My stomach curled itself into a fist. Our fight, the night I'd found the knife in Ryan's room. What had I said? What had she heard?

'Darling, Ryan didn't kill Pickles.'

'Well, if it wasn't true, why did you say it?'

I try not to smile at my daughter's perspective on the world. So pure, so innocent.

'I was scared, and sad, and I said things I shouldn't have. I'm sorry you heard Daddy and me speaking like that, it wasn't a conversation that you were meant to hear.'

Her bottom lip trembled, and I pulled her into my arms.

'I know you're sad about Pickles,' I said, and she sniffed into my chest, 'but it wasn't your brother's fault, OK?'

She'd sniffed again, her shoulders shaking.

'Cassie?' I lifted her from my body, holding her at arm's length. 'Do you understand? It wasn't Ryan.'

'OK, Mummy,' she said.

'So are you going to be nice to your brother now?'

She'd nodded, and I'd enveloped her little body once more.

The pain of what happened is starting to feel like a distant memory. Ryan and Cassie are getting along again, setting the house alarm every day has become like second nature, and the hunting knife has been disposed of, safely, and permanently. Life is back to normal, and tonight, with all three kids home from their school camp, and Cassie celebrating her birthday, I won't let anything burst the swelling sense of joy I'm feeling.

As I make my way towards the front door, I wipe my hands on the back of my jeans. I regret it immediately. I just washed these, and now they'll be covered in flour. I peer through the peephole and smile.

'Judy.' I smile as I open the door to my neighbour. But Judy isn't smiling.

'Is everything OK?' I ask, taking in her ashen face and frantically darting eyes.

'Have you seen Chance?'

Chance, Judy's pet rabbit, regularly escapes their fence and can be found snuffling in one of the front gardens of the houses along our street. My kids love it when he breaks free because they get to play with him for a few precious minutes before Judy comes looking.

'No,' I say. 'But I'm sure he's around here somewhere.'

Without warning, Judy bursts into tears.

'What's the matter?' I ask, reaching out to put a comforting hand on her shoulder.

'I'm just so worried,' she says between sobs.

'But he's always escaping,' I explain. 'Why are you so worried now?'

'Because he went missing last night,' she sniffs. 'I don't usually mind too much when he goes off, he always turns up after a few hours, but he didn't come home in the evening. That was unusual, but it's happened before, when a neighbour has let him into their house and then brought him around in the morning, but then no one did, and I've been walking around looking, but no one has seen him.'

I reach over and pull her into a hug.

'Come on,' I say, steering her by the shoulder into the house and through to the kitchen. 'Come and have a cup of tea, OK?'

She lets me lead her through to the kitchen table, and after a cup of tea and a couple of my best biscuits, she's calmed down enough to talk about her rabbit again.

'I'm sorry,' she says, looking embarrassed. 'I guess I just . . . I'm just worried, you know, after what happened to your cat. And then to the Singh family's pug.'

I ran into Indira Singh at school pick-up a few weeks ago, and the injuries she described on their family pet, Bubbles, sounded exactly like those that Pickles suffered. I shudder now at the thought, but I brush it away. I've been trying to forget about it since then.

'I know,' I say, 'but I'm sure it's nothing like that; you know what Chance is like.'

'I know,' she says. 'But what if what they're saying is true? What if there's some kind of sick pet killer out there?'

Even as I think it, I feel awful, but I can't help what's popped into my head, the only thing that matters after months of trying to convince myself of what I so desperately need to be true.

The kids are all at school camp. They were there yesterday, and the day before. Which means, if poor Chance has fallen into the hands of an awful animal killer, then it truly is just someone random.

Relief wells up inside me, and for a horrible moment I hope that Judy's rabbit does turn up like Pickles, just so I can prove to myself that the evidence is irrefutable. But I stop myself mid-thought. I don't need proof. I already know.

It's not one of my children. There can't be a killer living in my home.

Chapter 35

2017

DETECTIVE ADAM ADEBAYO

'Uh... Adam?' Christine's voice sounds unsure. Worried, even.

'Yeah, what's up?' I say, standing up so I can see her beyond the partition that separates us.

'Seen Twitter?'

'What about it?'

'Just take a look.'

Frowning, I sit back down and open a new tab in my browser.

'What am I looking for?' I ask, but then I see it. In the left-hand column, under London's trending topics. I don't realise I'm holding my breath as I click the link to see why people are talking about the Tinder Ripper now.

Breaking! reads a tweet from Channel Eight. Could the Tinder Ripper still be out there? Does this new letter prove he's free to kill again? Or is this nothing more than a chilling hoax?

I hurriedly click the link that takes me to a single paragraph of so-called news.

Exclusive: A letter, claiming to be from the Tinder Ripper himself, has been received by channel executives here at Channel Eight. Although Gina Mills' brother, Ryan Mills, has been charged for both of the murders that were discovered and live streamed by his sister, and is being held in custody awaiting trial, this new evidence could call into question who the Tinder Ripper really is. Channel Eight is working with authorities to alert them to the contents of the letter, but a full report will follow shortly. Click here to receive news alerts directly to your phone.

I let out a long, low whistle.

'I know,' Christine says.

'You don't actually believe there's a letter, do you?' I ask.

'Oh, I'm sure there's a letter,' she laughs. 'But it'll be some crazy guy just wanting a few minutes of fame. It's not going to do anything to calm down the media storm, though.'

Before we can debate the existence of the letter any further, Mia barks at us from across the office to join her in the incident room. As we walk over, a knot builds in my stomach. I'm sure we have the right guy – the evidence is all there – but Ryan's insistence on his innocence, the complete disbelief on his face when we showed him the images from the CCTV camera, and now this . . . it makes me uneasy, like the world is tilted a few degrees off centre, just enough to make me feel unbalanced.

'You may have seen the news,' Mia says as the last person closes the door behind her. 'But in case you haven't, a letter was delivered to Channel Eight today, claiming to be from the Tinder Ripper. News of the letter has already been leaked, but the woman who the letter is addressed to, an executive named Jacqueline Davies, called us right away to report it.'

A few people exchange confused glances. They mustn't have been on Twitter yet. Christine gives me a meaningful look at the mention of Gina's boss.

'Unfortunately, it seems as though they will be publishing the full contents of the letter shortly – we've tried to put a stop to it but it sounds like they'd rather face legal action than miss a breaking new story – so we need to strike now.'

She twists around to point the remote control at the screen behind her, and a photograph of the letter appears. It's typed, so nothing stands out to us immediately, but as Mia begins to read it aloud, goosebumps prickle my arms.

Dear Jacqueline,

I'm writing to let you know that the police have got the wrong person. You see, I am the Tinder Ripper. I murdered those women. You might not believe me, but why don't you ask Ryan what happened to the jewellery they were wearing, the pieces that went missing? I doubt he'll know about that, being that I am the one responsible for their deaths.

To be fair, he did kill them, so I suppose in a way the police are partially right. But he's nothing more than a puppet. A pawn. He is my hands, my feet, my eyes.

People have tried what I've achieved before. Even the CIA has attempted it (look up MK-Ultra if you don't believe me). But until now, no one has mastered what I've now proven to be possible.

I can control people's minds.

Not just anyone, obviously. Only those who are highly susceptible to suggestion, and who fill a number of other requirements (which I won't be sharing. My secrets are my currency).

I can see you scoffing, and I can imagine your scepticism as I type this. But rest assured, it's true. After years of research and testing, I've perfected my method to the point where I can make people do anything I want them to do, murder included. Plenty of frauds have claimed they've done this before, but they've done it behind the safety of a camera, where there's too much at stake to truly put their powers to the test. What I've achieved is so much more pure, and complex, and powerful. Because it's all real.

I imagine you're going to expect some kind of proof, so I have enclosed a photograph of the missing jewellery from both of the victims against today's newspaper.

Yours truly,

The Tinder Ripper

PS – Although I'm sure a team of media gurus probably spent a whole morning brainstorming my nickname, I'd much prefer being called The Puppeteer from now on, please. Thanks ever so much.

'Come *on*,' someone moans from the back of the room. 'We're not actually taking this seriously, are we?'

'We wouldn't be,' Mia says, 'if it weren't for this.'

She clicks the remote control again and two images appear on the screen, side by side, causing a surge of shock to pulse over the room.

It's the necklace. And the charm bracelet. On what looks like today's papers.

'I have digital forensics looking into these images to check their authenticity,' she says. 'But unless we hear otherwise, we need to treat this as though it's real. Jimi, I need you to go speak to Jacqueline, find out why she was the one who this letter was sent to.'

'Got it,' Jimi says.

'Are we thinking that whoever sent this could be some kind of accomplice to Ryan?' Christine asks.

'Could be,' Mia replies. 'Let's question Mr Mills again, see if he'll talk now.'

An hour later, I'm at the prison, sitting opposite Ryan in an interview room, wishing I could read people enough to know without any doubt whether he's telling me the truth. He's gaunt, and his skin is pallid, these past few days in prison already taking their toll. Judging by the dark smudges under his eyes, I'm guessing he's not getting a lot of sleep in here.

'Do you know anyone who goes by the name The Puppeteer?'

His face twists in confusion. This clearly wasn't the line of questioning he was expecting.

'The what?'

'The Puppeteer,' I repeat.

'No,' he says, the word coming out more as a question than a statement. 'What kind of name is that?'

'The name of the person claiming responsibility for the murders,' I say.

'Wait,' Ryan says, a light sparking behind his eyes. 'You mean you know it wasn't me?'

'Not exactly,' I say, handing him a printout of the letter that was published on the Channel Eight website just moments before I walked in here. As he reads the page the receptionist printed for me, his skin changes from white to a kind of washed-out grey colour. I think he might be sick.

He looks up at me, his eyes brimming with terror.

'What is this?' he asks, his hand shaking so much the paper is flapping against the table.

'We just received it today,' I explain. 'Along with these.'

I hand him another sheet of paper, which shows the two

photographs we received. His eyes grow even wider. He falls silent for a long moment, the claims of what he's just read sinking in.

'So it's real?' he asks eventually.

'We're trying to find that out right now,' I say. 'But, Ryan, if you had an accomplice, you could have your jail time reduced significantly for telling us who it is.'

He stares at me again, his expression stony.

'I don't have an accomplice,' he says, 'because I didn't do anything. You need to find whoever this is.' He jabs at the paper with a long, pale finger. 'This is the person responsible, not me. They even admit to it.'

'Are you suggesting to me that what The Puppeteer claims they did is true? That you've been brainwashed?'

Ryan slumps into his chair, defeated. There's no logical explanation for this, nothing that will make the letter make sense. What we need isn't a guess, or a desperate grasping at straws. We just need the unfiltered truth.

'I'm not saying I've been brainwashed,' he says, his eyes widening as though an idea has just occurred to him. 'But what if I've been hypnotised?'

I look hard at him. Is he having me on?

'Ryan, either you did it, or you didn't do it. If you think you could have somehow been manipulated into this, it means you did it. Is that really the way you want this to go?'

'Listen,' he says urgently. 'I've seen the pictures from the CCTV footage, and I can't explain it to you. I'm not lying, I just don't know how the hell I showed up on camera when I swear to you I was at home on the couch, asleep. Same for the DNA. I wasn't there. At least, consciously, I wasn't. What if this actually explains it?'

'But wouldn't you know if you'd been hypnotised?'

'I don't know,' he admits. 'I've never – to my knowledge – been hypnotised, so I couldn't tell you what it feels like.'

An icy cold finger runs a trail up my spine as I consider the implications of what he's suggesting – of what this person claiming to be The Puppeteer is suggesting.

'Think about it,' he urges. 'I'm assuming you know whether these pictures were photoshopped or not?'

'We're authenticating them now.'

'OK, but if they come back as being real, then what? Then you have to give weight to what this guy's saying. And you might not believe it but I've seen some pretty crazy hypnosis in my time. Haven't you seen that Derren Brown show where he made people rob an armed guard, or where that guy pushed someone off a roof?'

'Yes, I've seen them.' The shows he's talking about intrigued and horrified me in equal measure.

'So then you know. You know it's possible, if someone's suggestible enough, to make them do something crazy. Maybe there are some triggers or something that set me off, like songs or . . . I don't know, pictures or something.'

'Ryan, those shows are theatre. They're performance. The Puppeteer even hints at it in that note. No one can prove that what happens on those shows is legitimate, they could all be actors.'

'Come on. You don't actually believe that, do you? Just because you don't like the idea of people being manipulated doesn't mean it can't happen. And it's not just hypothetical; I'm not just clutching at straws here. I mean . . . I feel like a traitor to Gina for even suggesting this, but . . . You've seen what Julian can do, haven't you?'

Ryan pauses to let the meaning of his words sink in. My heart starts beating faster. And faster still, until it builds to a crescendo and my blood is racing through my veins. Julian.

He made a guy speak fluent Russian without skipping a beat. I saw the video. He's good. And it's true that other illusionists have made people do some crazy things under hypnosis.

'Do you really think . . . ?'

'Well,' Ryan says, 'it's not impossible. I know it sounds far-fetched, but the facts add up.'

I stare at him, calculating what he's saying. What if Julian really is that good? If he is, who's to say he couldn't hypnotise Ryan into murder? A perfect puppet, dangling on his strings.

'I have to go,' I say, standing up suddenly.

'Wait!' Ryan yells, getting to his feet. 'You believe me?'

I don't respond. I can't. 'I need to speak to Julian.'

Chapter 36

1996

SHARON

A high-pitched giggle drifts through the air from the back-yard, and I feel a smile teasing the corners of my mouth.

Judy found her rabbit, Chase. And my kids are, categoric-ally, not killers.

I feel awful for Judy, knowing exactly the pain and fear that she's experiencing, and terrified now that I know there really is someone out there murdering innocent creatures. The police suggested that it might have been a fox that killed her fluffy white pet, but she knows better. I do, too.

Tears spring to my eyes but I immediately scold myself for being weak. If the kids are moving on, so should I.

As I peel and chop potatoes, I savour the sound of their yelling as it reaches me from outside. They're probably play-ing pirates again, Ryan's favourite. Or princes and princesses, Cassie's favourite. Gina mostly has to go along with whoever is most dominant – the stronger, older brother or the baby of the family. They seem to be getting into whatever game they've decided on, as the volume is increasing, along with the intensity.

And then, suddenly, a wail.

My heart stops. I listen hard. Bill always tells me I'm too soft, that I should just let them play, let them fall and scratch themselves and learn from their mistakes. My instinct is to run to them, to kiss them better, to save them from even the smallest amount of pain. There will be enough of that later in life. They don't need it now, too. More often than not I can't hold back, and I run outside, frantic, only to find them laughing it off, or brushing themselves down, mocking silly Mummy for worrying. Again.

So I wait, stock-still, pleading silently for everything to be OK, waiting for a giggle to ring out so I can get back to making dinner.

But there's just silence. And then feet, pounding through the back door. In a few strides, I meet Ryan halfway, his pale eyes wide, his face a picture of fright.

'Mum, it's Cassie!'

'What happened?' I ask, already moving towards the back garden.

'You have to help,' he says, and my blood chills in my veins.

'Mum, I . . . she's hurt. She's not moving. I think she might be dead.'

Chapter 37

2017

GINA

'I don't know.'

It's the same three words I've repeated over and over again for the past hour. It's like I'm speaking into a void, except in reality my words are being recorded in multiple ways. There are the two cameras, peering at me from two corners of the room. I'm certain the audio is being saved somewhere. We're being observed through the two-way mirror I'm facing. And, of course, there are the notepads of the two detectives, currently being furiously scribbled in as though I've said something new.

I feel like I'm in some kind of loop with no chance of escape. *Groundhog Day*, but without the comedy. I'm sitting in the same interview room, with the same cops, holding the same cup of weak, tepid tea. Answering the same unanswerable questions.

'Why didn't you report him missing when he first disappeared?'

I stare at the detective in disbelief.

'I've already told you.'

'Why don't you explain it to me again? I'm struggling to understand.'

I sigh, and try to remain patient. I want Julian back as much as they do, although for completely different reasons.

'One,' I say, tapping my index finger, 'he texted me saying he was fine and not to worry. Two. He's a grown man, not a vulnerable child. And three, I kind of had bigger things to be worrying about than my boyfriend not calling me back, you know? Not sure if you heard, but my brother was just arrested and charged with murder.'

The final word catches in my throat. I swallow forcefully. These detectives have seen enough of my emotion to last a lifetime. Right now, I have to focus.

'And you have no idea where he might have disappeared to?'

'If I knew, don't you think I would have tried to get hold of him?'

'If you could just answer the question, please, Miss Mills—'

'No, I don't know where he's disappeared to. Look, we're going around in circles. I've already answered all of your questions – multiple times – so unless you're going to charge me for something, like not keeping tabs on my boyfriend, then I'm going home.'

It's not Constable Adebayo's fault – I know he's just doing his job – but I'm fed up, so he's bearing the brunt of it. All I want is to talk to Julian. I'm desperate to see his face, hear his voice, feel his arms around me.

'We're not arresting you,' says Constable Taylor, sounding deflated. 'You're free to go. But just so you know, we're currently processing a search warrant for Mr Hoskins' home, and when that comes through, we'll have a team arriving over there shortly.'

This catches me by surprise.

'Why are you searching his flat?'

'We can't discuss details of the case with you, I'm afraid, Miss Mills.'

'Why are you wasting time looking in his apartment? He's not there – I've already checked. Why aren't you looking for *him*?'

'As I said, I'm not able to discuss specific details of the case,' she says apologetically.

I breathe in deeply to calm myself, and stand up.

'Before you go,' the detective says. 'Are you certain he's never hypnotised you?'

'No! How many times do I have to tell you? I never wanted to try it, and he respected that. Why do you find that so hard to believe?'

'We're just covering all possible angles, Miss Mills. And to that effect, we're assigning an officer to watch your place, just in case Julian comes after you. At this point, we're concerned for your safety.'

'No you're not,' I say. 'You think, like Ryan does, that I'm some kind of ticking hypnosis time bomb, and you want to make sure I'm not going to go out and kill anyone.'

'Miss Mills—'

'You don't need to deny it,' I say. 'But I want you to know that you're wrong. And instead of supposedly worrying about my safety, maybe you should actually start worrying about Julian's safety. Because no matter what you think, Julian would never just leave me without an explanation. He's not like that. Something is seriously wrong, it has to be, and you're the only ones who can find out what it is. Please, please don't give up on him.'

Constable Taylor looks at me for a long moment, and then nods once, curtly.

'We're not giving up, Gina,' she says, shuffling her file. 'Believe me, we want answers just as much as you do.'

251

Chapter 38

DETECTIVE ADAM ADEBAYO

I ring the doorbell and wait. I'm not expecting him to come to the door, but you never know. This case has been one episode of crazy after another, so I'm not sure if anything would surprise me at this point.

Silence.

I try again, then force the end of the tool that I carried from the car into the doorjamb. It doesn't take much pressure for the wood to give way, and once the lock snaps with a metallic crunch I push the door easily, grateful for the Methods of Entry training I was sent on a few months ago. Without it, I'd have needed a whole team behind me to get inside.

'Julian Hoskins?' I shout. 'Julian, it's the Metropolitan Police. We have a search warrant, so officers are now entering your property. If you're here, please make yourself known immediately.'

Nothing. The silence doesn't come as a surprise. Unmarked cars have been monitoring the property since Julian's name was first uttered in relation to The Puppeteer yesterday, and there's been no sign of him in that time. As Gina claimed, he seems to have disappeared altogether.

'OK,' I say to Christine, who's waiting patiently behind me. 'Let's go.'

The place is pristine. Eerily so. Christine's sharp intake of breath next to me mirrors my thoughts.

'It's like a bloody display home,' she breathes.

The thing that strikes me most about the space at first is that it's so white. The floor is made up of glistening white tiles, the grout unblemished. The walls are perfectly white, and the few pieces of furniture scattered around the place – a sofa, a coffee table, a side table – are all white, too. He's even moved his books so the pages are facing outwards instead of the spines. It's consistent, clean . . . and completely soulless. Nothing in here is expensive – I think I have the same Ikea sideboard at home – but arranged the way it is, and with no clutter in sight, the whole effect is that of a space carefully arranged by someone with an eye for design.

The only splashes of colour, which, against the stark white surroundings, look positively garish, are a huge green plant in the corner of the living room and what looks like a reproduction Dali painting, if my high school art classes taught me anything. The gold, dripping clock and blue sky are so bright against all that white that I can't tear my eyes away from the canvas.

We walk slowly through each room, on high alert in case Julian is hiding . . . or worse. It doesn't take long to clear each of the rooms. The place is spotless. Not a speck of dust, or a single book out of place. The guy must be obsessive compulsive or a total germaphobe.

But there are a few signs of disorder, which we note as we go. A closet door left slightly ajar, empty coat hangers dotted between suits and shirts, and the slightly creased duvet. In my own room, this would be considered miraculously tidy, but here it creates an air of complete chaos.

'So we're going for fled rather than dead, yeah?' asks Christine.

'Looks like it,' I say. 'Although Gina's been here already, which could also explain the disruption. Still doesn't tell us anything though. I'll take the kitchen and hallway, you take the bedroom and bathroom, we'll both take the living room and see if we can find anything at all.'

I still don't know exactly what I suspect Julian of. Ryan was clearly the person who killed those women, but Julian's the key to all of our unanswered questions, I'm sure of it. The trouble is, to explain how I think he could be involved, I have to admit that I believe in The Puppeteer as a concept. Except I'm not even sure I do believe it. I keep going back and forth in my mind, scolding myself for being too gullible and then recalling the facts and deciding that maybe, just maybe, it *is* possible.

My willingness to even entertain the idea comes back to the look on Ryan's face when I showed him the pictures of himself in the CCTV footage. I've interviewed a lot of liars in my time, some of whom were incredibly talented. But you can't fake the kind of complete shock, the utter horror, that I saw in Ryan's eyes that day.

He wasn't upset in the way that most criminals are when they realise that the evidence against them is irrefutable. He wasn't annoyed that he'd been caught out in a lie, or defensive about the details. He was, quite simply, in disbelief.

He says he doesn't remember being out of the house on either of those evenings, and stands by his claims that he was at home, on the sofa, watching TV and quite possibly napping.

And then we have the facts about Julian. He's a hypnotist. Whether his skills are anywhere near as advanced as the so-called Puppeteer is questionable, but the Russian trick he pulled at his show was impressive, so much so that it's caught the attention of some high-profile magicians and illusionists. He knows Ryan and Gina extremely well. Whether he knows them well enough to manipulate them into murder, or colluding with him to murder someone... that, I don't know. But what I do know is that he's gone. And he disappeared right when the evidence started to point in his direction.

'Are you kidding me?' Christine had moaned when I'd told her I wanted a search warrant for Julian's house. 'You can't honestly believe this Puppeteer guy is for real? We have our guy. It's Ryan.'

'You can't just write it off because it's unlikely,' I'd argued. 'And I'm not saying I definitely believe it, but Julian's vanished, right when claims of mind control came out. And Julian can hypnotise people.'

'Yeah, he made some guy spout off some phrases in another language,' Christine had shot back. 'Murder is hardly the next trick in the book.'

'OK, but have you seen the TV illusionist who makes people rob the guy carrying cash at gunpoint?'

She'd rolled her eyes at me. 'That guy? He's just a showman. That wouldn't work in real life.'

'Maybe,' I'd replied. 'Maybe not. But will you just back me on this search. Please? If it's nothing, drinks are on me next time we go to the pub.'

'Fine,' she'd said. 'About time you bought a round anyway.'

The warrant was approved more easily than I'd expected, and now we're here and I'm mentally crossing my fingers and my toes that this search won't be in vain. There's a risk that Gina found – and removed – anything incriminating when she came here after Julian's disappearance. But there's also a chance that she missed something, or that she didn't think to look. She seems to be blindly positive that her boyfriend is innocent. A victim, even. Which only adds to my mounting suspicion that she's been hypnotised herself.

But I'm hopeful. In part, because if we don't find anything, I'll be the laughing stock of the office.

I've rummaged through the kitchen, lifting every plate and pot, and checking the underside of the countertop, and even the freezer. There's nothing there. Christine's gone through Julian's bedroom, and she's also come up short. She takes her search to the bathroom and I begin to scour the hallway, losing faith in myself with every passing minute.

I riffle through the pockets of each of the jackets hanging up at the front door, and then move on to the two pairs of shoes placed neatly side by side on the floor below, shaking them in case something's hidden in the toe. Nothing.

I move on to the sideboard, a glossy white thing with no visible handles and nothing cluttering the surface. I push the door and it pops open. Inside is a small collection of mail – bills, mostly – a set of keys, a shoe cleaning kit, and a box of old electrical cords and plugs. I pull them out, dropping a wall charger as I do so. It bounces off the floor and lands with a clunk underneath the sideboard.

Rummaging through the box reveals nothing but a tangle of cords, so I put it back and go through the rest of the sideboard bit by bit, making sure I haven't missed anything. I'm about to close it when I remember the charger. Usually, I'd just leave it. But there's something about the order of this place that makes me want to keep everything exactly as I found it.

Sighing, I get onto my knees and lean over until I can see under the sideboard. Julian must clean frequently – there's no dust, even in this hidden corner of the house.

I reach under and my fingers brush the edge of the plug. I stretch a bit further and flick it towards me. It slides easily along the tiles, and, along with it, something small skitters along the floor. I throw the plug back into the box, close the sideboard, and look around.

It's easy to spot – it's the only thing out of place. It looks like a bead, or a small piece of hardware.

As I move closer, my skin begins to tingle. Heat rushes to my face and I get down onto my hands and knees to get a better look at the tiny, silver object.

'Christine,' I yell. 'Christine, I think I've got something.'

She rushes into the hallway. 'What is it?'

'Careful,' I say, putting my arm out to stop her from accidentally stepping on it. 'Here. Take a look.'

She drops to the ground and peers at the tiny metal giraffe. It's about a centimetre tall, and very delicate, like one rough touch could snap it in two. On the giraffe's head is a tiny metal loop. The kind that's used to thread charms onto a bracelet.

'Oh my God,' she breathes. 'Do you think it's . . . ?'

'I don't know,' I say, 'but we need to get forensics over here.'

In what feels like just minutes, the house is swarming. There are people in white protective suits in every room of Julian's home. They're taking photographs, sweeping surfaces with cotton buds and bagging up his belongings. The eerie calm we walked into has now turned into a hive of activity.

'I'd say you've found a trophy,' says the forensic guy, whose name I can never remember – Casper? Carter? – with a grimace.

He's holding up a gloved hand, and pinched between his thumb and forefinger is the giraffe.

'Are we sure it's hers?'

'We can't be certain until we get the DNA results, but it matches the photograph we have of the bracelet.'

I know that picture. I've looked at it dozens of times. The chunky silver chain was exploding with charms: a horse and a pumpkin and a coffee cup and a hammer. All seemingly unrelated, but according to Angela's distraught mum, each one held significance for her. The giraffe, apparently, was to commemorate a family trip to the zoo.

Christine walks up to me and punches me lightly in the arm.

'Looks like I owe you a drink,' she says with a smile.

'Yeah, well, it's not really enough to give us any answers,' I say. 'It looks like he probably dropped it on his way out. There were so many charms on that bracelet that he wouldn't have noticed it was gone. And besides, he's still disappeared, hasn't he?'

'Cheer up,' Christine says. 'This is a win, and a bloody big one, too. Give yourself a break, OK? I just got off the phone to Mia and she's issuing a press release along with a reward for information leading to his arrest. You'll get your answers.'

I wish I could believe her. But if this guy can make someone kill for him, I'm certain he can make himself disappear. He's a magician, after all.

'Besides,' she continues, 'we've got Ryan. The evidence on him is solid. We got our killer, OK? And now we know who his accomplice was and what happened to the missing jewellery. We won. The bad guys lost. Justice prevails, or whatever cheesy platitude is going to make you see some sense.'

I offer her a thin smile. I should be pleased but there are too many unanswered questions still buzzing around in my head. It's not enough to just know *who* has the jewellery.

Now I need to know the why. And the how.

Because, right now, all of the evidence suggests that Julian is The Puppeteer, and that he really did what he claimed to have done.

'But if Ryan was hypnotised—' I begin, but my partner cuts me off with a groan.

'This again?' she says. 'Adam, you have to let that go. Here's what happened: Ryan killed those women, some kind of suppressed anger about what happened to his sister as a kid. He got the jewellery to Julian somehow, and made sure the kills happened on Gina's route home so he'd get the coverage, make a name for himself as a murderer. That's what most serial killers want, isn't it? Notoriety. And Julian wanted to be seen as some kind of master magician, which is why he went along with it, and now that he's got people talking about him, he's buggered off. End of story.'

I watch her as she tries to convince me of what everyone's been saying. But I can't accept it. It doesn't feel right. It doesn't feel like justice.

'Come on,' says Christine, sensing that she's not breaking through my doubts. 'Let's go get a drink, at least celebrate this win. Tomorrow you can start again, you can argue with me all you want. But right now, I need a beer and it looks like you do, too. And as it turns out, I'm buying.'

Chapter 39

RYAN

I think they might be right. It's possible that I am, in fact, a murderer.

But it doesn't ring true, despite the proof. It's as though someone has told me I'm a brain surgeon, and then shown evidence of me performing a complicated operation inside someone's head. I feel absolutely no connection to it, I know it's not possible, but somehow the facts check out. I roll the word around in my mouth – murderer – trying it on, determining whether it fits. It's uncomfortable and sharp. It lodges in my throat, suffocating me.

'Mills!'

I sit up, startled out of my thoughts, and turn to the window in my cell door, where the voice came from.

'Visitor.'

My heart leaps, and then sinks when I remember that it's probably just the police, here to ask me more of the same questions that I can't answer. I trudge behind the guard, trying to steel myself for the interrogation I know is coming. We get to the interview room, and the guard keeps walking.

'Where are we going?'

'Visitors' room,' he grunts, and my heart does a little flip before I force myself to expect nothing. I can't let myself hope. It could be anyone, I remind myself.

It's only when I see her sitting there, when I drink in that flaming hair and those vivid green eyes, that I allow myself to believe that she's all right.

'Gina,' I say, my lungs singing with relief. 'Thank goodness you're OK.'

She looks at me, takes me all in. I do the same to her, noticing how much her cheeks have hollowed, even in the last ten days, giving her face a sharper, more angular look.

'You are OK, right?'

Since the detective came to see me about the letter, since the idea of hypnosis first sparked, I've been terrified for my sister, convinced that Julian got to her, too. Because if he could somehow manipulate me into doing the unthinkable, how much more could he do with her, who he spent so much more time with, who he knew so much better? She trusted him implicitly. Which would make her the perfect puppet.

'Ryan,' she says, ignoring my question. Her voice is low and scratchy. 'Have you seen? They found evidence at Julian's house. I don't understand...'

She seems bewildered. When they told me about the charm from Angela's bracelet, when they said that they were searching for Julian as an accomplice, I'd not been surprised. It was relief I'd felt. Because if they're looking for Julian, based on the contents of that letter, then they must also believe in The Puppeteer. Which means there's hope for me.

When I'd next spoken to my lawyer, he'd broken the bad news.

'This doesn't change anything for you, Ryan,' he'd said bluntly. I'd come to appreciate his no-nonsense approach. It was like taking a shot of vodka, straight-up, no mixers. It made me wince, but the sting of it dissipated in a couple of seconds.

'But . . . they know Julian's The Puppeteer. That means I'm innocent, right?'

'They're not saying they believe all of his claims,' Thompson had said. 'They believe what the evidence tells them. So far all they have on Julian is the jewellery, which doesn't prove that he was directly responsible for either of the murders, and there's no proof whatsoever that this mind-control stuff is real. In any case, the jewellery could have been sent to him after the fact. You have to remember, Ryan, he was in completely different cities when the murders took place. His alibis are absolutely airtight. But the evidence on you is unchanged. Your trial is still going ahead, and we need to talk about our defence strategy.'

His defence strategy, I knew, was for me to claim some kind of mental incompetence. Diminished responsibility, he'd said, on the grounds of a psychotic break. It could mean a shorter sentence, or even some kind of psychiatric institution instead of prison.

And maybe that *is* what's really happened. At least, that's what I'm trying to convince myself of. Only . . . I don't know if psychosis is any better than the alternative, because either way, no one is claiming that I didn't kill Michelle and Angela. I'm trapped between two impossible theories: mind control or psychosis. There isn't a third option. There's no way out. It eats away at me, every minute of every bleak day.

I wake up in the morning feeling like there's a lead brick pressing on my ribs, crushing my lungs, my heart. My soul. I start my day knowing what they've told me about what I've done, the images of the women I supposedly killed waiting to greet me as I enter consciousness.

The panic is fresh, every day. It's crippling. The questions, so many of them, scream at me from inside my head until I feel like I might explode. I have to press my palms against my ears to try to block them. I hum, I shout until my voice is raw, but it doesn't work. The unanswerable questions persist. Maybe I *am* crazy. It's starting to feel like I'm coming unhinged, anyway. Because I *know* I didn't kill those women. But I also know I did. Which means I can't trust anything I feel, or think, or believe, any more.

I inspect my sister, silent, across the table from me, tears streaming down her face. I mentally slap myself. What an insensitive idiot. Whatever I believe about Julian, whatever I feel towards him, doesn't change the fact that my sister is heartbroken. And scared. I reach across the space between us and squeeze her hand.

'I'm really sorry, Gina,' I say. 'I can't imagine what you're going through right now. But you know, you deserve better than that—'

'What?'

She pulls her hand away from mine as though I've burned her.

'Julian is my soulmate,' she snaps. 'I don't deserve better, because there's no one else out there for me. Don't ever say that.'

'But the letter . . . Gina, he's The Puppeteer.'

'There's no proof of that!'

'Gina,' I say, keeping my voice down so our visit isn't cut short. 'Think about it. Julian disappeared. I was arrested for something I didn't do. Then that letter was sent to Jacqueline – who's his friend – talking about mind control, which is basically another word for hypnosis. You have to at least *consider* that it could be true.'

'But it's Julian. He'd never hurt anyone.'

'That's what he made you believe,' I say. 'But what if he's hypnotised you, too?'

She slaps her palm on the table. 'He'd never do that!'

'OK.' I hold my hands up. 'But will you at least promise me that you'll be extra careful? I know you don't believe Julian would do this, but just on the tiniest chance that he's not who you think he is, I'm just worried you're in danger. Or that he'll make you do something, like he did to me.'

She looks away, her jaw set. She doesn't make any such promise, but she doesn't refuse, either, which is a start.

Gina believes in Julian. Blindly. She thinks something terrible has happened to him. She's afraid that he's a victim.

I think something terrible has happened, too. Only I don't believe that Julian's the one she needs to be worried about. She won't believe me, I know that. But I want to somehow make her at least understand the danger she could be in. Because I'm behind bars. I can't hurt anyone now. But what if Gina has also been conditioned into doing something terrible?

What if the worst-case scenario is that I'm just the start of his plan?

Maybe she won't listen now, but if I push her away then I'll never have the chance to convince her. I have to tread carefully. I clear my throat.

'The prosecution is going to say he was my accomplice,' I say. 'At trial.'

'I heard,' she says softly. 'They also think I was hypnotised into finding those women.'

That's new information to me. I frown. 'How *did* you find them?'

Even before I was charged, back when I couldn't have even dreamed of becoming tangled up in all of this, I'd wondered the same thing. Everyone had. I'd asked, but she'd been vague. Evasive, even.

'I just . . . I just did, Ryan,' she says. 'I was just walking home, and there they were.'

'So it could have been hypnosis?'

'No,' she says firmly. 'Why doesn't anyone believe me? He would never hypnotise me, not without my permission. I just . . . I just found them. I can't explain it.'

I nod. I think, deep down, she knows that Julian is not who he said he was, that he's capable of terrible things. But she's not ready to admit it yet. I remember being envious of what Gina and Julian had, of their complete, unquestioning love for one another. But if loving someone so deeply can leave you this vulnerable, this blind . . . then I'm glad I've never found my soulmate.

'Look,' she says. 'I don't know what happened. But obviously there's an explanation they just haven't thought of yet, OK? I don't think anyone actually believes that what the letter said is true, but it just means they can wrap up their case and tell the public the bad guy is behind bars.'

Her eyes widen as she realises what she's just said.

'Ryan, I didn't mean—'

'It's fine,' I say. 'Bad guy is about the nicest thing I've been called lately.'

'Is it awful?' she asks. 'In here?'

'It's not great,' I admit wearily. 'But for now, because I haven't been convicted of a crime, it's not too bad. After the trial though . . .'

Thompson has never promised that the insanity plea will work. He wanted me to plead guilty all along, but I refused. The one thing I won't do is go down without a fight. But our play is risky. A jury might see my psychosis as an easy way out, as a get-out-of-jail-free card, rather than just another plot in this living nightmare. They'll be presented with compelling evidence, evidence that even I struggle to argue with, despite everything. I can't expect them to believe something different just because I'm telling the truth.

The realisation that I might spend my life behind bars has been sinking in, little by little, the horror of it matched with the very smallest portion of relief. In here, The Puppeteer can't get me. In here, I can't kill someone without remembering it.

I wake up multiple times each night, silent screams catching at my throat as I try to convince myself that I haven't killed someone else without realising. Mum, Dad, Gina, friends at work, casual acquaintances . . . they've all been found dead in my dreams, and I've been the one to blame. The evidence, of course, is irrefutable.

I'm scared. Of being here. Of never living my life again. But mostly, I'm scared of myself. I'm terrified that I'm truly a monster at heart. Because I've researched hypnosis. There's a book on it, here in the prison library. You can't be hypnotised, it claims, into doing something you wouldn't ordinarily do.

I haven't mentioned that to anyone. Because if it's true, and even if The Puppeteer is real, then no matter what he did, I am a killer. Whether I want to believe it or not.

'I went to see Cassie the other day,' Gina says in a whisper, changing the subject.

For a split second, my heart stops. A flare of hope sparks inside me, until logic takes hold once again and I realise what Gina means. Cassie, or what now remains of her, is in the cemetery near our house. I work hard to keep my expression neutral, to hide my irrational reaction.

'Oh, yeah?' I ask, concentrating on keeping the tremor from my voice. I'm annoyed at myself. I know she's gone. Why does my mind keep convincing me – even for a moment – that she's still around?

'I haven't been to her grave for so long,' she continues. 'I couldn't face it. But with you in here, and Julian . . . well,

I guess I just needed someone to talk to. I'm sorry, I know you don't want to hear about it—'

'No. No,' I insist. 'It's not that I don't want to hear about it. It's, well, you know. It's hard. Every time you say her name it brings it back, and I wish I could change the past. I really, really do. But I can't, so it's easier for me just to pretend she never existed. I know that's hard for you, and I know you wanted to talk about her. I just . . . I can't. I'm sorry.'

She looks down at her hands and my eyes follow her gaze. Her nails are ragged and torn, her cuticles raw. I imagine her sitting on the sofa at night, eyes wild, chewing her fingers with no one to talk to, her boyfriend vanished and her brother in jail.

'They're saying you got notes from her?' Gina asks, a tremor in her voice.

'I got a note, yeah,' I reply. 'From someone claiming they knew what happened to her. I know it can't have been from her, I know she's gone, but I couldn't explain it. I still can't.'

'Why didn't you tell me?'

'Really?' I ask. 'You really have to ask that? What would you have said if you'd come home and I told you that I got a note that sounded like it was from our dead sister?'

She winces, and looks down.

'OK, fair enough. Who do you think sent it though?'

'I wish I knew,' I say. I have my suspicions, of course. But I know exactly how she'll react if I try to blame him for something again, so I leave it. 'I feel like someone's been trying to mess with my head, and it's working. I had all these nightmares about Cassie. I even thought I saw her on the train one day.'

Gina's head whips up.

267

'It wasn't her,' I say forcefully. 'It can't have been. She's gone, Gina.'

She sighs. 'I know. I just ... I miss her, every day. Still.'

'Me too,' I say. 'I miss her, and I feel so guilty. Part of me thinks that I deserve to be here. Not just for those women, but for Cassie. Like finally my past is catching up with me.'

'That's not the same thing,' Gina says, frowning. 'You didn't mean—'

'Yes. I did. I didn't mean to kill her, obviously. But I was angry at her. It's what I've realised since I started having those nightmares. She thought I killed Pickles, and she kept saying it and I was so angry at her for not believing me, because of course I didn't kill the damn cat. I just wanted her to shut up, so I pushed her, and she tripped. And then—'

My voice breaks with emotion. Since the dreams started, since I saw my baby sister on the train that day, the memories have risen up like a geyser, the pressure of being suppressed rupturing the barrier I'd so carefully constructed, drowning me in the truth I never wanted to admit. That day, all those years ago, it's as vivid now as if it were yesterday, and I feel everything again when I let the recollection surface. Fear, anger, stark terror. And then the guilt. I swallow it down, and keep going. I have to say this. I have to face it, finally.

'And then I let you take the blame, Gina. I just convinced myself that because Mum said you did it, that maybe you really did do it, that maybe my push had nothing to do with Cassie's death, even though the coroner said it was the head injury. I let her hate you, and I let her treat you the way she did the whole time we were growing up, when it was me all along.'

'We were just kids, Ryan,' she says urgently. 'That doesn't

268

make you a killer. A coward, yes. A little boy with a temper, maybe. But you're not an animal.'

'Yes, I am,' I say. It feels good to get the words out. 'I know we were kids, but I still pushed her. And I've seen that CCTV footage, and the DNA reports. I can't keep making excuses, Gina. I'm a murderer. I killed those women. And I killed our sister.'

She stares at me, as if calculating my sincerity. Then she nods slowly.

'I've waited a long time for that,' she whispers.

'For what?'

'For you to finally admit what really happened with Cassie. I always thought you blamed me, like everyone else did. That's why I couldn't talk about it for years after. I'd had enough of that from Mum, I couldn't bear to be punished by you, too, not when I knew the truth. I thought it'd be better not to talk about it, to move on, to look forward rather than backwards. I saw you pushing her that day, I saw everything, but I've never had the guts to ask what you really thought about what happened. I couldn't bear for you to say that you thought I killed her, too.'

'This whole time, you thought I blamed you?' I ask, aghast.

'It doesn't matter now,' she says sharply. 'What's done is done.'

She sits back heavily in her chair, ending the subject. But I can't let it go that easily.

'I know it's probably far too late,' I say hesitantly, 'but do you think you'll ever be able to forgive me?'

'Forgive you?' Her eyes widen. 'What good is my forgiveness? It won't change the fact that you're here. Or that Cassie's dead, or that Mum and Dad are gone.'

'Still,' I say. 'I want it anyway.'

She smiles, and my chest swells with hope.

'Maybe,' she says, and I feel myself deflating a little. 'Maybe one day. But not yet.'

I nod. It's all I could have hoped for.

It's more than I deserve.

Chapter 40

1996

SHARON

In the years that are to come, I will analyse every single second of this afternoon. I'll go over and over and over the moments that followed Ryan's panicked entrance from the backyard, combing it for clues. I'll try to remember, I'll desperately attempt to find something new in my memories of that day. To understand. To get to the truth.

But I don't know that yet.

Right now, I am possessed by my own fear.

When I hear the words *I think she might be dead*, every cell in my body howls in terror. My mind grinds to a halt, goes completely blank, and then heaves forward at double speed, trying to process what my son has just told me.

He must be mistaken. Children are dramatic. She's probably just playing. Pretending. I should laugh it off, follow him to the back garden, playfully scold my munchkins for scaring me this way.

But what if he's not mistaken?

Oh, God. What if he's not mistaken?

My fingers tremble as I pull the phone from its place on the wall, hitting the number nine three times, forcefully. I wait for the operator, and I explain that I think my daughter's hurt, that I need an ambulance, that they have to hurry, and then I offer our address and hang up, staggering

271

through the kitchen and out the door, where I sprint for the back of the garden, without waiting for Ryan to follow.

I don't know how long it's been since he said those four words to me. It could be seconds or minutes. I'll probably never know.

As I stride across the lawn, dodging toys and colourful bottles once filled with juice, I see Gina huddled over a mess of pink fabric. Cassie. I'd let her dress herself when she got home from school this afternoon. She's headstrong about her clothes, and today I didn't feel like fighting. She flounced down the stairs in her favourite pink dress, the one usually reserved for birthday parties or our annual trip to church with my parents on Christmas morning, along with her purple wellies. And, of course, that Minnie Mouse watch that she got for her birthday, the one she refuses to take off, even at bath time. She was practically begging for a reaction, for a fight, but I didn't so much as raise an eyebrow.

Today, I didn't want an argument. They were all having fun, laughing together. I didn't want to ruin that over the thought of some extra washing.

But now she's lying with her legs folded under her, her dress torn on the side, her arms out as though she'd tried to regain her balance mid-fall.

Gina's body is blocking her face. I run, I stumble, I reach them and for just a second I don't see it. This is the moment – although I don't know it now – that I'll be forced to watch again and again in my dreams, in my nightmares. The moment that will spell the end of my family as I know it. That will change my life for ever.

But right now it's a moment that seeps in far too slowly, taking precious seconds to comprehend.

Gina is crouched over her sister, bent low, and as she

hears me approaching she springs back, making way for the sight I will never forget.

My baby girl's eyes are closed. And her head is resting in a puddle of red. The puddle is growing, seeping out of her, and I know, in that second, although every cell in my body wishes for it to be a lie.

Cassie is dead.

Chapter 41

2017

DETECTIVE ADAM ADEBAYO

'Cheers,' Mia says, raising her pint towards the middle of the table.

I clink my own glass against a few others, but my heart isn't in it. We shouldn't be acting like we've had some kind of victory. The case is still open, and it's a total mess. With countless loose ends, and so many holes in our theories, it's basically just a tangle of threads. So there's nothing satisfying about it, nothing to celebrate, and yet, here we are.

'You all did an exceptional job,' Mia is shouting above the noise of the pub. 'The circumstances were unusual at best, and definitely made the job harder, but each one of you rose to the challenge.'

More clinking glasses, more smiles I can't return.

'And I've been asked by the prosecutor on this case to say an enormous thank you to you all. They're confident that with the evidence you all uncovered, they'll secure a conviction quickly. So here's to a good night's sleep, at least for one night until the work begins again!'

There's spontaneous applause, laughter, and even more glass clinking. I can't handle the complete denial of the obvious that's going on right in front of me. With a scrape that makes me wince, I push my stool away from the table and take my beer outside. It's cold, but I don't care. At least out here I don't have to pretend to be elated.

A few moments later the door swings open and Christine walks out, a glass of wine in her left hand, a cigarette in the other.

'I thought you gave up,' I say accusingly.

'I did,' she says. 'I'm not actually going to smoke it. I just need something to do with my hands if I'm going to stand out here and talk you out of acting like such a grumpy git.'

I sigh, annoyed, and snap, 'I didn't ask you to come out here. Go back in, enjoy the party.'

'Don't be like that,' she says, looking hurt. 'I was just trying to make you laugh.'

I don't say anything. I'm sulking. I know it's childish, and I know that none of this is Christine's fault, but I can't very well have it out with Mia or her superiors. I'm using my partner as a punching bag, and I hate myself for it, but whenever I open my mouth it seems to just tumble out. So I stay silent.

'Look,' she says after taking a long sip of wine. 'I get it. I know why you're upset. This case was an absolute ball ache, and it messed with all of our heads. And trust me, Adam, I'd love to have some more closure. You think the rest of us don't have a million questions about what the hell really happened with those girls? Of course we do. But we know that you don't always get to tie up your cases in a neat, pretty bow. You know that, too. So yeah, we don't have all of the answers. And we haven't caught Julian yet. Hell, maybe he does have some crazy hypnosis skills, I don't know. But we got Ryan. The evidence is solid, no one can deny that. We know who killed those women, even if we don't understand all of the reasons, or how it happened. Forensics prove it was just one person, and that has to be Ryan, you know it does.

Julian wasn't in the same city. There's no evidence even suggesting that he murdered anyone, other than the claims in that letter. And we can't prove the letter was definitely from him. No, Adam, we can't. Besides, even Ryan has trouble denying that he's a killer. He's having to resort to an insanity plea to have any hope of getting out of a life sentence in prison.'

I take a deep swig of my beer, watching as Christine flicks the unlit cigarette, as though ridding it of non-existent ash. Old habits die hard, I guess.

'And you know what?' she continues, jabbing my chest fiercely. 'The killing has stopped. It's been weeks, and no more murders. Do you know why?'

She waits. I grit my teeth.

'Why?' I grunt.

'Because we caught the bloody killer!'

I shake my head at her. She doesn't get it, just like the rest of them don't get it. If Ryan really is just some unwilling pawn, and if Julian really has somehow mastered hypnosis to the point where he can manipulate someone into killing for him, what's stopping him from doing it again?

It's true that the killings have stopped – for now – but if Julian's the mastermind behind all of this, then he'll turn up again, and probably not out in the open where we can arrest him. His method has worked for him once. Who's to say that he hasn't programmed Gina to strike once the heat on this case has died down?

My stomach turns at the thought. But as much as I wish I could, I can't dismiss it. I think back to the way Gina was acting when we interviewed her after she discovered both of the bodies. I'd thought it was shock. And maybe it was. But she was acting strangely – even Christine can admit that – almost like she was in a trance. Like she was hypnotised.

'I wish I had your confidence,' I say eventually. 'But I'm just not convinced that this case is as simple as you believe it is.'

'Well,' Christine says, downing her drink. 'You can keep looking, my friend, but the resources are being pulled back for now, unless we can offer a solid lead. I suggest you keep those alerts live and try to forget about it until one of them pings. You'll only drive yourself crazy otherwise.'

My shoulders slump. If my own partner isn't on my side on this one, who else can I count on to keep chasing down leads with me? Not that we have any leads to chase. We tried them all, and they all led nowhere.

'Look on the bright side,' she says as she pockets her cigarette and heaves the pub door open. 'We've still got a reward out for Julian. If anything pops up, you'll be able to run wild again with your hypnotherapy theories.'

'Hypnosis,' I mutter, but she's already inside, in the warm glow of the pub, celebrating what she sees as a success. I suppose in a way it is. Ryan is behind bars. The case against him is strong, as strong as it could be without an actual video of him killing those women. And we do have some resources still on the hunt for Julian. The case isn't closed entirely.

But those questions keep needling at me, preventing me from getting that good night's sleep Mia mentioned. They're like a riddle that's taunting me, incessant and urgent, as though if I find just one right answer, the rest will fall into place.

I don't have the answers. I have no idea how Gina just happened to be the first person on the scene both times. Even if Julian or Ryan had suggested a specific route home, there was every chance she would have decided on a whim to catch a bus. The odds of her being in the exact right place at the exact right time must be impossibly low.

Who the hell sent that note to Ryan calling him a killer?

And if Julian is The Puppeteer, and he can do what he claims he can do, why did he choose Ryan? How did he select his victims? And what's he going to do now that he's a wanted man?

I shake my head.

Letting these questions spin around and around in my mind won't do any good. Christine's right about that.

But she's wrong about everything else. I don't have to forget about this case. Just because no one else believes in The Puppeteer, that doesn't mean I don't.

And it doesn't mean I can't keep an eye out, try to find answers . . .

Just in case.

Chapter 42

1996

SHARON

With something that sounds like a gurgle, I pour myself onto my baby girl.

She's bleeding heavily. There's a gash along the side of her head, and it's oozing glistening, dark blood, forming a halo in the dirt around her head. There's so much of it. I put my hand against the wound, gently but firmly, adrenalin coursing through me.

'Cassie? Cassie, darling, I'm here. Can you open your eyes for me, please? Cassie, baby...'

There's no response. Her eyes are closed, her little mouth is hanging ever so slightly open, whether in fear or surprise I can't tell.

Ryan's footsteps stop behind me. His breath is fast and shallow. I ignore him.

Tearing my cardigan off, I gently place it under my hand, onto Cassie's stained blonde curls. My fingers are sticky with blood. The bleeding won't stop, or even slow down. I'm sobbing, praying that the ambulance will arrive, but I can't hear a siren.

I tilt my head and see Gina, blood smeared across her arms and chest.

'What happened?' I scream at her, my own ferocity startling me.

She stares, her eyes wide and her face pale, but she doesn't reply.

'What happened to Cassie?' I ask again. She remains silent.

I can feel the cardigan getting warm and wet between my fingers. I know I should check for a pulse, but I'm too scared. What if I can't find one? I hear a wail in the distance, and my stomach lurches. The paramedics are on their way. They're coming. They'll help. They'll make sure Cassie is OK.

'Hold on, Cassie, honey. Hold on. The ambulance is almost here, they're almost here.'

I turn my head.

'Ryan, go let them in. Now!'

He runs towards the house, his limbs flailing, like he can't quite work out how to use them. Gina is still standing off to the side, motionless. I don't have time to work out exactly how this happened. I just need to get Cassie to the hospital. Voices filter out from the house, then footsteps rush towards me.

'Mrs Mills?'

The voice is calm, trustworthy. It takes a second for my brain to process the question, for my body to respond. I nod.

'I'm James, and I'm here to help your daughter. Here, I can take this from you, if you could just remove your hand for me, that's right, don't worry, I've got it—'

Once I've relinquished the cardigan to James's gloved hands, I'm immediately pulled away from Cassie by another paramedic whose name I forget the instant he offers it. I hover, trying to stay close enough to help Cassie, to be near her in case she needs me, in case I can comfort her.

'Please, Mrs Mills, if you could just step over here for me. That's right. Your daughter is in good hands, please don't worry, they're doing everything they can.'

'Is she going to be OK?'

'I haven't had a chance to take a look at her injuries yet, but we have the best people on it, I promise you. Can you tell me your daughter's name? Mrs Mills?'

'Cassie,' I stutter. 'It's Cassie. She's eight, she just turned eight.'

'That's great, thank you. And can you tell me what happened here?'

My eyes dart over to where Gina's standing, watching the paramedic working on her younger sister. What happened here? How was there so much blood?

'I don't know,' I admit, angry at this man for wasting time that could be spent on helping Cassie. I glance over to see her being carefully lifted onto a stretcher, the white bandage they've put on her head already soaked red.

'The kids were playing,' I say. 'I didn't see anything, I just... Ryan came in and told me to call for help.'

'OK,' he says calmly. 'That's OK. We'll discuss the details later. We're going to take Cassie to the hospital now, do you want to meet us there? Do you know where you're going?'

I nod. I have no idea if I'll be able to drive in this state. My head is buzzing, the noise so loud that I can hardly hear what this man is saying to me.

'No, wait!' I cry. 'I want to be with her. She'll be scared. I want to go with Cassie in the ambulance.'

'Is there someone who can look after the other children?'

I look at him blankly. It takes a few seconds to register what he's asked.

'No. Oh. No, I'll follow you there. Are you sure she'll be OK?'

'We're doing the best we can, Mrs Mills. Don't worry about her, she won't be scared, and we're taking very good care of her, OK?'

'OK,' I say, robotic.

'All right. When you get there, ask for emergency paediatrics. Have you got that?'

'Emergency paediatrics,' says a voice beside me. I look down, perplexed, and see Ryan. His face is so innocent, so plastered with worry, that I almost break down in tears. But then I remember Cassie. She needs me to be strong.

'Come on,' I say to Ryan, taking his hand. 'Let's go. Where's Gina?'

I look back towards the scene of the accident. Cassie's being carried carefully across the lawn towards the house, where she'll be lifted into the ambulance. Gina hasn't moved. Her eyes aren't on her sister's limp body, or the paramedics, or me.

She's staring at the jagged rock, the place where Cassie was lying just a few moments ago, the piece of earth that's covered in blood. Her sister's blood.

Chapter 43

2018

RYAN

If there's tension in the courtroom, I can't feel it.

It's not because I'm numb. I'm feeling so many things that I might explode. Emotion isn't the issue. It's just that I already know what the verdict will be. My lawyer keeps telling me that there's still hope, but this trial has felt like a farce, like some kind of theatrical performance that everyone knew the ending to before they even took their seats.

The jury is going to find me guilty. If I were one of the twelve, I would, too. For the past couple of weeks, I've been forced to listen to all of the reasons why it's impossible to believe I *didn't* kill Michelle and Angela. Right now, they're not interested in any theories about The Puppeteer. If they catch Julian, Thompson tells me, he'll be tried separately. All they need to know is whether or not I murdered two women.

They've done a good job of suggesting I did. Although I have absolutely no recollection of what they're saying I did, I don't see how it's possible for me not to have been the one who killed them. During the trial, more CCTV footage was given as evidence; footage I hadn't yet seen, showing me walking to and from the crime scenes, the timings too perfectly aligned with the victims' time of death to be co-incidence. There's nothing showing me actually doing it, but the video isn't all they had on me. If it were, I'd still argue my innocence, but that's just the tip of the incriminating iceberg.

As well as my DNA on Angela's neck, a fibre was discovered mixed in with the blood on her head wound. After searching my belongings, the police discovered that the fibre belonged to the jacket I was seen wearing on the night of her murder.

My lawyer is trying to argue that I wasn't in a fit mental state to know what I was doing at the time of the murders. He refused to present The Puppeteer angle, no matter how much I begged him to. Too unbelievable, he said. Psychosis is much easier to believe, to sympathise with.

Over the past seven months, since my arrest, I've visited more doctors and psychiatrists than I can count, most of whom weren't able to tell me what happened on those nights when I could have sworn I was at home, napping on the sofa. Only one offered an explanation that my lawyer believed could work in my favour, so of course that's what he's presented to the court. I suffered psychotic episodes, they said. This can be proved by my account of the morning I thought I saw Cassie on the train. A hallucination, they insisted, which is one of the symptoms of psychosis.

They brought up my dreams, my lack of memory, the fact that, for a moment in time, I questioned if my little sister really was dead. All of these things, the doctor said on the stand, point to psychosis, and that would mean I was mentally unable to tell right from wrong at the time of the crimes.

Part of me wants to cling to that, as though it's an irrefutable truth. After all, there's no other *logical* explanation. It just . . . it doesn't ring true to me. I wasn't hallucinating. I simply saw a woman who, for a split second, I thought was

Cassie. Is that a hallucination? Or just a misunderstanding? And my dreams... well, I don't know why they began a few months before this all started, but it can't be that abnormal to have nightmares about a traumatic event that happened in my childhood, can it?

It's strange that only now, while standing trial for something I don't even recall doing, I finally understand how Gina has felt for her whole life. I feel a spark of disappointment as I think about my sister – as I sense her absence, as physical as her presence would have been – and then scold myself for being so selfish.

Of course she doesn't have to stand by me as I'm convicted for murder. I shouldn't expect it, shouldn't even be allowed to want it. I try not to think about the family I have out in the real world, about Mum and Dad who refuse to come from Florida, who won't acknowledge me, their monster son, to match their monster daughter. I haven't seen Gina for over six months, since I admitted, after all this time, that I'd known she hadn't killed Cassie.

She even managed to avoid testifying at the trial. She submitted a written affidavit but her testimony wasn't considered to be reliable, given that she couldn't explain how she found the bodies, or what happened to the jewellery. Neither the defence nor the prosecution wanted to risk their arguments on a witness who could bring up more questions than she could answer. And as much as I'm glad she's being protected from all of this, from having to relive the trauma of last year, I'm selfishly devastated that she in't here.

I'm so alone, and so scared.

I look desperately around the courtroom as the jury takes their places and onlookers shuffle in their seats in anticipation. I begged for Gina to come. I didn't allow myself to hope that she would, but it doesn't sting any less that she's not here to be a familiar face in a sea of judgement. I need an anchor, a reminder of who I still believe myself to be. Or, at least, who I want to believe myself to be.

I glimpse a number of familiar faces. Journalists who have been at the trial since the first day. The jurors, whose faces are imprinted on my memory for ever. The families of the victims, whose constant presence has made this whole process even more surreal, if that's possible. I've watched their grief spilling over every day, their hatred towards me for something I don't recall doing, and have felt like a spectator to my own life. A bystander.

There's also my lawyer and his team members. The prosecutor and his cronies. The judge, of course. But no one from my life before all of this. No one who's ever known me as just plain old Ryan Mills.

My heart plunges into my feet as I realise that I'll have to hear this verdict alone. There won't even be someone I can focus on, a piece of my old life I can tether myself to as I transition into my new identity as a convicted murderer.

The judge asks if a verdict has been reached, and the jury spokesperson confirms that yes, a decision has been agreed upon. It's not surprising. They took the minimum amount of time to deliberate. If deliberate really is the right word for whatever happened in that room. I have a feeling they all agreed on my guilt early on, and had to sit and wait for the minimum time to pass. It's not a difficult case, I imagine. Even with all the questions still lingering in the air – the mysterious Tinder accounts, the jewellery, Gina's uncanny ability to find the bodies – even with all of that doubt, the weight of guilt still tips heavily against me.

'And what is your verdict?' the judge asks.

'Guilty.'

It's matter-of-fact. There are no gasps or cries. No one is

sad to see me go down for this. Simply some shuffling of paperwork, handshakes on the other side of the courtroom, and the judge setting a date for my sentencing.

And then I hear a cry.

I turn my head towards the sound, to the gallery overhead. There's a movement in my peripheral vision. I'm lightheaded after hearing the verdict. Even though I expected it, the word and all that it means for me has hit me like a physical force. There's no sadness; just a kind of aching disbelief. And so, despite all that's happening, I'm still able to be distracted by this sudden flicker of activity.

It's Gina.

My heart leaps, a tiny flicker of joy igniting in the darkness inside me. I have no idea how long she's been there, all the way at the back, shielded from my view when everyone was seated. But now she's getting up, pushing past the other people in her row. She notices me looking and freezes, as though caught in some terrible act, her eyes wide and locked right on mine.

We stay like that, our gazes fastened to each other, months of things unsaid passing between us. Instinctively, I smile. I'm happy to see her, and I want her to know how much joy this has brought me. But as soon as my lips stretch I know I've done the wrong thing. A frown dances across her forehead, and she blinks quickly, as though realising what's happening all of a sudden.

The spell is broken. She looks away, shoving past knees and feet to escape.

'Gina!' I yell, but it's too late.

She's gone. Before I have time to process what her presence means, fingers clasp the top of my arm to lead me away.

'I'm sorry,' my lawyer mumbles as I'm guided past him. But there's no feeling in his words. He doesn't mean it.

And just like that, there's no one left on my side. Not one person to help fight my battles.

I'm alone.

Chapter 44

1996

SHARON

'I'm so sorry, Mrs Mills,' says the doctor, and in that one sentence my world cracks apart, falling on the floor in a shower of tiny, jagged fragments.

I don't remember the next few moments. I don't notice what my other children, my living children, are doing, or thinking, or feeling.

There aren't any words that can describe what has happened to my heart, how it has been wrenched from my body, pulverised, and put back as though it is still able to do what it was designed to do, what it's been doing all my life. As though I have anything left to give to those who are still here with me.

I don't know who contacted him, or how – it might have even been me, although I have no memory of speaking to anyone – but suddenly Bill is by my side, holding me as I shatter in his arms. Small hands clutch at the hem of my T-shirt, the fabric still smeared with my little girl's blood, and I shove them away roughly.

'Here,' says Bill kindly, his voice thick and rough, but somehow still working. He holds me tightly with one arm and with the other he gathers Ryan and Gina close to him, stroking their heads as they weep, not truly understanding what's happened.

I have no concept of time but at some point a doctor allows us into a room to see Cassie, to say goodbye to our precious girl. I'm surprised that when I see her lying on the bed, still and pale, I don't collapse or faint. I'm ashamed at myself for staying upright and carrying on, for daring to live when I couldn't save her.

She's so small and fragile. Her head is bandaged, her hair gathered and draped in an attempt to hide the worst of her injury. Gina rushes past me to take the seat closest to her sister, and for a second the truth hits me. She's not my eldest daughter any more. She's my only daughter. It's a feeling so visceral that it knocks the wind from my lungs and I stop, taking a deep breath.

I turn my focus instead to my baby, silent and peaceful. Her barely-there lashes are resting on the tops of her cheeks, long and straight, so pale that they're almost invisible. I force myself to memorise the freckles on her nose, the small curl of hair that always hangs loose on the left-hand side of her forehead. I try to ignore the bandage, the proof of the head injury that killed her. It makes me dizzy, the thought of her lying there, on the ground, scared and bleeding, and with my entire being I wish that I could swap places with her, make it all go away, bring her back, somehow.

And then I see Gina, sitting next to her sister, and my heart turns cold. I don't know it in this moment, but it's here, in this hospital room, that everything changes. In this tiny sliver of time, there's the faintest flicker of suspicion playing at the edges of my consciousness.

Gina's eyes are locked on Cassie's face, her head tilted slightly to one side, not a trace of anguish or terror in her expression. Instead, the corner of her mouth is curved, tugging up towards her eyes, in . . . what is that?

Her pupils are large. Her chest is moving up and down

rapidly. And her gaze is locked on her fragile little sister, whose life was extinguished before her very eyes.

She can hardly hold it in. She looks like she's ready to burst with emotion.

And then I recognise it. I've seen it before, on her birthday, at Christmas, when her favourite meal is placed in front of her.

Gina's excited.

Chapter 45

GINA

Time freezes for just a moment, the verdict hanging from the lips of the woman who's speaking on behalf of the jury.

I shouldn't have come. I knew I'd regret it but it was as though a magnetic field was pulling me here, forcing me to sit through the trial. I stayed hidden. I couldn't bear for him to see me. Him seeing me would have meant an acknowledgement of some kind. I'm not ready for that. Not prepared to look him in the eye, to forgive him, to move on.

And yet, here I am. I need to know. Since that night in the alleyway, all those months ago, my life has been suspended, on hold, waiting for this very moment. The moment when all of this is put to rest for good.

I wish Julian were here. I imagine his hand curled around mine, savouring the fantasy of it. Then I remember where I am and what's happening, and reality takes over. My heart pounds and my lungs shrink. I can't suck enough air into my body.

And then the jury spokeswoman's lips are moving, and Ryan's future is about to be revealed.

'Guilty.'

The air all whooshes out of me in one heavy breath. I clutch a hand to my heart. So this is the end. This is how it finishes. After all of these months of not knowing, of my life being in limbo, of Ryan's fate being just a concept in a group of twelve strangers' hands, it's now written in stone. There was no ambiguity in their decision. They barely deliberated.

Guilty.

I don't look down to see my brother's reaction. I can't. Just imagining the horror he's feeling in this moment is making me unsteady. My hands tremble and my skin feels too tight. The walls feel like they're closing in on me. I need to get out of here, need to be free, to breathe fresh air, not the stale breath of the jurors and lawyers and family members.

'Excuse me,' I mutter to the woman next to me, not waiting for her to move before I barge past, knocking her knees with my own.

She yelps softly, but the sound echoes throughout the sparse courtroom. I freeze. I should just leave. He may have spotted me but I should put my head down and go, just get out of here. And yet, there's that magnetic force again, a tug from somewhere deep inside, pulling my gaze towards him. Nothing good will come of making eye contact, and yet I feel my head turning without my permission, my eyes sweeping the courtroom until they land on him.

It's like an electric current is ripping through my veins.

I'm completely stuck, wedged halfway between a stranger's knees and the back of the bench in front of me but I don't notice that. His eyes are locked with mine. Neither of us is willing to look away, like stags locked by their horns in a silent battle.

I can't decipher that look in his eyes, those eyes that, last time I looked into them, told the story of decades of lies and betrayal. Today, though, that's not what I see. Maybe he's feeling the exact same thing that I am, that pull of familiarity, of a lifetime of knowledge of one another. I *know* him. He's my brother. And now he's going to be sent to prison for murder.

The corners of his lips twitch. It's just for a second, the beginnings of a smile, an acknowledgement of all that is between us, heavy in the air, unspoken. It's the exact same smile he gave me when I turned up out of the blue after years of absolutely no contact. It's a look that says he wasn't expecting to see me, but he's glad. He's grateful. Relieved, even.

My stomach lurches and the spell is broken. I need to leave, I have to get out of here immediately. With all the strength I can muster, I tear my eyes away from Ryan's, and push past the rest of the people in my row, ignoring their protests. Gasping for breath, I run down the stairs and across the corridor, my footsteps echoing like gunshots across the tiles.

As soon as I burst through the main doors and onto the busy road, I let myself dissolve. The tears come, hot and bitter, rolling down my face without permission. My chest heaves with sobs, which wrack my body faster than I can gulp down air, so I'm left choking on my own anguish. I drop down onto the stone steps and rest my elbows on my knees as my emotions erupt.

A hand lands on my shoulder and I jump, startled. It's a man I've never seen before, dressed in a smart navy suit. His forehead is creased in concern.

'Are you OK?' he asks.

I can't speak, so I just nod miserably.

'Can I call someone for you?'

I shake my head, fresh tears falling, because there's no one to call. The man doesn't leave my side. Tears and snot are running into my mouth as my shoulders shake violently, and when I wipe my eyes my hand comes away smeared with black. No wonder a total stranger stopped to check that I was all right. I take a couple of long, shaky breaths until the sobs have subsided.

'I'm sorry,' I say to him, my voice thick with emotion. 'I just...'

I trail off. There's no way I can explain what I'm feeling to a complete stranger. I can't even explain it to myself.

'It's just been a tough day,' I say eventually. He sits on the step beside me and rubs my back. This unsolicited kindness almost makes me break into a fresh wave of sobs but I hold it together as we sit in silence for a couple of seconds. Eventually he speaks.

'You know it's going to get better, don't you? It always does. You just have to hang in there, OK?'

Before I can respond, he's up again and walking off in the stream of pedestrians who are passing by, oblivious to what just happened behind the doors of the court house. A man's future has just been irrevocably changed, and mine along with it, and yet the world keeps going and life continues as though it was just a normal day.

The stranger's words reverberate in my head as I sit, dazed and too weak to move, on the cold step outside the courts.

It's going to get better.

I know that. I've always known that.

All along, this was going to be the hardest part. Ryan's trial and subsequent verdict was never a certainty. Sure, his lawyers had the mental instability argument. And the prosecution had their science. But in any trial, the outcome is in the hands of a dozen imperfect people, each bringing with them their own prejudices and opinions. There was never a moment in time when I was certain how this was going to end.

But now I know.

The hardest part is over. The uncertainty has disappeared. And it *is* going to get better.

But it's also always going to be just a little bit worse.

Because despite what he did all those years ago, despite the anger I've had burning in me all this time, its glowing embers fuelling me, it turns out I love my brother. I miss my sister, of course I do, but now I've lost my brother, too.

I cling onto the pendant around my neck, its ridges worn down by my desperate need to be close to Julian again. It's him I need to make sure things start to get better.

I've had enough of not knowing. I've played the role of worried girlfriend, of grieving sister, of the broken woman for long enough now.

I sniff and wipe my nose with the back of my arm. I let my emotions get the best of me. I knew this would happen, it's why I knew I shouldn't have come. I breathe in deeply and stand up. I've had my moment. And now it's time.

It's time for things to get better.

Chapter 46

2018

DETECTIVE ADAM ADEBAYO

'Guilty?'

I hand Christine the folder I've been leafing through for the past ten minutes.

'They barely even deliberated,' I say.

She flips through the pages, taking a couple of seconds to skim each one.

'When's the sentencing?'

'Tomorrow,' I say, composing an email to Mia to summarise the court's findings.

'Do you want to talk about it?'

I look up at her, confused. 'About what?'

'About how you're feeling about the trial being done. I feel like you need another reminder that closure might never happen. You know that, right?'

'You've only told me about a hundred times, yes.'

'Well I just want to be sure you actually understand. Because... well, you know. You're a bit obsessed, quite frankly.'

'Of course I'm bloody obsessed!' I protest. 'Two women died and there's still no logical explanation for it, despite whatever the court says.'

'There's never a *logical* explanation for murder,' she snaps, throwing things into her handbag and shutting her computer down. 'You think anyone is justified in killing someone? Just because you can't explain this as easily as a gang stabbing doesn't mean it's any less solved.'

She's right, as usual. Murder is many things, but it's almost never logical. Sometimes there's a linear path that leads to the motive, but it's rarely a nicely packaged explanation, neatly spelling *THE END*. I know that. But there's something about this case that's burrowed deep under my skin and refusing to budge.

'I know I won't always get closure,' I say with as much patience as I can muster. 'But this case is just so twisted. And yes, I know we caught the guy who actually committed the murders, supposedly, but that doesn't change the fact that Julian's still out there. I just don't feel like those girls got the justice they deserve.'

'Women,' she says.

'Sorry?'

'They were women. Not girls. But I do know what you mean. It was a weird one. I just don't know if you've accepted that you might never catch him.'

He's evasive, and if it wasn't my job to catch him, I might even be impressed with his disappearing act. When we found the charm in his flat, I worked with our IT department to set up a number of alerts, allowing us to receive notifications if Julian did anything online. The searches were many and varied, mostly centred around keywords and phrases, based on previous identities we found on the hard drives we'd recovered from his desk. There's no telling how many instances of activity we've missed, but we put the searches in place in the hope that if Julian used any of the IP addresses or keywords we knew were associated with him, we'd be the first to know. And a couple of months ago, the searches finally paid off.

It had been a hive of activity that day in the office, as we frantically tried to track down the username that had popped up first thing that morning. As it turned out, Julian was using a method of encryption far superior to the decryption software we have access to. We had our best people on it but we couldn't find his location and he'd disappeared again later that day. We haven't heard from him since.

It wasn't a complete failure, though. We were able to see what he was doing, deep in the notoriously sinister forums of the dark web.

Master the skills of The Puppeteer, he'd boasted in the title of his forum post. It was cheesy, sure, but attention-grabbing all the same.

Many have tried to master mind control. And just as many have failed. Until now. In London, England, in 2018, I was able to pull off the most powerful public display of mind control and manipulation in human history.

The result? Two dead girls, one man arrested with absolutely no recollection of having murdered them, and all the evidence pointing his way. This isn't a case of framing someone for a crime they didn't do. He killed those women. He just didn't know he did it. He didn't choose to do it. I chose for him, because I am The Puppeteer.

You can read the headlines for yourself, if you must. But you're not here to brush up on world events. You're here for power. Not fake, self-confidence bullshit. You want the real thing. The ability to control another human being, to make them do whatever you want, whatever you command.

And I can teach you.

I didn't just pull it off once. I struck twice, and I could

have made my puppet kill again and again if I'd desired. But my aim has never been to play. It's been to teach. And empower.

What will it cost? Ten bitcoin, for a full, in-depth, practical training plan, including troubleshooting. Our connection will always be completely secure and untraceable (this is for my protection as well as yours) and you'll have my full and undivided attention for one month, after which we will reconnect monthly to track your progress and for me to answer any questions.

What will you gain? The ability to become a puppeteer. I don't want to do this alone. There are more out there with skills like mine, and with the right training, you, too, can manipulate others to do whatever you want without them even knowing. Think of the possibilities. Think of the return on your investment. And think of the power...

We'd tried to buy his services, of course, but something must have tipped him off, as that's when he vanished again. So we knew his game, now, and although what he was attempting to sell should have appalled me – and it did, of course – he was operating in a realm where much worse things were sold for a lot more money. The dark web was given that name for a reason.

The press got hold of it, and Julian made the headlines for a few days. I'm sure the attention pleased him immeasurably. My blood still simmers when I think about it.

'I know we might never catch him,' I lie to Christine. I don't believe that. Even if I have to keep looking until the day I retire, I'll find him. She raises an eyebrow at me.

'Really,' I insist. 'I'm not obsessed, I promise.'

She peers over the partition to judge my sincerity. I hold

my hands up, a sign of surrender. She nods as she puts her coat on.

'So how about that drink after work tomorrow?' I ask, a not-so-subtle change of subject.

'Sounds good,' she says. 'Are you going home soon? You've done loads today.'

'Yeah, just finishing some emails. I won't stay long.'

I catch the look she gives me.

'I swear,' I say. 'I'm going to the gym in a bit, anyway.'

'OK. See you tomorrow.'

'Bye.'

I have every intention of hitting the treadmill for a bit and then going home, but I send one email, and then another, and then catch up on some paperwork that's been piling up at my desk, and then I look up and the office is empty. I glance at the clock. It's gone ten. I really need to head home.

Yawning, I roll my head around to try to loosen the tension in my shoulders. I'm mid-stretch when Tim from IT appears at my desk, breathless and red in the face. His glasses are steaming up from the exertion.

'Mate. Are you OK?'

He nods and bends over to lean on his knees, wheezing.

'You need a puffer or something?'

He shakes his head.

'No, I just need to go to the bloody gym once in a while,' he squeezes out. 'Dunno why I took the stairs. Stupid me thought it'd be quicker.'

'What's the hurry?'

'We got a hit on Julian.'

All of a sudden I'm fully alert, adrenalin shooting from my heart to my fingertips, leaving them prickling.

After his first appearance, most people in the office

figured he'd found a buyer, and laid low since then. Ten bitcoin is something like fifty thousand pounds at today's rate, so depending where he's holed up, that could go a long way. A lot of my colleagues were convinced that he'd wait it out another couple of years, till the heat died down a little, before any of our searches got another credible hit.

'Where?'

'We can't trace *his* location,' Tim grimaces, 'but he's using an old username, one we discovered right when he disappeared, on one of the computers at his apartment. He's been communicating with someone here in London; they mustn't have the same level of security as he does, which is how we spotted it. He was only online for a couple of minutes, and we can't see what was said, but we tracked down the IP address of the computer he was communicating with here.'

'And?'

He hands me a piece of paper, wet and crumpled from being crushed inside his sweaty hand.

I glance at it, and my mouth falls open. It's an address.

'You know where that is?' Tim asks.

I look up at him.

'Yeah,' I say, stunned. 'That's Gina's house.'

'Gina, as in, his girlfriend?'

'The very one,' I say, standing up.

'Where are you going?'

'I have to go and find out what he said to her, and if it really is him.'

'Shouldn't you call it in, get some backup or something?'

'Come on, Tim,' I say. 'She's a victim as much as those women who were killed. I don't know if he's threatening her or something, but if I had to guess, I'd say she's just as surprised as we are to hear from him. I just want to find out what's going on.'

'OK,' Tim says uncertainly.

'I can protect myself. I am trained, you know.'

'I know, but don't you think it's weird timing – to show up the day that her brother is found guilty?'

'No,' I say. 'I think that's exactly the timing I'd expect from someone who wants to brag about how well they controlled another person.'

He shrugs. 'I'm just the IT guy,' he says. 'But I would be careful if I were you.'

'Noted,' I say as I pull my jacket on. 'Thanks for your good work, Tim. This is huge.'

My heart hammers in time with my fist bashing against her front door.

'Gina!'

There's a sudden flurry of movement, and then the door opens just enough to show me her face, a picture of confusion.

'Constable?'

I let go of the breath I've been holding in.

'You're OK,' I say, breathless.

'Of course I'm OK. Why wouldn't I be?'

'Uh . . . can I come in?'

I was too worried about her safety to think much further than just knowing that she's out of Julian's reach. Now that I'm here, I need to offer an explanation, and I need answers. I won't get them out here on her front doorstep.

Gina hesitates. She looks over her shoulder, and then back at me. Her eyes slide slowly from my shoes all the way up to my face. Butterflies erupt into action in my stomach. I tell my body to cut it out. She's a witness.

'Are you . . . are you here in an official capacity?'

She looks down at her feet. She's so vulnerable. Fragile.

I shuffle, embarrassed by my own thoughts.

'Actually, no,' I admit. 'I just finished a shift and this isn't a formal interview, just . . . were you talking to Julian earlier today, Gina?'

I'm not sure what reaction I expected, but this isn't it. She doesn't deny it, she doesn't look scared, she doesn't ask questions.

She bursts into tears.

Her sobs are so abrupt, and so consuming, that her whole body heaves with them. I stay completely still, unsure how to deal with such an unexpected outpouring of emotion.

'Come in,' she hiccups, and I obey.

I follow her down the hallway and into the living room where she gestures for me to sit. I sink onto the end of a sofa, looking around for a tissue I can offer her. There's nothing.

'Excuse me for a second,' she says, and disappears.

I hear Gina blowing her nose, water running, and then there's a tinkling noise, as though glassware is being arranged. I stare at a photo on the wall of Gina and Ryan together, smiling, and wonder what it's like knowing that your brother is capable of something as heinous as what he did.

When she returns, her face is red but she's otherwise composed. In one hand she's holding a bottle of wine. In the other, two glasses.

'I need a drink,' she announces. 'And I'm not drinking alone.'

'Oh, I really can't,' I say.

'I thought you said you were off the clock?'

'I am, I just . . . I shouldn't, I'm still working, even if it's not official.'

'I need to talk to someone,' she says, filling two glasses.

I pause, assessing her. She offers me a watery smile, and my resolve crumbles. I accept the glass she's holding out, and allow her to clink hers against it. She moves to the other side of the sofa and sits at the opposite end so we're both twisted awkwardly to face one another.

'Look, I'm really sorry about crying,' she says, taking a sip from her glass. I do the same. 'It's just been a horrible day.'

'Please don't apologise,' I say. I'm never sure how to respond to tears, so I leave it at that and hope she'll fill in the silence. I take another long sip.

'How did you know?' she asks after a pause. 'About the messages, I mean.'

'We're still tracking Julian,' I say. 'Those alerts I told you about last year? We're monitoring online activity that matches any of those keywords. Don't worry. We'll find him.'

'Well, it wasn't him,' she says simply.

'What do you mean?'

'Today. It wasn't him.'

'How can you be so sure?'

'Because I know him,' she says, shifting her body so she's facing me properly now. In the process, she's also moved slightly closer. I pretend not to notice.

'What happened?'

'Some guy messaged me, pretending to be him. He'd used a username I recognised from when Julian and I would chat online when we were first dating.'

She sighs and closes her eyes. This is painful for her. I shift my own weight so I'm facing her, too.

'For a second, I almost believed it was him,' she breathes. 'How sad is that? I'm so stupid, I forget that people can find all this stuff online, stuff I thought was private. In the end, it was just some loser sending me nasty sexual stuff, along with a few pictures I'd really rather forget.'

I grit my teeth. I'm disappointed that our intelligence was wrong, frustrated that this is another dead end, that we were duped just like Gina was. But I'm also angry.

'Show me,' I say, fury rising up. She's gone through enough. Sexual harassment is the last thing she needs. 'I'll find whoever it was, charge them. We take that kind of thing seriously.'

She doesn't move.

'It's just so hard,' she says, her voice hardly louder than a whisper. 'I lost him, and I lost Ryan, and I lost who I thought they both were, within a day of each other.'

'I'm sorry,' I say uselessly. She's crying again. Not great, gulping sobs, but a quiet stream of tears moving down her cheeks, pooling on her chin and dripping into her lap.

'I wish I was stronger. It's just difficult for me to have to deal with such a cruel joke, to have someone use my pain like that, after I'd just started feeling like I was able to move on.'

I can't help what happens next. It's an impulse, an urge to comfort her, that drives my hand to move, to land on her shoulder, to assure her that it's going to be all right. The gesture is tentative, awkward. But within seconds she's collapsed into me, the space between us now non-existent, her sobs muffled against my chest. I put my arms around her and hold her there, waiting for her emotion to drain away. When I breathe in, I can smell her perfume, sweet and intoxicating. I close my eyes and savour the feeling of being her protector, her comforter.

After a few seconds, however, the intimacy begins to feel uncomfortable. The reality of what's happening settles on me and I look around nervously, unsure what to do next, how to carry on, how to say the right thing. I really need to leave. I pat her back gently. She stirs, but she doesn't move away.

As I wait, I look around. The place is immaculate, aside from a shoe sitting in the middle of the floor. I frown. It's a running trainer, purple and black, the laces strewn across the wooden floorboards. I follow the white squiggles and spot a large shape in the corner. I shift my weight slightly to get a better view.

It's a suitcase, half open, clothes spilling out, items scattered around it. It's the picture of haste. The sight of it jolts me out of whatever it is that made me embrace Gina. I push her away from my body, my hands on her shoulders. Her face is blotchy, and her eyes are red-rimmed.

I remember why I'm here. I need answers. I have to concentrate on the case.

'Are you going somewhere?'

Silence hangs over us, and for a second I think she might dissolve into tears again. But then she takes a deep, shuddering breath.

'I was just scared,' she says. 'When I got those messages today, I just . . . I panicked. I know they were just nonsense, there was no actual threat, but I didn't feel safe. I felt like maybe I should go check into a hotel for a couple of nights.'

I keep my eyes locked on hers, assessing her words, testing them for truth. Fleeing over some lewd messages does seem a bit extreme, but then again, she's been through a number of incredibly frightening ordeals in the last year. Being a bit jumpy is completely understandable. Besides, I've never been sexually harassed. Who's to say I wouldn't do the same thing, if I was in her position?

'You don't need to run,' I say eventually. 'I'm here to help you, to protect you. But in order to do that, I need to take a look at the computer that you were using today when this person contacted you. I need to see those messages so that I can find whoever sent them.'

I notice a flash of frustration, as though she thinks I have no idea what it is she's dealing with. And she's right about that, but I have to try to help. It's my job, after all.

'The computer is in . . . well, it's in my bedroom,' she whispers, looking up at me, her eyes wide and innocent. She bites her lip, and my stomach clenches. I know I shouldn't be thinking about her like that, but the wine, and the embrace, and those eyes . . .

Before I have a chance to consider what's happening, she leans over in one smooth movement and presses her lips firmly against mine. I tense with the suddenness of it, but then I focus on her hands running through my hair, and I feel myself relaxing into the kiss.

'No!' I say, my better judgement kicking in.

I push her back, and look at her. I'm panting, and so is she.

'I can't,' I say.

'Why not?'

'My job, I . . . it's not right.'

'I won't tell anyone, Adam,' she says, her voice low and breathy. 'I want to. Don't you?'

My stomach simmers. I'm not thinking clearly. I know I'm not. But right now, there's no room in my brain for anything but her hands against my skin and her lips against mine.

And then, as though an unspoken agreement has been reached, we both lean in and the space between us disappears again. Before I know it, my shirt is on the floor, and then she's leading me to her bedroom, and I know I should be making an excuse and leaving, but I'm weak and I want her, and my hands are moving up inside her shirt. And I know I'm making a huge mistake.

But I can't stop.

Chapter 47

GINA

My eyes fly open.

I've kept them squeezed shut for what felt like minutes – but which must have only been for a couple of seconds – in a futile attempt to clear my head. To calm myself.

There's a thumping sound and my head snaps up to face my bedroom door. I hold my breath as I imagine it flying inwards, revealing an intruder.

My eyes flit back and forth blindly in the dark, until I realise.

That relentless beating. It isn't coming from outside. It's my own thrumming heart.

Adrenalin seeps from my pores as my temple and my pulse pound aggressively.

I count backwards from ten. I close my eyes again and focus on sounds in a bid to combat the darkness that's threatening to control my senses. My breath, sharp and shallow; my heart, its beat settling to a low, steady march, like an army advancing into battle. A siren in the distance. A fox wailing, its harrowing cry echoing under my prickling skin.

Taking a deep lungful of air, my breath catches at the taste in my mouth. Metallic. Sharp. I've felt this before, this tingling on my tongue.

Carefully, deliberately, as though keeping my movements steady will somehow slow the passing of time, I turn my head to look. To see. My eyes have adjusted now, and I slowly take in the details of the tableau that's spread out before me.

My gaze drifts from the shoes strewn carelessly in opposite corners of my room, to the trail of clothing that lies in motionless heaps. Clues, all pointing my way.

And me. Hands in my lap, tense, my body barely perched on the edge of my bed. My fingers, dark and glistening.

I am naked. And covered in blood.

I make out thick, dark smears streaked across my walls, my pillow, my stomach. My hands are shaking, dark red droplets dripping from my fingers into a puddle on the carpet by my feet. I try to remove myself from the pool, its surface glistening in the glow of the street lamp beyond my window.

I push myself further onto the bed, and as I scrabble into the corner, clutching the bed covers, my fingers close on something warm and sticky. For a split second, I let my hand linger. But I don't turn around to look. I already know what I'll see.

How did things go so wrong?

I try to clear my mind, to follow the thread of events that led to this. But it's not a linear path. It's convoluted. A tangled mess that, if it was picked apart and laid out thread by thread, would probably all end up here, anyway.

And somewhere deep in my gut, an instinct nags at me, reminding me of what I'd rather not acknowledge. Reality is slippery, out of reach, an ever-changing shadow. But there are certain facts as solid as the body in my bed. They're circling me like predators, screaming the truths I can't ignore, no matter how much I'd like to.

This isn't over, they snarl.

You started this.

And only you can finish it.

Leaping clear of my bed, I take a couple of deep breaths to calm myself down.

This wasn't part of the plan.

And yet.

I've had that feeling before, the one that took over me just moments ago, the knowledge that there was no other way out, the very idea of it making my blood rush around my veins and my heart quiver within my ribs.

Even as I recognised the sensation, I'd tried to stop it. Tried to suppress it like I have done for so many years. Nothing but sorrow and pain came from the last time I gave into it, almost twenty-two years ago.

The worst thing about what happened on that day is that I didn't even kill Cassie.

I'd had the urge, I'd taken action. I would have gone through with it, but I didn't need to, in the end. It was Ryan's fault. He pushed her. The head wound was what killed my sister, no matter what Mum believes.

Like the detective tonight, Cassie knew too much. But when she'd gone running towards the house to tell everyone who I really was, fate had been on my side. Ryan had thought she was yelling about him, saying that *he* was the one who killed Pickles. He'd got mad. He'd done the job. He'd killed her, really. I'd just been given all of the blame.

I shake my head. Now's not the time for reminiscing. Ryan's getting the justice he deserves. He's finally going down for being a murderer.

But there's no time to celebrate.

I open the lid of my laptop and navigate back to the portal Julian and I had spoken on earlier this evening, the password which he'd left me, engraved among the triangles on my pendant. Then I type in the words we agreed on, the phrase that means I need an emergency exit.

Time to fly.

I don't wait for him to reply. There's too much to do to fix this mess I somehow got myself into. Actually, it's not my fault. That detective came over here to snoop, right when I was in the middle of packing, and he'd started asking questions.

I'd panicked at the sight of him on my front doorstep. There had been so many months in which things could have gone horribly wrong, when all of the flaws in our plan could have brought us both down in a fiery heap, but, miraculously, we'd made it this far. There had been hitches, of course, but nothing that had completely derailed us. I literally had hours to go when Adam appeared with the capacity to ruin everything.

I'd wanted to scream, to strangle him there on the spot, at my front door. But I'd held it together, kept my cool, played my part like I'd been doing for months already. I'd had to remind myself that I'd been patient, I'd not messed up   too badly – so far, and I wasn't about to now, not when we were so close to freedom.

When he'd asked about the messages, my mind had fired warning shots. The sound was deafening. I thought the channel we had set up to communicate on was secure. When I'd messaged Julian to let him know that Ryan was found guilty, I'd never suspected that someone was watching us.

As I'd stared at the detective, I'd mentally riffled through my options, and a glimmer of a plan had started forming. It was stupid, I should have seen that. But I was thinking on my feet, trying to mentally calculate the risks of inviting him in versus trying to send him away. I knew this guy. He was dogged, and I didn't think a *now's not a great time* would have made him give up and walk away.

It had been a risky play, but it had worked. He'd seemed satisfied that it wasn't Julian who had contacted me, that I was still just scared, and confused.

Until he'd spotted the suitcase.

I'd tried to contain my frustration. I needed him to leave so I could finish packing and get the hell out. But I couldn't just send him away. He was suspicious. He'd probably come back in half an hour with a full team and a search warrant. Or worse – put some kind of alert on me so that at any border my face would sound all of the alarms. I was becoming agitated, too distressed by this unforeseen change in the plan to think clearly.

And so I'd done the one thing I could think of.

It only dawned on me as I pressed my mouth against his that I could have simply said I was going to visit my parents in Florida, that I needed some family support, and they needed me there. That would have been logical. He wouldn't have questioned that, he doesn't know they hate me. Stupid, stupid mistake. But it was too late to go back. I'd made a plan. I'd have to stick with it.

Things had moved quickly from there. Every kiss, every touch had made my stomach rage with disgust and self-loathing. Julian wouldn't mind. He knows I'd never cheat on him, not really. This was just me doing what it took to get myself out of this nightmare. But that didn't make it any easier, or any less sickening.

And then he was half naked and not showing signs of slowing down, and I knew there was only one way out of this.

314

The idea took hold, and as it formed and grew and came to life, I recognised the excitement rising up in me.

I'd tried to stop. Really, I had. But as my mind had imagined the scenario again and again, my heart rate quickening with every mental run-through, I'd realised that it could work. I'd realised that I wanted it to work. I'd realised that there was no other way.

Of course, the detective had taken my pounding heart and shortness of breath and dilated pupils to mean that I was just as keen on whatever was happening between us as he was. But that's the thing about the body's physical response to excitement. It can be easily misread. Which obviously worked in my favour during the aftermath of Ryan's murders. Excitement, fear . . . they look the same. People just make their own assumptions as to which one you're feeling.

And, with the detective's tongue pressing against mine in my room, I *was* feeling excited. Only it wasn't because of his hands finding their way under my shirt. It was because of what I was about to do.

Now that it's over, my heart rate is slowly settling back into its normal rhythm. But I can't wait around and revel in the satisfaction of what I've done. I can't savour the metallic smell of blood that's flooding my brain with childhood flashbacks, of mice and birds and Pickles and the Singh's pug and that stupid fluffy yappy dog that ruined everything.

It had found its way under the hole in the back of our fence that afternoon. Ryan and Cassie were playing something that hadn't interested me – as usual – and so I'd wandered off, lost in my own thoughts, content to be alone and explore the wildness that was the end of our back garden. I'd found the puppy there, white and fuzzy, growling at me like I was some kind of monster.

I'd been trying so hard to control the urges I had, those insistent, urgent tugs in the pit of my stomach that took hold every so often. It had been weeks since the pug. The neighbours were all in a frenzy about Chance the rabbit, even though that hadn't been me. It must have been a fox, just like the police suggested, because I was away at that stupid school camp.

But the pulling sensation was back. It was coming more quickly each time, now. At first, when it was just the mice and birds, I'd leave it a couple of months between each kill. It was easier then. I could blame Pickles, leave my victims at the back door, watch the horror unfolding on Mum's face as she found them. I used the hunting knife I'd heard Mum and Dad arguing about, when I'd pressed my ear against their bedroom door and he'd muttered the code to appease her paranoia. But I'd never meant to hurt Pickles.

I needed him so I could get away with what I was doing. But he'd scratched me while I was leaving a sparrow on the back doorstep. My own cat, my very own, had turned on me. Traitor.

The feeling had taken over then, the urge, tugging at me, and I'd not been able to control it. When it was over, the reality of it had settled on me heavily. I couldn't be found out, couldn't let my family see what I really was. And so I'd made it look like Ryan. I wasn't trying to get him in trouble, as such. I'd just wanted to get out of trouble myself. I didn't really care who else got blamed. But I was more careful after that, keeping my activities to the very end of our property, leaving them far away from our house in the middle of the night.

But on that terrible day in our back garden, I didn't want to give in to the urge. It was getting too dangerous. I'd looked down at the dog, mentally battling my own desires.

Each time, I came closer to being caught. I didn't know what would happen if they found out my secret, but I knew it wouldn't be good.

It had taken every morsel of strength in my little eleven-year-old body, but I'd done it. I'd turned around to walk away. And that's when I'd noticed. The dog was limping. It was hurt. I knew, then. I had to put it out of its misery. I'd picked it up, so gently, so carefully, and had cradled it in my arms. And then quickly, suddenly, without stopping to let logic take control again, I'd snapped its tiny neck, excitement flooding my veins, the rush taking over.

A shriek sounded in my ear, and I'd looked up in horror to see Cassie standing beside me, her eyes as wide as those chocolate coins she loved to eat, her mouth forming a perfect O.

There was a moment of complete silence, of utter dis-belief, that stretched between us, and then she'd turned to run, screaming at the top of her lungs.

'You're a killer!' she'd wailed. 'You killed Pickles.'

I'd lunged at her, blinded by the need to protect myself, to silence her, to make her stop screaming, but she'd been too quick. I'd chased her through the tangle of bushes and debris that littered the wild end of the garden, but she was faster than me, and more nimble.

Her curly blonde hair had bounced over her shoulders as she ran away, and then Ryan had appeared in front of us, laughing in delight at whatever game he believed they were still playing.

'You killed Pickles,' Cassie screamed again, her high-pitched voice drifting across the neighbourhood as she continued to run towards the house.

Ryan roared with frustration, or maybe it was fury, and reached out to shove his little sister. It wasn't a violent

317

push, but it was enough to tip her off balance. She wobbled, stepped backwards to steady herself, and caught her heel on a rock instead. I watched as she stayed where she was, suspended for just a moment, her arms flailing before she fell suddenly, and hard.

There was a hollow crack, and then silence. Peace.

The stillness settled over the world for a moment, maybe two, and then Ryan screamed.

'Mum!' he yelled, running towards the house. 'Muuuuum!'

I stepped forward, tentatively at first, and then with a few quick strides.

Leaning over her, I'd watched as blood seeped quickly from her skull and onto the stone it collided with. She wasn't moving. I'd pressed my ear to her chest. Her heart was still beating, pulsing the blood around her body, out of the wound in her head.

I'd leaned in close. I'd soothed my sister, my hands stroking her tiny head, her cheek, her arm. And then they had found their way to Cassie's delicate neck, and I'd pressed down tighter and tighter.

'It's OK,' I'd whispered to my sister's limp body. 'It'll be over soon. I practised on Pickles. He only struggled for a moment, too.'

I shake the memories away. I can't be distracted right now. The urgency to leave is far greater now than it was before the detective showed up. And there will be plenty of time to reminisce later, anyway.

I get into the shower and watch as the scalding water creates rivers of red down my torso, my legs, my arms, and between my toes. I stay there until the water runs clear, and then I inspect my hands. A few small scratches mark the side of my right pinkie, a Morse code tracing down to my wrist. They're still bleeding, so I carefully rummage through the bathroom cabinet and find plasters to patch up the wounds.

Then I walk back along the carpet, avoiding the bloody footprints I've left behind, and stand in the doorway of my bedroom. The scene is far more violent than I remembered. There's blood everywhere, as though a frenzied painter has covered it in angry swipes and splashes. Reminding myself of the time pressure I'm now under, I turn and walk down the stairs to Ryan's room, unchanged since he was arrested.

I rummage through his drawers until I find socks and a pair of gloves, then put them on before steeling myself to enter my room again. All I need is my phone and my passport. Everything else that matters is already packed.

When I have what I need, I run out into the hallway, throw Ryan's bloodied socks and gloves over my shoulder and dress quickly. There's no point cleaning the bathroom. They'll know what's happened the moment they walk into my room, anyway. I just need to make sure I look present-able enough to get through passport control. If I arrive at the airport covered in blood, they might have some questions for me.

I hoist my backpack over my shoulder, grab the handle of my suitcase and head towards the door. A text makes my phone vibrate in my pocket, and when I check it I see a flight confirmation from an unknown number. I smile. The flight is going to Punta Cana. The Dominican Republic is a non-extradition country, I remember that from our research. I didn't know which country he'd choose, but I'm glad this is where we'll be. It's a return ticket, but I have a feeling I won't be using the second part of it.

I take one last look around me, at the house where this

all began, at the home where I was never really loved, and never allowed to truly be me.

And then I square my shoulders and walk out of my front door, leaving the life I never wanted behind me.

Chapter 48

1997

SHARON

'It was an accident.' Bill speaks slowly, patiently, as though I might snap at any moment. To be fair to him, that's entirely possible.

I'm huddled on the floor in the corner of our bedroom, close to the wardrobe, my back against the wall and one arm wrapped around my legs. In my other hand I'm clutching Cassie's Minnie Mouse watch. The one I just found this afternoon in Gina's room. Hidden in the depths of her wardrobe, in a small box, the contents of which still make my stomach turn sour.

I'd been cleaning. Purging, more like.

When I'd woken up this morning, I'd thought, for the very first time since Cassie died, that maybe I could carry on. Maybe I could still live, face the day, function with the pain. It's been almost a year, but time doesn't mean much to me any more. Life after Cassie is one long stretch of grief that I no longer measure in hours or days or weeks.

But today was different. That tiny sliver of . . . what was it? Not hope, exactly. Acceptance, perhaps. Whatever it was, it had allowed me to put one foot in front of the other, start up my old routine, or at least try. I'd made the kids' lunches, had dropped them at school, and had come back home, seeing the mess and disorder for the first time. It had driven me to action, and I'd gone about the house in a frenzy, picking up stray clothes, scrubbing the bathroom sink, using the smallest attachment on the hoover to clean the nooks and crannies of Ryan and Gina's bedrooms. I hadn't set foot in Cassie's. I couldn't. Not yet.

I'd spotted a ball of dust in the furthest corner of Gina's wardrobe, and had moved all of her shoes and stray toys out of the way to reach it. I was packing everything back where it belonged when I'd found it. A small metal box, unfamiliar, and covered in dirt. I'd shaken it. The rattling noise made something inside me twist, even without seeing what the box contained. It was dry. Brittle. Like chalk.

I'd opened the lid, which squeaked in protest at the invasion.

I'd spotted the watch first. Cassie's watch. My heart had floundered and a wave of fresh grief had hit me. I'd stared at the tiny red strap and the cartoon mouse on the face, her arms pointing in unnatural directions, and tried to cling to the precious details of Cassie's final birthday, of the joy on her face when she opened the gift Bill had so carefully selected for her. I allowed myself to smile at the memory of her refusing to take it off to get in the bath or to go to sleep, and I was glad Bill had chosen the waterproof version.

A thought was nagging at me, more and more insistent, pushing against my brain, but I ignored it. I didn't want anything to interrupt the indulgence of remembering my beautiful little girl.

And yet, the thought pressed harder and harder until I'd been forced to acknowledge it, to break my reminiscing and focus. When I did, the realisation of what had been needling me made me gasp out loud. I'd sunk onto the floor, desperately remembering.

Cassie had been wearing her watch when they went out to play that day.

She wasn't wearing it at the hospital. I know, because I spent a full day staring at the items the nurses had handed back to us as we left the hospital. I wanted to bring my daughter home. Not a dress, a tiny pair of socks, wellington boots and a glittery hair clip. It wasn't right. I hated the nurses for it.

So Gina had stolen her sister's watch in the garden that day. Sitting there, the leather strap pinched between my fingers, I'd felt a pang of anger at Gina, but I flung it away just as quickly. She was just a kid. Maybe the watch had fallen off, and she'd pocketed it, and kept hold of it. That would be understandable. After all, she was grieving, too. We all processed our emotions differently, I reminded myself. I'd been reminding myself of this a lot since Cassie's death, since the moment in the hospital when Gina had looked so gleeful.

I'd sighed, and through tears I'd gone to replace the watch in Gina's box. And that's when I'd seen them.

The bones.

Tiny, white, and whisper thin. The remains of something delicate, fragile. Like a bird, I'd thought. Or a mouse. I'd shuddered. And then I'd seen the gold sphere at the bottom.

A bell.

Pickles's bell.

I'd turned it over in my fingers, trying to make sense of what I was seeing.

These bones, where had they come from?

Something else had caught my eye at the bottom of the box. I almost didn't want to see, didn't want to know, but I made myself. My fingers had scrabbled around in the corner to try to get a grip on the small silver item. I'd pinched it between my thumb and my forefinger, and brought it closer to my face to inspect it.

It was a metal disc. Engraved. I'd squinted to read the name.

Bubbles.

My hands had started shaking as recognition washed over me.

Bubbles was the Singh family's pet pug. The one who was killed, whose injuries sounded exactly like Pickles's.

Why would Gina have this name tag?

And why would she keep it with Pickles's bell . . . and Cassie's watch . . . ?

My stomach had lurched then, a quick and violent spasm that had sent me running to the bathroom, just in time to heave over the toilet bowl. It was there, with my cheek pressed against the porcelain, that my brain had caught up to what my body had already realised.

These items – they were trophies.

'Sharon,' Bill says to me now. 'The coroner confirmed that Cassie . . .'

He swallows firmly, and I keep my gaze fixed on his Adam's apple, which bobs up and down quickly.

'She died because of a head injury. And both Ryan and Gina say the same thing, that they were playing, and that Cassie fell, hitting her head on that rock.'

I'm shrinking further into the corner, like a wounded animal.

'But,' I whisper pathetically, 'what about the trophies?'

'Don't call them that,' Bill snaps. 'That's a terrible accusation to make against your own daughter.'

'Well, what are they, then?'

'I don't know.'

My husband pauses and stands up straight, staring at a spot on the wall above my head.

'I don't know,' he repeats. 'It's a little...macabre...I can see that, but it doesn't mean that Gina killed anything. Or anyone. Maybe this is just her way of dealing with death. Maybe she found Bubbles's name tag on the street.'

'No.' I shake my head. 'That's too convenient, Bill. And it doesn't explain the bones. Or the watch. She didn't know Cassie was dead when she took that, so it can't be her way of dealing with it. Besides, I told you how she looked at the hospital...'

I swallow the memory down. I can't focus on the look in her eyes. It makes my veins freeze over.

'You were in shock, Sharon. Who knows what your brain thinks you saw?'

'So now I'm crazy?' I spit venomously.

He squats down and balances on his haunches so his face is level with mine. He carefully places his hands on my knees.

'Of course you're not crazy. I would never think that, my love.'

'I know what she did.'

He pauses, but I don't say anything. I don't trust myself to speak.

'It was an accident, honey,' he says. 'A horrible, tragic, bloody unfair accident. But you can't punish the kids for it. We can't tell them how to grieve. Even if it is...unconventional.'

'But, Bill...we can't just ignore this. We have to say something.'

I don't know what we'd say. I don't know how to deal with this. I don't know anything, any more. My only daughter might be a monster. She might be a killer.

'Sharon, I know how difficult this is, I truly do. But we can't say anything. I just don't know what to say to convince you that it really wasn't anyone's fault. I miss her so much—'

At this, his voice cracks, and I commence my weeping.

'We can't say anything,' he whispers. 'We can't. They're too traumatised already. Nothing is going to bring Cassie back, especially not pointing the finger at Gina. And besides . . . what if you're wrong?'

I stare at him, weighing up his words.

What if I am mistaken? What if this is all a terrible misunderstanding? What if Gina really is just grieving, in her own way?

I could be wrong.

But there's one question that screams at me, louder than the rest.

What if I'm right?

Chapter 49

2018

GINA

I scan the faces that eagerly line the metal barrier. Bored-looking men in suits holding signs, families with balloons or flowers, small groups staring at every face that passes, looking disappointed when it's not the face they've been waiting for.

Julian isn't there.

A frown flits across my forehead. I look again at the name cards I ignored when I walked past, hoping to spot a Mills among the names I don't know. There is no sign for me.

A bubble of anxiety swells in my chest. I don't know anyone or anything here. I left in such a hurry that I had no time to research where I would go if no one was waiting to meet me. And I obviously can't use any of my bank cards from home. If Julian isn't here, I'm completely screwed.

'Hey, baby,' a voice murmurs in my ear.

I turn to see a man with a tangle of unkempt hair and a dark beard. I recoil in disgust and shrug away from the stranger. Then I freeze.

I look again. I see his eyes. Steely grey. Crinkled just a little at the sides in the beginnings of a smile. Mirrors to my soul.

'Julian!' I shriek. He laughs and throws his arms around me, picking me up and spinning me around. I close my eyes and savour the feeling of his skin against mine again, the smell of him, the very idea of being this close to him filling my stomach with a swarm of fluttery wings.

'I can't believe it's actually you,' I say, pulling away so I can see his face. I take in his mop of untidy locks and the hair that covers his face. 'I like the new look.' I smile. He winks at me and a warmth I hadn't even realised I was missing spreads from my chest and throughout my body, defrosting me, bringing me back to life.

'Let's get out of here,' he says, taking my hand. 'We really can't afford to be seen.'

The excitement drains out of me all at once and is replaced with nerves. Of course we can't be spotted. We may be in a non-extradition country, but the world knowing where we are would restrict us hugely in the future. And here I am making a scene. What an idiot.

'Sorry,' I mutter, peering over my shoulder as we walk out. No one seems to be looking at us. But now isn't the time to relax.

Julian drops some coins in the parking meter before throwing my suitcase in the boot of an old, rusty yellow car. We hop in, and as he backs the car out of his parking space, I steal another look at the man I've been waiting to see for what has felt like an eternity. Now that I'm here, I'm a tangle of nerves and excitement and utter disbelief that this is really happening.

'I'm so glad to see you,' I say.

He glances across and reaches over to squeeze my knee with a smile.

'I've missed you so much, Gina,' he says. 'We have so much to catch up on.'

Then, after a couple of seconds, 'Any trouble getting through?'

The airport had been an ordeal, with each new interaction bringing me closer to being discovered, arrested, exposed. But by some miracle – probably because the detective's body wouldn't have been discovered until I was well and truly out of British skies, and because the passport I'd had made long before all of this started was impossible to spot as a fake – I got through, I arrived, and here I am in the destination Julian has been hiding out in, building our new life for us, for all of this time.

'It was fine,' I say, as lightly as I can. It's over, so there's no point feeling sorry for myself over how stressful it was. Besides, I'm with Julian now, which means he can take responsibility for our future. It's his turn now. I'm the one who's put in all the hard work since Ryan's arrest.

I knew it would be difficult. But if I'd known exactly how this plan of ours would play out, if I'd recognised the depth of feeling I had for my brother, if I'd understood just how empty my life would be without Julian in it, I might never have agreed to it in the first place.

Although now, after all this time, after everything, I'm not sure whether I agreed to it, or whether I came up with it. Perhaps we both did.

It was like chemistry, how it all came together. Alone, neither of us was deadly. Sure, we had the capacity to kill, but unless we were mixed with the exact right ingredient, we never would have ignited.

We let one thing snowball into another, and without someone to rein us in, a glimmer of an idea became an incredibly detailed, unbelievably risky, plan.

Together, we were fire. The combination, it was instantaneous, burning white hot. Deadly.

The details of who said what, and whose idea it really was, are hazy. It doesn't matter. It was *our* idea, born of us and who we are together. I do remember the day it started though, the moment when the seed of a concept germinated and began to take on its own life.

We were lying in bed at my grim apartment, candles lit around us to distract us from the otherwise remarkably unromantic surroundings. My heart was pumping, my body tingling from my scalp to my toes. Julian had handed me a glass of water.

'How the hell did you do that?' I'd gasped, and he'd laughed.

'Hypnosis,' he'd said with a wink. 'It's not just for my shows.'

'It's so sexy,' I'd moaned.

'What?'

'You. Controlling someone. Well, me, but anyone. A man in control, it's irresistible.'

He'd kissed me deeply. 'Well, if it's a man in control you like, I'm happy to deliver.'

'Seriously though,' I'd insisted, my brain still spinning. 'Don't you love it? The power?'

'Of course I do,' he'd said. 'But there's only so much power I can wield on the stage without it getting incredibly creepy.'

'Well, why does it have to be on the stage?' I'd asked, immediately energised.

He'd looked at me curiously, waiting for me to elaborate.

'Why are you waiting to get famous from your shows? None of these agents are willing to represent you because they just don't see your potential. But I do. And I say you can do it without them, without having to slog your guts out for no money and no recognition.'

'What do you have in mind?' he'd asked me slowly. I could see the intrigue in his eyes, the hunger for more than what the people whose help he needed told him he would ever achieve.

'I don't know exactly,' I'd said uncertainly, my mind fizzing with possibility more than an actual plan. 'But I just think you shouldn't need a stage to put on a show. I mean, why not just prove to the world that you're the best – the most powerful – without having to rely on promotors or managers or whatever?'

'But I'm not the most powerful,' he'd protested.

'That's only because you haven't had a chance to really let loose. To properly test your limits. Who says you can't be better, and more impressive, than the best of them?'

He'd smiled, and kissed me, and I'd melted into him. The conversation had been dropped, but not forgotten.

A couple of days later, while I was painting my nails on the sofa and he was messing around with a deck of cards, he breathed in as though he was about to begin speaking. Then he closed his mouth.

'What is it?'

'No, I . . .'

'No really,' I'd insisted. 'What is it?'

'I was just . . . I was thinking about what we talked about the other day.'

He looked down and shuffled his cards with a flourish.

'What were we talking about?'

'You know,' he urged. 'About me not needing a stage to do my tricks.'

'What about it?'

'I think you might be on to something,' he'd said, and my chest had flared with – what was that – hope? Excitement? Perhaps a little of both. 'I do think I can do more than people think I can do. And I want so much more, I want to be famous, I want to be powerful. I love making people

331

do what I tell them to do. It's what I'm good at, it's what I was born to do.'

His face was flushed as he spoke, the words coming out too fast.

'I know,' I'd said simply.

We'd stared at each other for a couple of seconds, recognising each other – really seeing each other – before I'd spoken again.

'How far do you think you could take someone?'

'I don't know, I've never tried more than some stupid tricks to get a laugh.'

'Well, could you make a person strip naked in public?'

He'd frowned and considered it for just a second.

'Of course,' he'd said. 'That's easy. I'd have to find the right person, someone suggestible, but I'd just implant a trigger while they were hypnotised. Then all it would take is a word or a sound and they'd strip.'

'OK,' I'd said. 'How about . . . could you make someone steal for you?'

'Same thing,' he'd replied. 'Although a bit harder, because it goes against most people's morals. So I'd either have to find someone morally questionable, or make them believe that they were doing it for the right reasons. It's definitely not impossible, it'd just take a lot more work. You've seen that Derren Brown thing where he made people hold a guy up at gunpoint, right?'

'Yep,' I'd replied. 'I also saw the one where the guy pushed someone off a building. So I guess you could make someone commit murder, too?'

'Well, the guy that was pushed was on a harness, so he didn't actually kill anyone,' Julian had muttered. 'But the same concept applies, yeah. You'd just have to find someone who believed they had to do it.'

'Like making them believe they're in danger, like they'd be doing it for self-defence?'

'That would probably work,' he'd replied. 'But the groundwork would be insane. Months of setting up triggers and suggestion. It would be tough to do without that person getting suspicious. Hypothetically, of course.'

'Of course,' I'd said. 'Hypothetically.'

But we'd both known it wasn't hypothetical. There was something between us, an unspoken ripple that changed the very air around us that day. It was thick with the knowledge of what he *could* do, what we knew he was capable of. And once we knew he could, it was all we wanted. It was an addictive idea, and from that day we found our conversations circling back to the same topic with greater and greater frequency.

What started as nothing more than a concept grew at an alarming rate, ever expanding, becoming more exquisitely complex, until one day we stopped speaking in hypotheticals and began making solid plans.

Plans that would eventually incorporate the ignition of my own dreams, because, of course, an act as shocking, as powerful, as the one we were dreaming up, needed to be made known to the public. There would be no point becoming the most powerful hypnotist alive if no one knew you'd really done it. But if I was there, I could let the world know what was possible. Of course, we couldn't reveal his identity. Not yet. Not like that.

But if everything went to plan – and there were so many ways it could go wrong but we were willing to take the risk, to go down together if we needed to, a modern-day Bonnie and Clyde – if it actually worked, our names would be written in history books.

All we needed was our killer, our unwilling assassin.

He came to us unexpectedly, and all at once. A gift, practically tied up with a ribbon.

I'd been keeping tabs on my family. From a distance, of course. There was a kind of pull, a morbid curiosity to know what my life would have been like if Mum hadn't stopped loving me, if she'd believed the coroner and placed the blame for Cassie's death where it actually belonged: with Ryan.

It still hurt, knowing that even though my brother was the one whose actions led to our sister's death, he was the one who was loved and protected and favoured. There was a twisted kind of logic in the whole thing. Mum knew the facts, she knew what the coroner told her, that it was a terrible, tragic accident. She heaped Ryan with love and support, to help him get over the trauma of what had happened, of what he'd witnessed. And yet, somewhere deep inside her, she always believed that I was really responsible. It was as if her brain never really accepted the truth, no matter how many times it was presented to her.

And, of course, Ryan never admitted what really happened. I could have pointed the finger, but I was afraid. Mum *had* found Cassie's watch. And my other trophies. And even though I hadn't killed Cassie, I had killed Pickles. I couldn't explain the contents of that box. Not without answering a lot more questions.

She never confronted me about it. And I never asked what happened to the box in my wardrobe. But we both knew.

And so I was pushed aside, forgotten, the black sheep. Even Dad, battered by the death of his little girl, was too exhausted to feel strongly about anything that was happening. He retreated, he ignored the way his wife was treating their only remaining daughter. Maybe he suspected me, too, but he simply took the path of least resistance. Which meant that the little love they had left to give went to my brother, the killer.

As soon as I could, I left home, began my own life, free from my past and the rejection of the people who were supposed to love me unconditionally. I watched from a distance as Ryan got everything he wanted: a first-class degree from a top university, his dream job, weekly dinners where he was doted on by our parents.

And then one day, they packed up and left. They moved to Florida. Retired, they called it in their smug Facebook posts. They had a farewell party, where they had photographs with their successful son. Their only child, anyone would be forgiven for thinking.

They were gone. Ryan was given our home, our family home. An early inheritance, I saw him admitting sheepishly in a comment to a friend who had left a post on the invitation to his housewarming party, questioning how the hell he could afford a three-bedroom house in west London.

He was alone.

He had killed before.

And I knew that I could manipulate him into spending long periods of time with me. Months, if that's what it took for Julian to do what he needed to do.

In the end, it was easier than I'd expected to squeeze my way back into his life. He felt abandoned by our parents – imagine that! – and he practically welcomed me with open arms, barely asking anything about me before inviting me to move in with him. I'd played the poor, struggling PA role perfectly, convincing everyone around me that I was desperate to become a newsreader – it was easy enough because it was true. Well, it used to be. Until I set my sights higher.

It was perfect. Julian had befriended him easily. He's good like that; people let their guard down with him. He tested

Ryan to see how suggestible he was, hypnotised him secretly, gave him simple commands – stand up, sit down, go find a pink pen – and watched as he carried out each one without question.

Then it was time to plant the triggers. The word 'Pickles', for example, would lead him to recall every detail of Cassie's death. I'd whisper it over him while he was sleeping – one of the advantages of living in the same house – and watch as he twitched and moaned with the horror of that day unfolding again and again, reminding him that he was still a murderer, no matter what Mum had told him.

After that, the triggers became more complex, and more frequent. When he saw a young woman with blonde, curly hair, he'd believe it was his dead sister. When he thought of her, he'd feel a sense of danger. We needed to make him believe she was going to expose him for who he really was, that she'd ruin him, or our plan wouldn't work.

The note was my idea. After all, I *am* Ryan's other sister, the forgotten one, the child cast aside, thrown away, forgotten. He drew his own conclusions. He panicked.

In the meantime, Julian researched how to create email addresses that couldn't be traced, and set up our fake Tinder accounts. It was child's play to find women who looked the way I imagined an adult Cassie would have. Cute. Blonde. Bouncy curls. Making them believe we were the man of their dreams was a piece of cake, too. We planned the day and hour carefully, making sure Julian was away, far from suspicion's reach.

At the time we'd agreed, Julian had called Ryan – from a burner phone, the number of which I'd programmed into Ryan's phone with a ringtone that was another trigger, designed to put him into a state of high alert and suggestibility – saying that I'd just called, that I was in danger, that Cassie was trying to kill me.

We didn't know if it would work.

So much could have gone wrong.

But the combination of paranoia for his own reputation, fear for my safety, and being in a state of suggestibility meant Ryan was the ideal candidate for our particular job. The perfect puppet.

The rest had been a piece of cake. Ryan's trance state included washing his clothes and showering when he got home, and then forgetting everything he'd done while in the trance. I had pre-stamped, addressed envelopes in my bag to quickly send the trophies to our anonymous post office box, thanks to the nearby postboxes. We had to have proof that it was us. We couldn't let someone else take the credit for our work.

I acted strangely with the police, so later they'd think I was another victim of Julian's. And I got my time in the spotlight, as a newsreader. Enough people knew how desperate I was to present that it wasn't a huge stretch for me to have filmed the whole thing. I didn't get the lifelong career I once hoped for, but it stopped mattering, because what Julian and I were achieving together was so much bigger than anything I could – or wanted to – do alone. We were leaving a legacy.

I'd like to think it all went off without a hitch, but there were flaws in our plan. I hadn't accounted for the online hatred, which had been stupid and naive of me. Those threats – physical, real threats to my safety – left me weak with terror and questioning everything we'd worked so hard for. I'd tried to talk Julian out of the second victim, but he'd been adamant. And his argument had made sense, even if it scared me. One, and people might say it was a fluke. Two, and they can't deny what you're capable of.

I'd almost lost it altogether when I'd had to spend a night in that cell. I'd been frantic with worry. We hadn't been careful enough, I'd figured. They had me. I was going to end up in jail, separated from Julian, all of our plans for nothing. The reality of how badly everything was going wrong, of the potential consequences of our actions, had hit me then, and all I'd wanted was to turn the clock back, return to the time when all of this was just a hint of an idea, an exciting concept. Nothing more.

But they'd let me go. It had felt like I'd cheated death when I walked out the doors of the police station that day, hand in hand with Julian. Free.

When he'd left, as I knew he would, as we'd planned, my grief was real enough. I'd had to make a show of trying to find out where my boyfriend had gone, but there was nothing false about how much I missed him. Every second of the past seven months has been torturous, and I've questioned on most days whether the separation was worth it.

But in the end, Julian was right. It had all worked out, miraculously, and better than we could have imagined. And here I was, right where I belonged. Back with Julian.

'Penny for your thoughts,' he says as we drive alongside the impossibly blue ocean, past miles and miles of lush green vegetation. I'm lost in wonder at our new life, at our fresh start.

'I just can't believe it,' I say. 'We actually did it. All of it.'

'I know,' he laughs, his elbow resting on the window frame, the wind whipping through his wild hair. 'You did so brilliantly.'

'No, you did.'

'Honey,' he reaches over and laces his fingers between

mine, 'we're a team. We couldn't have done this without each other.'

'Bonnie and Clyde,' I say with a smile, my fingers stroking his warm, tanned skin.

'Bonnie and Clyde,' he repeats. We settle into silence for a couple more minutes, enjoying the air on our faces and the feeling of complete freedom.

'So have you got any students?' I ask. Our plan wasn't simply to make a splash for a few months. It has longevity. And financial reward.

'Three,' he says smugly.

'Three?' I squeal. I do the calculations in my head. 'Julian, imagine how rich we'll be in a few years. Especially when your students can testify that your training works.'

'And also because I'm doubling the price once I have that kind of proof.'

I can't stop grinning. It's like the past months of worry and longing and uncertainty were all just a blip, a tiny bump on the road.

'I'm sorry you couldn't make it to Ryan's sentencing,' Julian says gently. 'I saw this morning though, he got life.'

I look over at him, sharply. There's a hint of a smile playing on his lips. I breathe out.

'So it's over,' I say. 'I wish I could have been there. But there's no way I could have stayed after the detective showed up.'

I fill him in on what happened the previous night, the events that sparked my sudden SOS message to him.

He whistles softly. 'That must have been stressful. Are you all right?'

'Fine,' I say. 'Besides, now I'll be in the headlines too. We'll be famous. Both of us.'

He laughs and takes my hand. 'Oh, and baby?'

'Mmmm?' I ask, my eyes closed, basking in the warmth of our success.

'I looked into the assholes who threatened you.'

'Who was it?' I ask, suddenly alert.

'Just some loser trolls with nothing better to do,' he says.

For a moment I'm surprised. I'd been so convinced that Tash had double-crossed me, and orchestrated some kind of coordinated online attack. 'So it wasn't anyone I knew?'

'Well, Tash organised the petition. And the protest. And she must have been the one to take the picture of you in the office. But those other threats, they were just garden variety degenerates getting off on scaring you. Don't worry. I've taken care of them.'

'What did you do?'

'Nothing they didn't deserve,' he laughs. 'Let's just say I've planted some photos and documents on their computers that the police will be *very* interested in.'

'You didn't do that to Tash though, did you?'

As angry as I am about what she did, she's still my friend. She was there when no one else was. And although her actions were inexcusable, I can understand why she reacted the way she did. I don't want her to be punished. I just want to move on.

'Of course not, baby. I know she's your friend.'

He squeezes my hand. I start to squeeze it back, but then I hesitate. It's just for a split second, but despite being apart for so long, he can read me just as well as he always has. He looks over at me with concern.

'What is it?' he asks before focusing on the road again. 'We can mess with the trolls some more if you like?'

'No, it's not that. I just . . . I feel bad about Ryan,' I blurt out before I can stop myself.

Julian whips his head around to look at me, to see if I'm serious.

'What?'

'I just ... I don't know, Julian. It's just that when I went to see him, he admitted to killing Cassie, to letting Mum treat me the way she did. He seemed like he really was sorry. He asked for my forgiveness.'

'And you forgave him? Gina, you know what we did to him, right?'

'Of course I do,' I say. 'But I just don't know how I feel about him any more. I'm not angry like I used to be, and I ... well, I haven't forgiven him, but now I don't know if there's anything to forgive. He was just a boy. And it really was an accident.'

'Well, we can't take it back now,' Julian says softly. 'I'm sorry, Gina. I'm sorry you feel this way.'

'I just miss him,' I admit, a tear sliding from the corner of my eye. 'I didn't think I cared about him at all.'

'He's your brother,' Julian tries to soothe me, but he's driving. He has to keep his eyes on the road. 'Of course you care. But what happened to you, what he took from you as a child, that wasn't right.'

'No,' I say, my eyes once again dry, my resolve hardened. 'It wasn't right. But it wasn't his fault. Not completely.'

'What are you saying, Gina?'

I pause for a moment. What am I saying? I know I can't fix this for Ryan, not without losing everything. I can't change his future. But maybe I can right the wrongs of his past. And mine, too.

'You enjoyed this, didn't you – what we did?'

'Of course,' he replies immediately. 'You did too ... right?'

'Would you do it again?'

He looks at me, sideways.

'What do you have in mind?' he asks, a small smile playing at the side of his mouth.

'The one who's really responsible for what happened to Ryan and me needs to pay,' I say. 'How about we get some real justice this time? And we can add it to your list of successes – I'm sure the extra headlines will bring in more business.'

'Just tell me where, and I'm there.'

I smile widely again, and let the wind whip at my hair and the sun kiss my face as the car takes us past rows of candy-coloured houses.

'Florida,' I say firmly, my mind made up. 'Take me to Florida.'

Acknowledgements

Firstly, thank you to my wonderful agent, Ariella Feiner at United Agents, whose wisdom and patience I couldn't have done without.

Huge thanks also to my incredibly talented editor, Francesca Pathak, for your wisdom and enthusiasm, and to the rest of the hard-working team at Orion, especially Bethan, Lauren and Lynsey.

To Brendan, for supporting me even when our apartment walls have been covered in post-it notes. For that, and for every little thing you do for me every day, you're my hero.

Thanks to Niki for the coffees, the WhatsApp chats, and for the laughs. You've kept me sane, and I'm so grateful.

Thank you to Lucy for your constant encouragement, Monica for your endless motivation, Amie for being my US spy, Jules for being the best neighbour in the world, Rohin and Jackie for always making me laugh, and Hannah and Ed for the fun times and the invaluable detective knowledge.

I couldn't have written this book without the support of all of my friends, near and far, and I'm so grateful to each of you.

To Tam and Greg, please don't read anything into the characters in this book! I love you both. Mum and Dad, thanks for making reading such an integral part of my childhood. For that I'll be forever grateful.

And to all of my readers – I owe you the biggest thank you of all!

**If you were being framed for murder,
how far would you go to clear your name?**

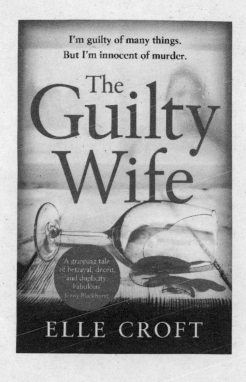

'I couldn't put this down' **Cass Green**

'An ending that pulls the rug from under your feet.'
Phoebe Morgan

'Kept me completely rapt' **KL Slater**

**Read on for an extract from Elle Croft's
gripping debut novel.**

Prologue

A helicopter pilot.

If you'd asked me what I was going to be when I grew up, back when I was a round-faced teenager, that would have been my answer. No hesitation. I knew I was born to fly, right up until the first time I boarded a plane and my family holiday was cut short by an unexpectedly crippling panic attack. I've never managed to shake that terror, and I haven't boarded an aircraft since.

But that fear, the lung-crushing, paralysing dread I experienced so long ago in my cramped window seat was nothing compared to this.

What I feel now is beyond panic.

Because ... someone knows.

My secrets are in their hands. Hands that were, just days ago, soaked in the blood of a man it should have been impossible to harm. Hands that could tear me apart just as effortlessly.

I suspect that they're enjoying this too much to kill me, though. For now, at least. They'll toy with me first, destroy everything I have.

Ruin me.

But before my dirty laundry is thrown out in a heap to be picked through and scrutinised, I feel like I should open the windows and let some fresh air diffuse a bit of truth into my situation.

I am not guilty.

But even I can admit that doesn't make me innocent.

Chapter One

'This is how Monday evenings should always look,' Calum announced, reminding me how different the world appeared to someone with no financial limitations.

I smiled and rolled my eyes, but couldn't help agreeing with him.

I was wrapped in my thickest scarf, the lingering warmth of the day not quite defending itself against the chill that cut through the evening air. We'd spent the last moments of sunshine basking on Calum's terrace and drinking in the view of London that spread out before us. When I turned my head I could see the top of Big Ben, his famous face peeking out across the tree line, surveying his city as it came alive in the unseasonal warmth. I'd suggested a walk, but Calum had shaken his head. No public outings; one of his many precautions. Instead, he had grabbed me by the hips and lifted me high, a figure-skater move that had elicited a squeal of surprise, and when he'd thrown me on his bed all thoughts of a walk had been swiftly forgotten.

Now he was running his thumb lightly across the back of my hand, watching with amusement as two sparrows bravely took it in turns to hop closer and closer to our table, daring one another to steal stray crumbs.

I smiled contentedly as I took in Calum's tousled hair and his shadow of dark stubble. He had the air of a man without a care or responsibility, not someone with an enormous company and a public persona to maintain. His forehead was for once uncreased by the frown that usually darkened his face and made his staff worry constantly that he was angry.

Noticing my gaze, he turned towards me, the corners of his mouth twitching upwards. Suddenly shy, I couldn't stop the warmth that began creeping into my cheeks. I felt silly for reacting that way, but however much I promised myself I'd stay cool in his presence, there was nothing I could do to stop it.

'You're so cute when you blush,' he said, and the heat spread to my chest.

'Stop it,' I pleaded. 'You know that just makes it worse.'

He laughed, and pulled me onto his lap.

'I'm sorry,' he whispered in my ear.

'Well, that doesn't stop you from teasing me every time it happens.'

'I can't help it. You make it too easy.'

'I wish you had some kind of flaw I could tease you about.'

'It's not a flaw,' he said, kissing my cheek. 'I think you look beautiful, even when you're embarrassed. And trust me, I'm far from perfect. You just don't see it yet.'

I laughed and leaned back, allowing myself to be lulled by the slow rise and fall of his chest. He ran his hand lightly up and down my back in a gentle rhythm as we stared at the park being drenched in the golden hue of a dying day.

'Oh,' I said suddenly. 'I almost forgot.'

'What's that?'

'Your present.'

'Ah,' he replied, raising an eyebrow.

I rummaged for a few seconds in my bag before handing Calum a tiny silver box tied with a blue ribbon.

'Happy birthday,' I said, kissing him lightly. 'I'm sorry it's so late, but . . . well, I haven't really seen you—'

'I totally understand,' he interrupted. 'Besides, I love an extended birthday.'

I watched him struggling with the knot I'd spent so long perfecting that afternoon, and mirrored his own mischievous smile when he lifted the lid.

He pulled the small black piece of plastic from its bed of tissue paper and leaned over to kiss me.

'Thank you,' he said. 'I love it.'

'Well, you haven't even seen what's on it yet,' I joked. 'It might just be a memory card full of puppy pictures.'

'I do love puppies. But probably not as much as I think I'll love what's on here.'

He kissed me again, but after a few seconds I pulled away.

'Calum,' I said, serious now, 'I know we've already spoken about it, but you really have to make sure no one sees these. Please promise me.'

'Bethany,' he said, his tone gentle. 'I would never show anyone, but are you sure you're comfortable with this? I know it was my idea, and I also know it's not the sort of thing you'd usually do – or the sort of thing I'd do, for that matter. So if you want me to get rid of it, we can just forget about the photos.'

The photos are the only gift I could possibly afford, I thought. What do you get the man who, quite literally, has everything? A steamy photo shoot featuring the two of you, apparently.

I studied his face, trying to decide if he meant it, if he really would destroy the memory card just because I was uncomfortable. But it was so difficult to make rational decisions when his eyes were fixed on me. That gaze was completely disarming.

'No, of course I don't want you to get rid of it,' I said eventually, meaning it. 'It's just not something I've ever done before. And anyway, I'm more confident being behind the lens, not in front of it.'

'Well, I thought you made an excellent model. Have you considered a career change?'

'I have, but I like burgers far too much.'

'You could have fooled me. With a figure like that, I'd have thought you lived off lettuce.'

Calum got up and reached for my hand.

'Come on.'

I laced my fingers through his and stood, following his lead towards the door. We walked in silence into his apartment, past the bed where the illicit photos had been taken and across the room to his desk, almost hidden in the furthest corner. He reached for a book on the second shelf and opened a drawer, which he rummaged through for a few seconds. He handed the book to me and I stared at him, waiting for an explanation. Not receiving one, I turned it over, then flipped through the pages. Nothing.

'A business self-help book?' I asked. 'Am I missing something here?'

He smiled, taking the book from me, and flicking to the back cover.

'Can you give me a piece of that please?' he asked, passing me a roll of tape.

I complied, frowning in confusion.

He stuck the memory card to the rectangle of tape I'd given him and secured it to the inside of the book's cover. Replacing it on the shelf with the rest of his serious non-fiction, he turned back to kiss me again. This time I kissed him back.

'Don't worry,' he said. 'No one but us will know it's there.'

'Thank you,' I whispered.

'You're welcome. And trust me. No one wants to keep our secret more than I do. Those photos are safe with me.'

Chapter Two

My husband reached for my hand as we stepped out of the Tube station and were greeted by the buzz of after-work revellers. Bars and pubs crawled with drinkers who had spilled onto the streets and lined the narrow pavements. There was a tangible excitement in the air, a ripple of electricity caused by the spurt of warm weather that had brought Londoners out in droves, despite it being a Tuesday night.

I felt a pull to join in the springtime festivities, to soak up the warmth of the evening, but instead, I took his hand and wrenched the heavy wooden door open. We blinked away the sunlight as our eyes adjusted to the darkness inside the restaurant.

I tried to stay focused on the conversations that unfolded during our meal, but I was relieved when we waved our friends goodnight and their cab turned the corner to disappear from sight.

Jason curled his arm around my waist and I leaned into him, glad that it was just the two of us again. He kissed the top of my head.

'Home?'

'Home,' I said, smiling up at him.

This probably comes as a surprise, given what I'd been up to the previous afternoon, but Jason and I were, by all accounts, happily married.

I was in love with my husband. Always had been, really.

Ever since the morning after I met him, in our first week of university. We'd been introduced at a party, the kind where there was lots of drinking, and lots of dancing. I'd foolishly worn a pair of brand-new heels, and by the end of the evening I was hobbling ungracefully on bleeding feet. The next morning when I dragged myself out of bed to take a shower, I tripped on a small blue box that was sitting in the hallway outside my door. Inside was a packet of blister plasters and a can of Coke, along with a note that said:

For your hangover. And your heels. I hope to see you again soon. J

We were official within days. He was my first serious boyfriend, and the only man I'd ever loved.

Until now.

Somehow, without meaning to, I'd found myself having an affair. An act of betrayal that I never imagined myself capable of. And to make matters even worse, the affair wasn't just about the sex. I really cared for Calum.

I hadn't fallen out of love with Jason. How could I? He was everything I could ask for in a husband. Supportive, handsome, loyal.

The opposite of me. I was a liar. A cheat. An adulterer.

And in love with two men at the same time.

Chapter Three

'Here, try this.'

Calum reached across the counter, holding a spoon out towards me. I leaned over and took a sip of the sauce that he'd spent the past half-hour perfecting.

'Wow,' I exclaimed. 'That tastes incredible.'

'Didn't I tell you I could cook?'

'You did. And I'm truly sorry that I didn't believe you.'

'It's OK,' he said lightly. 'For dessert I have a really nice slice of humble pie for you.'

I laughed and tried to flick him with the tea towel, but he moved away too quickly.

'Are you sure there's nothing I can do to help?'

'You can sit right there and relax,' he replied. 'Dinner won't be long.'

'I think I can manage that,' I said, closing my laptop. I'd been trying to review a week's worth of photos since I'd arrived at Calum's apartment for our meeting, but it was no use trying to concentrate when I was with him.

'Actually, can you do me a quick favour?' Calum asked.

'Of course,' I said.

'It's getting warm in here. Could you open the sliding doors? We can eat over by the lounge so it's a bit cooler.'

A fresh spring breeze accompanied our meal, which was an impressive dish of lamb chops and fried potatoes, all perfectly cooked.

I had just mopped up the last of the sauce on my plate with a warm bread roll when Calum's phone buzzed violently on the table. He snatched it up and I gathered the plates to take back to the kitchen.

I was scrubbing a frying pan, my arms covered in soap suds, when I felt Calum's hands curling around my waist. I smiled.

'Stay,' he whispered into my ear.

My smile dissolved.

'What?'

'Don't go home. Stay the night.'

I turned around to face him, expecting a playful wink, but he looked serious.

'I . . . well, aside from a whole bunch of other obvious reasons why I shouldn't, including how I'd explain it to Jason, what would you say to the security guys out there?' I waved towards the door as I dried my hands, pan forgotten.

'I can give them the night off,' he said. 'They're not prison guards.'

'OK, fine, but we've talked about this before,' I said. 'It's one of your paranoid rules.'

'How many times do I have to tell you it's not paranoia, Bethany?'

I sighed, and walked back to the table to collect the salt and pepper grinders.

'I get it. You feel bad about Kitty.'

I couldn't help but frown as I thought about the woman Calum had been seeing before me.

'I don't just feel *bad* about Kitty,' he said. 'I will never, ever forgive myself for what happened to her. It was my fault that she was attacked. I was the one who insisted she told the police about the stalking, and the threats she was getting. I was trying to protect her. If anyone had told me then that the cops would be the ones to leak our affair to the press, I probably would have called them paranoid, too. But it's not paranoia if it's true. The police were the only ones who knew about us, and the day after we told them, she was all over the news. And then she was attacked, and her whole life was ruined. I wanted to help fix things, but she wanted nothing to do with me. She hates me, and I don't blame her. Because all of it was my fault.'

His voice quavered, and I shifted my weight uneasily.

'I have to deal with the guilt of knowing I caused that, but I couldn't live with the responsibility of anything happening again. Not to you. All it takes is one news story for everything to go crazy, so please don't call me paranoid again, OK? You don't know what it's like. This system I use? It's for you. For your safety.'

'I'm sorry,' I said gently. 'I really am. I do understand, honestly, and I appreciate it. It's just ... frustrating sometimes.'

'I know,' he said. 'I just don't want you to lose sight of why we have to do things this way.'

'I won't. I promise. But I really can't stay, as much as I'd love to. I have to go home to Jason. And besides, I thought you said Claire was back later.'

'I thought she would be too, but she sent me a message,' he said, reaching for his phone.

He tapped the screen a few times and then read, ' "Won't be home tonight, darling. Still with Red Ferrari." '

'She's with a car?'

'Not a car.' He shook his head. 'It's a nickname for the man she's in California with; she doesn't tell me their real names. Plausible deniability or something. Last month it was Guitarist Five. She has a thing for musicians, apparently.'

I blinked, trying to decide if he was playing with me, but there was no hint of a smile, no telling spark in his eye.

'How can that not bother you, Calum? I mean, why do you even stay together when both of you are sleeping with other people? How can you call that a marriage?'

'Judge much?' he replied, his tone measured, a reined-in sort of anger. 'What makes you so much better, when you're sleeping with me? At least Claire and I have the decency not to pretend to be something we're not.'

I mentally clutched for words.

'Decency?' I finally blurted out as he walked a few paces away. 'That's what you call it? So as long she tells you she's cheating then it's totally fine. And what about you? You've not told her about us, so how are you so superior?'

Calum turned around, his face steely. He moved towards me and stopped when our faces were too close, his expression making me squirm uncomfortably.

'Bethany,' he said slowly, looking me directly in the eye. 'What Claire and I choose to do in our marriage is none of your business. She and I love each other, just not in a way that you find ... palatable. We've found a way to make our marriage work for both of us, and just because it doesn't fit into your little idea of what a relationship should be, you immediately get all self-righteous and judgy. Claire and I are honest with each other. We have an understanding. Boundaries. We're open with each other and we've discussed the way we choose to operate our marriage in great detail. She doesn't want to know if I'm sleeping with someone else, and I respect that.'

He was talking with his hands now, voice rising, brows meeting at the bridge of his nose.

'You, on the other hand, you act like you're just an innocent girl who never meant for anyone to get hurt, but what you're doing is deceitful and malicious. You're not honest with your husband, you're lying to him. You're waiting for life to make your decisions for you rather than knowing what you want and owning that choice. If you don't want me to judge you and your decisions, then you can't judge me and my marriage. You're not pure, you're not a victim here, and I won't be criticised. Not by you. Not when I thought we understood each other.'

I stood, slack-jawed, not sure what to say. When he spoke again, his voice was softer, but still simmering with anger.

'We've both got flaws. I just thought you'd accepted that.'

My cheeks burned with the humiliation of being berated, and his angry face wobbled through the tears that suddenly stung my eyes. I wanted to scream, to defend myself, but I knew that if I opened my mouth the only thing that would come out would be a sob. He wasn't going to see me cry.

Saying nothing, I spun around and walked towards the door, blinking furiously to stay my tears.

'Come on, Bethany,' he called from behind me, but I was already halfway across his apartment. I expected to hear footsteps following me, but the only noise that reached my ears was my own staccato breath.

I hauled my bag over my shoulder, shielded my pathetically watery eyes with sunglasses and stormed out of Calum's apartment, pulling the door forcefully. But the door, obviously designed to neutralise such dramatic exits, slid silently back into its frame without so much as a click.

The security guard barely glanced at me as he pressed the button on the wall, and we waited side by side in excruciating silence. I managed a tight smile as the light flashed, then hurried into the elevator. When I reached the ground floor I power-walked across the over-the-top lobby, head down, before exhaling into the evening air.

Crossing the road, I stepped into Kensington Gardens, tears suddenly flowing and hiccuppy gasps escaping from the depths of my lungs. I was a mess, but at least I was an anonymous mess; just another crazy person littering the streets of London. My crying barely drew a second glance.

I didn't want to join the throngs of tourists and office workers who were soaking up the last moments of sunshine. I needed to be alone, to bathe in my self-pity away from such palpable joy. Wiping my nose on the back of my arm, I walked purposefully towards my favourite part of the park, a flower garden near the Albert Memorial. I could never explain why I loved the depressingly gothic structure that had been built by Queen Victoria. It was somehow meant to prove her love for her dead husband, but it looked more sinister than romantic.

Finding an empty bench engulfed by a tangle of yellow and pink roses, I carefully turned Calum's words over in my head. Malicious. Deceitful. Self-righteous. Each of his accusations smarted like the smack of a gavel.

He was right. I knew he was. But that didn't mean I was willing to hear it.

I knew the situation I was in hadn't just *happened* – affairs never just happen – but it felt like one day I was happily married, innocently getting on with my life, and the next I was in love with another man. How had I let myself get into this mess?

Since I'd assumed the role of Mistress, I'd been refusing to face the decisions I inevitably needed to make. I'd ignored my conscience as it tugged like an impatient child, begging for attention while I declined to acknowledge its existence.

Life wasn't going to just make this decision for me, as much as I wished it would.

I knew the right thing to do. Of course I did. I should end

things with Calum, confess to Jason, beg for his forgiveness and spend the rest of my life trying to prove my love for him. Or, at the very least, I should end things with Calum, hope Jason never found out and carry on like nothing had ever happened.

It was hardly the worst outcome in the world, being married to a man I loved.

And yet, even knowing that, I couldn't bear the thought of never seeing Calum again, never looking into those eyes, never joking with him, laughing at his easy wit, being swept onto his bed.

I'd fallen in love with him, and I didn't know how to reverse that.

And honestly... I didn't want to.

Don't miss out on the rest of this gripping novel – order now.